MW01099060

欧·亨利短篇小说选集

Selected Short Stories of O Henry

美 国 文 学 卷

欧·亨利
O Henry

盛世教育西方名著翻译委员会
主　　任：黎小说　高民芳　屈丽娜
本册委员：周明明　周明瑞　魏彦平
　　　　　高　璐　章杰
美　　编：赵　旭

世界图书出版公司
上海·西安·北京·广州

图书在版编目（CIP）数据

欧·亨利短篇小说选集：中英对照全译本/（美）欧·亨利
（Henry, O.）著；盛世教育西方名著翻译委员会译. —上海：上海
世界图书出版公司，2009.5（2013.8 重印）

ISBN 978-7-5062-9935-0

I.①欧… II.①欧… ②盛… III.①英语－汉语－对照读物
②短篇小说－作品集－美国－近代 IV.①H319.4：I

中国版本图书馆 CIP 数据核字（2009）第 059423 号

欧·亨利短篇小说选集

[美] 欧·亨利 著

盛世教育西方名著翻译委员会 译

上海世界图书出版公司 出版发行

上海市广中路 88 号

邮政编码 200083

北京兴鹏印刷有限公司印刷

如发现印刷质量问题，请与印刷厂联系

（质检科电话：010-84897777）

各地新华书店经销

开本：880×1230 1/32 印张：13.25 字数：197 000

2013 年 8 月第 1 版第 4 次印刷

ISBN 978-7-5062-9935-0/H·919

定价：19.80 元

http://www.wpcsh.com.cn

http://www.wpcsh.com

前　言

　　通过阅读文学名著学语言，是掌握英语的绝佳方法。既可接触原汁原味的英语，又能享受文学之美，一举两得，何乐不为？

　　对于喜欢阅读名著的读者，这是一个最好的时代，因为有成千上万的书可以选择；这又是一个不好的时代，因为在浩繁的卷帙中，很难找到适合自己的好书。

　　然而，你手中的这套丛书，值得你来信赖。

　　这套精选的中英对照名著全译丛书，未改编改写、未删节削减，且配有权威注释、部分书中还添加了精美插图。

　　要学语言、读好书，当读名著原文。如习武者切磋交流，同高手过招方能渐明其间奥妙，若一味在低端徘徊，终难登堂入室。积年流传的名著，就是书中"高手"。然而这个"高手"，却有真假之分。初读书时，常遇到一些挂了名著名家之名改写改编的版本，虽有助于了解基本情节，然而所得只是皮毛，你何曾真的就读过了那名著呢？一边是窖藏了50年的女儿红，一边是贴了女儿红标签的薄酒，那滋味，怎能一样？"朝闻道，夕死可矣。"人生短如朝露，当努力追求真正的美。

　　本套丛书的英文版本，是根据外文原版书精心挑选而来；对应的中文译文以直译为主，以方便中英文对照学习，译文经反复推敲，对忠实理解原著极有助益；在涉及到重要文化习俗之处，添加了精当的注释，以解疑惑。

　　读过本套丛书的原文全译，相信你会得书之真意、语言之精髓。

　　送君"开卷有益"之书，愿成文采斐然之人。

CONTENTS

目 录

1. THE GIFT OF THE MAGI
1. 麦琪的礼物

One dollar and eighty-seven cents. That was all. And sixty cents of it was in pennies. Pennies saved one and two at a time by bulldozing the grocer and the vegetable man and the butcher until one's cheeks burned with the silent imputation of parsimony that such close dealing implied. Three times Della counted it. One dollar and eighty-seven cents. And the next day would be Christmas.

There was clearly nothing to do but flop down on the shabby little couch and howl. So Della did it. Which instigates the moral reflection that life is made up of sobs, sniffles, and smiles, with sniffles predominating.

While the mistress of the home is gradually subsiding from the first stage to the second, take a look at the home. A furnished flat at $8 per week. It did not exactly beggar description, but it certainly had that word on the lookout for the mendicancy squad.

In the vestibule below was a letter-box into which no letter would go, and an electric button from which no mortal

一块八毛七分钱。这就是全部的财产，其中还包括 60 美分。一想到这都是一分一分从杂货店老板、菜贩子、肉贩子那儿软磨硬泡才攒下来的，她就忍不住自惭形秽，觉得做这种锱铢必较的事实在是太丢人了。德拉来回数了三次，还是一块八毛七分钱。而明天就是圣诞节了。

除了一屁股坐在破沙发上嚎啕大哭之外，她没有其他任何办法。而坐在沙发上之后，她又陷入对当前生活深深的反思：那里充斥着啜泣、哽咽和微笑。而不幸的是，哽咽占了绝大多数时间。

当女主人的情绪渐渐平息下来的时候，让我们来好好看看这个家吧。一套每周租金八美元带一些简单家具的公寓，尽管难以确切地说这就是乞丐的境况，可是看起来还是体现了"乞丐"这个词儿的含义。

楼下的门廊里有个信箱，可从未有过来信。还有一个电铃，也从未被人按响过。此时，这个信箱上有一张卡片，上面赫然写

finger could coax a ring. Also apper-taining thereunto was a card bearing the name "Mr. James Dillingham Young."

The "Dillingham" had been flung to the breeze during a former period of prosperity when its possessor was being paid $30 per week. Now, when the in-come was shrunk to $20, though, they were thinking seriously of contracting to a modest and unassuming D. But when-ever Mr. James Dillingham Young came home and reached his flat above he was called "Jim" and greatly hugged by Mrs. James Dillingham Young, already in-troduced to you as Della. Which is all very good.

Della finished her cry and attended to her cheeks with the powder rag. She stood by the window and looked out dully at a gray cat walking a gray fence in a gray backyard. Tomorrow would be Christmas Day, and she had only $1.87 with which to buy Jim a present. She had been saving every penny she could for months, with this result. Twenty dollars a week doesn't go far. Expenses had been greater than she had calculated. They always are. Only $1.87 to buy a present for Jim. Her Jim. Many a happy hour she had spent planning for something nice for

着一个名字，"詹姆斯·迪林厄姆·杨先生"。

"迪林厄姆"这个教名是它的主人前一阵手头阔绰时随性加上去的，那时他每星期能挣30美元。而现在，他的收入只有每星期20美元，"迪林厄姆"这几个字也就显得有些垂头丧气，仿佛正严肃思考着是不是缩写成谦虚不招摇的字母D更合适些。不过，每次詹姆斯·迪林厄姆·杨回家走进楼上的公寓时，詹姆斯·迪林厄姆·杨太太（就是刚提到的德拉）总是会叫他"吉姆"并给他一个温暖的拥抱。这真是世上再好不过的事情了。

德拉哭完后，往毫无生气的两颊上擦了一些脂粉。然后呆呆地站在窗户旁，看见一只灰色的猫正沿着灰暗的篱笆，跳进一个灰蒙蒙的后院。明天就要过圣诞节了，而她只有一元八毛七分钱给吉姆买礼物。几个月以来，她竭尽全力节省每一枚便士，但也只攒到这么多。一周20美元实在不经花，生活费用远远超出了她的预算，这对于她们来说已经是家常便饭了。只有一元八毛七分钱可以给吉姆买礼物，她亲爱的吉姆。尽管她一直兴高采烈地计划着要送他一件称他心意的礼

---

him. Something fine and rare and sterling – something just a little bit near to being worthy of the honor of being owned by Jim.

There was a pier-glass between the windows of the room. Perhaps you have seen a pier-glass in an $8 flat. A very thin and very agile person may, by observing his reflection in a rapid sequence of longitudinal strips, obtain a fairly accurate conception of his looks. Della, being slender, had mastered the art.

Suddenly she whirled from the window and stood before the glass. Her eyes were shining brilliantly, but her face had lost its color within twenty seconds. Rapidly she pulled down her hair and let it fall to its full length.

Now, there were two possessions of the James Dillingham Youngs in which they both took a mighty pride. One was Jim's gold watch that had been his father's and his grandfather's. The other was Della's hair. Had the queen of Sheba lived in the flat across the airshaft, Della would have let her hair hang out the window some day to dry just to depreciate Her Majesty's jewels and gifts. Had King Solomon been the janitor, with all his treasures piled up in the basement,

物，一件精致、独特、纯正——配得上他，让他值得拥有的礼物。

在房间的窗子之间，有一面穿衣镜。想必你见过每周八美元租金公寓里的穿衣镜吧，那是只有苗条且行动灵活的人才能对付的。在观察了自己一连串纵向重影之后，才可能对自己的容貌体态有一个大致的了解。不过德拉，这位身材纤细的女主人，早已灵活掌握了这门照镜子的艺术。

德拉忽然从窗户边急转过身，站在穿衣镜前，眼睛里闪耀出灿烂的光芒，但紧接着她的双颊却迅速失去了血色。她迅速解开发辫，任由发丝随意散落开来。

詹姆斯·迪林厄姆·杨夫妇有两样他们视若珍宝的东西。一样是吉姆的金表，那是由他祖父和父亲传下来的；另一样则是德拉的秀发。假如住在天井对面公寓的是示巴女王[1]，德拉只需在洗过头后把秀发垂到窗外去晾干，她的秀发就足以使女王的奇珍异宝黯然失色；如果所罗门王是他那地下宝藏的看门人，吉姆每次路过，只要掏出金表，定会让所罗门王忌妒得拽自己的胡子。

Jim would have pulled out his watch every time he passed, just to see him pluck at his beard from envy.

So now Della's beautiful hair fell about her rippling and shining like a cascade of brown waters. It reached below her knee and made itself almost a garment for her. And then she did it up again nervously and quickly. Once she faltered for a minute and stood still while a tear or two splashed on the worn red carpet.

On went her old brown jacket; on went her old brown hat. With a whirl of skirts and with the brilliant sparkle still in her eyes, she fluttered out the door and down the stairs to the street.

Where she stopped the sign read: "Mme. Sofronie. Hair Goods of All Kinds." One flight up Della ran, and collected herself, panting. Madame, large, too white, chilly, hardly looked the "Sofronie."

"Will you buy my hair?" asked Della.

"I buy hair," said Madame. "Take yer hat off and let's have a sight at the looks of it."

Down rippled the brown cascade.

"Twenty dollars," said Madame, lifting the mass with a practised hand.

此时，德拉的秀发犹如褐色的瀑布散落在她的身后，微波起伏，闪闪发光。她的秀发长及膝下，使她看上去就像身披着一袭锦袍。但马上，她又有些神经质的迅速把头发梳好。梳好以后，她就呆呆地站在那儿，迟疑了一分钟，直到两滴泪珠溅落在红色的旧地毯上。

她穿戴好褐色的旧衣帽，裙摆翩然的步出房间，眼睛里仍然闪耀着奇异的光彩。她关上门走下楼梯来到街上。

这位女主人最终停留在一块招牌前，其上写着："索弗罗妮夫人——各式头发，一应俱全"。德拉飞快的跑上楼梯，气喘吁吁地定了定神。那位夫人可是个大块头，皮肤异常地白，盛气凌人，同"索弗罗妮"的雅号极不相称。

"你会买我的头发吗？"德拉问。

"我买，"索弗罗妮夫人回答。"把帽子摘了，让我看看货色品相如何。"

那褐色瀑布顿时倾泻下来。

"20美元，"夫人边说边非

"Give it to me quick," said Della.

Oh, and the next two hours tripped by on rosy wings. Forget the hashed metaphor. She was ransacking the stores for Jim's present.

She found it at last. It surely had been made for Jim and no one else. There was no other like it in any of the stores, and she had turned all of them inside out. It was a platinum fob chain simple and chaste in design, properly proclaiming its value by substance alone and not by meretricious ornamentation – as all good things should do. It was even worthy of The Watch. As soon as she saw it she knew that it must be Jim's. It was like him. Quietness and value – the description applied to both. Twenty-one dollars they took from her for it, and she hurried home with the 87 cents. With that chain on his watch Jim might be properly anxious about the time in any company. Grand as the watch was, he sometimes looked at it on the sly on account of the old leather strap that he used in place of a chain.

When Della reached home her intoxication gave way a little to prudence and reason. She got out her curling irons and lighted the gas and went to work

常熟练地托起长发。

"请快点给钱！"德拉说。

哦，接下来的两小时如插上美好的翅膀般一掠而过。不用在意这个蹩脚的比喻。她逛遍了各式商店，只为给吉姆买圣诞礼物。

最后她终于找到了，这件美好的东西就像是为吉姆量身定做的一样。她找遍了所有的店铺，再也没有比这更合适的了，一条简单大方的白金表链。正如一切品质优良的东西那样，它全靠本身质地尽显高贵，而非华而不实的装饰的点缀。它与吉姆的那只金表是多么的般配啊！她一眼就相中了这条链子，知道它是非吉姆莫属了。这条链子正如吉姆本人一样，低调而高贵——这一形容对两者真是恰到好处。付了21美元后德拉成了这条链子的主人。她带着仅剩的87美分急匆匆地赶回家。有了这条完美的表链，吉姆无论何时何地都可以骄傲地看时间了。那只表尽管贵重华丽，从前却是用一条旧皮带代替表链凑合系着，所以他也只能偶尔偷偷地瞥上一眼来确定时间。

回到家后，德拉从沉醉中回归平静和理智。她找出卷发钳，打开煤气，开始着手修补因慷慨

repairing the ravages made by generosity added to love. Which is always a tremendous task, dear friends – a mammoth task.

Within forty minutes her head was covered with tiny, close-lying curls that made her look wonderfully like a truant schoolboy. She looked at her reflection in the mirror long, carefully, and critically.

"If Jim doesn't kill me," she said to herself, "before he takes a second look at me, he'll say I look like a Coney Island chorus girl. But what could I do – oh! what could I do with a dollar and eighty-seven cents?"

At 7 o'clock the coffee was made and the frying-pan was on the back of the stove hot and ready to cook the chops.

Jim was never late. Della doubled the fob chain in her hand and sat on the corner of the table near the door that he always entered. Then she heard his step on the stair away down on the first flight, and she turned white for just a moment. She had a habit of saying a little silent prayer about the simplest everyday things, and now she whispered: "Please God, make him think I am still pretty."

The door opened and Jim stepped in

的爱所造成的损失——一整理头发。亲爱的朋友们，这是项巨大的工程——一件了不起的任务。

不到40分钟，她的头上就布满了密密的小卷发，使她看上去活像一个逃学的小男孩。她对着镜子，长久地、仔细地、挑剔地看着自己。

"假如吉姆在看我第二眼之前没把我宰掉的话，"她自言自语道，"他准会说我像科尼岛合唱队的卖唱女郎。但是我能怎么办呢？——老天，我能用一块八毛七分钱干什么呢？"

7点钟时，她煮好了咖啡，然后把煎锅放在热炉子上，准备做肉排。

吉姆从不晚回家。德拉把表链紧攥在手里，坐在靠近门口桌子的拐角处。接着，她听见楼梯响起了吉姆的脚步声，德拉紧张的脸色煞白。她习惯于为了最简单的生活琐事而默默祷告，此刻，她不由悄声祈祷："上帝保佑，让他觉得我依然漂亮吧。"

门开了，吉姆走进屋关上门。他看起来很消瘦而且一脸严肃。可怜的人啊，他才22岁，就得承担起一个家庭的全部责任！他需要一件新外套，还缺一副手套。

and closed it. He looked thin and very serious. Poor fellow, he was only twenty-two – and to be burdened with a family! He needed a new overcoat and he was without gloves.

Jim stopped inside the door, as immovable as a setter at the scent of quail. His eyes were fixed upon Della, and there was an expression in them that she could not read, and it terrified her. It was not anger, nor surprise, nor disapproval, nor horror, nor any of the sentiments that she had been prepared for. He simply stared at her fixedly with that peculiar expression on his face.

Della wriggled off the table and went for him.

"Jim, darling," she cried, "don't look at me that way. I had my hair cut off and sold because I couldn't have lived through Christmas without giving you a present. It'll grow out again – you won't mind, will you? I just had to do it. My hair grows awfully fast. Say 'Merry Christmas!' Jim, and let's be happy. You don't know what a nice – what a beautiful, nice gift I've got for you."

"You've cut off your hair?" asked Jim, laboriously, as if he had not arrived at that patent fact yet even after the hardest

吉姆一动不动地在门口站着，就好像猎犬嗅到了鹌鹑的气味。他的眼睛直直的盯着德拉，脸上有一种她读不懂的表情，这把她吓坏了。那不是愤怒，不是惊讶，不是不满，也不是恐惧，不是她所设想的任何一种表情。他仅仅是面带这种怪异的表情死死地盯着她。

德拉站起身沿着桌子向他走过去。

"吉姆，亲爱的，"她带着哭腔喊道，"不要这样看着我。我把头发剪掉卖了，因为如果不送你一件礼物，这个圣诞节我就没法过。头发还会再长长的——你不会介意的，对吗？我必须要这么做。我的头发长得可快了。说'圣诞快乐'吧吉姆！高兴点儿，你绝对猜不到我给你买了件多么称心如意、漂亮精致的礼物！"

"你把头发剪了？"吉姆结结巴巴地问道，似乎就算他绞尽脑汁也没办法弄明白这显而易见的事实。

"剪掉卖了，"德拉说，"不管怎么说，你还是会像以前一样喜欢我，对吗？头发剪了，可我还是我，不是吗？"

mental labor.

"Cut it off and sold it," said Della. "Don't you like me just as well, anyhow? I'm me without my hair, ain't I?"

Jim looked about the room curiously.

"You say your hair is gone?" he said, with an air almost of idiocy.

"You needn't look for it," said Della. "It's sold, I tell you – sold and gone, too. It's Christmas Eve, boy. Be good to me, for it went for you. Maybe the hairs of my head were numbered," she went on with sudden serious sweetness, "but nobody could ever count my love for you. Shall I put the chops on, Jim?"

Out of his trance Jim seemed quickly to wake. He enfolded his Della. For ten seconds let us regard with discreet scrutiny some inconsequential object in the other direction. Eight dollars a week or a million a year – what is the difference? A mathematician or a wit would give you the wrong answer. The magi brought valuable gifts, but that was not among them. This dark assertion will be illuminated later on.

Jim drew a package from his overcoat pocket and threw it upon the table.

"Don't make any mistake, Dell," he said, "about me. I don't think there's

吉姆还在好奇地四下张望。

"你说你的头发没有了,是吗?"他如白痴般地问道。

"别找了!"德拉说,"头发卖了,我告诉你——卖了,没了。现在是圣诞前夜,小伙子。请对我好一点,我可是为了你才这样做的。也许我的头发可以数的清根数,"她突然变得既严肃又甜蜜:"可我对你的爱,那是谁也数不清的。我可以做肉排了吗,吉姆?"

吉姆好像一下子从恍惚之中清醒过来,他紧紧地把他的德拉拥在怀里。就让我们用 10 秒钟的时间从另一角度认真思索一下一些无关紧要的事吧。每周八美元,或者一年 100 万美元——有什么区别?数学家或巧舌如簧的才子可能会给出错误的答案。麦琪带来了珍贵的礼物,但是那件不在其中。这句话的真正含义将在下文揭晓答案。

吉姆从外套兜里里掏出一个小包,往桌上一扔。

"不要误会,德拉,"他说,"无论你头发长短,有没有美容,用什么洗发水,我对你的爱一丝一毫都不会减弱。不过,你只要打开那包东西就会明白我刚才为

anything in the way of a haircut or a shave or a shampoo that could make me like my girl any less. But if you'll unwrap that package you may see why you had me going a while at first."

White fingers and nimble tore at the string and paper. And then an ecstatic scream of joy; and then, alas! a quick feminine change to hysterical tears and wails, necessitating the immediate employment of all the comforting powers of the lord of the flat.

For there lay The Combs – the set of combs, side and back, that Della had worshipped long in a Broadway window. Beautiful combs, pure tortoise shell, with jewelled rims – just the shade to wear in the beautiful vanished hair. They were expensive combs, she knew, and her heart had simply craved and yearned over them without the least hope of possession. And now, they were hers, but the tresses that should have adorned the coveted adornments were gone.

But she hugged them to her bosom, and at length she was able to look up with dim eyes and a smile and say: "My hair grows so fast, Jim!"

And then Della leaped up like a little singed cat and cried, "Oh, oh!"

什么变傻的原因了。"

白皙的手指灵巧地解开绳子，打开纸包。紧接着一声欣喜若狂的尖叫：哎呀！但紧接着变成了女性歇斯底里的哭泣和哀嚎，迫使这间公寓的男主人想尽一切办法去安慰和化解。

因为摆在桌上的是发卡：一整套发卡。包括两鬓用的和脑后用的，一应俱全。这是在百老汇的一个橱窗中陈列的让德拉眼热了很久的东西。这些漂亮的发卡，纯正的玳瑁制品，边上镶嵌着珠宝——颜色恰好跟她刚刚失去的秀发相匹配。她知道，这套梳子价格不菲，所以，她仅仅是羡慕，从未奢望过能拥有它们。如今，它们是她的了，可是那能配得上这渴望已久的装饰品的秀发已离她而去。

不过，她还是把发卡抱在怀里，最后，她抬起那双不再闪烁奇异光彩的眼睛望着吉姆，并且做出一个微笑："我的头发长得飞快，吉姆！"

随后，德拉活像一只被烫着了的小猫一样跳了起来，嘴里还喊道："喔！喔！"

吉姆还没看到给他的漂亮礼物。她热切地摊开手心，伸到他

Jim had not yet seen his beautiful present. She held it out to him eagerly upon her open palm. The dull precious metal seemed to flash with a reflection of her bright and ardent spirit.

"Isn't it a dandy, Jim? I hunted all over town to find it. You'll have to look at the time a hundred times a day now. Give me your watch. I want to see how it looks on it."

Instead of obeying, Jim tumbled down on the couch and put his hands under the back of his head and smiled.

"Dell," said he, "let's put our Christmas presents away and keep 'em a while. They're too nice to use just at present. I sold the watch to get the money to buy your combs. And now suppose you put the chops on."

The magi, as you know, were wise men – wonderfully wise men – who brought gifts to the Babe in the manger. They invented the art of giving Christmas presents. Being wise, their gifts were no doubt wise ones, possibly bearing the privilege of exchange in case of duplication. And here I have lamely related to you the uneventful chronicle of two foolish children in a flat who most un-wisely sacrificed for each other the

面前给他看，那没有知觉的贵重金属闪耀了一下，似乎要展现她的快乐和热忱。

"是不是很精致高雅，吉姆？我搜遍了全城才找到的。你现在每天都得把表掏出来看上个100遍。把表给我，让我看看它们配在一起是什么样子。"

吉姆没有这么做，相反，他往沙发上一倒，两手垫在脑后，笑了。

"德拉，"他说，"让我们把圣诞礼物放在一边，让它们自己待一会。东西实在太好了，我们最好都暂时别用。因为，给你买梳子的钱，是我卖掉手表换来的。好了，现在你开始给我做肉排吧。"

众所周知，麦琪[2]是有大智慧的人。当耶稣在马厩里出生时，他们带来礼物并送给他。并且还开创了圣诞节互赠礼物这门艺术。他们聪明过人，因此毋庸置疑，他们的礼物也都是聪明的礼物。万一礼物重样，也有特权调换。在此我已笨嘴拙舌地给你们讲述了一个平淡无奇的故事，主人公是住在经济型公寓的两个傻孩子，他们极不明智地为了对方而牺牲了自己最贵重的东西。不

greatest treasures of their house. But in a last word to the wise of these days let it be said that of all who give gifts these two were the wisest. Of all who give and receive gifts, such as they are wisest. Everywhere they are wisest. They are the Magi.

过，在下要对当今世上的聪明人说的是，在普天之下一切赠送礼物的人当中，那两个人是最聪明的。在一切馈赠又收受礼物的芸芸众生中，他们也是最聪明的。无论在世界上的任何地方，他们都是最富有智慧的人。他们就是圣贤麦琪。

1.示巴女王：Queen of Sheba，基督教《圣经》中朝觐所罗门王，以测其智慧的示巴女王，她以美貌著称。
2.麦琪（Magi，单数为 Magus）指圣婴基督出生时来自东方送礼的三贤人，见于《圣经》（新约全书）"马太福音"。

2. A SERVICE OF LOVE
2. 爱的奉献

When one loves one's Art no service seems too hard.

That is our premise. This story shall draw a conclusion from it, and show at the same time that the premise is incorrect. That will be a new thing in logic, and a feat in story-telling somewhat older than the great wall of China.

Joe Larrabee came out of the post-oak flats of the Middle West pulsing with a genius for pictorial art. At six he drew a picture of the town pump with a prominent citizen passing it hastily. This effort was framed and hung in the drug store window by the side of the ear of corn with an uneven number of rows. At twenty he left for New York with a flowing necktie and a capital tied up somewhat closer.

Delia Caruthers did things in six octaves so promisingly in a pine-tree village in the South that her relatives chipped in enough in her chip hat for her to go "North" and "finish." They could not see her f – , but that is our story.

当一个人热爱他所认准的艺术时，任何奉献都是不难做出的。

这是我们的前提。这篇故事会在这个前提得出结论的同时证明它是错误的。就逻辑学来说这是个新兴艺术，可就文学来说，这可是一门比中国的万里长城还要古老的艺术。

乔·拉雷毕来自中西部槲树参天的平原，他有着极高的绘画天赋。六岁的时候他就画了一幅画，画的是镇上的水泵，画上还有一个当地颇有声望的村民急匆匆从水泵旁边经过的情景。这件作品后来被装裱起来挂在了药房的橱窗里，药房旁边零落的长着几棵玉米，玉米棒子已经开始抽穗了。当他20岁的时侯，他离开家乡来到纽约。脖子上系着条领带，贴身藏着一个钱包。

德丽雅·加鲁塞斯来自南方一个长满松树的小村庄，她在六音阶方面大有前途，所以她的亲戚们给她凑了些学费，让她前往"北方"去"深造"。他们没能看到她完成学业，但这就是我们

Joe and Delia met in an atelier where a number of art and music students had gathered to discuss chiaroscuro, Wagner, music, Rembrandt's works, pictures, Waldteufel, wall paper, Chopin and Oolong.

Joe and Delia became enamoured one of the other, or each of the other, as you please, and in a short time were married – for (see above), when one loves one's Art no service seems too hard.

Mr. and Mrs. Larrabee began housekeeping in a flat. It was a lonesome flat – something like the A sharp way down at the left-hand end of the keyboard. And they were happy; for they had their Art, and they had each other. And my advice to the rich young man would be – sell all thou hast, and give it to the poor – janitor for the privilege of living in a flat with your Art and your Delia.

Flat-dwellers shall indorse my dictum that theirs is the only true happiness. If a home is happy it cannot fit too close – let the dresser collapse and become a billiard table; let the mantel turn to a rowing machine, the escritoire to a spare bedchamber, the washstand to an upright piano; let the four walls come

要讲的故事。

乔和德丽雅在一间画室相遇。那儿经常有许多研究美术和音乐的学生聚在一起，彼此讨论绘画的明暗对照法、瓦格纳、音乐、伦勃朗的作品、制图、瓦尔特杜弗、壁纸、肖邦以及乌龙茶。

乔和德丽雅倾慕彼此的才华，或说他们一见钟情，随你怎么说。很快他们就结婚了——当一个人爱好他所认准的艺术时，任何奉献都不难做出。

拉雷毕夫妇在一套公寓里开始了他们的家庭生活。那是一套颇为冷清的公寓——有点像钢琴键盘中最左端直线降低的A音。但是他们过得非常幸福，因为他们拥有所热爱的艺术，同时又拥有彼此。在此我也劝告那些有钱的年轻人——卖掉你所有的财产，把它分给穷苦的看门人，这样你就能专注的跟你所热爱的艺术和心爱的爱人共同生活了。

公寓的住户们一定赞成我的论断：他们的幸福是惟一真正的幸福。只要家庭幸福，房间再小又有什么关系呢？——梳妆台坍下来，可以当作台球桌；壁炉架可以改为划船练习器；写字桌可以充当临时卧榻；洗脸架则可用

together, if they will, so you and your Delia are between. But if home be the other kind, let it be wide and long – enter you at the Golden Gate, hang your hat on Hatteras, your cape on Cape Horn and go out by the Labrador.

Joe was painting in the class of the great Magister – you know his fame. His fees are high; his lessons are light – his high-lights have brought him re-nown. Delia was studying under Rosenstock – you know his repute as a disturber of the piano keys.

They were mighty happy as long as their money lasted. So is every – but I will not be cynical. Their aims were very clear and defined. Joe was to be-come capable very soon of turning out pictures that old gentlemen with thin side-whiskers and thick pocketbooks would sandbag one another in his studio for the privilege of buying. Delia was to become familiar and then contemptuous with Music, so that when she saw the orchestra seats and boxes unsold she could have sore throat and lobster in a private dining-room and refuse to go on the stage.

But the best, in my opinion, was the home life in the little flat – the ardent,

来当立式钢琴。如果四堵墙有可能合拢的话，别担心，反正你和你的德丽雅仍在其中没有分离。可如果家庭是另一个样子，那么房子再宽敞也没有用——你从金门[1]进去，把帽子挂在哈得拉斯，把披肩挂在合恩角，然后穿过拉布拉多出去了。

乔在著名的马杰斯脱班上学画画——这个班名气显赫，同时学费也十分的不菲，但课程是很轻松的——由于美名远扬而使然。德丽雅在罗森斯托克手下学习，她的老师爱跟键盘较劲是出了名的。

有钱时，他们过得很幸福。谁不这样呢？——不是因为我愤世嫉俗。他们的艺术目标清晰明了。乔很快就会有精彩的画作问世，到时候那些鬓须稀疏而荷包殷实的老绅士，都会争先恐后地挤到他的画室里来，以购买他的作品为荣。德丽雅先是精通音乐，后来她简直可以说是如鱼得水。当她看到剧院大厅和包厢里有空位时，就推诿说嗓子疼而拒绝登台，随后去一家私人餐厅享受美味的龙虾。

但在我看来，最美好的时光还是在那间小公寓里的家庭生

voluble chats after the day's study; the cozy dinners and fresh, light breakfasts; the interchange of ambitions – ambitions interwoven each with the other's or else inconsiderable – the mutual help and inspiration; and – overlook my artlessness – stuffed olives and cheese sandwiches at 11 p.m.

But after a while Art flagged. It sometimes does, even if some switch man doesn't flag it. Everything going out and nothing coming in, as the vulgarians say. Money was lacking to pay Mr. Magister and Herr Rosenstock their prices. When one loves one's Art no service seems too hard. So, Delia said she must give music lessons to keep the chafing dish bubbling.

For two or three days she went out canvassing for pupils. One evening she came home elated.

"Joe, dear," she said, gleefully, "I've a pupil. And, oh, the loveliest people! General – General A. B. Pinkney's daughter – on Seventy-first street. Such a splendid house, Joe – you ought to see the front door! Byzantine I think you would call it. And inside! Oh, Joe, I never saw anything like it before.

"My pupil is his daughter

活：追求艺术激情四溢的心灵体会；一天的学习后绵绵不绝的情话；令人惬意的晚饭和怡人适口的早餐；关于理想抱负的交流——他们的理想抱负是交织在一起的，否则就没有了意义——相互之间的帮助和鼓励。还有，恕我直言——晚上11点钟的菜裹肉片和奶酪三明治。

但是没过多久，艺术的醇美味道就开始变味了。即使意志坚定的人没有去刻意动摇，但生活就是如此。正如俗话所说，坐吃山空。他们已经没有钱支付马杰斯脱和罗森斯托克两位先生的学费了。当一个人热爱他所认准的艺术时，任何奉献都不难做出。于是，德丽雅说，她要去找份教音乐的家教，那样他们盘子里就会一直有热气腾腾的饭菜了。

为了招揽学生，她在外面奔走了两三天。一天晚上，她欢欣雀跃地回到了家里。

"乔，亲爱的，"她高兴地说，"我已经收到一个学生啦！哟，那真是最好的人家。一位将军——A·B·品克奈将军的女儿，住在第七十一街。他们的房子真是富丽堂皇！乔——你真该看看那大门，我想你会称它为拜占庭

Clementina. I dearly love her already. She's a delicate thing – dresses always in white; and the sweetest, simplest manners! Only eighteen years old. I'm to give three lessons a week; and, just think, Joe! $5 a lesson. I don't mind it a bit; for when I get two or three more pupils I can resume my lessons with Herr Rosenstock. Now, smooth out that wrinkle between your brows, dear, and let's have a nice supper."

"That's all right for you, Dele," said Joe, attacking a can of peas with a carving knife and a hatchet, "but how about me? Do you think I'm going to let you hustle for wages while I philander in the regions of high art? Not by the bones of Benvenuto Cellini! I guess I can sell papers or lay cobblestones, and bring in a dollar or two."

Delia came and hung about his neck.

"Joe, dear, you are silly. You must keep on at your studies. It is not as if I had quit my music and gone to work at something else. While I teach I learn. I am always with my music. And we can live as happily as millionaires on $15 a week. You mustn't think of leaving Mr. Magister."

"All right," said Joe, reaching for the

式大门[2]。还有屋子里面，喔！乔，我算是大开眼界了。

"我的学生，品克奈将军的女儿克蕾门蒂娜，我可真喜欢她。她是个娇弱的姑娘——总是穿着白色的衣服，她的一言一行都那么天真可爱！她才18岁，我一星期给她上三次课。你想想看，乔，一次课五块钱。尽管数目不大，不过我一点儿也不介意，等我再多找两三个学生，我就又可以到罗森斯托克先生那儿去学习了。好了亲爱的，别再皱眉头啦，让我们好好享受晚餐吧。"

"这对你来说不错，德丽，"乔说，同时用切肉刀和短柄小斧打开一罐豌豆罐头，"可是，你认为我会忍心让你四处奔波，而自己却在艺术的殿堂里追逐所谓的艺术吗？我以班范纽都·切利尼[3]的尸骨发誓，这绝不可能！我想我可以卖卖报纸，或者去铺石子，那样的话至少也可以挣个一两块钱。"

德丽雅走过来，搂住他的脖子。

"乔，亲爱的，你真傻！你必须继续你的学业。我并没有放弃音乐去干别的事，我可以边教边学。我永远跟我的音乐在一起。而且我们一星期可以有15块钱的收入，

blue scalloped vegetable dish. "But I hate for you to be giving lessons. It isn't Art. But you're a trump and a dear to do it."

"When one loves one's Art no service seems too hard," said Delia.

"Magister praised the sky in that sketch I made in the park," said Joe. "And Tinkle gave me permission to hang two of them in his window. I may sell one if the right kind of a moneyed idiot sees them."

"I'm sure you will," said Delia, sweetly. "And now let's be thankful for Gen. Pinkney and this veal roast."

During all of the next week the Larrabees had an early breakfast. Joe was enthusiastic about some morning-effect sketches he was doing in Central Park, and Delia packed him off breakfasted, coddled, praised and kissed at 7 o'clock. Art is an engaging mistress. It was most times 7 o'clock when he returned in the evening.

At the end of the week Delia, sweetly proud but languid, triumphantly tossed three five-dollar bills on the 8x10 (inches) centre table of the 8x10 (feet) flat parlour.

"Sometimes," she said, a little wea-

这样我们就可以像百万富翁一样快乐的生活了。你千万不能有离开马杰斯脱先生的想法啊。"

"那好吧,"乔边说边伸手去拿那个蓝色的扇贝形碟子。"但是我讨厌你去做什么家教,那不是艺术。但这恐怕是我们追求艺术的过程中不得不出的一张王牌了!"

"当一个人热爱他所认准的艺术时,做任何奉献都不难!"德丽雅说。

"马杰斯脱称赞了我在公园画的那幅素描里天空的部分。"乔说,"而且丁克尔也已经答应让我在他的橱窗里挂两幅画。要是恰好有有钱的白痴看上它,我就能卖掉它们了。"

"我相信你一定行的,"德丽雅甜蜜地说,"现在,先让我们来感谢品克奈将军和这盘烤小牛肉吧。"

接下来的整整一周,拉雷毕夫妇每天早早地便开始用餐。乔急于要去中央公园画几张具有晨光效果的速写,而德丽雅则要在早饭后撒一下娇、或者说几句赞美的话,然后和他吻别,在7点钟的时候送他出门。艺术真是个迷人的情妇。等他回到家时,大多数时候都已经是晚上7点钟了。

rily, "Clementina tries me. I'm afraid she doesn't practise enough, and I have to tell her the same things so often. And then she always dresses entirely in white, and that does get monotonous. But Gen. Pinkney is the dearest old man! I wish you could know him, Joe. He comes in sometimes when I am with Clementina at the piano – he is a widower, you know – and stands there pulling his white goatee. 'And how are the semiquavers and the demi-semiquavers progressing?' he always asks.

"I wish you could see the wainscoting in that drawing-room, Joe! And those Astrakhan rug portieres. And Clementina has such a funny little cough. I hope she is stronger than she looks. Oh, I really am getting attached to her, she is so gentle and high bred. Gen. Pinkney's brother was once Minister to Bolivia."

And then Joe, with the air of a Monte Cristo, drew forth a ten, a five, a two and a one – all legal tender notes – and laid them beside Delia's earnings.

"Sold that watercolour of the obelisk to a man from Peoria," he announced overwhelmingly.

到了周末，自豪而又疲倦的德丽雅得意洋洋地把三张五块钱的钞票扔在公寓客厅正中的那张宽八英寸、长十英寸的桌子上。

"有时候，"她有些厌倦地说，"克蕾门蒂娜也真够折腾人的。也许是她练得不够充分吧，我不得不一遍又一遍地教她同一个问题。而且她老是穿一身白，也让人感觉挺单调的。不过品克奈将军倒是一个很讨人喜欢的老头儿！我希望你能认识他，乔。我和克蕾门蒂娜练钢琴的时候，他有时候会进来看看，他是个鳏夫——经常会站在那儿捋他的白色山羊胡子。'十六分音符和三十二分音符教得怎么样啦？'他总是这样问。

"我真希望你能看看他们客厅的护壁板，乔！还有阿斯特拉罕呢门帘。克蕾门蒂娜总是咳嗽。我希望她能比看起来更强壮些。喔，我真是越来越喜欢她了，她是那么的温柔，又那么有教养。品克奈将军有一个弟弟曾经是驻波利维亚的公使。"

接着，乔摆出基度山伯爵的架势，掏出一张 10 元、5 元、2 元和 1 元的票子——全是柔软的合法钞票——放在了德丽雅挣来的钱旁边。

"Don't joke with me," said Delia, "not from Peoria!"

"All the way. I wish you could see him, Dele. Fat man with a woollen muffler and a quill toothpick. He saw the sketch in Tinkle's window and thought it was a windmill at first. He was game, though, and bought it any-how. He ordered another – an oil sketch of the Lackawanna freight depot – to take back with him. Music lessons! Oh, I guess Art is still in it."

"I'm so glad you've kept on," said Delia, heartily. "You're bound to win, dear. Thirty-three dollars! We never had so much to spend before. We'll have oysters to-night."

"And filet mignon with champignons," said Joe. "Where is the olive fork?"

On the next Saturday evening Joe reached home first. He spread his $18 on the parlour table and washed what seemed to be a great deal of dark paint from his hands.

Half an hour later Delia arrived, her right hand tied up in a shapeless bundle of wraps and bandages.

"How is this?" asked Joe after the usual greetings. Delia laughed, but not

"我把那幅方尖碑的水彩画卖给了一个从庇奥利亚[4]来的人",他郑重地宣布。

"别开玩笑了,"德丽雅说,"不可能是庇奥利亚来的!"

"千真万确!我希望你能见见他,德丽。他体型偏胖,围着羊毛围巾,叼着一根羽毛管牙签。他在丁克尔的橱窗里看到了那张素描,刚开始他还以为是风车呢。不过最后他还是心甘情愿把它买了下来。他还预定了一幅——勒加黄那货运车站的油画——准备带回家。音乐课!哦,我想艺术仍然存于其中。"

"我很高兴你能一直坚持,"德丽雅诚挚地说。"你一定会成功的,亲爱的。33块!我们从没有过这么多钱。今晚我们可以吃牡蛎啦。"

"还有香草炸嫩肉排,"乔说,"橄榄油叉子在哪?"

下一个星期六的晚上,乔先回到了家。他把18块钱摊在客厅的桌子上,然后去洗粘在手上许多类似于黑漆的东西。

半个小时以后,德丽雅回来了,她的右手被纱布和绷带缠得乱七八糟。

"这是怎么回事?"乔像往常

very joyously.

"Clementina," she explained, "insisted upon a Welsh rabbit after her lesson. She is such a queer girl. Welsh rabbits at 5 in the afternoon. The General was there. You should have seen him run for the chafing dish, Joe, just as if there wasn't a servant in the house. I know Clementina isn't in good health; she is so nervous. In serving the rabbit she spilled a great lot of it, boiling hot, over my hand and wrist. It hurt awfully, Joe. And the dear girl was so sorry! But Gen. Pinkney! – Joe, that old man nearly went distracted. He rushed downstairs and sent somebody – they said the furnace man or somebody in the basement – out to a drug store for some oil and things to bind it up with. It doesn't hurt so much now."

"What's this?" asked Joe, taking the hand tenderly and pulling at some white strands beneath the bandages.

"It's something soft," said Delia, "that had oil on it. Oh, Joe, did you sell another sketch?" She had seen the money on the table.

"Did I?" said Joe; "just ask the man from Peoria. He got his depot to-day, and he isn't sure but he thinks he wants

那样打了招呼后问道。德丽雅笑了一下,不过不是很快活。

"克蕾门蒂娜,"她解释道,"她真是个古怪的姑娘!下课后一定要吃威尔士干酪。下午5点钟的时候她说要吃,将军当时也在那儿。你没看到他跑过去拿盘子时的样子,乔,就好像家里没佣人一样。我知道克蕾门蒂娜身体不好,又有些神经质。当她端干酪的时候忽然撒出来许多,那些滚烫的干酪刚好掉在我的手和手腕上,真让人痛得要命。可是乔,那可爱的姑娘抱歉极了!还有品克奈将军!——乔,那老头儿简直惊慌失措。他冲到楼下去喊人——听说是喊烧锅炉或是在地下室里干活的人——让他们去药房买油膏和包扎用的东西。现在我已经感觉不怎么疼了。"

"这是什么?"乔问道,同时温柔地托起德丽雅的那只手,包住伤口的绷带下面的有几根白色的线。

"那是一些软纱。"德丽雅说,"你知道我涂了油膏的。呃,乔,你又卖掉了一幅素描是吗?"她看到了桌子上放着一些钱。

"你问我吗?"乔说,"去问问那个庇奥利亚人你就会知道了。他今天来取走了那幅车站风景画,

another parkscape and a view on the Hudson. What time this afternoon did you burn your hand, Dele?"

"Five o'clock, I think," said Dele, plaintively. "The iron – I mean the rabbit came off the fire about that time. You ought to have seen Gen. Pinkney, Joe, when – "

"Sit down here a moment, Dele," said Joe. He drew her to the couch, sat beside her and put his arm across her shoulders.

"What have you been doing for the last two weeks, Dele?" he asked.

She braved it for a moment or two with an eye full of love and stubbornness, and murmured a phrase or two vaguely of Gen. Pinkney; but at length down went her head and out came the truth and tears.

"I couldn't get any pupils," she confessed. "And I couldn't bear to have you give up your lessons; and I got a place ironing shirts in that big Twenty-fourth street laundry. And I think I did very well to make up both General Pinkney and Clementina, don't you, Joe? And when a girl in the laundry set down a hot iron on my hand this afternoon I was all the way home

他还想再要一幅公园风景画和一幅哈得逊河风景画呢。你今天下午什么时候把手烫伤的，德丽？"

"我想是5点左右吧，"德丽雅可怜巴巴地说。"那个熨斗——我是说干酪，恰巧就在那个时候做好。你真该看到品克奈将军当时的样子，乔，当时……"

"到这儿来坐一会儿吧，德丽，"乔说，然后把她拉到沙发上坐下，而他则坐在了她身边，搂住她的肩膀。

"告诉我，这两周你到底在做什么，亲爱的？"他问道。

她硬挺了一会儿，眼里充满了爱和固执，然后含糊不清地又念叨了两遍品克奈将军。但最终她还是低下头来，流着眼泪说出了实情。

"我一个学生都招不到，"她终于开始承认，"但我实在不忍心看你中断学业，于是我去找了个烫衬衫的活儿干，就在第二十四街那家大洗衣店里。我想我编的品克奈将军和克蕾门蒂娜的故事挺真实的不是吗？今天下午，洗衣店里的一个姑娘不小心把滚烫的熨斗放在了我手上，我一路上都在编那个威尔士干酪的故事，你不会生我的气对吗乔？我想如果我不做这份

making up that story about the Welsh rabbit. You're not angry, are you, Joe? And if I hadn't got the work you mightn't have sold your sketches to that man from Peoria."

"He wasn't from Peoria," said Joe, slowly.

"Well, it doesn't matter where he was from. How clever you are, Joe – and – kiss me, Joe – and what made you ever suspect that I wasn't giving music lessons to Clementina?"

"I didn't," said Joe, "until to-night. And I wouldn't have then, only I sent up this cotton waste and oil from the engine-room this afternoon for a girl upstairs who had her hand burned with a smoothing-iron. I've been firing the engine in that laundry for the last two weeks."

"And then you didn't – "

"My purchaser from Peoria," said Joe, "and Gen. Pinkney are both creations of the same art – but you wouldn't call it either painting or music."

And then they both laughed, and Joe began:

"When one loves one's Art no service seems – "

But Delia stopped him with her hand

工作，也许你就不可能把那幅画卖给那个庇奥利亚人了。"

"他不是庇奥利亚人，"乔慢吞吞地说。

"哎，算了，他是什么地方人都没有关系。你真是个聪明的男子汉。乔——亲亲我吧，告诉我——是什么使你怀疑我没去给克蕾门蒂娜上音乐课呢？"

"我什么都没怀疑，直到今天晚上。"乔说，"而且要不是今天下午我从机房里去给楼上的一个被熨斗烫伤的姑娘送棉纱和油膏的话，我是不会起疑心的。这两周以来，我就在那家洗衣店里烧锅炉。"

"这么说你没有……"

"我的那位庇奥利亚主顾，"乔说，"和品克奈将军一样都是同一门艺术的产物——不过这门艺术既不是绘画也不是音乐。"

他们两个都笑了起来，乔又说道：

"当一个人热爱他所认准的艺术时，任何奉献都……"

但德丽雅伸手捂住了他的嘴。"不，"她说——"只要'当

on his lips. "No," she said – "just 'When one loves.'"

一个人去爱的时候' 就足够了。"

1. 金门是美国旧金山湾口的海峡；哈得拉斯是北卡罗来纳州海岸的海峡，与英文的"帽架"谐音；合恩角是南美智利的海峡，与"衣架"谐音；拉布拉多是哈得逊湾与大西洋间的半岛，与"边门"谐音。
2. 拜占庭式为公元 6 世纪至 15 世纪间东罗马帝国的建筑式样，圆屋顶、拱门、细工镶嵌。
3. 班范纽都•切利尼（1500 年~1571 年）意大利著名雕刻家。
4. 庇奥利亚是伊利诺州中部的城市。

3. THE COP AND THE ANTHEM
3. 警察与赞美诗

On his bench in Madison Square Soapy moved uneasily. When wild geese honk high of nights, and when women without sealskin coats grow kind to their husbands, and when Soapy moves uneasily on his bench in the park, you may know that winter is near at hand.

A dead leaf fell in Soapy's lap. That was Jack Frost's card. Jack is kind to the regular denizens of Madison Square, and gives fair warning of his annual call. At the corners of four streets he hands his pasteboard to the North Wind, footman of the mansion of All Outdoors, so that the inhabitants·thereof may make ready.

Soapy's mind became cognisant of the fact that the time had come for him to resolve himself into a singular Committee of Ways and Means to provide against the coming rigour. And therefore he moved uneasily on his bench.

The hibernatorial ambitions of Soapy were not of the highest. In them there were no considerations of Mediterranean cruises, of soporific Southern skies drifting in the Vesuvian Bay. Three

躺在麦迪逊广场的长凳上，苏比不安地翻来覆去。每当大雁在夜空中引吭高鸣，每当没有海豹皮衣的女人对丈夫更加温存，每当苏比在街心公园的长凳上辗转反侧，这个时候你就该知道，冬天已经迫在眉睫了。

一片枯叶飘落到苏比的大腿上，那是杰克·弗洛斯特[1]的名片。杰克总是对麦迪逊广场的常住居民们厚爱有加，每年光临之际，总要热情地先打个招呼。他会先在十字街头把名片交给"露天公寓"的门仆"北风"，以便让居民们做好准备。

苏比明白，为了抵御这冬季的严寒，是他亲自出马组织一个单人财物委员会的时候了。为此，他在长凳上辗转反侧，难以入睡。

苏比的过冬计划不属于要求高的那种。他没打算去地中海旅游，也没有想过去南方晒那令人昏昏欲睡的太阳，更没想过要去维苏威海湾漂流。他梦寐以求的

months on the Island was what his soul craved. Three months of assured board and bed and congenial company, safe from Boreas and bluecoats, seemed to Soapy the essence of things desirable.

For years the hospitable Blackwell's had been his winter quarters. Just as his more fortunate fellow New Yorkers had bought their tickets to Palm Beach and the Riviera each winter, so Soapy had made his humble arrangements for his annual hegira to the Island. And now the time was come. On the previous night three Sabbath newspapers, distributed beneath his coat, about his ankles and over his lap, had failed to repulse the cold as he slept on his bench near the spurting fountain in the ancient square. So the Island loomed big and timely in Soapy's mind. He scorned the provisions made in the name of charity for the city's dependents. In Soapy's opinion the Law was more benign than Philanthropy. There was an endless round of institutions, municipal and eleemosynary, on which he might set out and receive lodging and food accordant with the simple life. But to one of Soapy's proud spirit the gifts of charity are encumbered. If not in coin you must pay in humiliation

仅仅是在岛上呆足三个月。整整三个月，不愁食宿，有意气相投的伙伴，并且不受"北风"[2]和警察的骚扰。在苏比看来，人生的乐趣也莫过于此了。

多年来，好客的布莱克韦尔岛一直是苏比冬天的最佳寓所。正如比他有福气的纽约人每年都要买票去棕榈滩[3]和里维埃拉过冬一样。现在又到了苏比为一年一度投奔小岛作必要准备的时候了。昨天晚上，他睡在老广场喷水池旁的一个长凳上，用三份星期日的报纸分别垫在外套里、包住脚踝、盖着大腿，也没能抵挡住刺骨的严寒。这不免使苏比的脑海中快速而清晰的浮现出岛上的情景。他瞧不起以慈善事业的名义对地方穷人所做的布施，在苏比看来，法律比救济更为仁慈。诚然，他可以去的地方多的是，有市政府办的，也有慈善机构办的。那些地方都能混吃混住，勉强度日。但对于苏比这样灵魂高傲的人来说，接受施舍是一种另人难以忍受的折磨。从慈善机构得到好处固然可以不用付钱，但是却必须遭受精神上的屈辱，正如恺撒对待布鲁图那样[4]。要睡慈善机构的床铺，都得被人押着先

of spirit for every benefit received at the hands of philanthropy. As Caesar had his Brutus, every bed of charity must have its toll of a bath, every loaf of bread its compensation of a private and personal inquisition. Wherefore it is better to be a guest of the law, which though conducted by rules, does not meddle unduly with a gentleman's private affairs.

Soapy, having decided to go to the Island, at once set about accomplishing his desire. There were many easy ways of doing this. The pleasantest was to dine luxuriously at some expensive restaurant; and then, after declaring insolvency, be handed over quietly and without uproar to a policeman. An accommodating magistrate would do the rest.

Soapy left his bench and strolled out of the square and across the level sea of asphalt, where Broadway and Fifth Avenue flow together. Up Broadway he turned, and halted at a glittering cafe, where are gathered together nightly the choicest products of the grape, the silk-worm and the protoplasm.

Soapy had confidence in himself from the lowest button of his vest upward. He was shaven, and his coat was decent and his neat black, ready-tied four-in-hand had

去洗澡；要吃一片免费的面包，就得先把自己的个人隐私交代个一清二楚。因此，还不如当个法律的客人。虽然法律循规蹈矩，但至少它不会过分地干涉一位绅士的私事。

既然打定主意要去岛上，苏比便开始准备实现他的计划。简单的办法倒真有不少，其中最舒服的莫过于去豪华餐厅美美地吃上一顿，然后声明自己身无分文，这样就可以被悄悄地、毫不声张地交到警察手里，剩下的事自会有一位随和的治安官来处理。

苏比离开长凳，踱出广场，穿过百老汇大街和第五大道交汇处那片平坦的柏油马路。来到百老汇大街，在一家灯火通明的咖啡馆前停了下来。每天晚上，这里都汇集了葡萄、蚕桑及原生质的最佳制品。[5]

苏比对自己马甲最下面一颗扣子以上的部分很有信心。他刮了胡子，上衣得体，佩戴的那条干干净净的黑领带是一位女教士

been presented to him by a lady missionary on Thanksgiving Day. If he could reach a table in the restaurant unsuspected success would be his. The portion of him that would show above the table would raise no doubt in the waiter's mind. A roasted mallard duck, thought Soapy, would be about the thing – with a bottle of Chablis, and then Camembert, a demi-tasse and a cigar. One dollar for the cigar would be enough. The total would not be so high as to call forth any supreme manifestation of revenge from the cafe management; and yet the meat would leave him filled and happy for the journey to his winter refuge.

But as Soapy set foot inside the restaurant door the head waiter's eye fell upon his frayed trousers and decadent shoes. Strong and ready hands turned him about and conveyed him in silence and haste to the sidewalk and averted the ignoble fate of the menaced mallard.

Soapy turned off Broadway. It seemed that his route to the coveted island was not to be an epicurean one. Some other way of entering limbo must be thought of.

At a corner of Sixth Avenue electric lights and cunningly displayed wares behind plate-glass made a shop window

在感恩节送给他的。如果在他到达餐桌之前没有让人起疑心的话，那么他就胜券在握了。他露在桌面的上半身还不至于引起侍者的怀疑。一只烤野鸭，苏比寻思着，这就差不多了——再来一瓶夏布利酒，一份卡门贝干酪[6]，一杯清咖啡和一根雪茄。只要一美元一根的雪茄就足够了，全部加在一起不能太贵，以免咖啡馆的店主发狠报复。吃下这顿饭后，他就可以心满意足、开开心心地踏上他的冬季避难旅程了。

可是，苏比刚迈脚踏入餐厅，侍者领班的目光便落在他那条旧裤子和那双破皮鞋上。一双粗壮有力的手掌推得他转了个身，安静而又迅速地把他打发回了人行道。那只险些遭到毒手的野鸭子，命运也因此被扭转。

苏比离开了百老汇大街，看来靠白吃白喝踏上朝思暮想的小岛，这个办法是行不通了。要进监狱，还得想想其他办法。

在第六大道的拐角处有一家商店，摆在灯火辉煌、装饰精巧的大玻璃橱窗内的商品尤为引人

conspicuous. Soapy took a cobblestone and dashed it through the glass. People came running around the corner, a policeman in the lead. Soapy stood still, with his hands in his pockets, and smiled at the sight of brass buttons.

"Where's the man that done that?" inquired the officer excitedly.

"Don't you figure out that I might have had something to do with it?" said Soapy, not without sarcasm, but friendly, as one greets good fortune.

The policeman's mind refused to accept Soapy even as a clue. Men who smash windows do not remain to parley with the law's minions. They take to their heels. The policeman saw a man half way down the block running to catch a car. With drawn club he joined in the pursuit. Soapy, with disgust in his heart, loafed along, twice unsuccessful.

On the opposite side of the street was a restaurant of no great pretensions. It catered to large appetites and modest purses. Its crockery and atmosphere were thick; its soup and napery thin. Into this place Soapy took his accusive shoes and telltale trousers without challenge. At a table he sat and consumed beefsteak, flapjacks, doughnuts and pie. And then to the waiter

注目。苏比捡起一块鹅卵石向橱窗砸去，人们纷纷从拐角处跑了过来，一位警察跑在最前面。苏比站着一动不动，双手插在裤兜里，对着离眼前越来越近的黄铜扣子[7]微笑。

"肇事者跑哪儿去了？"警察气急败坏地问。

"你难道看不出来我和这事有点关系吗？"苏比很友好地说，但语气中多少带点讽刺。仿佛好运马上就要降临了。

不过在警察看来，苏比连个证人都算不上。没有哪个人砸过橱窗还愿意留在现场与警察聊天的，他们早就逃之夭夭了。警察看到距这半条街的地方有个人正跑着想搭一辆车，便挥着警棍追了过去。苏比心里窝火极了，只得继续游荡。这已经是第二次失败了。

街对面有家不怎么起眼的餐厅，正适合胃口大钱包瘪的顾客。那里的餐具和环境都很粗糙，菜汤和餐巾也都薄的透亮。苏比穿着那双暴露身份的皮鞋和那条泄露真相的裤子进了这家餐厅，这一次他没遭到白眼。他在一个桌前坐下，享受了牛排、煎饼、炸面圈和馅饼。吃完后，他向侍者

be betrayed the fact that the minutest coin and himself were strangers.

"Now, get busy and call a cop," said Soapy. "And don't keep a gentleman waiting."

"No cop for youse," said the waiter, with a voice like butter cakes and an eye like the cherry in a Manhattan cocktail. "Hey, Con!"

Neatly upon his left ear on the callous pavement two waiters pitched Soapy. He arose, joint by joint, as a carpenter's rule opens, and beat the dust from his clothes. Arrest seemed but a rosy dream. The Island seemed very far away. A policeman who stood before a drug store two doors away laughed and walked down the street.

Five blocks Soapy travelled before his courage permitted him to woo capture again. This time the opportunity presented what he fatuously termed to himself a "cinch." A young woman of a modest and pleasing guise was standing before a show window gazing with sprightly interest at its display of shaving mugs and inkstands, and two yards from the window a large policeman of severe demeanour leaned against a water plug.

It was Soapy's design to assume the

坦白道：他与金钱素昧平生。

"现在，快去报警吧，"苏比催促道，"别让我等得太久。"

"用不着惊动警察，"嗓音油腻的像奶油蛋糕，眼睛红如曼哈顿鸡尾酒里浸泡的樱桃的侍者说，"阿康，过来！"

苏比被两个侍者干净利落地推倒在冷冰冰的人行道上，左耳着地。他费劲地把自己撑起来，就像木匠在打开一把折尺，然后掸去衣服上的尘土。被捕仿佛是一个美梦，小岛似乎遥不可及了。一个正站在两个门面之外药店前的警察，只是对着他笑了笑，便顺着街道走开了。

苏比一直走过五个街口，才再次鼓起勇气去设法被捕。这一次的机会好极了，他一厢情愿的以为这次肯定万无一失。一位衣着朴素讨人喜欢的年轻女士正站在一个橱窗前，兴趣盎然地看着陈列其中的修面缸和墨水瓶架。而两码之外，一位身材魁梧的警察正表情严肃地靠在救火水龙头上。

苏比计划扮成一个下流、令

role of the despicable and execrated "masher." The refined and elegant appearance of his victim and the contiguity of the conscientious cop encouraged him to believe that he would soon feel the pleasant official clutch upon his arm that would insure his winter quarters on the right little, tight little isle.

Soapy straightened the lady missionary's ready-made tie, dragged his shrinking cuffs into the open, set his hat at a killing cant and sidled toward the young woman. He made eyes at her, was taken with sudden coughs and "hems," smiled, smirked and went brazenly through the impudent and contemptible litany of the "masher." With half an eye Soapy saw that the policeman was watching him fixedly. The young woman moved away a few steps, and again bestowed her absorbed attention upon the shaving mugs. Soapy followed, boldly stepping to her side, raised his hat and said:

"Ah there, Bedelia! Don't you want to come and play in my yard?"

The policeman was still looking. The persecuted young woman had but to beckon a finger and Soapy would be practically en route for his insular haven. Already he imagined he could feel the

人讨厌的"小流氓"。他的对象是一位举止优雅的女士，而旁边这位尽忠职守的好警察，足以使他相信那双可爱的手很快就会落到自己的肩膀上，在岛上过冬总算有着落了。

苏比理了理女教士送给他的领带，把缩进去的袖子拉出来，再把帽子使劲往后推，使它歪得都快掉下来了。他侧着身子向那位女士靠过去，向她抛了个媚眼，又假装咳了几声，嬉皮笑脸、厚颜无耻地把一个"小流氓"该干的一切卑鄙下流的勾当都干尽了。他斜眼瞄着警察，看到他正目不转睛地盯着自己。那位年轻女士走了几步，又专心致志地看起那个修面缸。苏比跟了上去，大胆地走到她身边，把帽子向她举了举，说：

"啊哈，比德莉亚，你难道不想去我的院子玩玩儿吗？"

警察仍紧盯着他们。那遭人非礼的年轻女士只需一招手，苏比就可以踏上去安乐岛的旅程了。他想像着，仿佛已经感觉到警察局的温暖和舒适了。年轻的

cozy warmth of the station-house. The young woman faced him and, stretching out a hand, caught Soapy's coat sleeve.

"Sure, Mike," she said joyfully, "if you'll blow me to a pail of suds. I'd have spoke to you sooner, but the cop was watching."

With the young woman playing the clinging ivy to his oak Soapy walked past the policeman overcome with gloom. He seemed doomed to liberty.

At the next corner he shook off his companion and ran. He halted in the district where by night are found the lightest streets, hearts, vows and librettos. Women in furs and men in greatcoats moved gaily in the wintry air. A sudden fear seized Soapy that some dreadful enchantment had rendered him immune to arrest. The thought brought a little of panic upon it, and when he came upon another policeman lounging grandly in front of a transplendent theatre he caught at the immediate straw of "disorderly conduct."

On the sidewalk Soapy began to yell drunken gibberish at the top of his harsh voice. He danced, howled, raved and otherwise disturbed the welkin.

The policeman twirled his club, turned

女士转过脸来，伸出一只手挽住苏比的胳膊。

"当然啰，迈克，"她兴致勃勃地说，"不过先得破费你给我买杯啤酒。要不是那个警察老盯着我，我早就跟你搭讪了。"

年轻女士像常青藤一样紧紧攀附着苏比这棵橡树。苏比心中无比懊恼地从警察身旁走过。看来他的自由是命中注定的。

刚一拐弯，他便甩掉女伴跑掉了，一口气跑到另一个街区才停下来。这个地方一到晚上，到处都是最明亮的街道，最轻松的心情，最轻浮的誓言和最轻快的歌剧。身着轻裘大氅的淑女绅士们兴高采烈地在凛冽的寒风中来来往往。突然，苏比感到一阵恐惧，觉得仿佛有一种可怕的魔法镇住了他，使他免于被捕。这念头不免使他心里直发慌。但是，当看见一个警察大模大样地在灯火辉煌的剧院门前巡逻时，他立马抓住了"扰乱治安"这根近在眼前的救命稻草。

苏比在人行道上扯开他那破锣般的嗓子，发酒疯似的乱嚷嚷。他又是跳，又是吼，又是骂，使尽一切办法来扰乱这片天空。

his back to Soapy and remarked to a citizen.

"'Tis one of them Yale lads celebratin' the goose egg they give to the Hartford College. Noisy; but no harm. We've instructions to lave them be."

Disconsolate, Soapy ceased his unavailing racket. Would never a policeman lay hands on him? In his fancy the Island seemed an unattainable Arcadia. He buttoned his thin coat against the chilling wind.

In a cigar store he saw a well-dressed man lighting a cigar at a swinging light. His silk umbrella he had set by the door on entering. Soapy stepped inside, secured the umbrella and sauntered off with it slowly. The man at the cigar light followed hastily.

"My umbrella," he said, sternly.

"Oh, is it?" sneered Soapy, adding insult to petit larceny. "Well, why don't you call a policeman? I took it. Your umbrella! Why don't you call a cop? There stands one on the corner."

The umbrella owner slowed his steps. Soapy did likewise, with a presentiment that luck would again run against him. The policeman looked at the two curiously.

警察转着他的警棍,转身背对着苏比,跟一位市民解释道:

"这是耶鲁的小伙子在庆祝胜利呢!他们跟哈特福德学院赛球,请人家吃了个鸭蛋。这的确有点吵,但是不碍事。我们已经接到指示,让他们尽情地闹去吧。"

苏比怏怏地停止了白费力气的吵闹。难道就没有警察来抓他吗?在他的幻梦中,那岛屿已经俨然成为遥不可及的阿卡狄亚[8]了。他扣紧单薄的上衣,以抵御刺骨的寒风。

这时,他看见有一位衣着考究的人正在雪茄店里用摇曳的火光点烟。那个人进店时,把他的绸伞靠在门边放着。苏比走进店去,拿起绸伞,慢吞吞地退了出来。那个点烟人急忙追了出来。

"我的伞!他厉声喝道。

"噢,是吗?"苏比冷笑着说,在小偷小摸之上再加上条侮辱罪吧,"你为什么不叫警察呢?没错,是我拿的,你的伞!你为什么不叫警察?拐角那儿就有一个。"

绸伞的主人放慢了脚步,苏比也放慢了脚步。他忽然有一种预感,好运将再次与他擦肩而过

"Of course," said the umbrella man – "that is – well, you know how these mistakes occur – I – if it's your umbrella I hope you'll excuse me – I picked it up this morning in a restaurant – If you recognise it as yours, why – I hope you'll –"

"Of course it's mine," said Soapy, viciously.

The ex-umbrella man retreated. The policeman hurried to assist a tall blonde in an opera cloak across the street in front of a street car that was approaching two blocks away.

Soapy walked eastward through a street damaged by improvements. He hurled the umbrella wrathfully into an excavation. He muttered against the men who wear helmets and carry clubs. Because he wanted to fall into their clutches, they seemed to regard him as a king who could do no wrong.

At length Soapy reached one of the avenues to the east where the glitter and turmoil was but faint. He set his face down this toward Madison Square, for the homing instinct survives even when the home is a park bench.

But on an unusually quiet corner Soapy came to a standstill. Here was an

了。那位警察好奇地看着他们俩。

"当然，"绸伞主人说，"嗯……你知道有时会发生误会……我……要是这伞是你的，我希望你能原谅我……这是今天早上我在餐厅捡到的……要是你认出这伞是你的，那么……我希望你别……"

"当然是我的，"苏比凶巴巴地说。

绸伞的前主人走开了。那位警察急匆匆地跑去扶一位身穿晚礼服的金发高个儿女士过马路，免得她被从两条街之外驶来的电车撞到。

苏比朝东走去，穿过一条因翻修被弄得坑坑洼洼的街道。他忿忿地把绸伞猛地扔进一个坑里，嘟嘟囔囔地咒骂起那些头戴钢盔、手拿警棍的家伙来。他是一心只想落入他们手中，而他们却偏偏把他当成永不犯错的国王[9]来对待。

最后，苏比来到通往东区的一条马路上。这儿灯光昏暗，嘈杂声也隐隐约约。他顺着街道走向麦迪逊广场，即使他的家只是公园里的一条长凳，但他仍有归巢的本能。

但在一个僻静的拐角处，苏

old church, quaint and rambling and gabled. Through one violet-stained window a soft light glowed, where, no doubt, the organist loitered over the keys, making sure of his mastery of the coming Sabbath anthem. For there drifted out to Soapy's ears sweet music that caught and held him transfixed against the convolutions of the iron fence.

The moon was above, lustrous and serene; vehicles and pedestrians were few; sparrows twittered sleepily in the eaves – for a little while the scene might have been a country churchyard. And the anthem that the organist played cemented Soapy to the iron fence, for he had known it well in the days when his life contained such things as mothers and roses and ambitions and friends and immaculate thoughts and collars.

The conjunction of Soapy's receptive state of mind and the influences about the old church wrought a sudden and wonderful change in his soul. He viewed with swift horror the pit into which he had tumbled, the degraded days, unworthy desires, dead hopes, wrecked faculties and base motives that made up his existence.

And also in a moment his heart responded thrillingly to this novel mood.

比停下了脚步。这儿有一座古老的教堂，古色古香，布局稍显凌乱，是那种靠山墙的建筑。一缕柔和的灯光透过褪色的紫色玻璃窗透出来。很显然，风琴师为了练熟星期天的赞美诗，正在键盘上按来按去。苏比被这动人的音乐深深地吸引住了，他不由得紧紧地靠在了螺旋形的铁栏杆上。

明月当空，光辉静穆。车辆和行人都很稀少，屋檐下的麻雀在睡梦中偶尔啁啾几声——有那么一会儿，这情景犹如乡村中的教堂墓地。风琴师弹奏的赞美诗使铁栏杆前的苏比入了神。当他的生活中还拥有母爱、玫瑰、理想、朋友以及洁白无瑕的思想和衣领的时候，赞美诗对他来说是很熟悉的。

苏比觉醒的内心和老教堂潜移默化的作用交织在一起，使他的灵魂突然起了奇妙的变化。他幡然醒悟到自己已经坠入了深渊，那些堕落的日子、低俗的欲望、心灰意冷、才智枯竭、动机不良——这一切已经构成了他的存在。

就在那一刻，这种全新的思想境界令他激动不已。一股强烈

An instantaneous and strong impulse moved him to battle with his desperate fate. He would pull himself out of the mire; he would make a man of himself again; he would conquer the evil that had taken possession of him. There was time; he was comparatively young yet; he would resurrect his old eager ambitions and pursue them without faltering. Those solemn but sweet organ notes had set up a revolution in him. To-morrow he would go into the roaring downtown district and find work. A fur importer had once offered him a place as driver. He would find him to-morrow and ask for the position. He would be somebody in the world. He would—

Soapy felt a hand laid on his arm. He looked quickly around into the broad face of a policeman.

"What are you doin' here?" asked the officer.

"Nothin'," said Soapy.

"Then come along," said the policeman.

"Three months on the Island," said the Magistrate in the Police Court the next morning.

的冲动鼓舞他去挑战坎坷的命运。他要把自己拖出泥潭，他要重新做人，他要征服那个曾经奴役自己的恶魔。还有时间，他尚且年轻，他要重振当年的雄心壮志，并坚定不移地把它变为现实。庄重而甜美的管风琴音调在他的内心深处掀起了一场革命。明天，他要去繁华的市中心找工作。有个皮货进口商曾让他去当司机，明天就去找他，把这份差事接下来。他想做个大人物。他要……

忽然，苏比感觉有只手压在了他的胳膊上。他猛地回过头，看见一位警察的胖脸。

"你在这儿做什么？"警察问。

"没什么……"苏比回答道。

"那就跟我走一趟吧。"警察说。

第二天早晨，警察局法庭的治安官宣判："布莱克韦尔岛，三个月。"

1.杰克·弗洛斯特是"霜冻"的拟人化称呼；弗洛斯特是 frost（霜冻）的音译。

2.Boreas 希腊神话中北风之神；常指北风。

3.棕榈滩，美国佛罗里达州东南部城镇，冬令游憩胜地;里维埃拉，南欧沿地中海一段地区，在法国的东南部和意大利的西北部，是节假日旅游胜地。

4.恺撒，Julius Caesar(100 BC ~ 44 BC)，罗马统帅、政治家，罗马的独裁者，遭到共和派贵族的刺杀。布鲁图，Brutus(80BC ~ 42BC)，罗马贵族派政治家，刺杀恺撒的主谋，后逃出雅典，集结军队对抗安东尼和屋大维联军，战败自杀。

5.作者诙谐调侃的说法，分别指美酒、华丽衣物和上流人物。

6.夏布利酒,原产于法国的莎布利斯的一种无甜味的白葡萄酒；卡门贝干酪一种产于法国的软干酪。

7.黄铜扣子,指警察，因警察上衣的扣子是黄铜做的。

8.原为古希腊的一个山区，现位于伯罗奔尼撒半岛中部，以田园牧歌式的淳朴生活而著称，代指"世外桃源"。

9.来自英语谚语：国王不可能犯错误。

4. THE LAST LEAF
4. 最后一片常春藤叶

In a little district west of Washington Square the streets have run crazy and broken themselves into small strips called "places." These "places" make strange angles and curves. One street crosses itself a time or two. An artist once discovered a valuable possibility in this street. Suppose a collector with a bill for paints, paper and canvas should, in traversing this route, suddenly meet himself coming back, without a cent having been paid on account!

So, to quaint old Greenwich Village the art people soon came prowling, hunting for north windows and eighteenth-century gables and Dutch attics and low rents. Then they imported some pewter mugs and a chafing dish or two from Sixth avenue, and became a "colony."

At the top of a squatty, three-story brick Sue and Johnsy had their studio. "Johnsy" was familiar for Joanna. One was from Maine; the other from California. They had met at the table d'hôte of an Eighth street "Delmonico's," and

在华盛顿广场西面有一个小区，那里的街道都杂乱无章的延展开来，然后分叉成一条条狭窄的"胡同"，于是这些"胡同"便呈现出奇怪的角度和曲线。一条街自个就可以来回交叉一两次。曾有一个画家发现了这条街的价值所在：万一有个要账的跑到这来，讨要颜料、纸张和画布的钱，他会突然间发现自己两手空空、没有要到一分钱却原路而返了！

就这样，不久以后就有一些画家摸索到这个古老而精致的格林尼治村来了。他们看中的就是这儿朝北的窗户、18世纪的尖顶山墙、荷兰式的阁楼，以及廉价的房租。接着，他们又从第六街引进了一些白蜡酒杯和一两只火锅，这里便成了他们的地地道道的"艺术区"。

苏和琼西的画室在一座低矮的三层砖房的顶楼上。"琼西"是乔安娜的昵称。她俩一个来自缅因州，一个来自加利福尼亚州。在第八街的"台尔蒙尼歌之家"的餐桌上相遇，惊喜地发现两个人都喜欢

found their tastes in art, chicory salad and bishop sleeves so congenial that the joint studio resulted.

That was in May. In November a cold, unseen stranger, whom the doctors called Pneumonia, stalked about the colony, touching one here and there with his icy fingers. Over on the East Side this ravager strode boldly, smiting his victims by scores, but his feet trod slowly through the maze of the narrow and moss-grown "places."

Mr. Pneumonia was not what you would call a chivalric old gentleman. A mite of a little woman with blood thinned by California zephyrs was hardly fair game for the red-fisted, short-breathed old duffer. But Johnsy he smote; and she lay, scarcely moving, on her painted iron bedstead, looking through the small Dutch window-panes at the blank side of the next brick house.

One morning the busy doctor invited Sue into the hallway with a shaggy, gray eyebrow.

"She has one chance in – let us say, ten," he said, as he shook down the mercury in his clinical thermometer. "And that chance is for her to want to live. This way people have of lining-up

艺术、生菜色拉和时装，既然志趣相投，于是两人便合租了那间画室。

那是5月份的事了。11月时，一个冷酷的、肉眼看不见的陌生人——医生们把他称作"肺炎"，悄悄地来到艺术区游荡，用他那冰冷的手指头碰碰这里摸摸那里。在广场的东边，这个侵袭者更加地肆无忌惮，随意就击倒了几十个人，可到了宛若迷宫、狭窄而青苔满地的"胡同"，他也只能缓慢前行了。

肺炎先生不是你们所认为的那种具有武士风范的老绅士。这个挥舞着红色拳头、呼吸急促的老笨蛋根本不应该把一个身体瘦弱，连加利福尼亚州的西风都能让她毫无血色的弱女子当成猎物。可是，琼西却被击倒了。她一动不动地躺在那张被她漆过的铁床上，透过小小的荷兰式玻璃窗凝望着对面砖房子的那面空荡荡的墙。

一天早上，那个忙碌的医生抬了抬蓬松的灰色眉毛，示意苏到外面的走廊上去。

"要我说的话，她痊愈的几率只有十分之一。"医生边甩体温表里的水银柱边说，"如果她想要活下去，那么她就得拥有希望。有些人似乎不怎么想活下去，就喜欢关

on the side of the undertaker makes the entire pharmacopeia look silly. Your little lady has made up her mind that she's not going to get well. Has she anything on her mind?"

"She – she wanted to paint the Bay of Naples some day," said Sue.

"Paint? – bosh! Has she anything on her mind worth thinking about twice – a man, for instance?"

"A man?" said Sue, with a jew's-harp twang in her voice. "Is a man worth – but, no, doctor; there is nothing of the kind."

"Well, it is the weakness, then," said the doctor. "I will do all that science, so far as it may filter through my efforts, can accomplish. But whenever my patient begins to count the carriages in her funeral procession I subtract 50 per cent. from the curative power of medicines. If you will get her to ask one question about the new winter styles in cloak sleeves I will promise you a one-in-five chance for her, instead of one in ten."

After the doctor had gone Sue went into the workroom and cried a Japanese napkin to a pulp. Then she swaggered into Johnsy's room with her drawing board, whistling ragtime.

Johnsy lay, scarcely making a ripple

照殡仪馆的生意,这简直让整个医学界都束手无策。你的朋友看来是认定自己不会康复了。你知道她在想些什么吗?"

"她——她希望能去画那不勒斯海湾。"苏说。

"画画?——真是胡闹!她脑子里没有什么值得好好期待的事吗——比如说,一个男人?"

"男人?"苏带着像单簧口琴一样的鼻音问道,"难道男人值得——不,医生,没有这种事。"

"嗯,这就是不利的地方,"医生说,"我会用我所知的所有知识来治疗她。可要是我的病人已经开始考虑她出丧的时候会有多少辆马车,我就不得不把药效减掉一半了。要是你有法子让她对冬季最新款式的风衣袖子感兴趣的话,那我就可以向你保证,她康复的几率会变成五分之一,而不是十分之一。"

医生走后,苏走进工作室哭起来,泪水把一条日本餐巾弄成了纸浆。然后她拿起画板,装作神采奕奕的样子走进琼西的屋子,嘴里还哼着爵士乐。

琼西躺在床上,脸朝着窗外,

under the bedclothes, with her face toward the window. Sue stopped whistling, thinking she was asleep.

She arranged her board and began a pen-and-ink drawing to illustrate a magazine story. Young artists must pave their way to Art by drawing pictures for magazine stories that young authors write to pave their way to Literature.

As Sue was sketching a pair of elegant horseshow riding trousers and a monocle on the figure of the hero, an Idaho cowboy, she heard a low sound, several times repeated. She went quickly to the bedside.

Johnsy's eyes were open wide. She was looking out the window and counting – counting backward.

"Twelve," she said, and a little later "eleven;" and then "ten," and "nine;" and then "eight" and "seven," almost together.

Sue looked solicitously out the window. What was there to count? There was only a bare, dreary yard to be seen, and the blank side of the brick house twenty feet away. An old, old ivy vine, gnarled and decayed at the roots, climbed half way up the brick wall. The cold breath of autumn had stricken its leaves from the

被子里的身体几乎一动不动。苏还以为她睡着了，于是便停止了哼唱。

她支好画板，开始给杂志上的故事画钢笔插图。为了铺平通向艺术的道路，年轻的画家必须给杂志里的故事画插图，就像为了铺平通向文学的道路，年轻的作家也必须写故事一样。

苏正要给故事里的男主角——一个爱达荷州牧人着上一条马匹展览上的时髦马裤和一个单片眼镜，她听到一个声音在微弱的重复，她快步走到床前。

琼西正睁大眼睛望着窗外，数着……并且是倒数着。

"12……"她数道。过了一会儿又说到："11……"然后是"10"、"9"，接着差不多是同时数着"8"和"7"。

苏关切地朝窗外望去，同时纳闷有什么好数的？那儿只是一个寸草不生的沉闷的院子而已，20英尺以外还有一面空荡荡的墙。砖墙的半腰上攀着一棵年迈的常春藤，朽烂的根纠结在一起。秋日的寒风几乎把藤上的叶子吹光了，只剩下光秃秃的枝条还紧攀着剥落

vine until its skeleton branches clung, almost bare, to the crumbling bricks.

"What is it, dear?" asked Sue.

"Six," said Johnsy, in almost a whisper. "They're falling faster now. Three days ago there were almost a hundred. It made my head ache to count them. But now it's easy. There goes another one. There are only five left now."

"Five what, dear. Tell your Sudie."

"Leaves. On the ivy vine. When the last one falls I must go, too. I've known that for three days. Didn't the doctor tell you?"

"Oh, I never heard of such nonsense," complained Sue, with magnificent scorn. "What have old ivy leaves to do with your getting well? And you used to love that vine so, you naughty girl. Don't be a goosey. Why, the doctor told me this morning that your chances for getting well real soon were – let's see exactly what he said – he said the chances were ten to one! Why, that's almost as good a chance as we have in New York when we ride on the street cars or walk past a new building. Try to take some broth now, and let Sudie go back to her drawing, so she can sell the editor man with it, and buy port wine for her sick child, and pork

的砖墙。

"你在数什么，亲爱的？"苏问道。

"六片，"琼西耳语般地说，"它们现在落得更快了。三天前还有差不多一百来片，数得我头生疼。现在好了，又掉了一片。只剩下五片了。"

"五片什么，亲爱的？告诉你的苏娣吧。"

"叶子，常春藤上的叶子。等到最后一片叶子落去，我也就走到了尽头。三天前我就知道了，难道医生没告诉你吗？"

"哼，我可从来没听过这样的胡言乱语！"苏十分不屑地抱怨到，"那些老常春藤叶子和你的康复有什么关系？你说什么傻话，你不是很喜欢这棵树吗？别犯傻了！瞧，今天早上，医生还和我说了你会立即痊愈的，几率是——照他的原话说——有九成把握。噢，几乎和我们在纽约坐电车或是走路经过一栋新楼房的几率一样大。起来喝点肉汤吧，让我回去画我的画，画完好卖给编辑先生，等换了钱，就可以给她生病的孩子买点红葡萄酒，再给贪嘴的自个儿买点猪排了。"

chops for her greedy self."

"You needn't get any more wine," said Johnsy, keeping her eyes fixed out the window. "There goes another. No, I don't want any broth. That leaves just four. I want to see the last one fall before it gets dark. Then I'll go, too."

"Johnsy, dear," said Sue, bending over her, "will you promise me to keep your eyes closed, and not look out the window until I am done working? I must hand those drawings in by to-morrow. I need the light, or I would draw the shade down."

"Couldn't you draw in the other room?" asked Johnsy, coldly.

"I'd rather be here by you," said Sue. "Besides I don't want you to keep looking at those silly ivy leaves."

"Tell me as soon as you have finished," said Johnsy, closing her eyes, and lying white and still as a fallen statue, "because I want to see the last one fall. I'm tired of waiting. I'm tired of thinking. I went to turn loose my hold on everything, and go sailing down, down, just like one of those poor, tired leaves."

"Try to sleep," said Sue. "I must call Behrman up to be my model for the old hermit miner. I'll not be gone a minute.

"你犯不着再为我买酒了，"琼西的眼睛一直盯着窗外，"叶子又掉了一片……不，我不想喝什么肉汤，只剩下四片了。我想在天黑之前看最后一片叶子落下，然后我也要去了。"

"琼西，亲爱的，"苏俯身看着她，"你能不能答应我把眼睛闭上，不往窗外看。等我画完，好不好？明天我必须把这些插图交上，我需要光线，否则我一定会把窗帘拉下来！"

"你难道不能去另一间屋子画吗？"琼西冷冷地问。

"我喜欢和你在一起，"苏说，"再说，我不想让你老盯着那些愚蠢的常春藤叶子。"

"你画完就立刻告诉我，"琼西说着，然后闭上了双眼躺在床上，她脸色苍白，就像是一尊倒下的雕像。"我想看最后一片叶子落下来，我不愿意再等了，更不愿意再想了。我想丢下一切，就像一片可怜的疲倦的叶子一样坠落下去，坠落下去。"

"试着睡一会儿吧，"苏说，"我得下楼去叫贝尔曼给我当那个隐居老矿工的模特。我不到一分

Don't try to move 'till I come back."

Old Behrman was a painter who lived on the ground floor beneath them. He was past sixty and had a Michael Angelo's Moses beard curling down from the head of a satyr along the body of an imp. Behrman was a failure in art. Forty years he had wielded the brush without getting near enough to touch the hem of his Mistress's robe. He had been always about to paint a masterpiece, but had never yet begun it. For several years he had painted nothing except now and then a daub in the line of commerce or advertising. He earned a little by serving as a model to those young artists in the colony who could not pay the price of a professional. He drank gin to excess, and still talked of his coming masterpiece. For the rest he was a fierce little old man, who scoffed terribly at softness in any one, and who regarded himself as especial mastiff-in-waiting to protect the two young artists in the studio above.

Sue found Behrman smelling strongly of juniper berries in his dimly lighted den below. In one corner was a blank canvas on an easel that had been waiting there for twenty-five years to receive the first line of the masterpiece. She told him of

钟就回来，在我回来之前千万别乱动。"

老贝尔曼也是个画家，就住在她们的楼下。他六十多岁了，蓄着一把米开朗琪罗的摩西雕像那样的大胡子，这胡子从塞特（一个半人半兽的森林之神）的脑袋上长出来，又在小鬼似的身躯上卷曲地飘拂着。贝尔曼没能在艺术上取得成功。他挥舞了近四十年的画笔，却从来没有触摸到艺术女神的裙边。他老是说就要画一幅杰作，却迟迟没有动笔。几年来，除了时不时地涂鸦些商业广告之类的玩意儿，他没有真正的画过什么。就靠着给住在艺术区里那些没钱雇职业模特儿的年轻画家们当模特儿来挣点儿小钱勉强度日。他喝起杜松子酒来就没有节制，还时常提到打算画的那幅杰作。另外，他还是一个脾气暴躁的小老头，总是无情地嘲弄别人流露出来的柔情，却自诩是专门保护顶楼画室里那两个年轻女画家的看门狗。

苏在楼下那间光线惨淡的画室找贝尔曼的时候，他浑身都是杜松子酒的味道。在屋子的角落立着一个绷了空白画布的画架，那张画布已经足足等了那幅杰作25年了，可是迄今为止一根线条还没有等

Johnsy's fancy, and how she feared she would, indeed, light and fragile as a leaf herself, float away when her slight hold upon the world grew weaker.

Old Behrman, with his red eyes, plainly streaming, shouted his contempt and derision for such idiotic imaginings.

"Vass!" he cried. "Is dere people in de world mit der foolishness to die because leafs dey drop off from a confounded vine? I haf not heard of such a thing. No, I will not bose as a model for your fool hermit-dunderhead. Vy do you allow dot silly pusiness to come in der prain of her? Ach, dot poor little Miss Johnsy."

"She is very ill and weak," said Sue, "and the fever has left her mind morbid and full of strange fancies. Very well, Mr. Behrman, if you do not care to pose for me, you needn't. But I think you are a horrid old – old flibbertigibbet."

"You are just like a woman!" yelled Behrman. "Who said I will not bose? Go on. I come mit you. For half an hour I haf peen trying to say dot I am ready to bose. Gott! dis is not any blace in which one so goot as Miss Yohnsy shall lie sick. Some day I vill baint a master piece, and ve shall all go away. Gott! yes."

Johnsy was sleeping when they went

来。苏告诉他琼西的胡思乱想，说她害怕琼西对这个世界越来越没有留恋，最后真得会像一片叶子那样飘走。

老贝尔曼两眼发红，显然他在流泪，但他却非要大声的做出讥讽和嘲笑，说从没听过这种白痴般的胡思乱想。

"啥嘛！"他喊道，"这世上还真有人傻到以为当那些该死的常春藤叶子掉光以后，他们就会死掉？我从来没听说过这种事。不，我才不要当你那愚蠢的隐居矿工的模特儿呢。你怎么能让她想那些乱七八糟的东西呢？唉，可怜的琼西小姐。"

"她病得很严重，身子很虚弱，"苏说，"发烧发得头昏脑胀，满脑子都是怪念头。好吧！贝尔曼先生，你要是不愿意给我当模特儿就算了，可是说实话，我觉得你是个让人讨厌的老——老啰唆鬼！"

"你真够婆妈的！"贝尔曼大声嚷道，"谁说我不要当模特儿啦？走，我跟你一块儿去。这么半天了，我不是一直说着要给你当模特儿吗？老天，像琼西小姐这么好的姑娘，怎么能躺在这种地方生病呢。总有一天我要画一幅杰作，然后我们就一块儿搬出去。噢我的上

upstairs. Sue pulled the shade down to the window-sill, and motioned Behrman into the other room. In there they peered out the window fearfully at the ivy vine. Then they looked at each other for a moment without speaking. A persistent, cold rain was falling, mingled with snow. Behrman, in his old blue shirt, took his seat as the hermit-miner on an upturned kettle for a rock.

When Sue awoke from an hour's sleep the next morning she found Johnsy with dull, wide-open eyes staring at the drawn green shade.

"Pull it up; I want to see," she ordered, in a whisper.

Wearily Sue obeyed.

But, lo! after the beating rain and fierce gusts of wind that had endured through the livelong night, there yet stood out against the brick wall one ivy leaf. It was the last on the vine. Still dark green near its stem, but with its serrated edges tinted with the yellow of dissolution and decay, it hung bravely from a branch some twenty feet above the ground.

"It is the last one," said Johnsy. "I thought it would surely fall during the night. I heard the wind. It will fall to-day,

帝，我保证！"

他们上了楼，琼西正在睡觉。苏把窗帘一直拉到遮住窗台地方，然后朝贝尔曼打了个手势，让他到隔壁房间去。在那里，他们担惊受怕地瞄着那棵常春藤。然后，他们相对无言，说不出任何话来。外面不停地下着冰冷的雨，间或还夹杂着一些雪片。贝尔曼穿着他那破旧的蓝衬衣，把一把铁壶翻过来当作岩石，扮成隐居的矿工。

第二天早上，苏只睡了一个小时就醒过来，她看见琼西正睁着呆滞无神的双眼呆呆地地盯着拉下来的绿色窗帘。

"拉起窗帘，我想要看一看。"她轻声命令道。

疲惫的苏照她说的做了。

可是，看啊！经过一整夜猛烈的雨打风吹之后，还有一片叶子挂在砖墙上，这是常春藤上的最后一片叶子。它长在靠近茎部的地方，虽然锯齿状的叶子边缘已经枯萎发黄，但看起来仍然是深绿色的，这片叶子就勇敢地挂在一根离地20多英尺高的藤枝上。

"这是最后的一片叶子了，"琼西说道，"我以为昨天晚上它肯定会落了呢，因为我听见刮风的声

and I shall die at the same time."

"Dear, dear!" said Sue, leaning her worn face down to the pillow, "think of me, if you won't think of yourself. What would I do?"

But Johnsy did not answer. The lonesomest thing in all the world is a soul when it is making ready to go on its mysterious, far journey. The fancy seemed to possess her more strongly as one by one the ties that bound her to friendship and to earth were loosed.

The day wore away, and even through the twilight they could see the lone ivy leaf clinging to its stem against the wall. And then, with the coming of the night the north wind was again loosed, while the rain still beat against the windows and pattered down from the low Dutch eaves.

When it was light enough Johnsy, the merciless, commanded that the shade be raised.

The ivy leaf was still there.

Johnsy lay for a long time looking at it. And then she called to Sue, who was stirring her chicken broth over the gas stove.

"I've been a bad girl, Sudie," said Johnsy. "Something has made that last

音了。今天它一定会落的，然后我也就死去了。"

"哎呀，亲爱的，"苏把疲倦的脸庞靠在枕边对她说，"你不为自己想，也得想想我啊，你要是走了，可叫我怎么办呢？"

琼西没有回答。当一个灵魂准备踏上那神秘而又遥远的永恒之旅时，她就变成了这个世界上最寂寞的人。那些联系她同友谊以及大地之间的链条一条接着一条松开以后，她的妄想也变得越来越严重。

白天渐渐过去了，但在暮色中，她们仍然能看见那片惟一的藤叶紧紧地依附在靠墙的枝藤上。不久，黑夜到来了，随之而来的还有肆虐的北风，雨水依旧不停地拍打着窗子，然后从低垂的荷兰式屋檐上滴落下去。

天刚泛起微光，琼西就毫不留情地要求苏把窗帘拉起来。

那片藤叶还在那里。

琼西躺在床上，盯着它看了很久。然后开口呼唤正在煤气炉边给她煮鸡汤的苏。

"我真是差劲，亲爱的苏娣，"琼西说道，"冥冥之中有某种东西

leaf stay there to show me how wicked I was. It is a sin to want to die. You may bring me a little broth now, and some milk with a little port in it, and – no; bring me a hand-mirror first, and then pack some pillows about me, and I will sit up and watch you cook."

An hour later she said.

"Sudie, some day I hope to paint the Bay of Naples."

The doctor came in the afternoon, and Sue had an excuse to go into the hallway as he left.

"Even chances," said the doctor, taking Sue's thin, shaking hand in his. "With good nursing you'll win. And now I must see another case I have downstairs. Behrman, his name is – some kind of an artist, I believe. Pneumonia, too. He is an old, weak man, and the attack is acute. There is no hope for him; but he goes to the hospital to-day to be made more comfortable."

The next day the doctor said to Sue: "She's out of danger. You've won. Nutrition and care now – that's all."

And that afternoon Sue came to the bed where Johnsy lay, contentedly knitting a very blue and very useless woolen shoulder scarf, and put one arm around

把最后的那片藤叶留在那儿，以显示我是多么恶劣。的确，想死是有罪的。现在我想喝点鸡汤，最好再来点掺着葡萄酒的牛奶，还要——哦不，先给我一面小镜子吧，再帮我把枕头垫高，我想坐起来看着你做饭，亲爱的。"

一个小时之后，琼西又说：

"苏妲，我希望有一天能去画那不勒斯海湾。"

下午医生又来了，在他离开的时候，苏找了个借口来到走廊上。

"有五成的把握！"医生握住苏那颤抖着的纤瘦的手说，"好好照看她，她会好的。现在我得下楼去看看另一个病人，他叫贝尔曼——好像也是个画家。他也得了肺炎，但年纪大了，身子又弱，所以病得很厉害。他是没希望治好了，今天要把他弄到医院里，这样他会觉得更舒服一点。"

第二天，医生对苏说："她已经脱离危险了，你们成功了！现在就剩下营养和护理的问题了。"

当天下午，琼西正躺在床上一脸安然地织着一条没什么用处的深蓝色羊毛披肩，苏突然跑到她的床边，慌乱地用一只胳膊把琼西连

her, pillows and all.

"I have something to tell you, white mouse," she said. "Mr. Behrman died of pneumonia to-day in the hospital. He was ill only two days. The janitor found him on the morning of the first day in his room downstairs helpless with pain. His shoes and clothing were wet through and icy cold. They couldn't imagine where he had been on such a dreadful night. And then they found a lantern, still lighted, and a ladder that had been dragged from its place, and some scattered brushes, and a palette with green and yellow colors mixed on it, and – look out the window, dear, at the last ivy leaf on the wall. Didn't you wonder why it never fluttered or moved when the wind blew? Ah, darling, it's Behrman's masterpiece – he painted it there the night that the last leaf fell."

人带枕头一把抱住。

"我要告诉你一件事，小家伙，"她说，"贝尔曼先生因为肺炎今天在医院去世了。他只病了两天。头天早晨，看门人在楼下那间房子里发现他痛得不行，他的鞋子和衣服都湿透了，冰凉的瘆人。他们都不清楚在头一天那个可怕的晚上，他究竟上哪儿去了。后来，他们又发现一盏还燃着的灯笼；一把挪动过的梯子；几枝扔在地上的画笔和一块调色板，那上面残留着绿色和黄色的颜料！还有——快看窗子外面亲爱的，看看墙上最后那一片藤叶！你知道为什么刮风的时候，它既不摇晃也不动弹呢？哦天哪，亲爱的琼西，这正是贝尔曼先生的杰作啊！——在最后一片叶子掉落的那个夜晚，他把那片叶子永远地画在那儿了。"

5. A COSMOPOLITE IN A CAFE
5. 咖啡馆里的世界公民

At midnight the cafe was crowded. By some chance the little table at which I sat had escaped the eye of incomers, and two vacant chairs at it extended their arms with venal hospitality to the influx of patrons.

And then a cosmopolite sat in one of them, and I was glad, for I held a theory that since Adam no true citizen of the world has existed. We hear of them, and we see foreign labels on much luggage, but we find travellers instead of cosmopolites.

I invoke your consideration of the scene – the marble-topped tables, the range of leather-upholstered wall seats, the gay company, the ladies dressed in demi-state toilets, speaking in an exquisite visible chorus of taste, economy, opulence or art; the sedulous and largess-loving garcons, the music wisely catering to all with its raids upon the composers; the melange of talk and laughter – and, if you will, the Wüerzburger in the tall glass cones that bend to your lips as a ripe cherry sways on its

午夜时分，咖啡馆里面显得拥挤不堪。不知道为什么，从外面进来的顾客却对我所坐的那张小桌子视而不见，于是桌子旁边的两把空椅子尽量地伸开双臂，热情地迎接不断拥进来的人们。

终于，一位世界公民坐在了其中一把椅子上。这使我很高兴，因为我一直认定：自先祖亚当以来，还没有过一位真正意义上的世界公民诞生。我们仅仅是听说过而已，或者见到过大量像这样贴着异国标签的行李，但那仅仅是旅行者，而不是世界公民。

我恳请您留意以下的场景——镶嵌大理石桌面的桌子；靠墙摆放的皮革座椅；快乐的午夜同伴；女士们略施粉黛，微妙而又异口同声地谈论着经济、富裕的生活或者艺术；喜欢小费的侍者们小心翼翼地游弋其中；音乐很聪明地满足着所有顾客的口味而不惜违背作曲家的原意。人们都谈笑风生——如果你愿意，装在高脚玻璃杯的维尔茨堡酒[1]就在你的唇边，如同树枝上一枚熟

branch to the beak of a robber jay. I was told by a sculptor from Mauch Chunk that the scene was truly Parisian.

My cosmopolite was named E. Rushmore Coglan, and he will be heard from next summer at Coney Island. He is to establish a new "attraction" there, he informed me, offering kingly diversion. And then his conversation rang along parallels of latitude and longitude. He took the great, round world in his hand, so to speak, familiarly, contemptuously, and it seemed no larger than the seed of a Maraschino cherry in a table d'hôte grape fruit. He spoke disrespectfully of the equator, he skipped from continent to continent, he derided the zones, he mopped up the high seas with his napkin. With a wave of his hand he would speak of a certain bazaar in Hyderabad. Whiff! He would have you on skis in Lapland. Zip! Now you rode the breakers with the Kanakas at Kealaikahiki. Presto! He dragged you through an Arkansas post-oak swamp, let you dry for a moment on the alkali plains of his Idaho ranch, then whirled you into the society of Viennese archdukes. Anon he would be telling you of a cold he acquired in a Chicago lake breeze and how old Es-

透的樱桃在一只偷食的樫鸟嘴前招摇一样。一位来自莫克昌克的雕塑家告诉我,这里的景象是"真正巴黎式的。"

我身边的这位世界公民名叫E·拉什莫尔·科格兰,明年夏天他将会在科尼岛[2]出现——他向我透露说,他要在那儿建立一种新的"吸引力",并提供国王般的消遣。接着他的谈话就沿着经纬度的平行线铺展开来。他把这个巨大的圆形的世界玩弄于手掌,对它极其熟悉的又极其不屑,仿佛地求比做客时饭桌上黑樱桃酒里的樱桃核大不了多少。他无礼地谈论着赤道,时而说起这个大陆,时而说起那个大陆。他嘲笑地球的气候带,仿佛用餐巾就可以把公海给抹掉。他挥了挥手,谈论起海德拉巴邦[3]的某个集市。他吹一口气,就能让你在拉普兰[4]滑雪。他发出尖啸声,你就会在基莱卡希基同夏威夷土著一起乘风破浪。一眨眼的工夫,他已经拖着你穿过了阿肯色州那片长满星毛栎的沼泽地,又让你在他爱达荷州的大牧场那碱性的平原上晒上了一阵子,然后又旋风似的把你带到维也纳大公的上流社会去了。之后,他还会告诉你,有

camila cured it in Buenos Ayres with a hot infusion of the *chuchula* weed. You would have addressed a letter to "E. Rushmore Coglan, Esq., the Earth, Solar System, the Universe," and have mailed it, feeling confident that it would be delivered to him.

I was sure that I had found at last the one true cosmopolite since Adam, and I listened to his worldwide discourse fearful lest I should discover in it the local note of the mere globe-trotter. But his opinions never fluttered or drooped; he was as impartial to cities, countries and continents as the winds or gravitation.

And as E. Rushmore Coglan prattled of this little planet I thought with glee of a great almost-cosmopolite who wrote for the whole world and dedicated himself to Bombay. In a poem he has to say that there is pride and rivalry between the cities of the earth, and that "the men that breed from them, they traffic up and down, but cling to their cities' hem as a child to the mother's gown." And whenever they walk "by roaring streets unknown" they remember their native city "most faithful, foolish, fond; making her merebreathed name their bond upon

一次他在芝加哥湖感染了风寒，是布宜诺斯艾丽斯一位年长的埃斯卡米拉人用一种名叫丘丘拉的草煮成汤药，才把他治好的。你可以写信致"宇宙、太阳系、地球、E·拉什莫尔·科格兰先生"，而且他保证他肯定能收的到。

我确信，我终于找到了自亚当以来第一位真正的世界公民。我倾听着他那纵横世界的谈话，唯恐从中听出他仅仅是个有个地方口音的环球旅行者。他的见解总是不卑不亢，对待不同的城市、国家和大陆就像风或者万有引力一样不偏不倚。

就在 E·拉什莫尔·科格兰口若悬河地谈论着这个小小的星球时，我欣喜地想起了另一位伟大的几近世界公民的人来。他为整个世界写作，同时又献身于孟买[5]。他在一首诗中说，地球上的城市之间既有骄傲，又有敌意，"生于斯长于斯的人们，他们奔向四面八方，但又在故乡的城头留恋，就像孩子抓着母亲的睡袍一样。"当他们走在"繁华的异乡街道"上，就会想起家乡来，那"最为忠诚、笨拙、柔情的城市，一说出她的名字，他们就紧紧相连。"而我之所以欣喜是因

their bond." And my glee was roused because I had caught Mr. Kipling napping. Here I had found a man not made from dust; one who had no narrow boasts of birthplace or country, one who, if he bragged at all, would brag of his whole round globe against the Martians and the inhabitants of the Moon.

Expression on these subjects was precipitated from E. Rushmore Coglan by the third corner to our table. While Coglan was describing to me the topography along the Siberian Railway the orchestra glided into a medley. The concluding air was "Dixie," and as the exhilarating notes tumbled forth they were almost overpowered by a great clapping of hands from almost every table.

It is worth a paragraph to say that this remarkable scene can be witnessed every evening in numerous cafes in the City of New York. Tons of brew have been consumed over theories to account for it. Some have conjectured hastily that all Southerners in town hie themselves to cafes at nightfall. This applause of the "rebel" air in a Northern city does puzzle a little; but it is not insolvable. The war with Spain, many years' generous mint and watermelon crops, a few long-shot

为我发现吉卜林还需要打盹，而在这儿，我终于找到一个不平凡的人。他没有狭隘地夸耀自己的出生地或祖国。如果非说他吹牛的话，那他也是在向火星人和月球居民夸耀整个地球。

所有这些话题的阐述都是由坐在我面前桌子第三转角处的E·拉什莫尔·科格兰突然抛出来的。正当科格兰在给我描绘西伯利亚铁路沿线的地形时，乐队奏起了一个专辑。结束音乐是《迪克西》[6]，当振奋人心的音符不断推进时，每一张桌子的人们都在鼓掌，几乎把乐曲声都淹没了。

用一个段落来讲述纽约市众多的咖啡馆每天晚上随处可见的这种壮观场景是值得的，成吨的酒品被挥霍已经证明了这一点。有人草率地猜测，一旦夜幕降临，城里所有的南方人就都拥进了咖啡馆里。在一座北方城市里这种"反叛"气氛实在叫人有点费解，但并不是不可解释的。与西班牙的战争，薄荷和西瓜等农作物的连年丰收，冷门迭报的新奥尔良赛马场，以及由印第安纳和堪萨斯的居民所组成的"北卡罗来纳社团"举行的盛大宴会已经使南方在曼哈顿成为了一种"时尚"。

winners at the New Orleans race-track, and the brilliant banquets given by the Indiana and Kansas citizens who compose the North Carolina Society have made the South rather a "fad" in Manhattan. Your manicure will lisp softly that your left forefinger reminds her so much of a gentleman's in Richmond, Va. Oh, certainly; but many a lady has to work now – the war, you know.

When "Dixie" was being played a dark-haired young man sprang up from somewhere with a Mosby guerrilla yell and waved frantically his soft-brimmed hat. Then he strayed through the smoke, dropped into the vacant chair at our table and pulled out cigarettes.

The evening was at the period when reserve is thawed. One of us mentioned three Wüerzburgers to the waiter; the dark-haired young man acknowledged his inclusion in the order by a smile and a nod. I hastened to ask him a question because I wanted to try out a theory I had.

"Would you mind telling me," I began, "whether you are from – "

The fist of E. Rushmore Coglan banged the table and I was jarred into silence.

"Excuse me," said he, "but that's a

为你修剪指甲的人会小声嘀咕，说你的左手食指使她恰巧想起一位来自弗吉尼亚州里士满的绅士。呵呵，那是当然啰。不过，如今很多女人不得不工作——就是因为战争，我想你是知道的。

乐队正演奏着《迪克西》的时候，一个黑发的年轻小伙子不知道从什么地方窜了出来，像莫斯比[7]游击队队员那样吼叫着，疯狂地挥动着他那顶软毡帽。然后他穿过咖啡馆里层层叠叠的烟雾，来到我们桌旁的空椅子上坐下，并且抽出一支烟来。

夜已深，我们也就不再拘束。我们当中有人跟侍者点了三杯维尔茨堡酒，黑发的青年明白也有他的份，便微笑着点点头。趁此我赶紧问了他一个问题，因为我想验证一下自己的一种推测。

"请别介意，"我问道，"你是不是来自——"

E·拉什莫尔·科格兰一拳砸在桌上，把我的话噎了回去。

"抱歉，"他说，"但我决不喜欢听到这种问题！是哪里人又有什么关系呢？仅凭一个人的通讯地址来判断一个人，这公正吗？唉，我见过讨厌威士忌的肯塔基人，见过并不是波卡洪塔丝[8]

question I never like to hear asked. What does it matter where a man is from? Is it fair to judge a man by his post-office address? Why, I've seen Kentuckians who hated whiskey, Virginians who weren't descended from Pocahontas, Indianians who hadn't written a novel, Mexicans who didn't wear velvet trousers with silver dollars sewed along the seams, funny Englishmen, spendthrift Yankees, cold-blooded Southerners, narrow-minded Westerners, and New Yorkers who were too busy to stop for an hour on the street to watch a one-armed grocer's clerk do up cranberries in paper bags. Let a man be a man and don't handicap him with the label of any section."

"Pardon me," I said, "but my curiosity was not altogether an idle one. I know the South, and when the band plays 'Dixie' I like to observe. I have formed the belief that the man who applauds that air with special violence and ostensible sectional loyalty is invariably a native of either Secaucus, N.J., or the district between Murray Hill Lyceum and the Harlem River, this city. I was about to put my opinion to the test by inquiring of this gentleman when you interrupted with

后裔的弗吉尼亚人，见过没写过一部小说的印第安纳人，见过不穿沿着侧缝缀上银币丝绒裤的墨西哥人，也见过有趣的英国人，挥金如土的北方佬，冷血的南方人，小心眼儿的西方人，以及匆匆忙忙生活的纽约人。他们甚至不能在街上停下来，花上一小时瞅瞅杂货店里的独臂售货员是怎样把越橘装进纸袋子里去的。人就是人，不应该用任何地域标签来给他下定义。"

"请原谅我，"我说，"但我的好奇心不是没有根据的。我了解南方，每当乐队奏起《迪克西》的时候，我就开始观察。我相信那位为这支乐曲卖力喝彩、公然对南方表达忠心的人，一定是来自新泽西州的赛考库斯，或者是纽约的默里·希尔·吕克昂和哈莱姆河之间。我必须承认，我正打算询问这位绅士以验证我的观点时，恰好被你的高见所打断。"

这时黑发的青年开口跟我说话了，显然，他的思想也遵循着自己的一套常规运行。

"我倒愿意作一枝长春花，"

your own – larger theory, I must confess."

And now the dark-haired young man spoke to me, and it became evident that his mind also moved along its own set of grooves.

"I should like to be a periwinkle," said he, mysteriously, "on the top of a valley, and sing too-ralloo-ralloo."

This was clearly too obscure, so I turned again to Coglan.

"I've been around the world twelve times," said he. "I know an Esquimau in Upernavik who sends to Cincinnati for his neckties, and I saw a goat-herder in Uruguay who won a prize in a Battle Creek breakfast food puzzle competition. I pay rent on a room in Cairo, Egypt, and another in Yokohama all the year around. I've got slippers waiting for me in a tea-house in Shanghai, and I don't have to tell 'em how to cook my eggs in Rio de Janeiro or Seattle. It's a mighty little old world. What's the use of bragging about being from the North, or the South, or the old manor house in the dale, or Euclid avenue, Cleveland, or Pike's Peak, or Fairfax County, Va., or Hooligan's Flats or any place? It'll be a better world when we quit being fools about some mildewed

他表情诡秘地说，"生长于山谷之巅，歌唱嘟啦卢—拉卢。"

这话显然太令人费解了，于是我又转向科格兰。

"我已经周游世界12次了，"他说，"我认识一位住在厄珀纳维克的爱斯基摩人，他寄钱去辛辛那提[9]买领带。我在乌拉圭见过一个牧羊人，他在"小湾战斗"的早餐食品谜语竞赛中获了奖。我在埃及开罗租了间房，在日本横滨也租了一间，都是全年的。上海的一家茶馆专门为我准备了一双拖鞋，在里约热内卢或者西雅图，我也不需要告诉他们怎样给我煮鸡蛋。这个古老的世界实在太小了，北方人也好，南方人也好，山谷中的老庄园也好，克里夫兰市的欧几里德大街也好，派克峰[10]也好，弗吉尼亚的费尔法克斯县也好，胡利甘平川也好，其他任何地方也好，吹嘘自己的出生地有什么用呢？只有当我们能够对自己出生在某个发霉的城市或 10 英亩沼泽地带泰然处之时，世界才会变得更为美好。"

"看来你是个名副其实的世界公民，"我不无羡慕地说，"但是，你这样似乎有损于爱国主义。"

town or ten acres of swampland just because we happened to be born there."

"You seem to be a genuine cosmopolite," I said admiringly. "But it also seems that you would decry patriotism."

"A relic of the stone age," declared Coglan, warmly. "We are all brothers – Chinamen, Englishmen, Zulus, Patagonians and the people in the bend of the Kaw River. Some day all this petty pride in one's city or State or section or country will be wiped out, and we'll all be citizens of the world, as we ought to be."

"But while you are wandering in foreign lands," I persisted, "do not your thoughts revert to some spot – some dear and – "

"Nary a spot," interrupted E. R. Coglan, flippantly. "The terrestrial, globular, planetary hunk of matter, slightly flattened at the poles, and known as the Earth, is my abode. I've met a good many object-bound citizens of this country abroad. I've seen men from Chicago sit in a gondola in Venice on a moonlight night and brag about their drainage canal. I've seen a Southerner on being introduced to the King of England hand that monarch, without batting his eyes, the information that his grand-aunt

"爱国主义已经是石器时代的古董了!"科格兰激动地宣称,"四海之内皆兄弟——中国人、英国人、祖鲁人、巴塔哥尼亚人和住在考河湾的人都是兄弟。[11]总有一天,一切为自己出生的城市、州、地区或国家而感到自豪的那种小家子气式的自豪感将一扫而空,我们都会成为世界公民,因为我们生来理应如此。"

"但是当你在陌生的地方游历时,"我仍坚持问,"难道你就不思念某个地方——某个可爱而又……"

"从没有这样一个地方!"E·拉什莫尔·科格兰无礼地打断我,"这个由陆地构成、球形的、行星般运行的、两级略扁被人们称之为地球的地方,就是我的住所。在国外,我碰到过许多这个国家的公民,却还在被所谓的家乡所束缚。我在威尼斯见过一群芝加哥人,他们在月夜坐着凤尾船观光,却又吹嘘他们家乡的排水沟。我见过一位被引见给英格兰国王的南方人,见到国王时他的眼睛都直了,并且急忙向国王透露他母亲一方的一位姑婆嫁给了查尔斯顿[12]的珀金斯氏。我认识一位纽约人,他被几个阿富汗

on his mother's side was related by marriage to the Perkinses, of Charleston. I
knew a New Yorker who was kidnapped
for ransom by some Afghanistan bandits.
His people sent over the money and he
came back to Kabul with the agent.
'Afghanistan?' the natives said to him
through an interpreter. 'Well, not so
slow, do you think?' 'Oh, I don't know,'
says he, and he begins to tell them about a
cab driver at Sixth avenue and Broadway.
Those ideas don't suit me. I'm not tied
down to anything that isn't 8,000 miles in
diameter. Just put me down as E. Rushmore Coglan, citizen of the terrestrial
sphere."

My cosmopolite made a large adieu
and left me, for he thought he saw some
one through the chatter and smoke whom
he knew. So I was left with the would-be
periwinkle, who was reduced to Wüerzburger without further ability to voice his
aspirations to perch, melodious, upon the
summit of a valley.

I sat reflecting upon my evident cosmopolite and wondering how the poet
had managed to miss him. He was my
discovery and I believed in him. How
was it? "The men that breed from them
they traffic up and down, but cling to

的匪徒绑架了，等他的朋友送钱
去把他赎回来后，他同代理人一
起回到了喀布尔[13]。'阿富汗？'
当地人通过翻译问他说，'嗯，
你不认为那儿的生活节奏太慢了
点吗？''哦，我不知道，'他
说，然后便开始向他们讲起第六
大道和百老汇大街上一个出租车
司机的事。这些观念都不适合我。
我不会被束缚在任何直径不到
8000英里的地方。请记住我，E·拉
什莫尔·科格兰，整个地球的公
民。"

这个世界公民夸张地向我道
别后便离开了我，因为他越过闲
谈的人群和烟雾看见了某个认识
的人。因此，就剩下我和那位想
当长春花的青年了，他只顾着喝
维尔茨堡酒，再也没有闲暇去顾
及用悦耳的声音歌唱他那栖身于
山谷之巅的抱负了。

我坐在那儿，琢磨着那位使
我确信无疑的世界公民，想不通
究竟由于什么原因，竟使那位诗
人的成就高出了他？。我发现了
他，并且完全相信他。这到底是
怎么一回事？"生于斯长于斯的
人们，他们奔向四面八方，但又
在故乡的城头留恋，就像孩子抓
着母亲的睡袍一样。"

their cities' hem as a child to the mother's gown."

Not so E. Rushmore Coglan. With the whole world for his –

My meditations were interrupted by a tremendous noise and conflict in another part of the cafe. I saw above the heads of the seated patrons E. Rushmore Coglan and a stranger to me engaged in terrific battle. They fought between the tables like Titans, and glasses crashed, and men caught their hats up and were knocked down, and a brunette screamed, and a blonde began to sing "Teasing."

My cosmopolite was sustaining the pride and reputation of the Earth when the waiters closed in on both combatants with their famous flying wedge formation and bore them outside, still resisting.

I called McCarthy, one of the French garcons, and asked him the cause of the conflict.

"The man with the red tie" (that was my cosmopolite), said he, "got hot on account of things said about the bum sidewalks and water supply of the place he come from by the other guy."

"Why," said I, bewildered, "that man is a citizen of the world – a cosmopolite. He –"

E·拉什莫尔·科格兰可不会这样做，他把整个世界当作他的……

我的沉思忽然被咖啡馆另一边传来的激烈的争吵声打断了。从坐着的客人头顶望去，我看见E·拉什莫尔·科格兰正和一个陌生人扭打在一起。他俩在桌子之间打来打去，就像巨神堤坦[14]一样，玻璃杯被砸碎了，人们匆忙抓起帽子，还没来得及躲闪便被扑倒在地，一位浅黑肤色的女郎尖叫起来，而另一位金发女郎则开始唱《取笑》。

那位世界公民此刻还在为保持地球人的自豪感与声誉而奋力而战，侍者们只好用著名的飞速楔形结构把两个斗士围起来，硬把他俩往外驱逐，但他们一直都不屈不挠的反抗。

我把一名叫麦卡锡的法国侍者叫过来，问他这场争执发生的原因。

"那个打红领带的人"（就是我的世界公民），他说，"给惹火的原因是因为另一个家伙说他出生的那个地方的人行道和供水系统都很糟糕。"

"哦？"我不解地说，"那人可是个世界的公民呀——世界

"Originally from Mattawamkeag, Maine, he said," continued McCarthy, "and he wouldn't stand for no knockin' the place."

主义者。他……"

"他说他来自缅因州的马托瓦姆基格，"麦卡锡继续说道，"他容不得别人数落那个地方。"

1.Wüerzburger,维尔茨堡,德意志联邦的中南部城市，这里指该地所产的酒。
2.科尼岛,美国纽约布鲁克林区南部的一个海滨地带。
3.海德拉巴邦,巴基斯坦东南部城市。
4.拉普兰,北欧一地区名。
5.孟买,印度的一个海滨城市。
6.迪克西,美国南北战争时期在南部各州流行的战歌，现仍旧流行。
7.莫斯比(1833~1916)，美国内战时南方联盟别动队的首领。
8.波卡洪塔丝(1595~1617),北美波瓦坦印第安人部落联盟首领波瓦坦之女,曾搭救过英国殖民者 John Smith，1614 年与英国移民 John Rolf 结婚，1616 年前往英国后受到了上流社会的礼遇。
9.辛辛那提,美国俄亥俄州西部的城市。
10.派克峰,指科罗拉多州为纪念派克而命名的山峰。
11.祖鲁人,居住在南非纳塔尔;巴塔哥尼亚人,北欧一地区名,指拉普人居住的地区，包括挪威、瑞典、芬兰等国的北部和原苏联的科拉岛。
12.查尔斯顿,美国西弗吉尼亚州首府。
13.喀布尔,阿富汗首都。
14.巨神堤坦,希腊神话中天神以及大地女神之子。

6. MAMMON AND THE ARCHER
6. 财神与爱神

Old Anthony Rockwall, retired manufacturer and proprietor of Rockwall's Eureka Soap, looked out the library window of his Fifth Avenue mansion and grinned. His neighbour to the right – the aristocratic clubman, G. Van Schuylight Suffolk-Jones – came out to his waiting motor-car, wrinkling a contumelious nostril, as usual, at the Italian renaissancesculpture of the soap palace's front elevation.

"Stuck-up old statuette of nothing doing!" commented the ex-Soap King. "The Eden Musee'll get that old frozen Nesselrode yet if he don't watch out. I'll have this house painted red, white, and blue next summer and see if that'll make his Dutch nose turn up any higher."

And then Anthony Rockwall, who never cared for bells, went to the door of his library and shouted "Mike!" in the same voice that had once chipped off pieces of the welkin on the Kansas prairies.

"Tell my son," said Anthony to the answering menial, "to come in here be-

老安东尼·克韦尔是罗克韦尔尤雷卡肥皂厂的前任制造商兼厂长，当然他现在已经退休了。这一刻，他正从位于第五大街宅邸的书房窗户旁向外张望，咧嘴笑着。住在他右边的邻居——贵族俱乐部的花花公子，G·范·斯凯莱特·福克琼斯，正从家里走向等候他的汽车。像往常一样，朝矗立在这座肥皂宫殿正前方的意大利文艺复兴雕塑轻蔑地皱了皱鼻子。

"一无是处的小草包，你神气什么！"这位前肥皂大王嗤之以鼻道，"如果你再不老实点儿，伊登博物馆迟早会把你这个老掉牙的外来客内斯尔罗德[1]收进去。明年夏天，我要把我的房子粉刷成红白蓝三色[2]，看看你那荷兰鼻子还能翘多高。"

然后，安东尼·罗克韦尔走到书房门口大吼道，"迈克！"，他召唤佣人从不按铃。这一嗓子跟他当年划破堪萨斯草原苍穹的声音一样嘹亮。

"告诉少爷，"安东尼吩咐

fore he leaves the house."

When young Rockwall entered the library the old man laid aside his newspaper, looked at him with a kindly grimness on his big, smooth, ruddy countenance, rumpled his mop of white hair with one hand and rattled the keys in his pocket with the other.

"Richard," said Anthony Rockwall, "what do you pay for the soap that you use?"

Richard, only six months home from college, was startled a little. Hehad not yet taken the measure of this sire of his, who was as full of unexpectednesses as a girl at her first party.

"Six dollars a dozen, I think, dad."

"And your clothes?"

"I suppose about sixty dollars, as a rule."

"You're a gentleman," said Anthony, decidedly. "I've heard of these young bloods spending $24 a dozen for soap, and going over the hundred mark for clothes. You've got as much money to waste as any of 'em, and yet you stick to what's decent and moderate. Now I use the old Eureka – not only for sentiment, but it's the purest soap made. Whenever you pay more than 10 cents a cake for

前来的仆人，"让他出门之前到我这儿来一趟。"

小罗克韦尔走进书房的时候，老头子把报纸放在一边，光滑红润的大脸盘上带着慈爱而又严肃的神情看着他，用一只手胡乱拨弄着满头的银发，另一只手把口袋里的钥匙拨弄得叮当响。

"理查德，"安东尼·罗克韦尔说，"告诉我，你在买肥皂上花了多少钱？"

理查德从大学毕业才仅仅六个月，听了这话他感到有点吃惊，有时候他还拿不准他老爸的分寸。这老头子像第一次参加舞会的姑娘一样，经常问他很多令人意想不到的问题。

"6美元一打，爸爸。"

"衣服呢，花了多少钱？"

"差不多60美元左右吧。"

"你是个绅士！"安东尼斩钉截铁地说，"我听说那些年轻的公子哥儿用24美元买一打肥皂，穿的衣服超过100元。你跟他们一样有钱，可以挥霍，但你始终保持分寸和谦逊。如今我用老牌尤雷卡不仅仅是出于感情，而是因为它是最纯正的肥皂。你花十多美分买一块肥皂，买到手的只是劣质的香料连同它的商

soap you buy bad perfumes and labels. But 50 cents is doing very well for a young man in your generation, position and condition. As I said, you're a gentleman. They say it takes three generations to make one. They're off. Money'll do it as slick as soap grease. It's made you one. By hokey! it's almost made one of me. I'm nearly as impolite and disagreeable and ill-mannered as these two old Knickerbocker gents on each side of me that can't sleep of nights because I bought in between 'em."

"There are some things that money can't accomplish," remarked young Rockwall, rather gloomily.

"Now, don't say that," said old Anthony, shocked. "I bet my money on money every time. I've been through the encyclopaedia down to Y looking for something you can't buy with it; and I expect to have to take up the appendix next week. I'm for money against the field. Tell me something money won't buy."

"For one thing," answered Richard, rankling a little, "it won't buy one into the exclusive circles of society."

"Oho! won't it?" thundered the champion of the root of evil. "You tell me

标。不过，你们这一代有地位有身份的年轻人花50美分买一块肥皂也算合情合理。就像我刚才说的那样，你是一位绅士。人们都说三代才能造就一位绅士，那种说法早就过时了，钱就可以造就绅士，而且做起来像肥皂油脂一样顺滑。钱使你成了绅士。噢哈哈，差点也让我成了绅士。不过，我想我差不多和住在我旁边的两个荷兰佬一样无礼，没风度，并且令人厌恶。他们曾经两个晚上没睡着，就因为我在他们中间购置了房产。"

"可有些事情有钱也办不到。"小罗克韦尔十分忧郁地说。

"你怎么能那样想！"老安东尼惊愕地说，"我发誓钱是万能的。我查遍了整个百科全书，一直查到字母Y也没发现什么是钱买不到的，下星期我再查查附录。我相信钱能解决一切。你跟我说说，什么东西是钱买不到的？"

"但比如，"理查德有些懊恼地说，"就算有钱也不能帮助一个人挤进一个排外的社交圈。"

"啊！是这样吗？"这个罪恶之源的拥护者不禁大发雷霆，"那么你告诉我，要是第一个阿斯特[3]没钱买统舱船票来到美国，

where your exclusive circles would be if the first Astor hadn't had the money to pay for his steerage passage over?"

Richard sighed.

"And that's what I was coming to," said the old man, less boisterously. "That's why I asked you to come in. There's something going wrong with you, boy. I've been noticing it for two weeks. Out with it. I guess I could lay my hands on eleven millions within twenty-four hours, besides the real estate. If it's your liver, there's the *Rambler* down in the bay, coaled, and ready to steam down to the Bahamas in two days."

"Not a bad guess, dad; you haven't missed it far."

"Ah," said Anthony, keenly; "what's her name?"

Richard began to walk up and down the library floor. There was enough comradeship and sympathy in this crude old father of his to draw his confidence.

"Why don't you ask her?" demanded old Anthony. "She'll jump at you. You've got the money and the looks, and you're a decent boy. Your hands are clean. You've got no Eureka soap on 'em. You've been to college, but she'll overlook that."

你所说的排外的社交圈子又会在哪出现呢？"

理查德叹了口气。

"这正是我要跟你说的，"老头子的语气缓和了些，"也是我叫你来的原因。孩子，你最近有点不太对劲。我已经注意你两个星期了，说出来吧。我想24小时之内我可以调动1100万美元，这还没算上房地产。如果是你心上人的问题，逍遥号就停泊在港湾，上足了煤，两天内就可以把你们送到巴哈马群岛[4]。"

"爸爸，你猜得不错，差不多就是那么回事。"

"噢，"安东尼热切地问，"那么，告诉我她叫什么名字？"

理查德开始在书房里走来走去。他这位举止粗鲁的老爸对他殷切的关爱，使他开始恢复勇气。

"你为什么不向她求婚呢？"老安东尼追问道，"她一定会扑进你怀里。你不缺钱，又那么英俊，是个举止得体的小伙子。更重要的是，你自食其力，还上过大学！难道她会对这一切视而不见吗？"

"我还没能找到机会向她表达呢。"理查德说到。

"创造一个机会啊！"安东

"I haven't had a chance," said Richard.

"Make one," said Anthony. "Take her for a walk in the park, or a straw ride, or walk home with her from church. Chance! Pshaw!"

"You don't know the social mill, dad. She's part of the stream that turns it. Every hour and minute of her time is arranged for days in advance. I must have that girl, dad, or this town is a blackjack swamp forever more. And I can't write it – I can't do that."

"Tut!" said the old man. "Do you mean to tell me that with all the money I've got you can't get an hour or two of a girl's time for yourself?"

"I've put it off too late. She's going to sail for Europe at noon day after tomorrow for a two years' stay. I'm to see her alone to-morrow evening for a few minutes. She's at Larchmont now at her aunt's. I can't go there. But I'm allowed to meet her with a cab at the Grand Central Station to-morrow evening at the 8.30 train. We drive down Broadway to Wallack's at a gallop, where her mother and a box party will be waiting for us in the lobby. Do you think she would listen to a declaration from me during that six or eight minutes under those circumstances? No.

尼说，"带她去公园散步，或者驾车出游，或者陪她从教堂走回家。机会简直多得是！"

"爸爸，你不了解现在的社交界，而她则是大名鼎鼎的交际花，她的每一个小时甚至每分钟都在许多天前就安排好了。不过，我必须和她在一起，爸爸，否则从此这个城市对于我来说，就如同臭沼泽地一样不值得留恋。但我又不能写信去表白，我想我不能这么做。"

"呸！"老头儿说，"你意思是，我给你的所有钱都不能让一个姑娘陪你一两个小时吗？"

"我已经没时间做什么事情了。她后天中午就要乘船到欧洲去，在那儿她要待上两年。明天晚上我倒是能单独跟她待上几分钟，她现在还住在拉齐蒙特的姨妈家，但我不能去她姨妈家找她，她只允许我明天晚上坐马车去中央火车站接她，她的火车8：30到站。我们会一起乘马车经过百老汇街赶到沃拉克剧院，她母亲和一大群人会在大厅等着我们。你认为在那种情况下，在那六到八分钟内她会听我的表白吗？不会的！不论是在剧院里还是在看过戏之后，我还有什么机会了。

And what chance would I have in the theatre or afterward? None. No, dad, this is one tangle that your money can't unravel. We can't buy one minute of time with cash; if we could, rich people would live longer.There's no hope of getting a talk with Miss Lantry before she sails."

"All right, Richard, my boy," said old Anthony, cheerfully. "You may run along down to your club now. I'm glad it ain't your liver. But don't forget to burn a few punk sticks in the joss house to the great god Mazuma from time to time. You say money won't buy time? Well, of course, you can't order eternity wrapped up and delivered at your residence for a price, but I've seen Father Time get pretty bad stone bruises on his heels when he walked through the gold diggings."

That night came Aunt Ellen, gentle, sentimental, wrinkled, sighing, oppressed by wealth, in to Brother Anthony at his evening paper, and began discourse on the subject of lovers' woes.

"He told me all about it," said brother Anthony, yawning. "I told him my bank account was at his service. And then he began to knock money. Said money couldn't help. Said the rules of society

不，爸爸，这的确是一个你的金钱解决不了的难题，我们连一分钟的时间也买不到。如果我们可以的话，那么有钱人就会更长寿。在兰特里小姐启航之前，我想我不可能同她谈一谈了。"

"好啦，理查德，我的孩子，"老安东尼高高兴兴地说，"现在，你可以去你喜欢的俱乐部了，我很高兴不是你的肝脏出了问题。不过别忘了时不时去庙里，给掌管金钱的神烧烧香。你说钱买不到时间？嗯，当然了，你不能出个价钱让人包裹好永生邮递到家门口。但是我却见过时间老人穿过金矿的时候被捣蛋的石头弄得满脚伤痕。"

就在那天晚上，埃伦姑妈来看望她的弟弟了。她是个性情温和、多愁善感、满脸皱纹、爱长吁短叹并习惯受制于金钱的女人。她来的时候安东尼正在看晚报，于是他们开始讨论关于这对恋人们之间的烦恼。

"他全告诉我啦，"安东尼打着呵欠说，"我告诉他，我的银行户头听凭他调配，可他却开始贬低金钱，说钱根本没用。还说就算10个百万富翁加在一起也不能打破陈规。"

couldn't be bucked for a yard by a team of ten-millionaires."

"Oh, Anthony," sighed Aunt Ellen, "I wish you would not think so much of money. Wealth is nothing where a true affection is concerned. Love is all-powerful. If he only had spoken earlier! She could not have refused our Richard. But now I fear it is too late. He will have no opportunity to address her. All your gold cannot bring happiness to your son."

At eight o'clock the next evening Aunt Ellen took a quaint old gold ring from a moth-eaten case and gave it to Richard.

"Wear it to-night, nephew," she begged. "Your mother gave it to me. Good luck in love she said it brought. She asked me to give it to you when you had found the one you loved."

Young Rockwall took the ring reverently and tried it on his smallest finger. It slipped as far as the second joint and stopped. He took it off and stuffed it into his vest pocket, after the manner of man. And then he 'phoned for his cab.

At the station he captured Miss Lantry out of the gadding mob at eight thirty-two.

"We mustn't keep mamma and the

"唉，安东尼，"埃伦姑妈叹了口气，"我真希望你别把金钱看得太重。在真挚的感情面前，财富有时候一文不值，只有爱情才是万能的。要是他能早一点开口该多好，那个姑娘不可能有理由拒绝我们的理查德。但是现在恐怕真的太迟了，他根本没有机会向她表白，你所有的金子也买不来你宝贝儿子的幸福。"

第二天晚上8点，埃伦姑妈从一个陈旧的盒子里取出一枚精致的古董金戒指，交给理查德。

"今晚你就戴上它，我的侄子，"她央求说，"这是你母亲把它交给我的，她说过这能给爱情带来好运。我记得她要我在你找到意中人时把它交给你。"

小罗克韦尔恭敬地接过戒指，戴在小指头上试了试，可它只滑到第二个关节就动不了了。他取下来，按男人的习惯把它塞进背心的兜里，然后打电话叫了辆马车。

8点32分，他在火车站嘈杂的人群中找到了兰特里小姐。

"我们不能让妈妈和其他人等太久。"她说。

"沃拉克剧院，能多快就多快！"理查德如她所愿地吩咐到。

others waiting," said she.

"To Wallack's Theatre as fast as you can drive!" said Richard loyally.

They whirled up Forty-second to Broadway, and then down the white-starred lane that leads from the soft meadows of sunset to the rocky hills of morning.

At Thirty-fourth Street young Richard quickly thrust up the trap and ordered the cabman to stop.

"I've dropped a ring," he apologised, as he climbed out. "It was my mother's, and I'd hate to lose it. I won't detain you a minute – I saw where it fell."

In less than a minute he was back in the cab with the ring.

But within that minute across-town car had stopped directly in front of the cab. The cabman tried to pass to the left, but a heavy express wagon cut him off. He tried the right, and had to back away from a furniture van that had no business to be there. He tried to back out, but dropped his reins and swore dutifully. He was blockaded in a tangled mess of vehicles and horses.

One of those street blockades had occurred that sometimes tie up commerce and movement quite suddenly in the big

他们旋风般地从第四十二街奔向百老汇大街,经过一条灯火如繁星般的小巷,从昏暗的柔软草地很快到达了亮如白昼、高楼林立的街区。

等到了第三十四街的时候,小理查德推开车窗的隔板,请车夫停下来。

"我掉了一枚戒指,"他下车时抱歉地说,"那是我母亲留给我的,如果丢了我会抱憾终身。我已经看到它掉在哪里了,找回来误不了一分钟。"

果然,不到一分钟他就带着戒指回到了马车里。

但是就在那一分钟,一辆城区街车刚好停在了马车前面,车夫试着从左边穿过去,但左边有一辆笨重的邮车挡住了他。车夫试了试右边,但很快为了躲避一辆毫无缘由出现的家具搬运车而退了回来。他想后退,但是不慎弄掉了缰绳,他能做的只能是尽职尽责地咒骂起来,因为他的车已经被这一团糟的车辆和马匹团团围住。

的确,在大城市道路阻塞时有发生,有时会突然切断商业和其他所有活动。

"为什么不继续赶路了?"

city.

"Why don't you drive on?" said Miss Lantry, impatiently. "We'll be late."

Richard stood up in the cab and looked around. He saw a congested flood of wagons, trucks, cabs, vans and street cars filling the vast space where Broadway, Sixth Avenue and Thirty-fourth street cross one another as a twenty-six inch maiden fills her twenty-two inch girdle. And still from all the cross streets they were hurrying and rattling toward the converging point at full speed, and hurling themselves into the struggling mass, locking wheels and adding their drivers' imprecations to the clamour. The entire traffic of Manhattan seemed to have jammed itself around them. The oldest New Yorker among the thousands of spectators that lined the sidewalks had not witnessed a street blockade of the proportions of this one.

"I'm very sorry," said Richard, as he resumed his seat, "but it looks as if we are stuck. They won't get this jumble loosened up in an hour. It was my fault. If I hadn't dropped the ring we –"

"Let me see the ring," said Miss Lantry. "Now that it can't be helped, I don't care. I think theatres are stupid,

兰特里小姐不耐烦地问,"我们快要迟到了。"

理查德在车里站起来,四周看了看,只见货车、卡车、马车、搬运车和街车的洪流已经把百老汇街、第六大街和第三十四街交叉口处的广阔地段挤得水泄不通,就像一个26英寸腰围的姑娘,却硬要扎上一根22英寸长的腰带一样。而且就在这几条街上还有车辆正在不断地全速驶过,投入到这一团难分难解的乱麻之中,新加进来的车夫的咒骂吼叫声加重了原有的嘈杂喧嚣。曼哈顿的全部车辆似乎都堵在这附近了。人行道上挤了成千上万的围观者,但即便是其中最年长的纽约人也从没看见过如此大规模的交通阻塞。

"我真的很抱歉,"理查德重新坐回座位时说,"但是看样子我们被堵死了。一小时之内,这团乱麻不可能有任何松动,都是我的错。如果我没有弄掉戒指的话,我们……"

"让我看看这戒指吧,"兰特里小姐说,"既然没办法,我也就不在乎了。其实有时候,我觉得剧院挺没劲的。"

那夜11点,有人轻轻地敲安

anyway."

At 11 o'clock that night somebody tapped lightly on Anthony Rockwall's door.

"Come in," shouted Anthony, who was in a red dressing-gown, reading a book of piratical adventures.

Somebody was Aunt Ellen, looking like a grey-haired angel that had been left on earth by mistake.

"They're engaged, Anthony," she said, softly. "She has promised to marry our Richard. On their way to the theatre there was a street blockade, and it was two hours before their cab could get out of it.

"And oh, brother Anthony, don't ever boast of the power of money again. A little emblem of true love – a little ring that symbolised unending and unmercenary affection – was the cause of our Richard finding his happiness. He dropped it in the street, and got out to recover it. And before they could continue the blockade occurred. He spoke to his love and won her there while the cab was hemmed in. Money is dross compared with true love, Anthony."

"All right," said old Anthony. "I'm glad the boy has got what he wanted. I told him I wouldn't spare any expense in

东尼·罗克韦尔的门。

"进来吧！"安东尼吼道，他穿着红色的睡衣，正在读一本关于海盗探险的小说。

进来的是埃伦姑妈，她看上去像位误留在人间的灰发天使。

"他们订婚了，安东尼，"她轻柔地说，"那个姑娘已经答应嫁给我们的理查德了。在他们去剧院的路上发生了交通阻塞，两小时之后，他们的马车才得以脱身。

"看看吧，安东尼弟弟，再也别吹嘘金钱的能力了。一件象征真爱的信物——一枚代表永恒不变、金钱买不到的爱情的小小戒指，才是我们的理查德找到幸福的缘由。他在街上把戒指弄丢了，就下车去找，但就在他们继续赶路之前，发生了交通阻塞。就在堵车的时候，他向他所爱的人表白了，并赢得了她的芳心。跟真爱比起来金钱简直是粪土，你说是不是，安东尼。"

"很好，"老安东尼说，"我很高兴那孩子终于如愿以偿了。我告诉过他，在这件事上，我会不惜一切代价，只要……"

"可是，安东尼弟弟，你的钱做过什么呢？"

the matter if – "

"But, brother Anthony, what good could your money have done?"

"Sister," said Anthony Rockwall. "I've got my pirate in a devil of a scrape. His ship has just been scuttled, and he's too good a judge of the value of money to let drown. I wish you would let me go on with this chapter."

The story should end here. I wish it would as heartily as you who read it wish it did. But we must go to the bottom of the well for truth.

The next day a person with red hands and a blue polka-dot necktie, who called himself Kelly, called at Anthony Rockwall's house, and was at once received in the library.

"Well," said Anthony, reaching for his chequebook, "it was a good bilin' of soap. Let's see – you had $5,000 in cash."

"I paid out $300 more of my own," said Kelly. "I had to go a little above the estimate. I got the express wagons and cabs mostly for $5; but the trucks and two-horse teams mostly raised me to $10. The motor men wanted $10, and some of the loaded teams $20. The cops struck me hardest – $50 I paid two, and the rest $20 and $25. But didn't it work beautiful, Mr.

"姐姐，"安东尼·罗克韦尔说，"我的海盗正在危难关头，他的船刚被凿沉，他对金钱的价值有着绝好的判断力，因此决不会让自己淹死。我希望你能让我继续读完这一章。"

我们的故事在这儿本该结束了，我跟这个故事的读者们一样真诚地希望如此。不过，我们必须打破砂锅问到底才能发现真相。

第二天，有个双手通红、系着蓝点领带的人来找安东尼·罗克韦尔，这个自称凯利的人立刻在书房受到了接见。

"嗯，"安东尼边说边伸手去拿支票本，"这一锅肥皂汤熬得不错。我们来看看，你已经支了5 000美元现金了。"

"我自己还垫了300块呢，"凯利说，"我不得不超出预算一点，大多数邮车和马车付五美元，但卡车和双驾马车很多都提价到10美元。汽车司机要10美元，一些载满货的要20美元。警察敲诈得最厉害，有两个一起跟我要50美元，剩下的一个20，一个25。不过罗克韦尔先生，这个表演真是太精彩了！我很高兴威廉·阿·布雷迪[5]没有亲眼看到那场户外车辆拥挤的场景，因为我

Rockwall? I'm glad William A. Brady wasn't onto that little outdoor vehicle mob scene. I wouldn't want William to break his heart with jealousy. And never a rehearsal, either! The boys was on time to the fraction of a second. It was two hours before a snake could get below Greeley's statue."

"Thirteen hundred – there you are, Kelly," said Anthony, tearing off a check. "Your thousand, and the $300 you were out. You don't despise money, do you, Kelly?"

"Me?" said Kelly. "I can lick the man that invented poverty."

Anthony called Kelly when he was at the door.

"You didn't notice," said he, "any-where in the tie-up, a kind of a fat boy without any clothes on shooting arrows around with a bow, did you?"

"Why, no," said Kelly, mystified. "I didn't. If he was like you say, maybe the cops pinched him before I got there."

"I thought the little rascal wouldn't be on hand," chuckled Anthony. "Good-by, Kelly."

不希望他因忌妒而心碎。在完全没有彩排过的情况下！伙计们都很准时，连一秒不差。交通堵塞的那两个小时内连一条蛇也没办法从格里利⁶塑像下钻过去。"

"这1 300美元给你，凯利，"安东尼说着，撕下一张支票，"1000美元是你的报酬，300美元是你垫的。你不鄙视金钱对吗，凯利？"

"我？"凯利说，"我想鞭打那个发明了贫困的家伙。"

凯利刚走到门口，安东尼就把他叫住了。

"难道你没注意，"他说，"在交通阻塞的地方有个赤裸的胖男孩⁷拿着弓箭在那儿乱射？"

"怎么？没有啊，"凯利迷惑不解地说，"我什么都没看到。如果他像你所说的那样，也许我还没走到他跟前，警察就把他抓走了。"

"我想，这个小流氓也不会在现场的。"安东尼咯咯地笑着，"再见，凯利。"

1.德籍俄罗斯政治家，代指外来客。

2.荷兰国旗的三种颜色。

3.约翰·罗伯特·阿斯特，原籍德国，移民美国，是美国皮毛商兼金融家。

4.拉丁美洲著名旅游胜地。

5.美国著名的剧院经理。

6.贺瑞斯·格里利，美国新闻记者、作家、编辑、政治家，是纽约论坛报的创始人。

7.丘比特,爱神。

7. AFTER TWENTY YEARS
7. 20 年以后

The policeman on the beat moved up the avenue impressively. The impressiveness was habitual and not for show, for spectators were few.The time was barely 10 o'clock at night, but chilly gusts of wind with a taste of rain in them had well nigh de-peopled the streets.

Trying doors as he went, twirling his club with many intricate and artful movements, turning now and then to cast his watchful eyes down the pacific thoroughfare, the officer, with his stalwart form and slight swagger, made a fine picture of a guardian of the peace. The vicinity was one that kept early hours. Now and then you might see the lights of a cigar store or of an all-night lunch counter; but the majority of the doors belonged to business places that had long since been closed.

When about midway of a certain block the policeman suddenly slowed his walk. In the doorway of a darkened hardware store a man leaned, with an unlighted cigar in his mouth. As the policeman walked up to him the man spoke up

一位值勤的警察沿着大街惹人注目地走着。这种惹人注目是习惯性的，并非是为了作秀，因为此刻几乎没有观众。才刚到夜里 10 点钟，但一阵冷飕飕的风夹杂着雨水已将街道清理得空无一人了。

他一边走一边注意各家各户的门有没有关严实，手里还转着他的警棍，玩儿出各种令人眼花缭乱的花样来。他警惕的目光不时地投向这平静的大道。这位警官以他坚定的外形和轻微的摆动描绘了一幅和平卫士的图景。附近的街区关门很早，你偶尔可能会看到一家雪茄店或者是一家彻夜营业的速食店柜台的灯光。但大多数商业店铺的门早就已经关了。

在一个街区的中央，警察突然放慢了他的脚步。一个嘴里叼着根没点燃的雪茄烟的人靠在一家已经熄了灯的五金商店门前。当警察走向他的时候，他迅速搭话道：

quickly.

"It's all right, officer," he said, reas-suringly. "I'm just waiting for a friend. It's an appointment made twenty years ago. Sounds a little funny to you, doesn't it? Well, I'll explain if you'd like to make certain it's all straight. About that long ago there used to be a restaurant where this store stands – 'Big Joe' Brady's restaurant."

"Until five years ago," said the po-liceman. "It was torn down then."

The man in the doorway struck a match and lit his cigar. The light showed a pale, square-jawed face with keen eyes, and a little white scar near his right eye-brow. His scarf pin was a large diamond, oddly set.

"Twenty years ago to-night," said the man, "I dined here at 'Big Joe' Brady's with Jimmy Wells, my best chum, and the finest chap in the world. He and I were raised here in New York, just like two brothers, together. I was eighteen and Jimmy was twenty. The next morn-ing I was to start for the West to make my fortune. You couldn't have dragged Jimmy out of New York; he thought it was the only place on earth. Well, we agreed that night that we would meet here

"一切安好，警官先生。"他令人放心地说，"我只是在这儿等一位老友。这是20年前定下的一个约定。听起来很滑稽，是不是？好吧，如果你想确定一切正常，我就解释给你听。大约20年前，那个时候这个店铺现在所占的地方是一家餐馆,叫做'大乔'布兰迪餐馆。"

"五年前餐馆就被拆了。"警察接着说。

门口的男子划了根火柴，点燃了他的雪茄。亮光中显现出一张苍白的脸。他下巴方阔，目光敏锐，右眉毛附近有一块小小的白色伤疤。他的领带夹是一块很大的钻石，但戴上去使人感觉很奇怪。

"20年前的今晚，"男子说，"我和吉米·维尔斯在'大乔'布兰迪餐馆共进晚餐。吉米是我最要好的朋友，也是这个世界上最好的人。我俩都在纽约长大，情同手足。我18岁，吉米20岁。当时，我第二天早上便准备动身到西部去谋生。你不可能把吉米拖出纽约，因为他认为这是地球上惟一的地方。当时我们俩约定：20年后的同一日期、同一时间，

again exactly twenty years from that date and time, no matter what our conditions might be or from what distance we might have to come. We figured that in twenty years each of us ought to have our destiny worked out and our fortunes made, whatever they were going to be."

"It sounds pretty interesting," said the policeman. "Rather a long time between meets, though, it seems to me. Haven't you heard from your friend since you left?"

"Well, yes, for a time we corresponded," said the other. "But after a year or two we lost track of each other. You see, the West is a pretty big proposition, and I kept hustling around over it pretty lively. But I know Jimmy will meet me here if he's alive, for he always was the truest, stanchest old chap in the world. He'll never forget. I came a thousand miles to stand in this door to-night, and it's worth it if my old partner turns up."

The waiting man pulled out a handsome watch, the lids of it set with small diamonds.

"Three minutes to ten," he announced. "It was exactly ten o'clock when we parted here at the restaurant door."

我们俩将来到这里再次相会，不管我们的境遇如何，不管我们身在何方。我们认为 20 年后我们两个都会找到各自的归宿，不管我们会成为什么样的人。"

"这听起来倒挺有意思的。"警察说，"但依我看从分离到见面的时间有点长。分手以后，你就没有收到过那位朋友的信吗？"

"哦，收到过。有一段时间我们曾经相互通信。"那个男子说，"可是一两年之后，我们就失去了联系。你知道，西部地大物博。而我呢，又总是疲于奔命。可我相信，只要吉米还活着，他就一定会来这儿和我相会的，因为他是这个世界上最真诚最忠实的朋友，他决不会忘记的。我赶了几千里的路，只为了能在今晚来到这个门口，只要我的老伙计出现，这一切都是值得的。"

这个正在等待的男子从口袋里掏出一块精美的手表。表盖上镶着小钻石。

"9 点 57 分了。"他说，"当年我们是 10 点整在这儿的餐馆门口分手的。"

"Did pretty well out West, didn't you?" asked the policeman.

"You bet! I hope Jimmy has done half as well. He was a kind of plodder, though, good fellow as he was. I've had to compete with some of the sharpest wits going to get my pile. A man gets in a groove in New York. It takes the West to put a razor-edge on him."

The policeman twirled his club and took a step or two.

"I'll be on my way. Hope your friend comes around all right. Going to call time on him sharp?"

"I should say not!" said the other. "I'll give him half an hour at least. If Jimmy is alive on earth he'll be here by that time. So long, officer."

"Good-night, sir," said the policeman, passing on along his beat, trying doors as he went.

There was now a fine, cold drizzle falling, and the wind had risen from its uncertain puffs into a steady blow. The few foot passengers astir in that quarter hurried dismally and silently along with coat collars turned high and pocketed hands. And in the door of the hardware store the man who had come a thousand miles to fill an appointment, uncertain

"你在西部干得不错,是吧?"警察问道。

"当然啰!吉米要是能赶上我一半就好了。他是个好人,但是做事有点拖拉。我跟最聪明的人竞争才积攒下现在的财富。人在纽约就要按惯例办事,但在西部人们就得刀光剑影地生活了。"

警察转了转警棒,走了一两步。

"我得走了,希望你的朋友很快就到。假如他不能按时赶来,你会离开吗?"

"不会的,"那个男子说,"我至少要等他半小时。如果吉米还活在这个世界上,他一定会按时来到这儿。再见,警官先生。"

"晚安,先生。"警察一边说着,一边继续巡逻,看看各家各户的门有没有关好。

又是一阵冷飕飕的风穿街而过,风已经从轻呼变成怒吼了。途经那个角落的少数几个人都在默默地赶路,他们外衣的领子翻得高高的,手插在口袋里面。五金商店门口那个男人抽着雪茄在等待着。他只是为了实现那个与儿时朋友许下的近乎荒谬的诺言,不远万里来到这里。

almost to absurdity, with the friend of his youth, smoked his cigar and waited.

About twenty minutes he waited, and then a tall man in a long overcoat, with collar turned up to his ears, hurried across from the opposite side of the street. He went directly to the waiting man.

"Is that you, Bob?" he asked, doubtfully.

"Is that you, Jimmy Wells?" cried the man in the door.

"Bless my heart!" exclaimed the new arrival, grasping both the other's hands with his own. "It's Bob, sure as fate. I was certain I'd find you here if you were still in existence. Well, well, well! – twenty years is a long time. The old restaurant's gone, Bob; I wish it had lasted, so we could have had another dinner there. How has the West treated you, old man?"

"Bully; it has given me everything I asked it for. You've changed lots, Jimmy. I never thought you were so tall by two or three inches."

"Oh, I grew a bit after I was twenty."

"Doing well in New York, Jimmy?"

"Moderately. I have a position in one of the city departments. Come on, Bob; we'll go around to a place I know of, and

男子等了 20 分钟, 这时, 一个身材高大的人匆匆地从街的另一头径直走向等待的那个男人。他的大衣领向上翻着, 盖住了耳朵。

"是你吗, 鲍勃? "他迟疑地问道。

"你是吉米·维尔斯? "门口的男子大声喊道。

"保佑我的灵魂吧! "来人惊呼道, 并握紧了男子的双手。"不错, 你是鲍勃。我坚信如果你还在世, 我就会在这儿见到你的。啧, 啧, 啧! 20 年的时间真不短啊! 鲍勃! 原来的那个饭馆已经不在啦! 我真希望它没拆, 那样我们就可以再一次在这里面共进晚餐了! 老朋友, 你在西部怎么样? "

"呵, 西部给了我想要的一切。你变了很多啊, 吉米。我从来没想到你会长这么高, 长了有两三英寸吧。"

"哦, 我 20 岁以后是长高了一点儿。"

"吉米, 你在纽约混得不错吧? "

"马马虎虎。我在一个市政

have a good long talk about old times."

The two men started up the street, arm in arm. The man from the West, his egotism enlarged by success, was beginning to outline the history of his career. The other, submerged in his overcoat, listened with interest.

At the corner stood a drug store, brilliant with electric lights. When they came into this glare each of them turned simultaneously to gaze upon the other's face.

The man from the West stopped suddenly and released his arm.

"You're not Jimmy Wells," he snapped. "Twenty years is a long time, but not long enough to change a man's nose from a Roman to a pug."

"It sometimes changes a good man into a bad one," said the tall man. "You've been under arrest for ten minutes, 'Silky' Bob. Chicago thinks you may have dropped over our way and wires us she wants to have a chat with you. Going quietly, are you? That's sensible. Now, before we go onto the station here's a note I was asked to hand you. You may read it here at the window. It's from Patrolman Wells."

The man from the West unfolded the

部门上班。来，鲍勃，咱们去一个我知道的地方好好叙叙旧。"

两个人手挽手在街上走着。那个来自西部的，因为成功而自我膨胀的人开始描述他的发家史。另一个缩在他的外套里面，饶有兴致地听着。

街角处有一家药店，里面灯火通明。来到亮处以后，两人都不约而同地互相打量起对方的脸。

突然间，那个从西部来的男子停住了脚步，松开了手。

"你不是吉米·维尔斯！"他吼道，"20年的时间虽然不短，但还不足以使一个人面目全非。"

"然而，20年的时间却有可能使一个好人变成坏人。"高个子说，"你已经被捕十分钟了，狡猾的鲍勃。芝加哥的警方猜到你会到我们这里来，于是他们给我们打电报说想要跟你'聊聊'。没话说了吧？想悄无声息地逃走，是吗？在我们去警察局之前，先给你看一张字条，你可以现在在窗户口看一下。这是巡逻员维尔斯写给你的。"

这个来自西部的男人打开了

little piece of paper handed him. His hand was steady when he began to read, but it trembled a little by the time he had finished. The note was rather short.

"Bob: I was at the appointed place on time. When you struck the match to light your cigar I saw it was the face of the man wanted in Chicago. Somehow I couldn't do it myself, so I went around and got a plain clothes man to do the job. JIMMY."

递给他的小纸条。刚开始的时候，他的手还握得很稳，但读完以后却微微颤抖着。便条上的内容很短：

"鲍勃：刚才我准时到了我们的相约之地。当你划亮火柴点烟的时候，我发现你正是芝加哥警方所通缉的那个人。不管怎样，我不忍心亲自逮捕你，所以我只好找了个便衣警察来做这件事。吉米"

8. THE FURNISHED ROOM
8. 带家具出租的房间

Restless, shifting, fugacious as time itself is a certain vast bulk of the population of the red brick district of the lower West Side. Homeless, they have a hundred homes. They flit from furnished room to furnished room, transients forever – transients in abode, transients in heart and mind. They sing "Home, Sweet Home" in ragtime; they carry their *lares et penates* in a bandbox; their vine is entwined about a picture hat; a rubber plant is their fig tree.

Hence the houses of this district, having had a thousand dwellers, should have a thousand tales to tell, mostly dull ones, no doubt; but it would be strange if there could not be found a ghost or two in the wake of all these vagrant guests.

One evening after dark a young man prowled among these crumbling red mansions, ringing their bells. At the twelfth he rested his lean hand-baggage upon the step and wiped the dust from his hatband and forehead. The bell sounded faint and far away in some remote, hollow depths.

在纽约西区南部的红砖房那一带，绝大多数居民都较为动荡不定、不停迁移、来去匆匆，正如时光本身一样。他们没有自己的家，但同时他们又有上百个家。他们不时地从一间带家具出租的房间搬到另一间，永远都是那么飘忽不定——住的地方是如此，情感和理智上也是如此。他们唱着"家，甜美的家"的爵士乐曲，拿着一个装有全部家当的硬纸箱，阔边帽上的装饰就是他们的葡萄藤，橡胶做的拐杖就是他们的无花果树。

所以，这一带的房子拥有上千的房客，也就有上千的故事可以讲述。当然，大多数的故事都很无聊。不过，要是在这么多漂泊过客经过之后，却找不出一两个鬼魂来，那才是怪事哩。

一天傍晚，天黑以后，有个青年男子在这些失修崩塌的红砖房中间转悠，挨家挨户地按门铃。走到第12家门前时，他把干瘪的手提行李包放在台阶上，然后擦去帽檐和额头上的灰尘。从遥远、

To the door of this, the twelfth house whose bell he had rung, came a housekeeper who made him think of an unwholesome, surfeited worm that had eaten its nut to a hollow shell and now sought to fill the vacancy with edible lodgers.

He asked if there was a room to let.

"Come in," said the housekeeper. Her voice came from her throat; her throat seemed lined with fur. "I have the third floor back, vacant since a week back. Should you wish to look at it?"

The young man followed her up the stairs. A faint light from no particular source mitigated the shadows of the halls. They trod noiselessly upon a stair carpet that its own loom would have forsworn. It seemed to have become vegetable; to have degenerated in that rank, sunless air to lush lichen or spreading moss that grew in patches to the staircase and was viscid under the foot like organic matter. At each turn of the stairs were vacant niches in the wall. Perhaps plants had once been set within them. If so they had died in that foul and tainted air. It may be that statues of the saints had stood there, but it was not difficult to conceive that imps and devils had dragged them forth in the

空旷的房屋深处传来了微弱的门铃声。

这是他按响的第 12 家门铃。铃声响过之后，女房东出来开门。她的样子让他想起一只令人厌恶、营养过剩的蛆虫。坚果已经被它吃得只剩下了空壳，现在正想寻找可以充饥的房客来填补空房间。

他问了问有没有房间出租。

"进来吧，"女房东说，她的声音从喉咙里发出，似乎上面覆盖了一层皮毛。"三楼阴面还有个房间，空了一个星期了。你想看看吗？"

年轻人跟她上了楼。不知从哪儿透出来的一线微光缓和了走廊上的阴影。他们在楼梯上不声不响地走着，脚下的地毯破烂不堪，可能连制造出它的织布机都不愿意承认这是自己的作品。在阴暗潮湿、缺少阳光的空气中，它仿佛变成植物了，堕落成一块块茂盛的地衣和蔓延的苔藓，一直长到楼梯上，踩在脚下就像踩在有机物上一样黏乎乎的。每个楼梯转角处的墙上都有空着的壁龛，也许里面曾经摆放过花草。如果摆放过的话，那些花草也早已在污浊腐臭的空气中死去了。

darkness and down to the unholy depths of some furnished pit below.

"This is the room," said the housekeeper, from her furry throat. "It's a nice room. It ain't often vacant. I had some most elegant people in it last summer – no trouble at all, and paid in advance to the minute. The water's at the end of the hall. Sprowls and Mooney kept it three months. They done a vaudeville sketch. Miss B'retta Sprowls – you may have heard of her – Oh, that was just the stage names – right there over the dresser is where the marriage certificate hung, framed. The gas is here, and you see there is plenty of closet room. It's a room everybody likes. It never stays idle long."

"Do you have many theatrical people rooming here?" asked the young man.

"They comes and goes. A good proportion of my lodgers is connected with the theatres. Yes, sir, this is the theatrical district. Actor people never stays long anywhere. I get my share. Yes, they comes and they goes."

He engaged the room, paying for a week in advance. He was tired, he said, and would take possession at once. He counted out the money. The room had been made ready, she said, even to towels

壁龛里面也许曾供奉过圣像,但是不难想象,黑暗中形形色色的魔鬼早就把圣人拽出来,一直拽到下面某间带家具的客房里的邪恶深渊里去了。

"就是这间,"房东说道,还是那副沙哑的盖着毛皮的嗓子。"房间很不错,常常会有人来住。今年夏天这儿还住过一些特别文雅的人呢——从不给我们添麻烦,而且总是提前付房租,从不拖欠。自来水在走廊尽头。斯普罗尔斯和穆尼在这里住了三个月。他们演过轻松喜剧。布雷塔·斯普罗尔斯小姐——也许你曾经听说过她——喔,那是她的艺名儿——就在那张梳妆台上边挂着她的镶了边框的结婚证书。煤气在这儿,壁橱的空间也很大。这房间人人都喜欢,从来没有空过很长时间。"

"你这里住过很多演戏的人吗?"年轻人问。

"他们总是来了又走。我的房客中有很多人的工作与剧院有关。对了,先生,这一带是剧院区。演戏的人从不在任何一个地方住太长的时间。到我这儿来住的人也不少,是的,他们总是来了又走。"

and water. As the housekeeper moved away he put, for the thousandth time, the question that he carried at the end of his tongue.

"A young girl – Miss Vashner – Miss Eloise Vashner – do you remember such a one among your lodgers? She would be singing on the stage, most likely. A fair girl, of medium height and slender, with reddish, gold hair and a dark mole near her left eyebrow."

"No, I don't remember the name. Them stage people has names they change as often as their rooms. They comes and they goes. No, I don't call that one to mind."

No. Always no. Five months of ceaseless interrogation and the inevitable negative. So much time spent by day in questioning managers, agents, schools and choruses; by night among the audiences of theatres from all-star casts down to music halls so low that he dreaded to find what he most hoped for. He who had loved her best had tried to find her. He was sure that since her disappearance from home this great, water-girt city held her somewhere, but it was like a monstrous quicksand, shifting its particles constantly, with no foundation, its upper

他租下了这间房，预付了一个星期的租金。他说他累了，想立刻住下来。他点好钱付了租金。女房东说房间早就布置妥当了，连毛巾和水都准备好了。正当女房东要离开的时候，他把挂在嘴边的问题又问了出来，这已经是他第1000次问了。

"有个姑娘——瓦西纳小姐——埃卢瓦丝·瓦西纳小姐——你记得有过这个房客吗？她大概是在舞台上演唱的，皮肤白嫩，中等身高，身材苗条，头发呈现有些微红的金黄色，左边的眉毛旁边有颗黑痣。"

"不，我不记得这个名字。那些演员们，换名字跟换房间一样快，他们总是来了就走。不，我不记得有这个名字。"

不，总是不！五个月来不间断地打听询问，答案却总是否定的。白天去找剧院经理、经纪人、戏剧学校和合唱团打听，晚上则夹在剧院观众中间去寻找。什么样的剧院他都去过了，不管是明星会演的剧院，还是低俗下流的歌舞杂耍戏院，尽管他害怕在那种地方找到他最想找的人。这么长时间了，深爱着她的他一心要找到她。他确信，自从她从家里

granules of to-day buried to-morrow in ooze and slime.

The furnished room received its latest guest with a first glow of pseudo-hospitality, a hectic, haggard, perfunctory welcome like the specious smile of a demirep. The sophistical comfort came in reflected gleams from the decayed furniture, the ragged brocade upholstery of a couch and two chairs, a foot-wide cheap pier glass between the two windows, from one or two gilt picture frames and a brass bedstead in a corner.

The guest reclined, inert, upon a chair, while the room, confused in speech as though it were an apartment in Babel, tried to discourse to him of its diverse tenantry.

A polychromatic rug like some brilliant-flowered rectangular, tropical islet lay surrounded by a billowy sea of soiled matting. Upon the gay-papered wall were those pictures that pursue the homeless one from house to house – The Huguenot Lovers, The First Quarrel, The Wedding Breakfast, Psyche at the Fountain. The mantel's chastely severe outline was ingloriously veiled behind some pert drapery drawn rakishly askew like the sashes of

失踪之后，这座河水环绕的大城市一定把她藏在了某个角落。但是这座城市就像一大团流沙，每一颗沙粒都在不断地改变着自己的位置，没有根基，今天还浮在上层的小颗粒明天就会被淤泥和黏土覆盖住了。

客房以假惺惺的热情迎接了新到的客人，就像面容枯槁的娼妓堆起满脸的假笑，例行公事、敷衍马虎地招呼客人一样。腐朽的家具、沙发上破烂不堪的织花布套、两把椅子、窗户间一码宽的廉价穿衣镜、一两个烫金相框、角落里的铜床架——所有这一切都折射出一种勉为其难的舒适。

房客慵懒地斜靠在一把椅子上，客房就如同巴比伦通天塔的一个套间，尽管口齿不清，仍然竭力地把曾在这里住过的不同房客向他娓娓道来。

一张杂色地毯铺在地面上，就像一个鲜花盛开的长方形热带小岛，周围是肮脏的垫子组成的波涛汹涌的大海。灰色的纸裱过的墙上，贴着追随无家可归的人四处漂泊的图片——"胡格诺情人"、"第一次争吵"、"婚礼早餐"、"泉边美女"。壁炉的样式典雅而庄重，外面却歪歪扭

the Amazonian ballet. Upon it was some desolate flotsam cast aside by the room's marooned when a lucky sail had borne them to a fresh port – a trifling vase or two, pictures of actresses, a medicine bottle, some stray cards out of a deck.

One by one, as the characters of a cryptograph become explicit, the little signs left by the furnished room's procession of guests developed a significance. The threadbare space in the rug in front of the dresser told that lovely woman had marched in the throng. Tiny finger prints on the wall spoke of little prisoners trying to feel their way to sun and air. A splattered stain, raying like the shadow of a bursting bomb, witnessed where a hurled glass or bottle had splintered with its contents against the wall. Across the pier glass had been scrawled with a diamond in staggering letters the name "Marie." It seemed that the succession of dwellers in the furnished room had turned in fury – perhaps tempted beyond forbearance by its garish coldness – and wreaked upon it their passions. The furniture was chipped and bruised; the couch, distorted by bursting springs, seemed a horrible monster that had been slain during the stress of some grotesque convulsion. Some

扭地挂了条花哨的布帘，像亚马逊舞剧里女人用的腰带。壁炉上面还有一些零碎物品，都是那些房客在幸运的风帆把他们载到新码头时丢弃的物件——一两个劣质的花瓶、女演员的画片、药瓶儿和一些零散的扑克牌。

渐渐地，线索一个接着一个变得清晰起来，先后居住过这间客房的人留下的一些细小痕迹也有了特殊的含义。梳妆台前那片几乎被磨破的地毯，告诉我们曾经有许多漂亮的女人在上面走过。墙上留下的小小指纹告知我们有多少小囚犯曾在这里努力探索通向阳光和空气的道路。还有一团溅开的污渍，就像炸弹爆炸后的碎片，是杯子或瓶子和里面所盛的东西一起被砸在墙上的见证。穿衣镜镜面上有人用钻石歪歪扭扭地刻着"玛丽"这个名字。似乎连续到来的房客们——或许是房间令人反感的俗艳装饰和冷漠让他们感到难以忍受——把一腔愤怒发泄在这个房间上。家具上面有不少破损之处；长沙发因凸起的弹簧而变了形，看上去像一头在痛苦痉挛中被宰杀的令人恐怖的怪物。还有某次威力更大的动荡使得大理石壁炉被砍掉了

more potent upheaval had cloven a great slice from the marble mantel. Each plank in the floor owned its particular cant and shriek as from a separate and individual agony. It seemed incredible that all this malice and injury had been wrought upon the room by those who had called it for a time their home; and yet it may have been the cheated home instinct surviving blindly, the resentful rage at false household gods that had kindled their wrath. A hut that is our own we can sweep and adorn and cherish.

The young tenant in the chair allowed these thoughts to file, soft-shod, through his mind, while there drifted into the room furnished sounds and furnished scents. He heard in one room a tittering and incontinent, slack laughter; in others the monologue of a scold, the rattling of dice, a lullaby, and one crying dully; above him a banjo tinkled with spirit. Doors banged somewhere; the elevated trains roared intermittently; a cat yowled miserably upon a back fence. And he breathed the breath of the house – a dank savour rather than a smell – a cold, musty effluvium as from underground vaults mingled with the reeking exhalations of linoleum and mildewed and rotten wood-

一大块。地板的每一块木板都是一个不同的斜面，并且似乎是因为各自的剧痛而在发出尖叫。令人难以置信的是，那些恶意破坏这个房间的人竟然是一度把它称之为自己的家的人；但是也许正是这被欺骗的、却仍然盲目坚持的恋家本能以及对虚假的护家神的仇恨点燃了他们胸中的怒火。只要是属于我们自己的家，就算是茅草屋，我们也会把它打扫得干干净净，装饰得漂漂亮亮，好好珍惜爱护它。

年轻房客坐在椅子上，任由这些思绪缓缓地萦绕心间。与此同时，楼中传来真实的声音和气味，他听见一个房间传来傻傻的不能自已的放声大笑；别的房间有人在滔滔不绝地诅咒别人，传来掷骰子的格格声，催眠曲和呜呜的哭泣声；楼上有人在情绪高涨地弹班卓琴。不知哪里的门砰砰地关上；火车时不时咆哮着驶过；一只猫在后面篱墙上凄惨地哀鸣。他呼吸到这座房子的气味。这不是什么气味儿，而是一种潮味儿，就像地窖里恶臭的油布和发霉的朽木混在一起发出的阴冷的腐烂味道一样。

work.

Then, suddenly, as he rested there, the room was filled with the strong, sweet odour of mignonette. It came as upon a single buffet of wind with such sureness and fragrance and emphasis that it almost seemed a living visitant. And the man cried aloud: "What, dear?" as if he had been called, and sprang up and faced about. The rich odour clung to him and wrapped him around. He reached out his arms for it, all his senses for the time confused and commingled. How could one be peremptorily called by an odour? Surely it must have been a sound. But, was it not the sound that had touched, that had caressed him?

"She has been in this room," he cried, and he sprang to wrest from it a token, for he knew he would recognize the smallest thing that had belonged to her or that she had touched. This enveloping scent of mignonette, the odour that she had loved and made her own – whence came it?

The room had been but carelessly set in order. Scattered upon the flimsy dresser scarf were half a dozen hairpins – those discreet, indistinguishable friends of woman-kind, feminine of gender, in-finite of mood and uncommunicative of

他就这样坐在那里休息，突然间，房间里充满了木樨草浓烈香甜的气息，一丝风把它吹散了过来，这香气如此真实，如此浓郁，如同真实的来客一般。年轻人忍不住大声喊道："是你吗？亲爱的？"他听到好像有人喊他似的。他一跃而起，四处张望。浓郁的香气扑面而来，环绕在他的周围，他伸出手臂去拥抱香气。他的感觉全部都混乱了，交织在了一起。香气怎么能如此轻易地将人召唤？唤起他的肯定是声音。难道这不是曾经抚摸过、安慰过他的声音吗？

"她在这个房间里住过。"他大声说，并奋力寻找起来，硬想搜出什么证据，因为他确信他能辨认出她的或是她碰触过的任何微小的东西。这沁人心脾的木樨花香，她喜爱的、唯她独有的芬芳，到底是从哪儿来的？

房间只是被人马马虎虎地收拾了一下。薄薄的不结实的梳妆台桌布上有五六个发夹——都是些女人用的东西，具有女性的特征，但是不代表任何心境或时间。他没去仔细琢磨，因为这些东西

tense. These he ignored, conscious of their triumphant lack of identity. Ransacking the drawers of the dresser he came upon a discarded, tiny, ragged handkerchief. He pressed it to his face. It was racy and insolent with heliotrope; he hurled it to the floor. In another drawer he found odd buttons, a theatre programme, a pawnbroker's card, two lost marshmallows, a book on the divination of dreams. In the last was a woman's black satin hair bow, which halted him, poised between ice and fire. But the black satin hair-bow also is femininity's demure, impersonal, common ornament, and tells no tales.

And then he traversed the room like a hound on the scent, skimming the walls, considering the corners of the bulging matting on his hands and knees, rummaging mantel and tables, the curtains and hangings, the drunken cabinet in the corner, for a visible sign, unable to perceive that she was there beside, around, against, within, above him, clinging to him, wooing him, calling him so poignantly through the finer senses that even his grosser ones became cognisant of the call. Once again he answered loudly: "Yes, dear!" and turned, wild-eyed, to gaze on vacancy, for he could not yet

显然缺乏个性。他把梳妆台抽屉搜了个底朝天，发现了一条被人遗弃的破旧小手绢。他把它蒙在脸上，天芥菜花刺鼻的怪味扑面而来。他把手绢扔到了地上。在另一个抽屉里，他发现几颗扣子、一张节目单、一张当铺老板的名片、两颗吃剩的果汁软糖和一本解梦的书。最后一个抽屉里有一个女人用的黑缎蝴蝶发结，他倏地惊呆了，心情处在冰与火、失望与兴奋之间。但是黑缎蝴蝶发结也只是娴静女子大众化的装饰，不能提供任何证据。

之后他就在房间里四处搜寻，像一条猎狗那样闻闻嗅嗅，扫荡四周。他趴在地上仔细观察拱起的地毯的角落，检查壁炉和桌子，窗帘、门帘和角落里东倒西歪的酒柜，试图发现一个有形的物体。他没法证明她就在这里，证明她就在他旁边、在他四周、前面、心里、上面，紧紧地粘着他、追逐他，通过一种细密的感觉尖锐的向他发出如此令人心碎的呼唤，以至于连他迟钝的感官都能发觉到这一声呼唤。他再次大声回答："我来了，亲爱的！"然后转过身，睁大眼睛，呆呆地

discern form and colour and love and outstretched arms in the odour of mignonette. Oh, God! whence that odour, and since when have odours had a voice to call? Thus he groped.

He burrowed in crevices and corners, and found corks and cigarettes. These he passed in passive contempt. But once he found in a fold of the matting a half-smoked cigar, and this he ground beneath his heel with a green and trenchant oath. He sifted the room from end to end. He found dreary and ignoble small records of many a peripatetic tenant; but of her whom he sought, and who may have lodged there, and whose spirit seemed to hover there, he found no trace.

And then he thought of the housekeeper.

He ran from the haunted room downstairs and to a door that showed a crack of light. She came out to his knock. He smothered his excitement as best he could.

"Will you tell me, madam," he besought her, "who occupied the room I have before I came?"

"Yes, sir. I can tell you again. 'Twas Sprowls and Mooney, as I said. Miss B'retta Sprowls it was in the theatres, but

注视着空荡荡的房间，因为他在木樨花香中无法辨认实体、色彩、爱情和张开的双臂。唔，上帝啊，那芳香是从哪儿来的？从什么时候起香味具有了呼唤的力量？他就这样不停地四处寻找着。

他搜遍了墙角和裂缝，只找到一些瓶塞和烟蒂，他对这些东西不屑一顾。有一次他在地毡里发现了一支抽了半截的雪茄，他狠狠地咒骂了一声，用脚后跟把它踩得稀烂。他把整个房间从一头到另一头筛查了一遍，发现了许许多多过客留下的无聊、可耻的记录。但是，关于她，他正在寻找的可能曾经住过这儿，灵魂好像仍徘徊在这里的她，但却没有丝毫痕迹。

这时他想到了女房东。

他从灵魂萦绕的房间跑下楼，来到透出一线灯光的门前。听到有人敲门，女房东开门出来。而他则尽力克制着自己的兴奋。

"请您告诉我，夫人，"他哀求道，"我住进来之前还有谁住过那个房间？"

"好吧，先生。我可以再跟你说一遍。以前住的是斯普罗尔斯和穆尼夫妇，我已经说过了。布雷塔·斯普罗尔斯小姐是演戏

Missis Mooney she was. My house is well known for respectability. The marriage certificate hung, framed, on a nail over – "

"What kind of a lady was Miss Sprowls – in looks, I mean?"

"Why, black-haired, sir, short, and stout, with a comical face. They left a week ago Tuesday."

"And before they occupied it?"

"Why, there was a single gentleman connected with the draying business. He left owing me a week. Before him was Missis Crowder and her two children, that stayed four months; and back of them was old Mr. Doyle, whose sons paid for him. He kept the room six months. That goes back a year, sir, and further I do not remember."

He thanked her and crept back to his room. The room was dead. The essence that had vivified it was gone. The perfume of mignonette had departed. In its place was the old, stale odour of mouldy house furniture, of atmosphere in storage.

The ebbing of his hope drained his faith. He sat staring at the yellow, singing gaslight. Soon he walked to the bed and began to tear the sheets into strips. With the blade of his knife he drove them

的，也就是穆尼夫人。我的房子声誉一直都很好。他们的结婚证就挂在墙上的钉子上，还镶了框……"

"斯普罗尔斯小姐是什么样女人——我是说，她的相貌？"

"喔，先生，黑头发，矮个子，身材很胖，五官长得很滑稽。他们一个星期前刚刚搬走，就是上星期二。"

"在他们以前谁还住过？"

"咳，有个单身男人，是个运货的。他还欠一个星期的房租没付呢。在他以前是克劳德夫人和她两个孩子，住了四个月，再以前是多伊尔老先生，房租是他儿子付的，他住了六个月。这都是一年以前的事了，再远的我就记不得了。"

他谢过她之后，慢腾腾地回到房间。房间里显得死气沉沉。曾让它充满生机的香气已经离去，木樨花香已经消失殆尽，扑面而来的是发霉家具老朽、腐烂的臭气以及储藏室发霉的气息。

希望的破灭让他觉得心灰意冷。他坐在那儿，呆呆地望着咝咝作响的煤气灯发出的黄色光芒。没过一会儿，他便走到床边，开始撕拉床单，把床单都撕成了

tightly into every crevice around windows and door. When all was snug and taut he turned out the light, turned the gas full on again and laid himself gratefully upon the bed.

It was Mrs. McCool's night to go with the can for beer. So she fetched it and sat with Mrs. Purdy in one of those subterranean retreats where house-keepers foregather and the worm dieth seldom.

"I rented out my third floor, back, this evening," said Mrs. Purdy, across a fine circle of foam. "A young man took it. He went up to bed two hours ago."

"Now, did ye, Mrs. Purdy, ma'am?" said Mrs. McCool, with intense admiration. "You do be a wonder for rentin' rooms of that kind. And did ye tell him, then?" she concluded in a husky whisper, laden with mystery.

"Rooms," said Mrs. Purdy, in her furriest tones, "are furnished for to rent. I did not tell him, Mrs. McCool."

"'Tis right ye are, ma'am; 'tis by renting rooms we kape alive. Ye have the rale sense for business, ma'am. There be many people will rayjict the rentin' of a room if they be tould a suicide has been after dyin' in the bed of it."

"As you say, we has our living to be

一条一条，然后用刀刃把撕好的布条塞进门窗周围的每一条缝隙里。当一切都收拾好之后，他把灯关掉，心存感激地躺在床上，把煤气打开并且开到最大。

今晚轮到麦克库尔夫人拿罐头和买啤酒了。她把酒拿回来后，和珀迪夫人在一个隐蔽的地下室里坐下。这是房东们碰头、也是蛆虫肆虐的地方。

"今晚我把三楼后面的房间租了出去，"珀迪夫人说，她杯中的啤酒泡沫显得满满的。"一个年轻人租了它。两个钟头以前他就上床休息了。"

"嗬，你可真厉害，珀迪夫人，"麦克库尔夫人赞叹道，"你可真是个能人啊，连那种房子你都能租出去。那你告诉他那件事了吗？"她压低了粗哑的嗓音，看起来充满神秘。

"房间，"珀迪夫人用她极嘶哑的声音说，"房间配了家具，就是为了把它租出去。我当然没告诉他那件事，麦克库尔夫人。"

"你做得对，我们就是靠出租房子混饭吃的。你很有生意头脑，夫人。如果大家都知道有人在这个房间里自杀，并且死在了床上，哪会有人来租它呢。"

making," remarked Mrs. Purdy.

"Yis, ma'am; 'tis true. 'Tis just one wake ago this day I helped ye lay out the third floor, back. A pretty slip of a colleen she was to be killin' herself wid the gas a swate little face she had, Mrs. Purdy, ma'am."

"She'd a-been called handsome, as you say," said Mrs. Purdy, assenting but critical, "but for that mole she had a-growin' by her left eyebrow. Do fill up your glass again, Mrs. McCool."

"当然嘛，我们总得养家糊口啊。"珀迪夫人说。

"对喽，夫人，这才是实话。一个星期前我才帮你把三楼后面的房间收拾出来。那姑娘就用煤气在里面自我了结了——她那小脸蛋儿长得多甜啊，珀迪夫人。"

"正如你所说，她长得挺标致，"珀迪夫人说，同意的同时又很挑剔的说了一句，"只是她左边眉毛旁边的痣长得不怎么好看。再来一杯吧，麦克库尔夫人。"

9. HEARTS AND HANDS
9. 心与手

At Denver there was an influx of passengers into the coaches on the eastbound B. & M. express. In one coach there sat a very pretty young woman dressed in elegant taste and surrounded by all the luxurious comforts of an experienced traveler. Among the newcomers were two young men, one of handsome presence with a bold, frank countenance and manner; the other a ruffled, glum-faced person, heavily built and roughly dressed. The two were handcuffed together.

As they passed down the aisle of the coach the only vacant seat offered was a reversed one facing the attractive young woman. Here the linked couple seated themselves. The young woman's glance fell upon them with a distant, swift disinterest; then with a lovely smile brightening her countenance and a tender pink tingeing her rounded cheeks, she held out a little gray-gloved hand. When she spoke her voice, full, sweet, and deliberate, proclaimed that its owner was accustomed to speak and be heard.

"Well, Mr. Easton, if you will make

丹佛站，一群旅客拥上了从波士顿向东开往缅因的特快列车。在其中一节车厢里坐着一位非常漂亮的年轻女人，她衣着端庄文雅，周围放满了一个有经验的旅行者才能想到的奢侈享受品。刚上车的人群里有两位年轻男子，一个很英俊，面容和风度显得勇敢和坦诚；另一位身材笨重，面容阴郁，衣冠不整。两个人被手铐铐在了一起。

他们沿着车厢的过道往前走，惟一空着的位子就剩下了这位颇具魅力的年轻女士对面的座位。这两个铐在一起的人就在这儿坐了下来。年轻的女士先是用冷漠疏远的目光瞥了他们一眼，继而脸上露出了可人的甜蜜微笑，圆圆的脸颊也显得微微泛红。她伸出了一只带着灰色手套的小手。声音饱满、甜美，清晰，一开口就听得出她是位爱聊天、很健谈的人。

"哎，阿斯顿先生，如果您

me speak first, I suppose I must. Don't you ever recognize old friends when you meet them in the West?"

The younger man roused himself sharply at the sound of her voice, seemed to struggle with a slight embarrassment which he threw off instantly, and then clasped her fingers with his left hand.

"It's Miss Fairchild," he said, with a smile. "I'll ask you to excuse the other hand; "it's otherwise engaged just at present."

He slightly raised his right hand, bound at the wrist by the shining "bracelet" to the left one of his companion. The glad look in the girl's eyes slowly changed to a bewildered horror. The glow faded from her cheeks. Her lips parted in a vague, relaxing distress.Easton, with a little laugh, as if amused, was about to speak again when the other forestalled him. The glum-faced man had been watching the girl's countenance with veiled glances from his keen, shrewd eyes.

"You'll excuse me for speaking, miss, but, I see you're acquainted with the marshall here. If you'll ask him to speak a word for me when we get to the pen he'll do it, and it'll make things easier for me

一定要让我打破沉默，我想我也必须这样了。在西部见到老朋友，你都认不出来了吗?"

这嗓音让那位年轻一些的男人突然一怔。他看起来有些尴尬，但他立刻就摆脱了这种尴尬，赶紧用左手握住了她的手指。

"原来是费切尔德小姐，"他笑着说，"请原谅我不能用右手，因为它这会儿正有事儿呢。"

他轻轻地扬起右手，一副闪闪发亮的"手镯"将他的右手腕与他同伴的左手腕铐在了一起。姑娘眼中喜悦的神情慢慢变成了惶恐，泛起的红晕也从她的脸颊上消退。她的嘴巴微微张开，显得很是紧张。阿斯顿微微地笑了笑，好像这是很有趣的一件事一样。他刚要说话，却被另外那位男士抢先开了口。这个一脸阴郁的男人一直在用他那双敏锐炽热的双眼观察着这个姑娘的表情。

"请原谅我插话，小姐。但我看得出您跟这位警官很熟。如果您能为我说几句好话，在我们抵达监狱之后，他一定会善待我的。这样我在那儿的日子便会好

there. He's taking me to Leavenworth prison. It's seven years for counterfeiting."

"Oh!" said the girl, with a deep breath and returning color. "So that is what you are doing out here? A marshal!"

"My dear Miss Fairchild," said Easton, calmly, "I had to do something. Money has a way of taking wings unto itself, and you know it takes money to keep step with our crowd in Washington. I saw this opening in the West, and – well, a marshalship isn't quite as high a position as that of ambassador, but – "

"The ambassador," said the girl, warmly, "doesn't call any more. He needn't ever have done so. You ought to know that. And so now you are one of these dashing Western heroes, and you ride and shoot and go into all kinds of dangers. That's different from the Washington life.You have been missed from the old crowd."

The girl's eyes, fascinated, went back, widening a little, to rest upon the glittering handcuffs.

"Don't you worry about them, miss," said the other man. "All marshals handcuff themselves to their prisoners to keep them from getting away. Mr. Easton knows his business."

过的多了。我因犯伪造罪要在利文沃斯监狱待上七年。"

"噢！"姑娘说，边深深地吸了口气，她的脸颊上又泛出了光彩，"所以，这就是您离开这儿后要做的事，警官！"

"我亲爱的费切尔德小姐，"阿斯顿冷静地说，"我总得干点什么吧。钱总是有办法让自己长上翅膀飞走。你知道，如果要跟在华盛顿那帮人保持步伐一致，得花好多的钱。我知道西部这个职位空缺，就……唉，警官虽说不像外交官那样位高权重，但是……"

"那位大使，"姑娘热切地说，"现在不用再打电话了。他再也不用那么做了，你应该知道这一点。这么说你现在是英勇的西部英雄中的一员了！你骑马、射击，历经危险、九死一生，过着与在华盛顿完全不同的生活。老朋友们可都惦着你呢。"

姑娘迷人的眼睛四处看了看，好奇的目光又转回来落到闪闪发光的手铐上。

"小姐，别为他担心，"另外那个男人说，"所有的警官都把自己同罪犯铐在一起以防他们逃跑，阿斯顿先生在这方面很专

"Will we see you again soon in Washington?" asked the girl.

"Not soon, I think," said Easton. "My butterfly days are over, I fear."

"I love the West," said the girl irrelevantly. Her eyes were shining softly. She looked away out the car window. She began to speak truly and simply without the gloss of style and manner: "Mamma and I spent the summer in Denver. She went home a week ago because father was slightly ill. I could live and be happy in the West. I think the air here agrees with me. Money isn't everything. But people always misunderstand things and remain stupid – "

"Say, Mr. Marshal," growled the glum-faced man. "This isn't quite fair. I'm needing a drink, and haven't had a smoke all day. Haven't you talked long enough? Take me in the smoker now, won't you? I'm half dead for a pipe."

The bound travelers rose to their feet, Easton with the same slow smile on his face.

"I can't deny a petition for tobacco," he said, lightly. "It's the one friend of the unfortunate. Good-bye, Miss Fairchild. Duty calls, you know." He held out his hand for a farewell.

业的。"

"我会很快在华盛顿再见到你吗？"姑娘问。

"我想不会太快，"阿斯顿说，"恐怕我像蝴蝶一样逍遥的日子已经终结了。"

"我爱西部，"她突兀地说，眼睛里闪烁着温柔的光。她抬头向车窗外望去，言谈开始变得简单质朴，摒弃了那光鲜的外表，"妈妈和我夏天是在丹佛度过的，因为爸爸有些不舒服。一周前她就回家了。在西部我生活的很快乐，我感觉这儿的空气很适合我。金钱不代表一切，可人们总是误解，而且执迷不悟……"

"我说，警官先生，"一脸阴郁的男人抱怨道，"这可真有点儿不公平。我想喝水，而且一整天都没抽烟了。你们聊得还不够吗？把我带到吸烟区去好不好？我想抽烟，都快想疯了！"

于是绑在一起的两个人起身离开，阿斯顿的脸上还带着不变的迟缓的笑容。

"我不能拒绝一个吸烟的请求，"他轻快地说，"它是这个不幸的人惟一的朋友。再见，费切尔德小姐，你知道，这是职责所在啊。"他挥手道别。

"It's too bad you are not going East," she said, reclothing herself with manner and style. "But you must go on to Leavenworth, I suppose?"

"Yes," said Easton, "I must go on to Leavenworth."

The two men sidled down the aisle into the smoker.

The two passengers in a seat near by had heard most of the conversation. Said one of them: "That marshal's a good sort of chap. Some of these Western fellows are all right."

"Pretty young to hold an office like that, isn't he?" asked the other.

"Young!" exclaimed the first speaker, "why – Oh! didn't you catch on? Say – did you ever know an officer to handcuff a prisoner to his right hand?"

"你不去东部太糟糕了，"她说，此时她又恢复了之前的风度，"可我想你必须继续前进去利文沃斯吧？"

"是呀，"阿斯顿说，"我必须继续到利文沃斯去。"

这两个男人侧身沿着走道到吸烟区去了。

附近座位上的两位旅客听到了这些谈话的大部分内容，其中一位说："那位警官是个好警察，有些西部人确实是不错。"

"你的意思是,他那么年轻就坐上这样一个职位，是不是？"另一位问道。

"年轻!"先开口那个人惊呼道，"怎么……噢!你没弄明白吗？我说，你以前听说过把罪犯拷在自己右手上的警官吗？"

10. THE PRINCESS AND THE PUMA
10. 公主与美洲狮

There had to be a king and queen, of course. The king was a terrible old man who wore six-shooters and spurs, and shouted in such a tremendous voice that the rattlers on the prairie would run into their holes under the prickly pear. Before there was a royal family they called the man "Whispering Ben." When he came to own 50,000 acres of land and more cattle than he could count, they called him O'Donnell "the Cattle King."

The queen had been a Mexican girl from Laredo. She made a good, mild, Colorado-claro wife, and even succeeded in teaching Ben to modify his voice sufficiently while in the house to keep the dishes from being broken. When Ben got to be king she would sit on the gallery of Espinosa Ranch and weave rush mats. When wealth became so irresistible and oppressive that upholstered chairs and a centre table were brought down from San Antone in the wagons, she bowed her smooth, dark head, and shared the fate of the Danae.

To avoid lese-majeste you have been

当然，这个故事里必须有国王和王后。国王是个可怕的老头，身上总戴着几支六响手枪和几根马刺，吼起来声如洪钟，连草原上的响尾蛇都会被吓得钻进他们在仙人掌下的洞穴里。在皇室成立之前，人们管他叫"小嗓门本"。当他拥有了五万英亩土地和连他自己都数不清的牛时，人们就都管他叫"牛王"奥唐奈了。

王后是一个来自拉雷多的墨西哥姑娘。现在她已经成为一个地地道道的温柔贤惠的科罗拉多妻子，她甚至成功教会了本在家里尽量控制嗓门，以免他的嗓门震破碗盏。本还没当上国王时，她常常坐在刺荆牧场正宅的走廊上飞快地编织草席。等到财源滚滚而进时，马车便从圣安东尼运来了豪华的软垫椅子和大圆桌，之后，她便低下了有着顺滑黑发的头，分享达纳埃的命运了。

为了避免大逆不道，我先向

presented first to the king and queen. They do not enter the story, which might be called "The Chronicle of the Princess, the Happy Thought, and the Lion that Bungled his Job."

Josefa O'Donnell was the surviving daughter, the princess. From her mother she inherited warmth of nature and a dusky, semi-tropic beauty. From Ben O'Donnell the royal she acquired a store of intrepidity, common sense, and the faculty of ruling. The combination was one worth going miles to see. Josefa while riding her pony at a gallop could put five out of six bullets through a tomato-can swinging at the end of a string. She could play for hours with a white kitten she owned, dressing it in all manner of absurd clothes. Scorning a pencil, she could tell you out of her head what 1545 two-year-olds would bring on the hoof, at $8.50 per head. Roughly speaking, the Espinosa Ranch is forty miles long and thirty broad – but mostly leased land. Josefa, on her pony, had prospected over every mile of it. Every cow-puncher on the range knew her by sight and was a loyal vassal. Ripley Givens, foreman of one of the Espinosa outfits, saw her one day, and made up his mind to form a royal

你们介绍了国王和王后。其实他们在这个可以被叫做《公主编年史、奇妙的想法和大煞风景的狮子》的故事里根本没有戏份。

公主约瑟法·奥唐奈是他们仅存的女儿。她从母亲那里继承了热情的天性和那种暗黑色的亚热带式的美;从父亲本·奥唐奈那儿获得了勇气、常识和统治之才。就是这样一个尤物,就算千里迢迢跑去看她一眼也是值得的。约瑟法可以一边骑着她的小马奔驰,一边瞄准挂在绳上摇摆的西红柿罐头,六枪五中。她还可以和自己的小白猫连续玩上好几个钟头,给它穿各种好笑的衣服。她鄙视铅笔,光凭脑子就能迅速告诉你:如果每头小牛值八块五毛钱,那么 1545 头两岁的小牛总共值多少钱。总的说来,长 40 英里、宽 30 英里的刺荆牧场——不过大部分土地是租来的,每一个角落约瑟法都骑着她的小马勘测过了。牧场上的每一个牛仔全都一眼就能认出她来,而且都对她忠心耿耿。里普利·吉文斯是刺荆牧场里一个牛队的领头,在某天见过她以后,便下定决心要与王室联姻。这是痴心妄

matrimonial alliance. Presumptuous? No. In those days in the Nueces country a man was a man. And, after all, the title of cattle king does not presuppose blood royalty. Often it only signifies that its owner wears the crown in token of his magnificent qualities in the art of cattle stealing.

One day Ripley Givens rode over to the Double Elm Ranch to inquire about a bunch of strayed yearlings. He was late in setting out on his return trip, and it was sundown when he struck the White Horse Crossing of the Nueces. From there to his own camp it was sixteen miles. To the Espinosa ranch it was twelve. Givens was tired. He decided to pass the night at the Crossing.

There was a fine water hole in the river-bed. The banks were thickly covered with great trees, undergrown with brush. Back from the waterhole fifty yards was a stretch of curly mesquite grass – supper for his horse and bed for himself. Givens staked his horse, and spread out his saddle blankets to dry. He sat down with his back against a tree and rolled a cigarette. From somewhere in the dense timber along the river came a sudden, rageful, shivering wail. The pony

想吗？不是的。那个时候，纽埃西斯的男子都是顶天立地的大丈夫。而且，话又说回来，牛王的头衔并不昭示着王室血统。通常，它只表明该头衔的拥有者盗牛艺术超凡，仅此而已。

一天，里普利·吉文斯骑马到双榆树牧场去打听一群走失的小牛的消息。因为出发的晚，所以当他回来到达纽埃西斯河的白马渡口时，太阳已经下山了。而从渡口到他自己的营地有16英里的路程，到刺荆牧场也有12英里。吉文斯累了，于是他决定在渡口过夜。

河床上有个清澈的水潭，两岸长满了密密地树丛和灌木。离水潭50码之外有一片卷曲的豆灌木丛——他的马有吃的了，他也有可以睡觉的地方了。吉文斯把马拴在桩子上，摊开鞍褥子晾干。然后背靠着一棵树坐下，卷了一支烟。突然，从河边茂密的树林里传来了一声雷霆般的怒吼，那声音让人不寒而栗。小马驹在绳子那头窜动起来，害怕地尖声打着响鼻。吉文斯悠闲地抽着烟，

danced at the end of his rope and blew a whistling snort of comprehending fear. Givens puffed at his cigarette, but he reached leisurely for his pistol-belt, which lay on the grass, and twirled the cylinder of his weapon tentatively. A great gar plunged with a loud splash into the waterhole. A little brown rabbit skipped around a bunch of catclaw and sat twitching his whiskers and looking humorously at Givens. The pony went on eating grass.

It is well to be reasonably watchful when a Mexican lion sings soprano along the arroyos at sundown. The burden of his song may be that young calves and fat lambs are scarce, and that he has a carnivorous desire for your acquaintance.

In the grass lay an empty fruit can, cast there by some former sojourner. Givens caught sight of it with a grunt of satisfaction. In his coat pocket tied behind his saddle was a handful or two of ground coffee. Black coffee and cigarettes! What ranchero could desire more?

In two minutes he had a little fire going clearly. He started, with his can, for the water hole. When within fifteen yards of its edge he saw, between the bushes, a side-saddled pony with down-dropped

不慌不忙地伸手去摸草地上的枪套皮带，然后试着转了转子弹筒。一条巨大的雀鳝扑通一声跃入水潭，溅起一阵水花。一只棕色的小兔子跳过一丛猫爪草，坐下来抖动着胡须，滑稽地看着吉文斯。小马继续低头吃草。

太阳落山时分，如果有墨西哥狮子在干涸的河床边唱起女高音，那么警惕一些总是没错的。因为它歌词的大意很可能就是：小牛和肥羊太少了，吃荤的它很想认识认识你。

草丛里躺着一只空了的水果罐头，是以前过路的人扔掉的。吉文斯一看到它，便满意地咕哝了一句。在他那拴在马鞍后面的上衣口袋里还有一把碾碎了的咖啡豆。黑咖啡和烟！还有什么不满足的？

只用了两分钟，他干净利落地生起了火，然后拿着空罐头铁罐向水潭走去。在离水潭不到15码的地方，他看到左边不远处的灌木丛中有一匹装有女鞍的小

reins cropping grass a little distance to his left. Just rising from her hands and knees on the brink of the water hole was Josefa O'Donnell.She had been drinking water, and she brushed the sand from the palms of her hands. Ten yards away, to her right, half concealed by a clump of sacuista, Givens saw the crouching form of the Mexican lion. His amber eyeballs glared hungrily; six feet from them was the tip of the tail stretched straight, like a pointer's. His hind-quarters rocked with the motion of the cat tribe preliminary to leaping.

Givens did what he could. His six-shooter was thirty-five yards away lying on the grass. He gave a loud yell, and dashed between the lion and the princess.

The "rucus," as Givens called it afterward, was brief and somewhat confused. When he arrived on the line of attack he saw a dim streak in the air, and heard a couple of faint cracks. Then a hundred pounds of Mexican lion plumped down upon his head and flattened him, with a heavy jar, to the ground. He remembered calling out: "Let up, now – no fair gouging!" and then he crawled from under the lion like a worm,

马,正搭拉着僵绳在啃草吃。水潭边上,有个人刚刚从地上站起来,那人正是约瑟法·奥唐奈。刚才她一直在跪着喝水,现在她正在擦手掌上的泥沙。吉文斯还发现,在离她右边十来码的地方,一只墨西哥狮子正在荆棘丛中若隐若现。它琥珀色的眼球放射出饥饿的光,眼睛后面六英尺的地方是像猎狗一样伸得笔直的尾巴尖。它的后腿正在轻轻摆动,那是猫科动物腾跃前的明显征兆。

吉文斯做了他该做的。他的六响手枪正躺在 35 码外的草地上。于是他大喝一声,窜到了狮子和公主中间。

这场"格斗"(吉文斯事后这么叫它)很简短,同时又有点混乱。当他刚到达战争一线时,只见空中掠过一道黑影,接着听见两声隐约的枪响。然后,重达一百磅的墨西哥狮子突然砸在他头上,使他重重地摔倒在地上,把他整个都压扁了。他还记得自己大喊了一声:"起来——这样打不公平!"然后,他像虫子一样从狮子身体下面爬出来,满嘴

with his mouth full of grass and dirt, and a big lump on the back of his head where it had struck the root of a water-elm. The lion lay motionless. Givens, feeling aggrieved, and suspicious of fouls, shook his fist at the lion, and shouted: "I'll rastle you again for twenty –" and then he got back to himself.

Josefa was standing in her tracks, quietly reloading her silver-mounted .38. It had not been a difficult shot. The lion's head made an easier mark than a tomato-can swinging at the end of a string. There was a provoking, teasing, maddening smile upon her mouth and in her dark eyes. The would-be-rescuing knight felt the fire of his fiasco burn down to his soul. Here had been his chance, the chance that he had dreamed of; and Momus, and not Cupid, had presided over it. The satyrs in the wood were, no doubt, holding their sides in hilarious, silent laughter. There had been something like vaudeville – say Signor Givens and his funny knockabout act with the stuffed lion.

"Is that you, Mr. Givens?" said Josefa, in her deliberate, saccharine contralto. "You nearly spoilt my shot when you yelled. Did you hurt your head when you

都是草和泥。因为刚才磕在了水榆树的树根上，后脑勺还鼓起了一个大包。狮子纹丝不动地瘫在地上。吉文斯愤愤不平，怀疑狮子犯了规。他冲狮子挥舞着拳头，嚷道："我要再跟你打上20个……"。就在这个时候，他突然明白了。

约瑟法一直站在她原来的位置，若无其事地给她那把配有银枪套的三八口径手枪重新上膛。刚才那一枪难度并不高，比起挂在绳子上摇摆的西红柿罐头，狮子的头实在是太容易被击中了。约瑟法的嘴角上和黑眼睛里带着挑衅、嘲讽和令人恼火的笑意。吉文斯，这位本来想英雄救美的骑士感到惨败的怒火直逼灵魂。这本来是他的机会，他梦寐以求的机会，可是掌管这个机会的不是丘比特而成了莫摩斯。毫无疑问，森林中的精灵们一定正在捧腹大笑，虽然它们没有发出声音。这里刚刚上演了一出好戏——就叫吉文斯先生与他吃饱了的狮子共同上演的滑稽闹剧。

"吉文斯先生，是你吗？"约瑟法用她深沉甜美的女低音问道，"你一声大叫害我差点儿脱靶。你摔倒时弄伤脑袋了吗？"

fell?"

"Oh, no," said Givens, quietly; "that didn't hurt." He stooped ignominiously and dragged his best Stetson hat from under the beast. It was crushed and wrinkled to a fine comedy effect. Then he knelt down and softly stroked the fierce, open-jawed head of the dead lion.

"Poor old Bill!" he exclaimed mournfully.

"What's that?" asked Josefa, sharply.

"Of course you didn't know, Miss Josefa," said Givens, with an air of one allowing magnanimity to triumph over grief. "Nobody can blame you. I tried to save him, but I couldn't let you know in time."

"Save who?"

"Why, Bill. I've been looking for him all day. You see, he's been our camp pet for two years. Poor old fellow, he wouldn't have hurt a cottontail rabbit. It'll break the boys all up when they hear about it. But you couldn't tell, of course, that Bill was just trying to play with you."

Josefa's black eyes burned steadily upon him. Ripley Givens met the test successfully. He stood rumpling the yellow-brown curls on his head pen-

"哦，没事，"吉文斯平静地说，"没伤到。"他弯下腰，把他那顶最好的斯特森毡帽从那只野兽身下拽出来，觉得脸面被丢尽了。帽子已被压得皱皱巴巴，看起来颇具喜剧效果。接着，他跪下来，温柔地抚摸着那个凶猛的、张着血盆大口的狮子脑袋。

"可怜的老比尔！"他悲痛地呼喊起来。

"这是怎么回事？"约瑟法尖声问道。

"你当然不知道，约瑟法小姐，"吉文斯说，带着一副用慷慨来战胜悲伤的神情，"没人会责怪你。我本来想救它，但我没能及时让你知道。"

"救谁？"

"唉，当然是比尔。我找它一整天了。你知道，它做我们的营地宠物已经有两年了。可怜的老家伙，它甚至连棉尾兔都不会伤害。兄弟们听到这个消息肯定会心碎的。不过，你当然不会看出来比尔只是想跟你玩玩而已。"

约瑟法的黑眼睛炯炯有神地盯着他看，里普利·吉文斯感到已经成功地通过了这个测试。他忧心忡忡地站着，把那头黄褐色的卷发拨弄得乱七八糟。在他那

sively. In his eye was regret, not unmingled with a gentle reproach. His smooth features were set to a pattern of indisputable sorrow. Josefa wavered.

"What was your pet doing here?" she asked, making a last stand. "There's no camp near the White Horse Crossing."

"The old rascal ran away from camp yesterday," answered Givens readily. "It's a wonder the coyotes didn't scare him to death. You see, Jim Webster, our horse wrangler, brought a little terrier pup into camp last week. The pup made life miserable for Bill – he used to chase him around and chew his hind legs for hours at a time. Every night when bedtime came Bill would sneak under one of the boy's blankets and sleep to keep the pup from finding him. I reckon he must have been worried pretty desperate or he wouldn't have run away. He was always afraid to get out of sight of camp."

Josefa looked at the body of the fierce animal. Givens gently patted one of the formidable paws that could have killed a yearling calf with one blow. Slowly a red flush widened upon the dark olive face of the girl. Was it the signal of shame of the true sportsman who has brought down ignoble quarry? Her eyes grew softer,

痛惜的眼神中，还掺杂着一丝温柔的谴责，他那光滑的脸庞显出一种无可非议的哀恸，使约瑟法不禁犹豫起来。

"那你们的宠物到这儿来干什么？"她最后反诘道，"白马渡口附近又没有营地。"

"昨天这个老家伙从营地里跑了出来，"古文斯毫不迟疑地答道，"野狼没把它吓死真是个奇迹。你知道，吉姆·韦伯斯特，我们管马的牛仔，上周弄了只小猎狗到营地去。那只小狗让比尔的日子很不好过——它常常连续几个钟头追着比尔到处跑，追上了就啃它的后腿。每天晚上，一到睡觉时间，比尔就会钻到其中一位仁兄的被窝里去睡觉，为的就是不让小狗发现它。我猜它一定是愁断肠了，否则它是不会逃跑的。平常，只要营地不在它的视野之内，它就会感到害怕。"

约瑟法看着这头猛兽的尸体。吉文斯轻拍着狮子的一只爪子，那只可以一下子就要了小牛的命的可怕爪子。慢慢地，姑娘深橄榄色的脸上泛起了一片红晕。那是真正的猎人在打到不光彩的猎物时心生羞愧的信号吗？她的目光也变得柔和起来，低垂

and the lowered lids drove away all their bright mockery.

"I'm very sorry," she said humbly; "but he looked so big, and jumped so high that – "

"Poor old Bill was hungry," interrupted Givens, in quick defence of the deceased. "We always made him jump for his supper in camp. He would lie down and roll over for a piece of meat. When he saw you he thought he was going to get something to eat from you."

Suddenly Josefa's eyes opened wide.

"I might have shot you!" she exclaimed. "You ran right in between. You risked your life to save your pet! That was fine, Mr. Givens. I like a man who is kind to animals."

Yes; there was even admiration in her gaze now. After all, there was a hero rising out of the ruins of the anti-climax. The look on Givens's face would have secured him a high position in the S.P.C.A.

"I always loved 'em," said he; "horses, dogs, Mexican lions, cows, alligators – "

"I hate alligators," instantly demurred Josefa; "crawly, muddy things!"

"Did I say alligators?" said Givens. "I meant antelopes, of course."

的眼睑把她原先那显而易见的嘲讽一扫而光。

"非常抱歉,"她谦恭地说,"不过它看起来那么大,又跳得那么高,所以……"

"可怜的老比尔饿了,"吉文斯打断她的话,立即替死去的狮子辩护道,"在营地里,我们总是让它跳起来去够它的美餐,它还会为了一块肉躺下打滚。当它看到你的时候,它还以为能从你那儿得到一点儿吃的。"

约瑟法突然把眼睛瞪大了。

"刚才那一枪也许会打到你!"她嚷道,"你刚好跑到中间。你竟然冒着生命危险救你的宠物!真是太伟大了,吉文斯先生。我喜欢对动物有爱心的人!"

没错,现在她的目光里甚至有了些许爱慕。不管怎样,一位英雄正在从一败涂地的残迹中冉冉升起。吉文斯脸上的表情完全可以替他在"禁止虐待动物协会"里谋得一个高位。

"我一向热爱它们,"他说,"马啊,狗啊,墨西哥狮子啊,牛啊,鳄鱼啊……"

"我讨厌鳄鱼,"约瑟法马上提出异议,"它们满身是泥,让人感觉毛骨悚然!"

Josefa's conscience drove her to make further amends. She held out her hand penitently. There was a bright, unshed drop in each of her eyes.

"Please forgive me, Mr. Givens, won't you? I'm only a girl, you know, and I was frightened at first. I'm very, very sorry I shot Bill. You don't know how ashamed I feel. I wouldn't have done it for anything."

Givens took the proffered hand. He held it for a time while he allowed the generosity of his nature to overcome his grief at the loss of Bill. At last it was clear that he had forgiven her.

"Please don't speak of it any more, Miss Josefa. 'Twas enough to frighten any young lady the way Bill looked. I'll explain it all right to the boys."

"Are you really sure you don't hate me?" Josefa came closer to him impulsively. Her eyes were sweet – oh, sweet and pleading with gracious penitence. "I would hate anyone who would kill my kitten. And how daring and kind of you to risk being shot when you tried to save him! How very few men would have done that!" Victory wrested from defeat! Vaudeville turned into drama! Bravo, Ripley Givens!

"我刚才说鳄鱼了吗？"吉文斯说，"当然，我的意思是说鹅和鱼。"

约瑟法的良心促使她想做进一步的补偿。她愧疚地伸出手，眼里含着两颗晶莹的泪珠。

"请原谅我好吗？吉文斯先生，你看，我只是一介女流，一开始我吓坏了。我开枪打死了比尔，真的非常非常抱歉。你不知道我心中多羞愧。早知道真相的话，我无论如何也不会这么做。"

吉文斯握住那只伸过来的手，直到他宽容的本性抑制住失去比尔带来的哀伤，才把它放开。最后，很显然，他原谅了约瑟法。

"请你别再提这件事了，约瑟法小姐，比尔的样子足以吓坏任何一位年轻女士。我会向兄弟们好好解释的。"

"你真的不会恨我吗？"约瑟法情不自禁地向他靠近了一些。她的眼睛很迷人——啊，迷人中还带着落落大方的忏悔，好像在乞求原谅，"要是有人杀了我的小猫，我一定会恨他，而你居然冒着中弹的危险去营救它，这是多么勇敢，多么仁慈啊！能这样做的人实在是太少了！"里普利·吉文斯就这样转败为胜啦！

It was now twilight. Of course Miss Josefa could not be allowed to ride on to the ranch-house alone. Givens resaddled his pony in spite of that animal's reproachful glances, and rode with her. Side by side they galloped across the smooth grass, the princess and the man who was kind to animals. The prairie odours of fruitful earth and delicate bloom were thick and sweet around them. Coyotes yelping over there onthe hill! No fear. And yet—

Josefa rode closer. A little hand seemed to grope. Givens found it with his own. The ponies kept an even gait. The hands lingered together, and the owner of one explained:

"I never was frightened before, but just think! How terrible it would be to meet a really wild lion! Poor Bill! I'm so glad you came with me!"

O'Donnell was sitting on the ranch gallery.

"Hello, Rip!" he shouted – "that you?"

"He rode in with me," said Josefa. "I lost my way and was late."

"Much obliged," called the cattle king. "Stop over, Rip, and ride to camp in the morning."

But Givens would not. He would push

杂耍变成戏剧啦！真是太棒了，里普利·吉文斯！

当时天色已晚，当然不应该让约瑟法小姐孤身一人骑马回牧场。吉文斯没理会小马哀怨的眼神，重新给它上完鞍后，便陪着约瑟法上路了。公主和这位善待动物的人并肩飞驰过柔软的草地，肥沃的土地上开满了娇艳的花朵，花香和泥土的芬芳交织在一起。野狼在远处的小山上嚎叫！不要害怕，然而——

约瑟法策马靠近吉文斯。一只小手似乎在摸索，吉文斯用自己的手找到了它。两匹小马齐头并进。两只手缠绕在一起，一只手的主人解释道：

"我以前从来没有害怕过，可是想想看：如果真遇到一头野生狮子，那该多可怕呀！可怜的比尔！真高兴你能陪我一起走！"

奥唐奈正坐在屋子的回廊上。

"喂，里普！"他叫喊着，"是你吗？"

"他陪我骑回来的。"约瑟法说，"我迷路了，天也晚了。"

"非常感谢。"牛国王喊道，"在这儿过夜吧，里普，明早再回营地去。"

on to camp. There was a bunch of steers to start off on the trail at daybreak. He said good-night, and trotted away.

An hour later, when the lights were out, Josefa, in her night-robe, came to her door and called to the king in his own room across the brick-paved hallway:

"Say, pop, you know that old Mexican lion they call the 'Gotch-eared Devil' – the one that killed Gonzales, Mr. Martin's sheep herder, and about fifty calves on the Salado range? Well, I settled his hash this afternoon over at the White Horse Crossing. Put two balls in his head with my .38 while he was on the jump. I knew him by the slice gone from his left ear that old Gonzales cut off with his machete. You couldn't have made a better shot yourself, daddy."

"Bully for you!" thundered Whispering Ben from the darkness of the royal chamber.

但是吉文斯不愿意。他得赶回营地，黎明时分还有一批牛要上路。他道过晚安，骑着马小跑着离开了。

一小时后，灯熄了，约瑟法身披睡袍，走到她的卧房门口，向住在青砖过道对面的牛王喊道：

"喂，老爸，你知道那头人称'缺耳朵魔鬼'的墨西哥老狮子吗？——就是吃了马丁先生的牧羊人以及冈萨勒斯和萨拉达牧场50头小牛的那头。嘿，今天下午我在白马渡口把它给消灭了。当它正要跳起来时，我用三八口径手枪朝它的脑袋开了两枪。我认出它来是因为它的左耳朵被老冈萨勒斯用弯刀砍掉了一片。爸爸，就算您亲自出马，恐怕也就是我这个效果。"

"好样的！"只听'小嗓门本'在寝宫的暗处雷霆般地吼道。

11. TWO THANKSGIVING DAY GENTLEMEN
11. 两位感恩节的绅士

There is one day that is ours. There is one day when all we Americans who are not self-made go back to the old home to eat saleratus biscuits and marvel how much nearer to the porch the old pump looks than it used to. Bless the day. President Roosevelt gives it to us. We hear some talk of the Puritans, but don't just remember who they were. Bet we can lick 'em, anyhow, if they try to land again. Plymouth Rocks? Well, that sounds more familiar. Lots of us have had to come down to hens since the Turkey Trust got its work in. But somebody in Washington is leaking out advance information to 'em about these Thanksgiving proclamations.

The big city east of the cranberry bogs has made Thanksgiving Day an institution. The last Thursday in November is the only day in the year on which it recognizes the part of America lying across the ferries. It is the one day that is purely American. Yes, a day of celebration, exclusively American.

And now for the story which is to

有一天是属于我们自己的。在那天,所有的美国人,只要不是从石头里蹦出来的,都会回自己的老家,一边吃着苏打饼干,一边纳闷门口的旧水泵怎么看起来比以前更靠近门廊了。祝福那一天吧。是罗斯福总统[1]把它送给我们的。我们也听过一些关于清教徒的传说,可就是记不得他们到底是什么人。无论如何,要是他们还想在这里登陆的话,我们准能打败他们。普利茅斯岩石[2]?嗯,这听起来就让人觉得熟悉多了。自从火鸡托拉斯垄断市场以来,我们中的许多人不得不退而求其次,改吃母鸡了。不过华盛顿有人走漏了风声,把感恩节[3]公告提前告诉了他们。

位于酸果蔓沼泽地[4]东边的那个大城市已经把感恩节定为法定节日。只有在每年11月的最后一个星期四,那个大城市才承认渡口对岸的那部分是美国。也只有这一天是完完全全属于美国的。是的,它是专属于美国的庆祝日。

prove to you that we have traditions on this side of the ocean that are becoming older at a much rapider rate than those of England are – thanks to our git-up and enterprise.

Stuffy Pete took his seat on the third bench to the right as you enter Union Square from the east, at the walk opposite the fountain. Every Thanksgiving Day for nine years he had taken his seat there promptly at 1 o'clock. For every time he had done so things had happened to him – Charles Dickensy things that swelled his waistcoat above his heart, and equally on the other side.

But to-day Stuffy Pete's appearance at the annual trysting place seemed to have been rather the result of habit than of the yearly hunger which, as the philanthropists seem to think, afflicts the poor at such extended intervals.

Certainly Pete was not hungry. He had just come from a feast that had left him of his powers barely those of respiration and locomotion. His eyes were like two pale gooseberries firmly imbedded in a swollen and gravy-smeared mask of putty. His breath came in short wheezes; a senatorial roll of adipose tissue denied a fashionable set to his upturned coat collar.

现在有个故事可以向你们证明：我们在海洋这边，也有一些传统，这些传统过时的速度可比在英国要快得多——这都是因为我们的活力和进取心。

如果你从东面进入联合广场的话，就会看见斯塔弗·皮特坐在喷水泉对面人行道右边的第三条长凳上。九年了，每到感恩节，他总是准时在下午 1 点钟坐在他的那个座位上。他每次都这么干，总有什么意外的遭遇——查尔斯·狄更斯式的遭遇，能让他的马甲膨胀到胸前，当然背后也是一样。

但是今天看起来似乎是出于习惯的原因，而不同于往年出现的饥饿，斯塔弗·皮特才又出现在一年一度的约会地点。慈善家们似乎认为，只有经过这么长的时间间隔，穷人才会遭到饥饿的折磨。

皮特当然不饿。来之前，他刚刚大快朵颐了一顿，吃得他只剩下呼吸和移动的力气了。他的眼睛活像两颗暗淡的醋栗，结结实实地嵌在一张浮肿的、满面油灰的面具上。他艰难而又短促地呼吸着，脖子上长着一圈参议员特有的脂肪组织，使得他翻上来

Buttons that had been sewed upon his clothes by kind Salvation fingers a week before flew like popcorn, strewing the earth around him. Ragged he was, with a split shirt front open to the wishbone; but the November breeze, carrying fine snowflakes, brought him only a grateful coolness. For Stuffy Pete was over-charged with the caloric produced by a super-bountiful dinner, beginning with oysters and ending with plum pudding, and including (it seemed to him) all the roast turkey and baked potatoes and chicken salad and squash pie and ice cream in the world. Wherefore he sat, gorged, and gazed upon the world with after-dinner contempt.

The meal had been an unexpected one. He was passing a red brick mansion near the beginning of Fifth avenue, in which lived two old ladies of ancient family and a reverence for traditions. They even denied the existence of New York, and believed that Thanksgiving Day was declared solely for Washington Square. One of their traditional habits was to station a servant at the postern gate with orders to admit the first hungry wayfarer that came along after the hour of noon had struck, and banquet him to a finish.

的大衣领看起来没有丝毫的时髦感。一个礼拜以前，仁慈的救世修女亲手给他缝在衣服上的钮扣，现在像爆米花一样四处飞散开来，在他身边铺了一地。他衣衫褴褛，衬衫的前襟裂开露出了胸口，可是11月里携带着美丽雪花的微风只让他感觉到一种带着感激的凉意，因为斯塔弗·皮特现在负载了过多的热量——都是那顿过于丰盛的晚餐制造的。他先吃了牡蛎，最后以葡萄干布丁结束，在他看来，那顿饭包含了全世界的烤火鸡、煮土豆、鸡肉色拉、南瓜馅饼和冰淇淋。因此，他现在肚子撑得饱饱地坐在那里，用一种吃饱喝足后的轻蔑神情看着这个世界。

那顿饭完全是他意料之外的。当时他正路过第五大街街头的一幢红砖墙宅子，那里面住着两位老太太，她们出生于古老的家族，因此对传统怀有敬畏之情。她们甚至拒绝承认纽约的存在，坚决地认为感恩节单单是为了华盛顿广场而设置的。她们有一个传统习惯，就是派一个佣人站在侧门口，让他把正午过后看见的第一个饥饿的过路人请进门，请他随便大吃大喝一顿，直到吃饱

Stuffy Pete happened to pass by on his way to the park, and the seneschals gathered him in and upheld the custom of the castle.

After Stuffy Pete had gazed straight before him for ten minutes he was conscious of a desire for a more varied field of vision. With a tremendous effort he moved his head slowly to the left. And then his eyes bulged out fearfully, and his breath ceased, and the rough-shod ends of his short legs wriggled and rustled on the gravel.

For the Old Gentleman was coming across Fourth avenue toward his bench.

Every Thanksgiving Day for nine years the Old Gentleman had come there and found Stuffy Pete on his bench. That was a thing that the Old Gentleman was trying to make a tradition of. Every Thanksgiving Day for nine years he had found Stuffy there, and had led him to a restaurant and watched him eat a big dinner. They do those things in England unconsciously. But this is a young country, and nine years is not so bad. The Old Gentleman was a staunch American patriot, and considered himself a pioneer in American tradition. In order to become picturesque we must keep on doing one

为止。斯塔弗·皮特在去往公园的路上经过了那儿，就被管家们请了进去，成全了城堡里的传统。

斯塔弗·皮特直直地瞪着他眼前的一切长达 10 分钟。之后，才意识到自己想换个更丰富多彩的视野。他憋足了劲，才慢慢把头转到左面。然后他的眼球恐惧地凸了出来，停止了呼吸，他的短腿上穿着的破皮鞋来回摩擦着沙砾地，发出沙沙的声响。

因为那位老绅士正穿过第四大街，朝他坐着的长凳走来。

九年来，一到感恩节，这位老绅士就上这儿来找坐在长凳上的斯塔弗·皮特。看来，老绅士正在试着把这件事变成一种传统。九年中，每逢感恩节，他总能在这儿找到斯塔弗，然后把他带到一家饭馆，看着他饱餐一顿。这种事情如果是在英国的话，那是很自然的。可是美国还很年轻，他能这么坚持九年真是很不错。那位老绅士是坚定的美国爱国主义者，并且自认为开创了美国传统的先锋之一。为了引人注目，我们必须长时间的做同一件事情，一点儿也不能马虎，像是每

thing for a long time without ever letting it get away from us. Something like collecting the weekly dimes in industrial insurance. Or cleaning the streets.

The Old Gentleman moved, straight and stately, toward the Institution that he was rearing. Truly, the annual feeding of Stuffy Pete was nothing national in its character, such as the Magna Charta or jam for breakfast was in England. But it was a step. It was almost feudal. It showed, at least, that a Custom was not impossible to New Y – ahem! – America.

The Old Gentleman was thin and tall and sixty. He was dressed all in black, and wore the old-fashioned kind of glasses that won't stay on your nose. His hair was whiter and thinner than it had been last year, and he seemed to make more use of his big, knobby cane with the crooked handle.

As his established benefactor came up Stuffy wheezed and shuddered like some woman's over-fat pug when a street dog bristles up at him. He would have flown, but all the skill of Santos-Dumont could not have separated him from his bench. Well had the myrmidons of the two old ladies done their work.

"Good morning," said the Old Gen-

周收几毛钱的工业保险费啦，或者是打扫街道之类的。

老绅士庄严地朝着他所建立的制度径直走去。不错，每年喂饱斯塔弗·皮特并不像英国的大宪章或者早餐吃的果酱那样具有国家性的特点，但是它仍代表着朝前迈进了一步。这多少有点封建意味。至少，它证明了在纽……啊！——是在美国，建立一种习俗不是不可能的。

老绅士六十来岁，瘦高个。他全身穿着黑衣服，架着一副老式眼镜，那副眼镜始终不能乖乖地戴在他的鼻子上。比起去年来，他的头发更白，也更稀疏了，同时他好像也更依赖那支粗大的有很多节的曲柄拐杖了。

眼看着老恩人走过来，斯塔弗·皮特不禁呼吸困难，浑身打颤，就好像某位太太那过于肥胖的狮子狗看见一条野狗鄙视它时那个样子。他本想逃走，可是就算是桑托斯·杜蒙[5]也没办法让他和长凳分开。看来那两位老太太的忠实家仆任务完成的可真是好。

tleman. "I am glad to perceive that the vicissitudes of another year have spared you to move in health about the beautiful world. For that blessing alone this day of thanksgiving is well proclaimed to each of us. If you will come with me, my man, I will provide you with a dinner that should make your physical being accord with the mental."

That is what the old Gentleman said every time. Every Thanksgiving Day for nine years. The words themselves almost formed an Institution. Nothing could be compared with them except the Declaration of Independence. Always before they had been music in Stuffy's ears. But now he looked up at the Old Gentleman's face with tearful agony in his own. The fine snow almost sizzled when it fell upon his perspiring brow. But the Old Gentleman shivered a little and turned his back to the wind.

Stuffy had always wondered why the Old Gentleman spoke his speech rather sadly. He did not know that it was because he was wishing every time that he had a son to succeed him. A son who would come there after he was gone – a son who would stand proud and strong before some subsequent Stuffy, and say:

"早上好。"老绅士说，"看到又一年的变迁并没有影响到你，你依然健康地享受着这个美好世界，我真的很高兴。就冲着这个祝福，今天这个感恩节对我们两人真是意义重大。我的朋友，要是你愿意跟我一起来，我就请你吃顿饭，让你的身心都一样健康。"

这就是每次老绅士都会说的话，九年来的每一个感恩节都是如此，这些话本身几乎成了一个制度。除了《独立宣言》之外，还没有什么可与之比拟的。以前，这话被斯塔弗听在耳朵里，会觉得它们就像音乐般美妙。但是现今他却满脸痛苦，眼含泪水地仰头看老绅士的面庞。精美的雪花落到他淌满汗水的额头上，几乎发出了咝咝的响声。但是老绅士却在微微颤抖，此刻他正转过身子，背朝着风。

斯塔弗一直想知道，为什么老绅士说这番话时神情颇有些哀伤。他不了解那是因为老绅士每次都希望能有个儿子来继承自己的事业。他希望自己逝世以后，能有个儿子来到这里——一个身材结实，充满自豪的儿子，站在斯塔弗的某个后继者面前说："为

"In memory of my father." Then it would be an Institution.

But the Old Gentleman had no relatives. He lived in rented rooms in one of the decayed old family brownstone mansions in one of the quiet streets east of the park. In the winter he raised fuchsias in a little conservatory the size of a steamer trunk. In the spring he walked in the Easter parade. In the summer he lived at a farmhouse in the New Jersey hills, and sat in a wicker armchair, speaking of a butterfly, the ornithoptera amphrisius, that he hoped to find some day. In the autumn he fed Stuffy a dinner. These were the Old Gentleman's occupations.

Stuffy Pete looked up at him for a half minute, stewing and helpless in his own self-pity. The Old Gentleman's eyes were bright with the giving-pleasure. His face was getting more lined each year, but his little black necktie was in as jaunty a bow as ever, and the linen was beautiful and white, and his gray mustache was curled carefully at the ends. And then Stuffy made a noise that sounded like peas bubbling in a pot. Speech was intended; and as the Old Gentleman had heard the sounds nine times before, he rightly construed them

了纪念我的父亲。"那样的话，一个制度就真正建立起来了。

然而老绅士没有什么亲戚。他在公园东面一条僻静街道上的一座陈旧的褐色砂石建筑里租了几个房间。冬天的时候，他在一个蒸汽机箱大小的温室里种些倒挂金钟。春天来了，他会参加复活节的游行。夏天，他住在新泽西州山间的农舍里，坐在柳条编织的扶手椅里，谈论着他希望有一天能找到的某种扑翼蝴蝶。到了秋天，他就请斯塔弗吃顿饭。这就是老绅士的全部事业。

斯塔弗抬头看了他一小会儿，无助地沉浸在自怨自艾中。老绅士的眼睛因为施与的快乐而迸发出光芒。一年又一年，他脸上的皱纹不断加深，但是他那小小的黑领结却依然神气，白色的亚麻衬衫十分漂亮，他那两撇灰白的胡子优美地翘起来。斯塔弗发出一种声音，听起来像是锅里煮豌豆的那种汩汩声。他本来打算说些什么，这些话老绅士也已经听过九次了，他理所当然地认为，这是斯塔弗表示接受时说的客套话。

into Stuffy's old formula of acceptance.

"Thankee, sir. I'll go with ye, and much obliged. I'm very hungry, sir."

The coma of repletion had not prevented from entering Stuffy's mind the conviction that he was the basis of an Institution. His Thanksgiving appetite was not his own; it belonged by all the sacred rights of established custom, if not, by the actual Statute of Limitations, to this kind old gentleman who bad preempted it. True, America is free; but in order to establish tradition some one must be a repetend – a repeating decimal. The heroes are not all heroes of steel and gold. See one here that wielded only weapons of iron, badly silvered, and tin.

The Old Gentleman led his annual protege southward to the restaurant, and to the table where the feast had always occurred. They were recognized.

"Here comes de old guy," said a waiter, "dat blows dat same bum to a meal every Thanksgiving."

The Old Gentleman sat across the table glowing like a smoked pearl at his corner-stone of future ancient Tradition. The waiters heaped the table with holiday food – and Stuffy, with a sigh that was mistaken for hunger's expression, raised

"谢谢您，先生。非常感激，我会跟您一起去。我饿坏了，先生。"

尽管斯塔弗因为吃太饱已经有些头晕，但是他并没有动摇心中的信念：他坚信自己是某种制度的基石。他感恩节的胃口并不只属于自己，而是属于这位拥有特权的和蔼的老绅士。就算不考虑现行的限制法令，也得考虑到既定习俗所拥有的所有神圣权利。是的，美国是个自由的国度。但是为了建立传统，总得有人来做循环节——哪怕是一个循环小数。英雄们不一定都是铁打金塑的。看这儿就有一位英雄，挥着惟一的铁质武器，武器上镀了些劣质的银和锡。

老绅士领着他一年一度的受惠者朝南走去，走向那家年年举行盛宴的饭馆里的那张桌子。已经有人认出了他们。

"老家伙来啦，"一个侍者说道，"一到感恩节，他都会请同一个流浪汉吃上一顿。"

老绅士坐在桌子对面，对着他那将要成就古老传统的基石，脸上闪现着只有被烟熏过的珍珠才会有的光芒。侍者在桌子上堆满了节日的食物——斯塔弗叹了口气，却被误以为是饥饿的表现。

knife and fork and carved for himself a crown of imperishable bay.

No more valiant hero ever fought his way through the ranks of an enemy. Turkey, chops, soups, vegetables, pies, disappeared before him as fast as they could be served. Gorged nearly to the uttermost when he entered the restaurant, the smell of food had almost caused him to lose his honor as a gentleman, but he rallied like a true knight. He saw the look of beneficent happiness on the Old Gentleman's face – a happier look than even the fuchsias and the ornithoptera amphrisius had ever brought to it – and he had not the heart to see it wane.

In an hour Stuffy leaned back with a battle won. "Thankee kindly, sir," he puffed like a leaky steam pipe; "thankee kindly for a hearty meal." Then he arose heavily with glazed eyes and started toward the kitchen. A waiter turned him about like a top, and pointed him toward the door. The Old Gentleman carefully counted out $1.30 in silver change, leaving three nickels for the waiter.

They parted as they did each year at the door, the Old Gentleman going south, Stuffy north.

Around the first corner Stuffy turned,

他举起刀叉,为自己雕刻了一顶不朽的桂冠,让自己毫无退路。

就算在敌人的队列里冲锋陷阵的英雄也不会比他更英勇。火鸡呀、肉排呀、汤呀、蔬菜呀、馅饼呀,一端上来他就吞到肚子里。当他走进饭馆的时候,他的肚子几乎已经撑到极限了,食物的气味几乎让他丧失了作为一个绅士的荣耀,但他却重整旗鼓地奋斗着,像一个真正的骑士一样。他看到老绅士脸上浮现出因为行善而得到的快乐——就是倒挂金钟和扑翼蝴蝶也不能让他如此快乐——他不忍心让这快乐消逝。

一小时之后,斯塔弗靠在椅背上,大获全胜。"多谢您,先生,"他像一根漏气的蒸气管一样喘着气说,"多谢您慷慨的大餐。"然后,他两眼放光,奋力站起身来,朝厨房走去。一个侍者就像扭陀螺似地把他转过来,推到门口。老绅士小心翼翼地数出一块三毛钱的碎银币,还给侍者留了三镍币的小费。

跟往年一样,他们在门口就分开了,老绅士朝南走,斯塔弗朝北走。

斯塔弗转过第一个拐角,停

and stood for one minute. Then he seemed to puff out his rags as an owl puffs out his feathers, and fell to the sidewalk like a sunstricken horse.

When the ambulance came the young surgeon and the driver cursed softly at his weight. There was no smell of whiskey to justify a transfer to the patrol wagon, so Stuffy and his two dinners went to the hospital. There they stretched him on a bed and began to test him for strange diseases, with the hope of getting a chance at some problem with the bare steel.

And lo! an hour later another ambulance brought the Old Gentleman. And they laid him on another bed and spoke of appendicitis, for he looked good for the bill.

But pretty soon one of the young doctors met one of the young nurses whose eyes he liked, and stopped to chat with her about the cases.

"That nice old gentleman over there, now," he said, "you wouldn't think that was a case of almost starvation. Proud old family, I guess. He told me he hadn't eaten a thing for three days."

下来站了一会儿。然后，他的破衣服像猫头鹰的羽毛一样膨胀起来，他像一匹中暑的马一样摔倒在人行道上。

救护车来的时候，年轻的外科医生和司机都在低声咒骂着他的体重。他身上没有威士忌的味道，因此不能把他转交给警察的巡逻车，于是斯塔弗和他吃下的两顿饭就被一并带到了医院。在那里，他们把他平放在病床上，开始检查他是不是得了什么怪病，并希望解剖尸体的时候能有机会发现问题。

看吧！一个小时以后，又一辆救护车把老绅士也带来了。他们把他放在另一张病床上，讨论着可以做盲肠炎手术，因为他看起来能付得起这笔医药费。

但是很快，一位年轻的医师碰到一个年轻的护士。他很喜欢这个护士的眼睛，于是他停下来，跟她聊起病人的病情。

"现在躺在那儿的那位体面的老绅士，"他说，"你根本想不到，他就快要饿死了。我猜他以前大概是什么大家族的。他告诉我他已经三天没吃过东西了。"

1.这里的罗斯福总统指西奥多·罗斯福（1858~1919），1901 年至 1909 年在任。

2. 普利茅斯岩石，位于马萨诸塞州普利茅斯港口，据说首批清教徒在此登陆美洲，其实准确的登陆地点应该是普罗文斯敦的科德角。

3. 感恩节：1620 年，英国清教徒为逃离宗教压迫，乘坐"5 月花号"船到达美洲普利茅斯，船上有 102 人，包括英格兰、苏格兰和爱尔兰移民。这些人定居后的第二年，为庆祝第一次收获，感谢上帝给予他们的恩惠，设置了感恩节，后来变成美国的法定节日，一般是每年 11 月的最后一个星期四。

4. 酸果蔓沼泽地东面的那个大城市：即纽约。

5 桑托斯·杜蒙（1873~1932），巴西气球驾驶员，1901 年乘气球从法国的圣克卢至埃菲尔铁塔往返飞行一次，1906 年和 1909 年还试飞过风筝式飞机和单翼飞机。他是欧洲第一个驾驶自制飞机上天的探险家,也是第一个当众试飞成功的探险家。

12. WITCHES' LOAVES
12. 女巫的面包

Miss Martha Meacham kept the little bakery on the corner (the one where you go up three steps, and the bell tinkles when you open the door).

Miss Martha was forty, her bank-book showed a credit of two thousand dollars, and she possessed two false teeth and a sympathetic heart. Many people have married whose chances to do so were much inferior to Miss Martha's.

Two or three times a week a customer came in in whom she began to take an interest. He was a middle-aged man, wearing spectacles and a brown beard trimmed to a careful point.

He spoke English with a strong German accent. His clothes were worn and darned in places, and wrinkled and baggy in others. But he looked neat, and had very good manners.

He always bought two loaves of stale bread. Fresh bread was five cents a loaf. Stale ones were two for five. Never did he call for anything but stale bread.

Once Miss Martha saw a red and brown stain on his fingers. She was sure

玛莎·米查姆小姐在街角开了一家小面包店（就是你上三级台阶，开门的时候铃声叮当作响的那家店）。

玛莎小姐 40 岁，在银行有 2000 元的存款，还有两颗假牙和一颗富有同情心的心脏. 许多男人碰巧娶的女人比起玛莎小姐的条件来可差得远啦。

玛莎小姐对一个一周来两三次的客人产生了兴趣。他是个中年男子，戴着眼镜，棕色的胡子修剪得很得体。

他说的英语带有很浓重的德国口音。他的衣服有的地方被磨破了补过，有的地方皱皱巴巴已经松弛。但他的外表看起来是那么整洁，又那么有风度。

他总是买两个过期的面包。买新鲜面包一个就要五分钱，而过期的面包两个才要五分钱。除了过期面包，他从来没买过别的什么东西。

有一次，玛莎小姐看到他的手指上有一块红褐色的污渍。从

then that he was an artist and very poor. No doubt he lived in a garret, where he painted pictures and ate stale bread and thought ofthe good things to eat in Miss Martha's bakery.

Often when Miss Martha sat down to her chops and light rolls and jam and tea she would sigh, and wish that the gen-tle-mannered artist might share her tasty meal instead of eating his dry crust in that draughty attic. Miss Martha's heart, as you have been told, was a sympathetic one.

In order to test her theory as to his occupation, she brought from her room one day a painting that she had bought at a sale, and set it against the shelves be-hind the bread counter.

It was a Venetian scene. A splendid marble palazzio (so it said on the picture) stood in the foreground – or rather forewater. For the rest there were gon-dolas (with the lady trailing her hand in the water), clouds, sky, and chiaroscuro in plenty. No artist could fail to notice it.

Two days afterward the customer came in.

"Two loaves of stale bread, if you blease."

"You haf here a fine picture, ma-

那时起她就确定他是个贫穷的艺术家。毫无疑问他住在阁楼,他在那里画画。边啃着过期的面包,边想着玛莎小姐面包店里的好吃的。

玛莎小姐坐下来吃她的肉排、面包卷、果酱和茶的时候经常叹气,她希望那个有绅士风度的艺术家能够分享她美味的食物,而不是待在漏风的阁楼里啃他的硬面包。正如我之前告诉你们的那样,玛莎小姐的心灵非常富有同情心。

为了验证她对这个客人职业的猜想,一天,她从屋里把以前在拍卖会上买来的一幅画搬出来,靠在面包柜台后面的架子上。

那是一幅威尼斯风景画。一座宏伟的大理石宫殿(画上这么写的)矗立在前景——或者是前水景。因为剩下的就是几条平底船了(船上坐着的女士伸手划过水面),云彩、天空和许多明暗配合。没有艺术家可以忽视它。

两天后,那个客人来了。

"请拿两个过期面包。"

"夫人,您这儿有一幅不错

dame," he said while she was wrapping up the bread.

"Yes?" says Miss Martha, revelling in her own cunning. "I do so admire art and" (no, it would not do to say "artists" thus early) "and paintings," she substituted. "You think it is a good picture?"

"Der balance," said the customer, "is not in good drawing. Der bairspective of it is not true. Goot morning, madame."

He took his bread, bowed, and hurried out.

Yes, he must be an artist. Miss Martha took the picture back to her room.

How gentle and kindly his eyes shone behind his spectacles! What a broad brow he had! To be able to judge perspective at a glance—and to live on stale bread! But genius often has to struggle before it is recognized.

What a thing it would be for art and perspective if genius were backed by two thousand dollars in bank, a bakery, and a sympathetic heart to – But these were day-dreams, Miss Martha.

Often now when he came he would chat for a while across the showcase. He seemed to crave Miss Martha's cheerful words.

He kept on buying stale bread. Never a

的画。"当她用纸包裹面包时，他说。

"是吗？"玛莎小姐说，并为自己的计谋而感到洋洋得意，"我非常爱好艺术和……（不，这么早就说"艺术家"是不合适的）和绘画。"她改口说，"你认为这幅画怎么样？"

"这宫殿，"客人说，"画得不太好。透视法用得不真切。再见，夫人。"

他拿起面包，弯腰鞠躬，然后匆匆忙忙地走了。

是的，他一定是个艺术家。玛莎小姐把画搬回她的房间。

他镜片后的眼睛闪耀着多么温柔和善的光芒啊！他的额头是多么地宽广！看一眼就可以判断透视法——却要靠过期面包生活！不过天才常常要奋斗一番才能被认可的。

假如天才有 2 000 元的银行存款、一家面包店和一颗富有同情心的心作为支持，艺术和透视法将会获得多大的成就啊——但这些都是白日梦罢了，玛莎小姐。

最近，他来时往往会隔着货柜聊上一会儿。看起来他似乎很渴望听到玛莎小姐愉快的言语。

他继续买他的过期面包。但

cake, never a pie, never one of her delicious Sally Lunns.

She thought he began to look thinner and discouraged. Her heart ached to add something good to eat to his meagre purchase, but her courage failed at the act. She did not dare affront him. She knew the pride of artists.

Miss Martha took to wearing her blue-dotted silk waist behind the counter. In the back room she cooked a mysterious compound of quince seeds and borax. Ever so many people use it for the complexion.

One day the customer came in as usual, laid his nickel on the showcase, and called for his stale loaves. While Miss Martha was reaching for them there was a great tooting and clanging, and a fire-engine came lumbering past.

The customer hurried to the door to look, as any one will. Suddenly inspired, Miss Martha seized the opportunity.

On the bottom shelf behind the counter was a pound of fresh butter that the dairyman had left ten minutes before. With a bread-knife Miss Martha made a deep slash in each of the stale loaves, inserted a generous quantity of butter, and pressed the loaves tight again.

从未买过蛋糕、馅饼，或是她店里美味的萨利伦甜饼。

她觉得他开始消瘦和颓唐。她的心渴望在他买的寒酸的食物里加上一点好吃的，但是她没有足够的勇气去付诸行动。她不敢冒犯他。她了解艺术家的傲气。

玛莎小姐开始穿起她那件蓝点子的丝绸背心站在柜台后面。她在后房熬了一种神秘的柏树种子和硼砂的混合物，有很多人一直用它来养颜。

一天，那个客人又像往常一样来了，他把镍币放在柜台上，要买过期的面包。玛莎小姐去拿面包的时候，响起了一阵喇叭声和警钟声，一辆消防车呼啸而过。

那个客人急忙跑到门口张望，遇到这种情况，任何人都会这么做。玛莎小姐灵机一动，抓住了这个机会。

柜台后面最底下一格的架子上放着一磅牛奶工十分钟前刚送来的新鲜黄油。玛莎小姐用面包刀把两个过期面包都切开一条深深的口子，塞进一大堆黄油，再把面包压紧。

When the customer turned once more she was tying the paper around them.

When he had gone, after an unusually pleasant little chat, Miss Martha smiled to herself, but not without a slight fluttering of the heart.

Had she been too bold? Would he take offense? But surely not. There was no language of edibles. Butter was no emblem of unmaidenly forwardness.

For a long time that day her mind dwelt on the subject. She imagined the scene when he should discover her little deception.

He would lay down his brushes and palette. There would stand his easel with the picture he was painting in which the perspective was beyond criticism.

He would prepare for his luncheon of dry bread and water. He would slice into a loaf – ah!

Miss Martha blushed. Would he think of the hand that placed it there as he ate? Would he –

The front door bell jangled viciously. Somebody was coming in, making a great deal of noise.

Miss Martha hurried to the front. Two men were there. One was a young man smoking a pipe – a man she had never

当那个客人再进来的时候，她已经在用纸包面包了。

他们格外开心地聊了几句。客人走后，玛莎小姐自顾自地笑起来，除此以外，心头还有点砰砰乱跳。

她是不是过于大胆了呢？他会感到被冒犯了吗？绝对不会的。食物不会说话，黄油并不代表不守妇道。

那天，她的心在很长一段时间里都在想这件事。她想像着当他发现她的小骗术时的情景。

他会放下画笔和调色板。画架上放着他正在画的画，那幅画的透视法一定是无可挑剔。

他会准备拿干面包和水当午饭。他会切开一个面包……哦！

玛莎小姐脸红了。他吃的时候，会不会想到那只把黄油塞在里面的手呢？他会不会……

前门的铃铛恼人地响了起来。有人吵吵闹闹地走进来。

玛莎小姐赶到大堂。那儿站着两个男人。一个是抽着烟斗的年轻人——她之前从来没见过，

seen before. The other was her artist.

His face was very red, his hat was on the back of his head, his hair was wildly rumpled. He clinched his two fists and shook them ferociously at Miss Martha. *At Miss Martha.*

"*Dummkopf!*" he shouted with extreme loudness; and then "*Tausendonfer!*" or something like it in German. The young man tried to draw him away.

"I vill not go," he said angrily, "else I shall told her."

He made a bass drum of Miss Martha's counter.

"You haf shpoilt me," he cried, his blue eyes blazing behind his spectacles. "I vill tell you. You vas von *meddingsome old cat!*"

Miss Martha leaned weakly against the shelves and laid one hand on her blue-dotted silk waist. The young man took the other by the collar.

"Come on," he said, "you've said enough." He dragged the angry one out at the door to the sidewalk, and then came back.

"Guess you ought to be told, ma'am," he said, "what the row is about. That's Blumberger. He's an architectural draftsman. I work in the same office with

另一个就是她的艺术家。

艺术家的脸涨得通红，帽子戴到了后脑勺上，头发被抓得乱哄哄的。他紧握着两个拳头，凶狠地朝玛莎小姐挥舞，朝玛莎小姐！

"笨蛋！"他撕破了嗓门高声叫喊，接着又用德语喊了一声五雷轰顶，或者类似的话。那个年轻人在试图把他拉走。

"我不走，"他愤怒地说，"我一定要告诉她。"

他擂鼓似地敲打着玛莎小姐的柜台。

"你把我给毁了。"他叫嚷着，镜片后面的蓝眼睛冒着火光。"我告诉你，你是个令人讨厌的老猫！"

玛莎小姐无力地靠在货架上，一只手放在那件蓝点子的丝绸背心上。抽烟斗的年轻人抓住他同伴的衣领。

"走吧，"他说，"你已经骂够了。"他把那个愤怒的人拖到对着人行道的门外面，然后回到屋里。

"夫人，我认为你理应知道这场吵闹的原因，"他说，"那个人是布卢姆伯格。他是个建筑图纸设计师。我和他在同一家事

him.

"He's been working hard for three months drawing a plan for a new city hall. It was a prize competition. He finished inking the lines yesterday. You know, a draftsman always makes his drawing in pencil first. When it's done he rubs out the pencil lines with handfuls of stale bread crumbs. That's better than India rubber.

"Blumberger's been buying the bread here. Well, to-day – well, you know, ma'am, that butter isn't – well, Blumberger's plan isn't good for anything now except to cut up into railroad sandwiches."

Miss Martha went into the back room. She took off the blue-dotted silk waist and put on the old brown serge she used to wear. Then she poured the quince seed and borax mixture out of the window into the ash can.

务所里工作。

"这三个月以来他一直在非常辛苦地绘制新市政厅的图纸，那是个有奖比赛。他昨天刚完成上墨。你知道，制图员总是先用铅笔画图，完成后就用大量的过期面包屑擦去铅笔画的线，过期面包比橡皮擦好用得多。

"布卢姆伯格一向在你这儿买面包。嗯，今天——嗯，你知道，夫人，里面的黄油可不——嗯，现在布卢姆伯格的图纸除了裁开去包三明治之外，再没有其他用途了。"

玛莎小姐走进后房。她脱下蓝点子的丝绸背心，换上那件以前她经常穿的很旧的棕色粗布衣服。之后，她把柏树种子和硼砂的混合物倒在窗外的垃圾箱里。

13. SPRINGTIME A LA CARTE
13. 菜单上的春天

It was a day in March.

Never, never begin a story this way when you write one. No opening could possibly be worse. It is unimaginative, flat, dry and likely to consist of mere wind. But in this instance it is allowable. For the following paragraph, which should have inaugurated the narrative, is too wildly extravagant and preposterous to be flaunted in the face of the reader without preparation.

Sarah was crying over her bill of fare.

Think of a New York girl shedding tears on the menu card!

To account for this you will be allowed to guess that the lobsters were all out, or that she had sworn ice-cream off during Lent, or that she had ordered onions, or that she had just come from a Hackett matinee. And then, all these theories being wrong, you will please let the story proceed.

The gentleman who announced that the world was an oyster which he with his sword would open made a larger hit than he deserved. It is not difficult to open an

这是三月里的一天。

如果你写故事，可千万千万别这么开头。大概没有比这更糟糕的开头了。它缺乏想像力，平淡，干瘪，充其量只会让人想到风。不过，就是在当下还是可以的。因为接下来这段本来应该是故事的开头，只是由于过于不着边际和荒谬，一下子放在毫无思想准备的读者的面前，会让人有点不知所云。

莎拉正对着她的菜单哭泣。

想像一下，一个纽约女孩在对着菜单流眼泪！

这是怎么回事呢？也许你会想，因为菜单上没龙虾了，或者她曾起誓四旬斋期间绝对不吃冰淇淋了，或者她点了洋葱，又或者她刚刚看完海克特日戏回来。不过，你全都猜错了，还是请让我把这个故事继续讲下去吧。

有位先生曾经说过，整个世界就是一个大牡蛎，他用剑就能把它劈开，并因此出了名。用剑剖开一个牡蛎并非难事，可是你见过有什

oyster with a sword. But did you ever notice any one try to open the terrestrial bivalve with a typewriter? Like to wait for a dozen raw opened that way?

Sarah had managed to pry apart the shells with her unhandy weapon far enough to nibble a wee bit at the cold and clammy world within. She knew no more shorthand than if she had been a graduate in stenography just let slip upon the world by a business college. So, not being able to stenog, she could not enter that bright galaxy of office talent. She was a free-lance typewriter and canvassed for odd jobs of copying.

The most brilliant and crowning feat of Sarah's battle with the world was the deal she made with Schulenberg's Home Restaurant. The restaurant was next door to the old red brick in which she ball-roomed. One evening after dining at Schulenberg's 40-cent, five-course *table d'hôte* (served as fast as you throw the five baseballs at the coloured gentleman's head) Sarah took away with her the bill of fare. It was written in an almost unreadable script neither English nor German, and so arranged that if you were not careful you began with a toothpick and rice pudding and ended with soup

么人用打字机打开这种陆栖双壳生物吗？你愿意等着一打生牡蛎被这么打开吗？

莎拉设法用她那不爽利的武器把牡蛎打开得足够大，以便在那冷冰冰，粘腻腻的壳内世界里细细地咬上一小口。她的速记法丝毫不比商业大学的速记毕业生差——社会上只容得那些人。因为当不成速记员，所以她便成不了办公室里显赫人才中的一员。她是一个自由打字员，尽量找些打字的零活儿干干。

莎拉同这个世界进行的最辉煌的一场战役就是她和舒伦伯格家庭餐馆做成的一项交易。她住在一幢旧红砖房子的一间大厅里，隔壁就是这家餐馆。那天晚上，她在舒伦伯格餐馆吃了一份 40 美分 5 个菜的套餐（上菜的速度和你把 5 个棒球丢到有色人种绅士的头上一样快）。走的时候莎拉顺手带上了菜单。菜单上的字是手写的，既不是英文，也不是德文，简直就没法看，一不小心，你就会以牙签和大米布丁开饭，最后才看见汤和星期几。

---

and the day of the week.

The next day Sarah showed Schulenberg a neat card on which the menu was beautifully typewritten with the viands temptingly marshalled under their right and proper heads from "hors d'oeuvre" to "not responsible for overcoats and umbrellas."

Schulenberg became a naturalized citizen on the spot. Before Sarah left him she had him willingly committed to an agreement. She was to furnish typewritten bills of fare for the twenty-one tables in the restaurant – a new bill for each day's dinner, and new ones for breakfast and lunch as often as changes occurred in the food or as neatness required.

In return for this Schulenberg was to send three meals per diem to Sarah's hall room by a waiter – an obsequious one if possible – and furnish her each afternoon with a pencil draft of what Fate had in store for Schulenberg's customers on the morrow.

Mutual satisfaction resulted from the agreement. Schulenberg's patrons now knew what the food they ate was called even if its nature sometimes puzzled them. And Sarah had food during a cold, dull winter, which was the main thing

第二天，莎拉拿出一张卡片给舒伦伯格看，上面是用打字机打得整洁齐整的菜单，菜名被赏心悦目地排列在合适的位置上，从"开胃菜"一直到"衣帽雨伞，各自负责"。

舒伦伯格立即变成了被归化的市民。莎拉离开以前，他自愿和她达成了一项协议。莎拉给餐馆里的 21 张餐桌提供打印的菜单——每天要为晚餐打一份新菜单，要是早餐和午餐变了花样，或者是菜单弄脏了，就另打一份干净的菜单。

作为回报，舒伦伯格每天派一个侍者——可能是溜须拍马的家伙——把三餐送到莎拉的房间，每天下午还送去一张用铅笔写好的菜单草稿，上面列着第二天命运女神给舒伦伯格家的顾客所准备的饭菜。

这项协议让双方都很满意。现在那些到舒伦伯格餐馆用餐的顾客知道他们吃的菜到底叫什么名字了，尽管有时候这些菜的原料让他们感到困惑。而对莎拉来说，能在寒冷又沉闷的冬天里三餐不愁

with her.

And then the almanac lied, and said that spring had come. Spring comes when it comes. The frozen snows of January still lay like adamant in the cross-town streets. The hand-organs still played "In the Good Old Summertime," with their December vivacity and expression. Men began to make thirty-day notes to buy Easter dresses. Janitors shut off steam. And when these things happen one may know that the city is still in the clutches of winter.

One afternoon Sarah shivered in her elegant hall bedroom; "house heated; scrupulously clean; conveniences; seen to be appreciated." She had no work to do except Schulenberg's menu cards. Sarah sat in her squeaky willow rocker, and looked out the window. The calendar on the wall kept crying to her: "Springtime is here, Sarah – springtime is here, I tell you. Look at me, Sarah, my figures show it. You've got a neat figure yourself, Sarah – a – nice springtime figure – why do you look out the window so sadly?"

Sarah's room was at the back of the house. Looking out the window she could see the windowless rear brick wall of the box factory on the next street. But the

是最主要的事情了。

然后，就如历书上说的那样，春天已经来了，其实完全不是那么回事。春天要在它该来的时候才来。一月份冻得硬邦邦地的积雪覆盖在横穿市区的街道上。手拿乐器的乐手还在演奏着《在昔日往昔美好的夏天》这首曲子，带着 12 月的活力和神情。看门人已经关了暖气。逢此情形，人们就会知道，这座城市仍然处于冬天的掌控之下。

一天下午，莎拉在她精致的小卧室里冻得浑身打颤，"房屋暖和，纤尘不染，便捷舒适，眼见为实。"，手头除了舒伦伯格的菜单外，她无事可做。莎拉坐在她吱嘎作响的柳木摇椅上望着窗外，墙上的月历朝她不停叫唤："春天来了，莎拉，我跟你说，春天来了。看着我，看我的样子你就知道了。你有这么匀称的身材，莎拉，犹如春天般美好的体形，你为什么如此伤感地望着窗外呢？"

莎拉的房间在这幢房子的后面。从窗子里望出去，她能看到下一条街道上一家制盒厂的没有窗子的后砖墙。莎拉对这堵墙视而不

wall was clearest crystal; and Sarah was looking down a grassy lane shaded with cherry trees and elms and bordered with raspberry bushes and Cherokee roses.

Spring's real harbingers are too subtle for the eye and ear. Some must have the flowering crocus, the wood-starring dogwood, the voice of bluebird – even so gross a reminder as the farewell hand-shake of the retiring buckwheat and oyster before they can welcome the Lady in Green to their dull bosoms. But to old earth's choicest kin there come straight, sweet messages from his newest bride, telling them they shall be no stepchildren unless they choose to be.

On the previous summer Sarah had gone into the country and loved a farmer.

(In writing your story never hark back thus. It is bad art, and cripples interest. Let it march, march.)

Sarah stayed two weeks at Sunnybrook Farm. There she learned to love old Farmer Franklin's son Walter. Farmers have been loved and wedded and turned out to grass in less time. But young Walter Franklin was a modern agricul-turist. He had a telephone in his cow house, and he could figure up exactly what effect next year's Canada wheat

见。她只看见了樱桃树和榆树的树荫掩盖的山梅矮树丛和切罗基玫瑰花围绕的绿色小路。

对于眼睛和耳朵来说，春天真实的预兆太过微妙了。有些人非得看到绽放的番红花，星星点点的山茱萸，听到蓝知更鸟的鸣唱——即使迹象如此明显，也要跟过季的荞麦和牡蛎握手道别后，才迟钝的把春姑娘抱进他们的怀里。但对于古老地球最疼惜的亲属来说，他的新娘直接送来了让人欢喜的消息，告诉他们除非他们愿意，否则他们将没有继子女。

前一年的夏天，莎拉到乡下去，爱上了那儿的一个农夫。

（您写故事的时候可别这样倒叙，这手法太拙劣了，会磨掉人的兴趣。我们还是继续吧。）

莎拉在森尼鲁克农场待了两个礼拜，就在那儿，她爱上了老农民富兰克林的儿子沃尔特。农民们总是很快恋爱，结婚，然后又继续忙于自己的牧活。不过年轻的沃尔特·富兰克林是个充满现代气息的农艺家。他在牛圈里安装了电话，他还能准确地指出加拿大来年的小麦产量对在暗夜里种植的马铃

crop would have on potatoes planted in the dark of the moon.

It was in this shaded and raspberried lane that Walter had wooed and won her. And together they had sat and woven a crown of dandelions for her hair. He had immoderately praised the effect of the yellow blossoms against her brown tresses; and she had left the chaplet there, and walked back to the house swinging her straw sailor in her hands.

They were to marry in the spring – at the very first signs of spring, Walter said. And Sarah came back to the city to pound her typewriter.

A knock at the door dispelled Sarah's visions of that happy day. A waiter had brought the rough pencil draft of the Home Restaurant's next day fare in old Schulenberg's angular hand.

Sarah sat down to her typewriter and slipped a card between the rollers. She was a nimble worker. Generally in an hour and a half the twenty-one menu cards were written and ready.

To-day there were more changes on the bill of fare than usual. The soups were lighter; pork was eliminated from the entrees, figuring only with Russian turnips among the roasts. The gracious spirit

薯会有什么样的影响。

就在这偏僻的布满了山梅的地方,沃尔特向她求爱,并赢得了她的心。他们坐在一起编了一个蒲公英花冠,他帮她戴在头上。他大肆地赞美蒲公英的黄色花朵映衬着她那棕色头发所产生的效果,她把花冠留在那里,手中挥舞着草帽回到住所。

沃尔特说,他们来年春天就结婚,一有了春天的征兆就结婚。然后莎拉就回到城里继续做打字员了。

一阵敲门声打断了莎拉对幸福日子的幻想,一位侍者带来了家庭餐馆第二天的菜单,上面满是潦草的铅笔字迹,是老舒伦伯格用他那双瘦削的手写的。

莎拉坐到打字机旁,往滚轴里塞了一张卡片。她干起活来十分敏捷,21张菜单卡片通常一个半小时就全部打好了。

今天菜单上的变动比往常要多。汤清淡了一些,主菜里没有了猪肉,烤肉的配菜只有俄国芜菁,整个菜单洋溢着春天的气息。前些日子还在渐渐绿起来的山坡上奔

of spring pervaded the entire menu. Lamb, that lately capered on the greening hillsides, was becoming exploited with the sauce that commemorated its gambols. The song of the oyster, though not silenced, was *dimuendo con amore*. The frying-pan seemed to be held, inactive, behind the beneficent bars of the broiler. The pie list swelled; the richer puddings had vanished; the sausage, with his drapery wrapped about him, barely lingered in a pleasant thanatopsis with the buckwheats and the sweet but doomed maple.

Sarah's fingers danced like midgets above a summer stream. Down through the courses she worked, giving each item its position according to its length with an accurate eye. Just above the desserts came the list of vegetables. Carrots and peas, asparagus on toast, the perennial tomatoes and corn and succotash, lima beans, cabbage – and then –

Sarah was crying over her bill of fare. Tears from the depths of some divine despair rose in her heart and gathered to her eyes. Down went her head on the little typewriter stand; and the keyboard rattled a dry accompaniment to her moist sobs.

跑的山羊，现在被做成了酱羊肉以纪念它的欢跃。牡蛎的歌声，虽然尚未消弭，但也渐唱渐弱了。被限制在烘烤用具仁慈的栅条后的油煎锅似乎已怠惰了。馅饼的条目多了，比较油腻的布丁不见了，香肠、香肠纸与荞麦粉在愉悦地消逝的同时几乎未作任何逗留，而糖果注定是槭糖。

莎拉的手指在打字机上跃动着，宛如夏日小溪上空飞舞的小虫。她从上到下仔细地审视着菜名，按长度把它们打在合适的位置上。餐后甜点的上方是蔬菜的目录，胡萝卜、豌豆、吐司芦笋、四季不间断的番茄、玉米、豆煮玉米、菜豆和卷心菜——然后是——

莎拉对着她的那张菜单哭了起来。泪水从她绝望的灵魂深处的某个地方涌上来，在她的眼睛里积聚起来。她的头一直抵在打字机的小桌子上。单调的键盘声给她的啜泣加上了伴奏。

For she had received no letter from Walter in two weeks, and the next item on the bill of fare was dandelions – dandelions with some kind of egg – but bother the egg! – dandelions, with whose golden blooms Walter had crowned her his queen of love and future bride – dandelions, the harbingers of spring, her sorrow's crown of sorrow – reminder of her happiest days.

Madam, I dare you to smile until you suffer this test: Let the Marechal Niel roses that Percy brought you on the night you gave him your heart be served as a salad with French dressing before your eyes at a Schulenberg *table d'hôte*. Had Juliet so seen her love tokens dishonoured the sooner would she have sought the lethean herbs of the good apothecary.

But what a witch is Spring! Into the great cold city of stone and iron a message had to be sent. There was none to convey it but the little hardy courier of the fields with his rough green coat and modest air. He is a true soldier of fortune, this *dent-de-lion* – this lion's tooth, as the French chefs call him. Flowered, he will assist at love-making, wreathed in my lady's nut-brown hair; young and callow and unblossomed, he goes into the boil-

因为她已经两个礼拜没有收到沃尔特的来信了，而菜单上的下个菜名正好是蒲公英——蒲公英和某种鸡蛋——管它是什么鸡蛋！——蒲公英，沃尔特正是用蒲公英，那金黄色的花朵为他的爱情王后，未来妻子做了一个花冠——蒲公英啊，这位春天的使者，她悲伤中那悲伤的花冠——她不由地回想起那些快乐的日子。

夫人，您要是没有这种经历，肯定会觉得好笑：想像一下，您把心奉献给了珀西，他送给您的尼尔元帅玫瑰就在您面前被公开摆上斯家餐馆的公共餐桌，成了一道配了法国调料的色拉。要是朱丽叶看到她的爱情信物遭受如此侮辱，她也会立即去找高明的药剂师寻求忘忧草。

然而春天真像个女巫！一定会有什么信息送到这个满是石头钢筋的冰冷的大城市里来的。除了身穿着毛茸茸绿衣服的田野信使蒲公英——法国厨师称他为狮子的牙齿——还会有谁来传达春天到来的信息呢！一但开花，它就盘绕在姑娘的深棕色头发上帮助成全好事；稚嫩未开时，他就跳进沸腾的锅中，给他至高无上的女主人传递消息。

ing pot and delivers the word of his sovereign mistress.

By and by Sarah forced back her tears. The cards must be written. But, still in a faint, golden glow from her dandeleonine dream, she fingered the typewriter keys absently for a little while, with her mind and heart in the meadow lane with her young farmer. But soon she came swiftly back to the rock-bound lanes of Manhattan, and the typewriter began to rattle and jump like a strike-breaker's motor car.

At 6 o'clock the waiter brought her dinner and carried away the typewritten bill of fare. When Sarah ate she set aside, with a sigh, the dish of dandelions with its crowning ovarious accompaniment. As this dark mass had been transformed from a bright and love-indorsed flower to be an ignominious vegetable, so had her summer hopes wilted and perished. Love may, as Shakespeare said, feed on itself: but Sarah could not bring herself to eat the dandelions that had graced, as ornaments, the first spiritual banquet of her heart's true affection.

At 7:30 the couple in the next room began to quarrel: the man in the room above sought for A on his flute; the gas

不久，莎拉强忍住不哭。菜单还得打出来。蒲公英美梦发出的微弱的金色光芒尚在，有一阵子她心不在焉地敲打着打字机，她的整个心思都还徘徊在牧场的草地上和她的年轻农夫身上。但很快，她又回到曼哈顿的石砌建筑中来，打字机开始像出了故障的汽车一样咔嗒咔嗒地跳动起来。

下午6点钟，侍者送来了晚饭，并取走了打好的菜单。吃饭时，莎拉叹了口气，把那碟蒲公英与撒在上面的各式各样的配菜推到一旁。随着那鲜艳明亮的、为爱作证的花朵变成了可耻的蔬菜，又变成这团黑糊糊的东西，她的夏日憧憬也渐渐枯萎凋谢了。就像莎士比亚说的，爱能从自身中得到满足：但是莎拉可无法吃下这蒲公英，因为它曾装饰了她心中最真的爱恋——她的第一次精神盛宴。

七点半的时候，隔壁房间里的两个人开始吵架；在楼上那个房间住的男人一直找不准笛子的A调；

went a little lower; three coal wagons started to unload – the only sound of which the phonograph is jealous; cats on the back fences slowly retreated toward Mukden. By these signs Sarah knew that it was time for her to read. She got out The Cloister and the Hearth, the best non-selling book of the month, settled her feet on her trunk, and began to wander with Gerard.

The front door bell rang. The landlady answered it. Sarah left Gerard and Denys treed by a bear and listened. Oh, yes; you would, just as she did!

And then a strong voice was heard in the hall below, and Sarah jumped for her door, leaving the book on the floor and the first round easily the bear's. You have guessed it. She reached the top of the stairs just as her farmer came up, three at a jump, and reaped and garnered her, with nothing left for the gleaners.

"Why haven't you written – oh, why?" cried Sarah.

"New York is a pretty large town," said Walter Franklin. "I came in a week ago to your old address. I found that you went away on a Thursday. That consoled some; it eliminated the possible Friday bad luck. But it didn't prevent my hunt-

煤气灯的光变暗了，三辆煤车开始卸煤——这是惟一让留声机嫉妒的声音；后院篱笆那儿传来猫叫的声音。根据这些迹象，莎拉知道她看书的时间到了。她拿出了当月最不畅销的书《患难与忠诚》，把脚搁在箱子上，开始跟着杰拉德一起流浪。

前门的铃响了，房东太太去开门，莎拉任由熊把杰勒德和丹尼斯赶到树上，仔细地听着。噢，是的，要是你，也会像她那样做的。

接着楼下门厅里传来洪亮的声音，莎拉跳起来去开门，书被丢到了地板上，她如同熊扑向猎物的第一回合般急切地去开门。你已经猜出来了。她到达楼梯口时，她的农夫恋人也正一步跨三阶地跑上楼来，把她搂在怀里，她的整个身心全都给这拾穗人收捡了去。

"你为什么没写过信？啊？为什么？"莎拉哭喊道。

"纽约可真是个大城市，"沃尔特·富兰克林说，"一星期前我照着原来的地址去找你，结果发现你礼拜四就离开了。这稍稍安慰了一下我，消除了礼拜五可能的坏运气。但是从那以后，我一直通过警

ing for you with police and otherwise
ever since!

"I wrote!" said Sarah, vehemently.

"Never got it!"

"Then how did you find me?"

The young farmer smiled a springtime
smile.

"I dropped into that Home Restaurant
next door this evening," said he. "I don't
care who knows it; I like a dish of some
kind of greens at this time of the year. I
ran my eye down that nice typewritten
bill of fare looking for something in that
line. When I got below cabbage I turned
my chair over and hollered for the proprietor. He told me where you lived."

"I remember," sighed Sarah, happily.
"That was dandelions below cabbage."

"I'd know that cranky capital W 'way
above the line that your typewriter makes
anywhere in the world," said Franklin.

"Why, there's no W in dandelions,"
said Sarah, in surprise.

The young man drew the bill of fare
from his pocket, and pointed to a line.

Sarah recognized the first card she had
typewritten that afternoon. There was
still the rayed splotch in the upper
right-hand corner where a tear had fallen.
But over the spot where one should have

察局和别的办法到处找你!"

"我曾给你写过信!"莎拉说。

"我从来没收到过!"

"那你怎么找到我的呢?"

年轻的农民露出一个春日般
温暖的笑容。

"今天晚上,我顺便走到隔壁
的那家家庭餐馆去了,"他说,"我
才不管它有没有名气,每年这个时
候,我喜欢随便吃些绿色蔬菜。我
看着那份打印精美的菜单,想在里
面找点吃的,当我看到卷心菜下面
的那道菜时,就把椅子弄翻了,我
叫来了老板。他告诉我你住在哪
儿。"

"我记得,"莎拉快活地呼了
口气,"卷心菜下面是蒲公英。"

"无论在哪里,我都能认出你
的打字机打在线条上的歪歪斜斜
的大写'W'。"富兰克林说。

"可是,蒲公英的拼写里没有
'W'呀?"莎拉诧异地说道。

年轻人从口袋里抽出那张菜
单,指着其中的一行。

她认出这是她那天下午打的
第一张卡片,还能看见它右上角那
里带着边纹的眼泪的痕迹。因为对
那金色花朵的联想记忆,她在顾客
本应该看到的是一种蔬菜名的位

read the name of the meadow plant, the clinging memory of their golden blossoms had allowed her fingers to strike strange keys.

Between the red cabbage and the stuffed green peppers was the item:

"*DEAREST WALTER, WITH HARD-BOILED EGG.*"

置上打上了其他的字。

在红叶卷心菜和酿青椒两道菜之间，有这么一个菜名：

"最亲爱的沃尔特和白煮鸡蛋。"

14. ROADS OF DESTINY
14. 命运之路

I go to seek on many roads
What is to be.
True heart and strong, with love to light –
Will they not bear me in the fight To order, shun or wield or mould My Destiny?

Unpublished Poems of David Mignot.

我踏上许多条道路
追寻人生的真义。
带着真心和坚定，以爱照亮征程——
难道真心和爱情
在人生之战中不愿为我佑护，让我主宰、选择、左右或铸造我的命运？
大卫·米尼奥未发表的诗

The song was over. The words were David's; the air, one of the countryside. The company about the inn table applauded heartily, for the young poet paid for the wine. Only the notary, M. Papineau, shook his head a little at the lines, for he was a man of books, and he had not drunk with the rest.

David went out into the village street, where the night air drove the wine vapour from his head. And then he remembered that he and Yvonne had quarrelled that day, and that he had resolved to leave his home that night to seek fame and honour in the great world outside.

"When my poems are on every man's tongue," he told himself, in a fine exhilaration, "she will, perhaps, think of the

歌唱完了。歌词是大卫写的，乡村音乐的风格。小酒馆里，人们围着桌子，热情鼓掌，因为这位年轻的诗人为他们付了酒钱。只有公证人帕皮诺先生摇了摇头，不赞同这几行歌词，因为他读过很多的书，也没和其他人一起喝酒。

大卫走出门，来到村子的街道上。夜晚的风吹散了他脑袋里的酒气。随后他想起来，白天他刚和伊冯娜吵过架。他已经下定决心在那晚离家出走，到外面的大世界去追寻荣耀和名望。

"等到全世界的人都吟诵我的诗歌的那一天，"他乐滋滋地遥想着，"或许她会后悔今天说

hard words she spoke this day."

Except the roysterers in the tavern, the village folk were abed. David crept softly into his room in the shed of his father's cottage and made a bundle of his small store of clothing. With this upon a staff, he set his face outward upon the road that ran from Vernoy.

He passed his father's herd of sheep, huddled in their nightly pen – the sheep he herded daily, leaving them to scatter while he wrote verses on scraps of paper. He saw a light yet shining in Yvonne's window, and a weakness shook his purpose of a sudden. Perhaps that light meant that she rued, sleepless, her anger, and that morning might – But, no! His decision was made. Vernoy was no place for him. Not one soul there could share his thoughts. Out along that road lay his fate and his future.

Three leagues across the dim, moonlit champaign ran the road, straight as a ploughman's furrow. It was believed in the village that the road ran to Paris, at least; and this name the poet whispered often to himself as he walked. Never so far from Vernoy had David travelled before.

了那些难听的话。"

除了酒馆里的人还在热闹喧哗以外，全村的人都已经入睡。他悄声钻进他的房间，那是在他父亲的茅草房边搭起的一间棚子，他把衣物打成一个包，然后用木棒把它撬起搭在肩上，昂首踏上了离开维尔诺瓦的路。

他经过父亲的羊群，夜里它们都蜷缩在圈栏中——他每天放它们出去吃草，任它们四处奔跑，自己则在小纸片上写诗。他看见伊冯娜的窗户还亮着灯，瞬间，有一种柔情动摇着他的决心。灯光或许意味着她无法入睡，正在后悔不该发火，说不定到了早晨她就……可是，不行！他已下定决心。维尔诺瓦不是他的福地。这儿没有一个人能理解他。他的命运和未来就在前面这条路上。

马路横穿过暗淡月光下的原野，有三英里长，如耕地人的犁沟一般笔直。至少村里的人认为这条路是通向巴黎的。诗人一边走，一边在嘴里念着这个名字。大卫以前从来没有离开维尔诺瓦去那么遥远的地方。

THE LEFT BRANCH

Three leagues, then, the road ran, and turned into a puzzle. It joined with another and a larger road at right angles. David stood, uncertain, for a while, and then took the road to the left.

Upon this more important highway were, imprinted in the dust, wheel tracks left by the recent passage of some vehicle. Some half an hour later these traces were verified by the sight of a ponderous carriage mired in a little brook at the bottom of a steep hill. The driver and postilions were shouting and tugging at the horses' bridles. On the road at one side stood a huge, black-clothed man and a slender lady wrapped in a long, light cloak.

David saw the lack of skill in the efforts of the servants. He quietly assumed control of the work. He directed the outriders to cease their clamour at the horses and to exercise their strength upon the wheels. The driver alone urged the animals with his familiar voice; David himself heaved a powerful shoulder at the rear of the carriage, and with one harmonious tug the great vehicle rolled up on solid ground. The outriders

左岔道

这条路向前延伸了三英里，然后便看不清楚了。它与另一条更宽的路相交成直角。大卫站立着，犹豫了一阵，然后踏上了左边的岔道。

在这条更重要的公路上，清晰的车轮印在了路面上，那是刚经过的车辆留下的。大约半小时后，推测便被证实了。陡峭的山脚下，一辆笨重的大马车陷在一条小溪里面，车夫和左马御者都在对着马大声吆喝，不停地拽着马缰。路边站着一个穿黑衣服的魁梧的先生和一个纤瘦的女人，她的身子裹在一件薄薄的长大衣里。

大卫看出来佣人们没少卖力，但是缺乏技巧。他没有打招呼，很自然地就上前去指挥工作了。他吩咐侍从们不要向马吼叫，而是用力去推车轮，只让车夫一个人用马熟悉的声音呼唤它。大卫自己则用有力的臂膀去推马车的后部。在大家的通力合作下，只用了一次，马车就驶上了硬地面。侍从们攀上马车，在原先的位置上坐了下来。

climbed to their places.

David stood for a moment upon one foot. The huge gentleman waved a hand. "You will enter the carriage," he said, in a voice large, like himself, but smoothed by art and habit. Obedience belonged in the path of such a voice. Brief as was the young poet's hesitation, it was cut shorter still by a renewal of the command. David's foot went to the step. In the darkness he perceived dimly the form of the lady upon the rear seat. He was about to seat himself opposite, when the voice again swayed him to its will. "You will sit at the lady's side."

The gentleman swung his great weight to the forward seat. The carriage proceeded up the hill. The lady was shrunk, silent, into her corner. David could not estimate whether she was old or young, but a delicate, mild perfume from her clothes stirred his poet's fancy to the belief that there was loveliness beneath the mystery. Here was an adventure such as he had often imagined. But as yet he held no key to it, for no word was spoken while he sat with his impenetrable companions.

In an hour's time David perceived through the window that the vehicle

大卫单脚站了一会儿。那位身材魁梧的先生手臂一挥。"你上车吧。"他说，嗓门和他的身材一样大，但由于修养和习惯而显得文雅了些。在这样的声音所到之处，只有服从。年轻诗人才犹豫了片刻，就被另一声命令打断。大卫登上马车的踏板。黑暗中他微微可见后座上那女人的身形。他正要坐在对面的位子上，那声音突然再次发出命令："坐在这位女士的旁边吧。"

这位先生转过庞大的身躯，在前排坐了下来。马车继续朝山上行驶。女人蜷缩在角落里，一句话也不说。大卫看不出她究竟年老还是年轻，但她的衣服散发出的一丝幽柔淡雅的芳香，搅得他浮想联翩，是他相信这神秘之下一定藏着美丽。这正是他常常幻想过的艳遇。但是他还没有想出应对的办法，因为，他和这些猜不透的同伴们坐在一起，而他们之间一个字还没有说过。

一小时以后，大卫透过窗户看见马车正行驶在一座小镇的街

traversed the street of some town. Then it stopped in front of a closed and darkened house, and a postilion alighted to hammer impatiently upon the door. A latticed window above flew wide and a night-capped head popped out.

"Who are ye that disturb honest folk at this time of night? My house is closed. 'Tis too late for profitable travellers to be abroad. Cease knocking at my door, and be off."

"Open!" spluttered the postilion, loudly;"open for Monsiegneur the Marquis de Beaupertuys."

"Ah!" cried the voice above. "Ten thousand pardons, my lord. I did not know – the hour is so late – at once shall the door be opened, and the house placed at my lord's disposal."

Inside was heard the clink of chain and bar, and the door was flung open. Shivering with chill and apprehension, the landlord of the Silver Flagon stood, half clad, candle in hand, upon the threshold.

David followed the Marquis out of the carriage. "Assist the lady," he was ordered. The poet obeyed. He felt her small hand tremble as he guided her descent. "Into the house," was the next

上。一会儿，马车停在了一座关着门、没开灯的房子前面。一个侍从下了马车，不耐烦地猛敲着大门。楼上一扇花格窗户猛地开了，一个戴着睡帽的头探了出来。

"是谁在三更半夜敲门，打扰我们这些安分人啊？店已经关门啦。想掏钱住店，太晚啦。别敲了，走吧！"

"开门！" 侍从大声喊着，"开门！德博佩杜依斯侯爵大人要进来。"

"啊！"上面的声音惊叫道，"大人，请万分包涵。恕我不知……都这么晚了……马上就开，大人请随便用房。"

门内传来链条和横闩的叮当声，大门敞开了。银酒杯旅店的老板又冷又怕，抖个不停。他站在门槛上，手里举着一支蜡烛，连衣服都没有穿好。

大卫跟在侯爵后面下了车。"扶小姐一把。"侯爵吩咐他。诗人遵从了他的命令。扶她下车时，他感觉到她的小手在颤抖。"进屋去。"又来了一声命令。

command.

The room was the long dining-hall of the tavern. A great oak table ran down its length. The huge gentleman seated himself in a chair at the nearer end. The lady sank into another against the wall, with an air of great weariness. David stood, considering how best he might now take his leave and continue upon his way.

"My lord," said the landlord, bowing to the floor, "h – had I ex- expected this honour, entertainment would have been ready. T – t – there is wine and cold fowl and m – m – maybe –"

"Candles," said the marquis, spreading the fingers of one plump white hand in a gesture he had.

"Y – yes, my lord." He fetched half a dozen candles, lighted them, and set them upon the table.

"If monsieur would, perhaps, deign to taste a certain Burgundy – there is a cask –"

"Candles," said monsieur, spreading his fingers.

"Assuredly – quickly – I fly, my lord."

A dozen more lighted candles shone in the hall. The great bulk of the marquis overflowed his chair. He was dressed in

这间房是旅店的长餐厅。一张长方形橡木桌几乎占去了整间屋子。魁梧的先生在桌子近首的一张椅子上坐了下来。小姐瘫到了靠墙的一张椅子上,看上去很是疲倦。大卫站在一边,心里面盘算着怎样才能巧妙得体地告辞,继续上路。

"大人,"店老板说,深深鞠了一躬,"要……要是我早晓得您会大驾光临,我会老早做好准备招待您的。现在只剩……剩些酒和冷肉,可能还、还……"

"蜡烛。"侯爵说,以他独有的姿势伸出一只又白又胖的手,展开手指。

"是,是,大人。"店老板拿来半打蜡烛,点燃,然后放在桌上。

"不知大人是否愿意赏个脸尝尝我们的勃艮第红酒……我们还有一桶……"

"蜡烛。"大人说,同时展开他的手指。

"遵命……马上就好……我会很快的,大人。"

大厅里又点亮了一打蜡烛。侯爵庞大的身躯把椅子填得满满

fine black from head to foot save for the snowy ruffles at his wrist and throat. Even the hilt and scabbard of his sword were black. His expression was one of sneering pride. The ends of an upturned moustache reached nearly to his mocking eyes.

The lady sat motionless, and now David perceived that she was young, and possessed of pathetic and appealing beauty. He was startled from the contemplation of her forlorn loveliness by the booming voice of the marquis.

"What is your name and pursuit?"

"David Mignot. I am a poet."

The moustache of the marquis curled nearer to his eyes.

"How do you live?"

"I am also a shepherd; I guarded my father's flock," David answered, with his head high, but a flush upon his cheek.

"Then listen, master shepherd and poet, to the fortune you have blundered upon to-night. This lady is my niece, Mademoiselle Lucie de Varennes. She is of noble descent and is possessed of ten thousand francs a year in her own right. As to her charms, you have but to observe for yourself. If the inventory pleases your shepherd's heart, she be-

的。他从头到脚都以黑色为装束，甚至连他的剑炳和剑鞘也是黑色的，只有袖口和领口的褶边露出白色。他的表情是透着讥讽的傲慢。小胡子向上翘着，几乎要碰到他那双蔑视的眼睛了。

小姐坐在那儿，纹丝不动。大卫现在看出来了，她很年轻，有一种忧伤而动人的美丽。侯爵浑厚的声音让他从对她凄凉美艳的沉醉中惊醒过来。

"什么名字？做什么的？"

"大卫·米尼奥。一名诗人。"

侯爵的胡子向上弯了弯，离眼睛更近了。

"你以什么为生？"

"我也是个牧羊人，照看我父亲的羊群。"大卫回答说，昂着头，但他的脸红了。

"那牧羊人兼诗人少爷，听从你磕绊的命运今晚为你作出的安排吧。这位小姐是我的侄女，叫露西·德瓦内斯。她血统高贵，根据继承权每年有一万法郎的收入。要说她的魅力，你只需自己作出判断。这些条件若是能打动你这颗牧羊人的心，你只需表个态，她马上就可以成为你的妻子。

comes your wife at a word. Do not interrupt me. To-night I conveyed her to the château of the Comte de Villemaur, to whom her hand had been promised. Guests were present; the priest was waiting; her marriage to one eligible in rank and fortune was ready to be accomplished. At the alter this demoiselle, so meek and dutiful, turned upon me like a leopardess, charged me with cruelty and crimes, and broke, before the gaping priest, the troth I had plighted for her. I swore there and then, by ten thousand devils, that she should marry the first man we met after leaving the château, be he prince, charcoal-burner, or thief. You, shepherd, are the first. Mademoiselle must be wed this night. If not you, then another. You have ten minutes in which to make your decision. Do not vex me with words or questions. Ten minutes, shepherd; and they are speeding."

The marquis drummed loudly with his white fingers upon the table. He sank into a veiled attitude of waiting. It was as if some great house had shut its doors and windows against approach. David would have spoken, but the huge man's bearing stopped his tongue. Instead, he stood by the lady's chair and bowed.

别打我岔。今天晚上，我将她送到孔德·德维尔莫庄园，她本来是去结婚的。客人们都到齐了，神父也在恭候着，眼看着这桩地位和财富上都门当户对的婚事就要完成。可是在圣坛面前，这位往日温顺而本分的小姐，突然像母豹一样向我冲来，当着目瞪口呆的神父的面，控诉我的残酷和罪行，并撕毁了我替她订的婚约。我当场对天起誓，她必须嫁给我们在离开庄园后碰上的第一个男人。管他是王子也好，烧炭的也罢，或者是个贼也无所谓，她都得嫁。而你，牧羊人，你就是这第一个男人。小姐必须在今晚结婚。不是你，就会是另外一个人。你有十分钟的时间考虑。不要拿问题或废话来烦我。只有十分钟，牧羊人，时间过得很快的。"

侯爵用他白嫩的手指敲着桌子，就跟打鼓一样响。他在等待着，看不出在想什么。大院子的门窗好像已经被关得严严实实，不再允许客人进入了。大卫本想要说点什么，但侯爵的态度止住了他的舌头。他只好站到小姐的椅子旁边，鞠躬致意。

"Mademoiselle," he said, and he marvelled to find his words flowing easily before so much elegance and beauty. "You have heard me say I was a shepherd. I have also had the fancy, at times, that I am a poet. If it be the test of a poet to adore and cherish the beautiful, that fancy is now strengthened. Can I serve you in any way, mademoiselle?"

The young woman looked up at him with eyes dry and mournful. His frank, glowing face, made serious by the gravity of the adventure, his strong, straight figure and the liquid sympathy in his blue eyes, perhaps, also, her imminent need of long-denied help and kindness, thawed her to sudden tears.

"Monsieur," she said, in low tones, "you look to be true and kind. He is my uncle, the brother of my father, and my only relative. He loved my mother, and he hates me because I am like her. He has made my life one long terror. I am afraid of his very looks, and never before dared to disobey him. But to-night he would have married me to a man three times my age. You will forgive me for bringing this vexation upon you, monsieur. You will, of course, decline this mad act he tries to force upon you. But let me thank you for

"小姐，"他开口道。他惊异自己竟然能在如此优雅和美貌的人儿面前，流利顺畅地说话，"你已经听到，我是个牧羊人。时而我也会幻想自己是一位诗人。如果崇拜和怜香惜玉是对诗人的考验，那么我的梦想现在变得更加强烈了。我能为你效劳吗，小姐？"

年轻女人抬起头来望着他，那双眼睛干涩而哀婉。他那坦率、炙热的脸庞因这场奇遇而变得庄重严肃；他身材健硕而挺直；他的蓝眼睛里流着同情；也许，因为她心里正充满对久求未得的帮助和善良的需求——这一切，突然将她融化，她的泪水奔涌而下。

"先生，"她说，音调低低的，"你看上去真诚而善良。他是我的叔叔，我父亲的兄弟，我现在惟一的亲人。他爱我母亲，因为我长得像她，所以他恨我。他把我的人生变成了一个长长的噩梦。我害怕看见他的样子，以前从来不敢违背他。可是，今天晚上他差点把我嫁给一个年龄是我三倍的人。先生，原谅我把你扯进这场烦怨中来。当然，你是不会屈就于他的压力，答应这门荒唐的婚事的。但是我至少要感

your generous words, at least. I have had none spoken to me in so long."

There was now something more than generosity in the poet's eyes. Poet he must have been, for Yvonne was forgotten; this fine, new loveliness held him with its freshness and grace. The subtle perfume from her filled him with strange emotions. His tender look fell warmly upon her. She leaned to it, thirstily.

"Ten minutes," said David, "is given me in which to do what I would devote years to achieve. I will not say I pity you, mademoiselle; it would not be true – I love you. I cannot ask love from you yet, but let me rescue you from this cruel man, and, in time, love may come. I think I have a future; I will not always be a shepherd. For the present I will cherish you with all my heart and make your life less sad. Will you trust your fate to me, mademoiselle?"

"Ah, you would sacrifice yourself from pity!"

"From love. The time is almost up, mademoiselle."

"You will regret it, and despise me."

"I will live only to make you happy, and myself worthy of you."

Her fine small hand crept into his from

谢你慷慨的言语。很久都没有人跟我说过话了。"

诗人的眼里现在不只含着慷慨了。他一定算得上个真正的诗人了，因为伊冯娜已被遗忘了，这位新结识的精致可爱的美人清新而优雅，把他给迷住了。她身上散发出的幽香让他春心荡漾。他热切地向她倾注着柔情。而她，如饥似渴，倾向他的柔情。

"10分钟的时间，"大卫说，"就可以让我做我本来需要好多年才能完成的事情。我不会说我可怜你，小姐，那不是真话——我爱你。我还没有机会向你求爱，但让我把你从这个残暴的男人手中救出来吧，爱情可能会随之而来。我觉得我会有一个光明的未来，不会永远做一位牧羊人。现在，我将全心全意呵护你，让你的生命中少一些伤痛。你愿意把你的命运托付给我吗，小姐？"

"呵，你只是出于怜悯而牺牲自己吧。"

"出于爱。时间就要到了，小姐。"

"你会后悔，你会嫌弃我。"

"我今后就是为你的幸福而活，并使自己配得上你。"

她纤巧的小手从大衣里伸出

beneath her cloak.

"I will trust you," she breathed, "with my life. And – and love – may not be so far off as you think. Tell him. Once away from the power of his eyes I may forget."

David went and stood before the marquis. The black figure stirred, and the mocking eyes glanced at the great hall clock.

"Two minutes to spare. A shepherd requires eight minutes to decide whether he will accept a bride of beauty and income! Speak up, shepherd, do you consent to become mademoiselle's husband?"

"Mademoiselle," said David, standing proudly, "has done me the honour to yield to my request that she become my wife."

"Well said!" said the marquis. "You have yet the making of a courtier in you, master shepherd. Mademoiselle could have drawn a worse prize, after all. And now to be done with the affair as quick as the Church and the devil will allow!"

He struck the table soundly with his sword hilt. The landlord came, knee-shaking, bringing more candles in the hope of anticipating the great lord's whims. "Fetch a priest," said the marquis,

来，滑进他的手心。

"我愿意，"她轻声说，"把我的生命托付给你。还有……爱……也许不像你想的那么遥远了。告诉他。远离了他那双眼睛的魔力，我就可以忘掉从前。"

大卫走过去，站在侯爵面前。黑色的身躯动了起来，他嘲弄的眼睛瞟了一眼大壁钟。

"还剩两分钟。一个放羊的竟然用了八分钟来考虑愿不愿意接受美貌而富有的新娘！放羊的，快说，你同意成为这位小姐的丈夫吗？"

大卫自豪地站在那里，说："小姐已经屈尊应求，答应做我的妻子，鄙人不胜荣幸。"

"说得好啊！"侯爵说，"你倒是有求爱的天才，牧羊少爷。如果不是你，小姐没准会碰到更差劲的人呢。现在，只要教堂和恶魔准许，我们就尽快把这件事给办了吧。"

他用剑柄把桌子抽得巨响。店老板应声赶来，双腿打颤，拿来了更多的蜡烛，希望是猜准了大人的奇思异想。"去找个神父来，"侯爵说，"神父。明白吗？

"a priest; do you understand? In ten minutes have a priest here, or – "

The landlord dropped his candles and flew.

The priest came, heavy-eyed and ruffled. He made David Mignot and Lucie de Verennes man and wife, pocketed a gold piece that the marquis tossed him, and shuffled out again into the night.

"Wine," ordered the marquis, spreading his ominous fingers at the host.

"Fill glasses," he said, when it was brought. He stood up at the head of the table in the candlelight, a black mountain of venom and conceit, with something like the memory of an old love turned to poison in his eyes, as it fell upon his niece.

"Monsieur Mignot," he said, raising his wineglass, "drink after I say this to you: You have taken to be your wife one who will you're your life a foul and wretched thing. The blood in her is an inheritance running black lies and red ruin. She will bring you shame and anxiety. The devil that descended to her is there in her eyes and skin and mouth that stoop even to beguile a peasant. There is your promise, monsieur poet, for a happy life. Drink your wine. At last, mademoiselle, I am

给你10分钟,把神父叫到这儿来,要不然……"

店老板丢下蜡烛,立即往外奔。

神父来了,眼皮还在打架,惶恐不安。他宣布大卫·米尼奥和露西·德瓦内斯正式结为夫妻,把侯爵抛过来的金条揣进口袋,然后拖着脚步消失在了夜色中。

"拿酒来。"侯爵命令道,朝店主展开他那不祥的手指。

"斟酒。"酒拿上来后他说。在烛光的映影下,他站在桌子尽头,仿佛一座恶毒又自负的黑山。他转向他的侄女,在他的眼光里,好像对旧爱的记忆全化为了毒计。

"米尼奥先生,"他举起酒杯说,"我把话说完就干杯:你已经和她结为夫妻,她会让你的人生充满危险和不幸。她的血液里流淌着弥天大谎和血腥的灾难。她会给你带去耻辱和焦虑。她的眼睛、皮肤、嘴巴都被附着在她身上的魔鬼控制着,她甚至愿意卑躬屈膝,去勾引一个区区乡巴佬。诗人先生,这就是你期待的未来幸福生活。干了吧!小姐,我终于摆脱你这个累赘了。"

rid of you."

The marquis drank. A little grievous cry, as if from a sudden wound, came from the girl's lips. David, with his glass in his hand, stepped forward three paces and faced the marquis. There was little of a shepherd in his bearing.

"Just now," he said, calmly, "you did me the honor to call me 'monsieur.' May I hope, therefore that my marriage to mademoiselle has placed me somewhat nearer to you in – let us say, reflected rank – has given me the right to stand more as an equal to monseigneur in a certain little piece of business I have in my mind?"

"You may hope, shepherd," sneered the marquis.

"Then," said David, dashing his glass of wine into the contemptuous eyes that mocked him, "perhaps you will condescend to fight me."

The fury of the great lord outbroke in one sudden curse like a blast from a horn. He tore his sword from its black sheath; he called to the hovering landlord: "A sword there, for this lout!" He turned to the lady, with a laugh that chilled her heart, and said: "You put much labour upon me, madame. It seems I must find

侯爵把酒干了。这时女孩发出一声悲伤的叫喊,好像突然受伤一般。大卫端着他的杯子,朝前迈了三步,站到侯爵的面前。他举手投足间全然没有了牧羊人的影子。

"刚才,"他镇定地说,"你把我称作'先生',这是我的荣幸。既然我和小姐已经成婚,你我也算亲戚了,地位上也就更加接近了,所以我有资格在某件小事上和你平起平坐。可以吗?"

"可以啊,放羊的,"侯爵嘲弄地说。

"那么,"大卫一边说,一边把酒泼进那双讥笑他的眼睛,"也许你愿意屈尊和我决斗。"

随着一声咒骂,侯爵大人暴怒而起,来势如号角吹出的气流那般突然。他猛然把剑抽出黑鞘,对站在一旁手足无措的店老板大叫:"拿把剑来,给这个笨蛋!"他转向小姐,笑得让她心里直发寒,说:"小姐,你太让我费神了。看来,我得在同一个晚上,

you a husband and make you a widow in the same night."

"I know not sword-play," said David. He flushed to make the confession before his lady.

"I know not sword-play," mimicked the marquis. "Shall we fight like peasants with oaken cudgels? Hola! Francois, my pistols!"

A postilion brought two shining great pistols ornamented with carven silver, from the carriage holsters. The marquis tossed one upon the table near David's hand. "To the other end of the table," he cried; "even a shepherd may pull a trigger. Few of them attain the honour to die by the weapon of a De Beaupertuys."

The shepherd and the marquis faced each other from the ends of the long table. The landlord, in an ague of terror, clutched the air and stammered: "M – M – Monseigneur, for the love of Christ! not in my house! – do not spill blood – it will ruin my custom –" The look of the marquis, threatening him, paralyzed his tongue.

"Coward," cried the lord of Beaupertuys, "cease chattering your teeth long enough to give the word for us, if you can."

既给你找个丈夫，又要让你守寡。"

"我不会比剑，"大卫说。在自己的女人面前承认这点，他的脸刷的一下红了。

"我不会比剑，"侯爵模仿他的语调说，"那么我们要像乡巴佬一样比橡木棍？好啊！弗朗索瓦，把我的枪拿来！"

侍从从马车的枪套里抽出两支锃亮的大号手枪，上面还镶着银徽。侯爵顺手抓起一把，扔到了桌上大卫的手边。"站到桌子另一头去，"侯爵大叫着，"就算是放羊的也应该会扣板机吧。没有几个牧羊人有这等荣幸，死在姓德博佩杜依斯的枪下。"

牧羊人和侯爵在长桌两头对视而立。店老板被吓得可不轻，一边用手比划着，一边结结巴巴地说："先……先生，看在耶稣的份上，不要在我的店里打！别见血呀……那会把我的顾客都吓跑的……"侯爵用威胁的眼神瞪着他，店老板吓得连话都说不出来了。

"胆小鬼！"博佩杜依斯大人大叫，"别再让你的牙齿发抖了。如果你能行，不如替我们发口令。"

Mine host's knees smote the floor. He was without a vocabulary. Even sounds were beyond him. Still, by gestures he seemed to beseech peace in the name of his house and custom.

"I will give the word," said the lady, in a clear voice. She went up to David and kissed him sweetly. Her eyes were sparkling bright, and colour had come to her cheek. She stood against the wall, and the two men levelled their pistols for her count.

"Un – deux – trois!"

The two reports came so nearly together that the candles flickered but once. The marquis stood, smiling, the fingers of his left hand resting, outspread, upon the end of the table. David remained erect, and turned his head very slowly, searching for his wife with his eyes. Then, as a garment falls from where it is hung, he sank, crumpled, upon the floor.

With a little cry of terror and despair, the widowed maid ran and stooped above him. She found his wound, and then looked up with her old look of pale melancholy. "Through his heart," she whispered. "Oh, his heart!"

"Come," boomed the great voice of the marquis, "out with you to the carriage!

店老板扑通跪倒在地上。他一个字都说不出来，连声音也发不出来了。不过，他比划了几下，好像在为他的店子和客人乞求安宁。

"我来发令。"小姐说，嗓音清亮。她走到大卫身边，甜蜜地吻了他一下。她的双眼晶莹闪亮，脸颊升起红晕。她背墙站着，两个男人举起手枪等她报数。

"一——二——三！"

两声枪响几乎同时发出，烛光只颤动了一下。侯爵微笑着站在那儿，左手指伸展开，撑在桌子的边缘。大卫依然挺直站着，他缓缓转过头来，眼睛搜寻着他的妻子。接着，他披着的外衣滑了下来，他也散架了，瘫倒在地板上。

成了遗孀的小姐轻轻发出一声惊恐的叫唤，跑过去俯身看他。她找到了伤口，然后抬起头来，原来那层灰暗的忧愁又回到了脸上。"射穿了他的心，"她喃喃道，"噢，他的心啊！"

"走吧，"侯爵浑厚的声音说，"给我出去，上车！天亮之

Daybreak shall not find you on my hands. Wed you shall be again, and to a living husband, this night. The next we come upon, my lady, highwayman or peasant. If the road yields no other, then the churl that opens my gates. Out with you into the carriage!"

The marquis, implacable and huge, the lady wrapped again in the mystery of her cloak, the postilion bearing the weapons – all moved out to the waiting carriage. The sound of its ponderous wheels rolling away echoed through the slumbering village. In the hall of the Silver Flagon the distracted landlord wrung his hands above the slain poet's body, while the flames of the four and twenty candles danced and flickered on the table.

THE RIGHT BRANCH

Three leagues, then, the road ran, and turned into a puzzle. It joined with another and a larger road at right angles. David stood, uncertain, for a while, and then took the road to the right.

Whither it led he knew not, but he was resolved to leave Vernoy far behind that night. He travelled a league and then passed a large château which showed

前，我要把你再嫁出去。你得再结一次婚，嫁给一个活人，就今夜。嫁给下一个碰到的人，我的小姐，不管是强盗，或是农民。如果路上碰不到人，就嫁给替我开门的贱鬼。滚出去，上车！"

侯爵看上去难以消气，高大威严。小姐又裹上了外套，装扮得神秘难测。侍从们收起手枪——所有的人都出了门，上了等在外面的马车。巨轮滚滚，声音回荡在沉睡的村庄里。银酒杯旅店里，心神紊乱的老板搓着双手，俯身看着被击毙的诗人的身体；24 支蜡烛的火焰在桌子上空摇曳着。

右岔道

这条路向前延伸了三英里，然后便看不清楚了。它与另一条更宽的路相交成直角。大卫站立着，犹豫了一阵，然后踏上了右边的岔道。

这条路通向何处，他不晓得，但他下定决心在当晚远离维尔诺瓦。他走了一英里，经过了一座大庄园。看得出来，庄园不久前

testimony of recent entertainment. Lights shone from every window; from the great stone gateway ran a tracery of wheel tracks drawn in the dust by the vehicles of the guests.

Three leagues farther and David was weary. He rested and slept for a while on a bed of pine boughs at the roadside. Then up and on again along the unknown way.

Thus for five days he travelled the great road, sleeping upon Nature's bal-samic beds or in peasants' ricks, eating of their black, hospitable bread, drinking from streams or the willing cup of the goatherd.

At length he crossed a great bridge and set his foot within the smiling city that has crushed or crowned more poets than all the rest of the world. His breath came quickly as Paris sang to him in a little undertone her vital chant of greeting – the hum of voice and foot and wheel.

High up under the eaves of an old house in the Rue Conti, David paid for lodging, and set himself, in a wooden chair, to his poems. The street, once sheltering citizens of import and conse-quence, was now given over to those who ever follow in the wake of decline.

才招待过客人。每扇窗户里的灯都亮着，在通向大门的宽敞石路上，客人们的车辆印下了纵横交错的痕迹。

又走了三英里，大卫觉得疲倦了。他在路边歇息，以松树的枝干为床睡了一会儿。随后他又起来，继续踏上未知的路途。

他就这样在大路上走了五天，睡在有大自然芳香的床上或农舍边的干草垛里，吃着农夫们慷慨施舍的白面包，喝着小河里的水或放羊娃主动送来的小杯水。

终于，他走过了一座大桥，在那座微笑着的城市里住了下来，那里被埋没或加冕过的诗人比世界上其他任何城市都要多。在巴黎轻声向他哼唱着充满活力的欢迎曲之下——那是说话声、脚步声和车轮声混合而成的嗡鸣，他的呼吸不禁变得急促起来。

又走过了一段路，他来到孔第街一座老房子的屋檐下，付钱开了房间，坐在一把木椅上，开始写诗。这条街上曾住着有声望的家庭，但现在住的却都是些衰败没落的人。

The houses were tall and still possessed of a ruined dignity, but many of them were empty save for dust and the spider. By night there was the clash of steel and the cries of brawlers straying restlessly from inn to inn. Where once gentility abode was now but a rancid and rude incontinence. But here David found housing commensurate to his scant purse. Daylight and candlelight found him at pen and paper.

One afternoon he was returning from a foraging trip to the lower world, with bread and curds and a bottle of thin wine. Halfway up his dark stairway he met – or rather came upon, for she rested on the stair – a young woman of a beauty that should balk even the justice of a poet's imagination. A loose, dark cloak, flung open, showed a rich gown beneath. Her eyes changed swiftly with every little shade of thought. Within one moment they would be round and artless like a child's, and long and cozening like a gypsy's. One hand raised her gown, undraping a little shoe, high-heeled, with its ribbons dangling, untied. So heavenly she was, so unfitted to stoop, so qualified to charm and command! Perhaps she had seen David coming, and had waited for

街上的房屋都很高大，损毁的外表下面仍然透露着尊贵的气息。但大多数房子都空荡荡的，只剩下尘埃和蜘蛛了。到了晚上，只听得见铁器的碰撞声和人们吵闹着慌忙奔走在一个接一个的旅店找住处的声音。昔日上流人士的豪宅大院现已变成腐臭烂朽的荒淫之所。可是，大卫发现这一带的房租正配得上他寒碜的腰包。不管是白天还是夜里，他都伏案于纸笔之间。

一天下午，他买完食物回到他那简陋的房间，带回了一些面包、凝乳和一瓶低度酒。在楼梯上，他遇见——应该说是偶然碰见，因为她正坐在楼梯上休息——一个年轻的女子。她如此的美丽以至于连诗人的想像都无法与她比拟。她那松散、深黑的外套敞开着，可以看到里面富贵的睡衣。她的眼神随思绪的每一细小变化而变化着，可以在一刹那间从孩子般的浑圆天真变成吉普赛人般的细长狡黠。她一只手提起睡衣，露出一只娇小的鞋，高跟的鞋带散着吊在那里。她美若天仙，生来就不会屈尊俯就，施魔指挥才是她的权利！她可能已看见大卫走过来，所以坐在那儿

his help there.

Ah, would monsieur pardon that she occupied the stairway, but the shoe!the naughty shoe! Alas! it would not remain tied. Ah! if monsieur would be so gracious!

The poet's fingers trembled as he tied the contrary ribbons. Then he would have fled from the danger of her presence, but the eyes grew long and cozening, like a gypsy's, and held him. He leaned against the balustrade, clutching his bottle of sour wine.

"You have been so good," she said, smiling. "Does monsieur, perhaps, live in the house?"

"Yes, madame. II think so, madame."

"Perhaps in the third story, then?"

"No, madame; higher up."

The lady fluttered her fingers with the least possible gesture of impatience.

"Pardon. Certainly I am not discreet in asking. Monsieur will forgive me? It is surely not becoming that I should inquire where he lodges."

"Madame, do not say so. I live in the —"

"No, no, no; do not tell me. Now I see that I erred. But I cannot lose the interest I feel in this house and all that is in it.

等他帮忙。

哦,请先生原谅她占住了楼道,可是,瞧那鞋!讨厌的鞋!唉!这鞋带居然散掉了。哦,但愿先生好心帮忙!

在系那打结的鞋带时,诗人的手指都在发抖。系完后他想赶紧逃开,因为她的存在对他来说很危险。可是她的眼睛变得像吉普赛人般细长狡黠,让他不禁呆住了。他靠在楼梯扶手上,手中紧握着那瓶酒。

"你真好,"她说,嫣然一笑,"请问,先生也住这所房子?"

"是,夫人。我……我想是的,夫人。"

"住在三楼吗?"

"不,夫人。还要高一些。"

夫人的手指动了动,似乎有一丁点儿不耐烦。

"请原谅。我这样问实在有些冒昧。请先生宽恕。打听您住在哪儿,真是太不合适了。"

"夫人,请别这么说。我住在……"

"算了,算了,不要告诉我了,我知道错了。只是我对这所房子很感兴趣,包括里面的一切。这儿曾是我的家。我常到这儿来,

Once it was my home. Often I come here but to dream of those happy days again. Will you let that be my excuse?"

"Let me tell you, then, for you need no excuse," stammered the poet. "I live in the top floor – the small room where the stairs turn."

"In the front room?" asked the lady, turning her head sidewise.

. "The rear, madame."

The lady sighed, as if with relief.

"I will detain you no longer then, monsieur," she said, employing the round and artless eye. "Take good care of my house. Alas! only the memories of it are mine now. Adieu, and accept my thanks you're your courtesy."

She was gone, leaving but a smile and a trace of sweet perfume. David climbed the stairs as one in slumber. But he awoke from it, and the smile and the perfume lingered with him and never afterward did either seem quite to leave him. This lady of whom he knew nothing drove him to lyrics of eyes, chansons of swiftly conceived love, odes to curling hair, and sonnets to slippers on slender feet.

Poet he must have been, for Yvonne was forgotten; this fine, new loveliness held him with its freshness and grace.

往日的幸福却只能是梦想了。这样的借口你相信吗？"

"就让我告诉你吧，因为你没有必要解释，"诗人结结巴巴地说，"我住在顶楼——楼梯拐角处的小房间里。"

"是正面那间？"夫人问，头偏向一侧。

"是背后那间，夫人。"

夫人叹了一口气，如释重负。

"那我就不再耽误你了，先生，"她说，眼睛又变得圆圆的，天真无邪，"好好照料我的房子。哦，现在我只拥有对它的记忆了。再见，感谢你的殷勤礼貌。"

她走开了，只留下一个微笑和一缕甜蜜的芳香。大卫梦游似的爬上楼梯。但他从梦中醒过来以后，那微笑和芳香却一直萦绕着他，从此再也没有真正离开过。这位他一无所知的女人促发了他的灵感，他写下了赞扬明眸的情诗，为一见钟情歌颂的吟唱，为蜷蜷秀发颂出的赋诗，以及为纤足拖鞋构思的十四行诗。

他一定算得上个诗人，因为伊冯娜已经被遗忘了。这位新结识的美人精致可爱，她的清新和

The subtle perfume about her filled him with strange emotions.

On a certain night three persons were gathered about a table in a room on the third floor of the same house. Three chairs and the table and a lighted candle upon it was all the furniture. One of the persons was a huge man, dressed in black. His expression was one of sneering pride.The ends of his upturned moustache reached nearly to his mocking eyes. Another was a lady, young and beautiful, with eyes that could be round and artless, as a child's, or long and cozening, like a gypsy's, but were now keen and ambitious, like any other conspirator's. The third was a man of action, a combatant, a bold and impatient executive, breathing fire and steel. he was addressed by the others as Captain Desrolles.

This man struck the table with his fist, and said, with controlled violence:

"To-night. To-night as he goes to midnight mass. I am tired of the plotting that gets nowhere. I am sick of signals and ciphers and secret meetings and such baragouin. Let us be honest traitors. If France is to be rid of him, let us kill in the open, and not hunt with snares and traps.

风雅把他给迷住了。她身上发出的幽香让他春心荡漾。

一天晚上，这座房子三楼的一间屋子里，有三个人围坐在桌子旁。房间里的这张桌子、三把椅子和桌上亮着的蜡烛就是所有的家具。三人当中有一个人身材魁梧，穿着黑衣。他的表情是透着讥讽的傲慢。小胡子向上翘着，几乎要碰到他那双嘲笑的眼睛了。第二个人是位夫人，年轻而美丽。她的眼睛有时像小孩那样，圆圆的，饱含天真；有时又像吉普赛人那样，长长的，充满狡黠。此时，她的眼睛锐利而充满野心，和任何一个密谋者的眼睛一样。第三个人是个实干者，一个格斗者，胆大心急的操刀人，浑身透着炙热与刚毅。另外两人称他作德罗尔斯上尉。

这人一拳扎在桌上，强压着怒火说：

"就在今晚。今天晚上，趁他半夜去做弥撒的时候动手。我厌倦了没有结果的密谋策划。我烦透了信号、密码、密会和接头暗号。我们就公开当叛国贼吧。如果法兰西需要除掉他，就让我们公开杀了他吧，不用设计陷阱和圈套去引他上钩。今天晚上就

To-night, I say. I back my words. My hand will do the deed. To-night, as he goes to mass."

The lady turned upon him a cordial look. Woman, however wedded to plots, must ever thus bow to rash courage. The big man stroked his upturned moustache.

"Dear captain," he said, in a great voice, softened by habit, "this time I agree with you. Nothing is to be gained by waiting. Enough of the palace guards belong to us to make the endeavour a safe one."

"To-night," repeated Captain Desrolles, again striking the table. "You have heard me, marquis; my hand will do the deed."

"But now," said the huge man, softly, "comes a question. Word must be sent to our partisans in the palace, and a signal agreed upon. Our stanchest men must accompany the royal carriage. At this hour what messenger can penetrate so far as the south doorway? Ribouet is stationed there; once a message is placed in his hands, all will go well."

"I will send the message," said the lady.

"You, countess?" said the marquis, raising his eyebrows. "Your devotion is

干，就这么定了。我说到做到。我亲手来做。今天晚上，在他半夜去做弥撒的时候动手。"

贵妇人兴奋地看他一眼。女人，无论对密谋多么驾轻就熟，对这般粗犷的勇气也不禁卑躬三分。大个子男人则捋着他上翘的小胡子。

"亲爱的上尉，"他说，声音响亮，并习惯地清了清嗓子，"这一次我和你想的一样。等下去是不会有结果的。我们有足够的宫廷卫士，可以保证这次计划万无一失。"

"就今晚，"德罗尔斯上尉重复道，又一拳击在桌上，"我说过了，侯爵，我要亲自动手。"

"可是现在，"大个子男人轻声说，"还有一个问题。我们得给宫廷里的自己人送信，跟他们约好暗号。我们的主力必须跟随皇家马车。都这么晚啦，上哪儿去找信使潜到宫廷南门？里布在那儿值勤，只要把信送到他手上，一切就顺利了。"

"信我来送，"贵妇人说。

"你送吗，伯爵夫人？"侯爵问，扬起眉毛，"你献身的勇气很伟大，这我们了解，可

great, we know, but – "

"Listen!" exclaimed the lady, rising and resting her hands upon the table; "in a garret of this house lives a youth from the provinces as guileless and tender as the lambs he tended there. I have met him twice or thrice upon the stairs. I questioned him, fearing that he might dwell too near the room in which we are accustomed to meet. He is mine, if I will. He writes poems in his garret, and I think he dreams of me. He will do what I say. He shall take the message to the palace."

The marquis rose from his chair and bowed. "You did not permit me to finish my sentence, countess," he said. "I would have said: 'Your devotion is great, but your wit and charm are infinitely greater.'"

While the conspirators were thus engaged, David was polishing some lines addressed to his *amorette d'escalier*. He heard a timorous knock at his door, and opened it, with a great throb, to behold her there, panting as one in straits, with eyes wide open and artless, like a child's.

"Monsieur," she breathed, "I come to you in distress. I believe you to be good and true, and I know of no other help. How I flew through the streets among the

是……"

"听我说！"贵妇人大声喊道，她站了起来，双手撑在桌上，"这幢房子的阁楼里住着一个外省来的年轻人，天真无邪、温驯善良，就跟他在乡下照看的羊羔一个样。我在楼梯上遇到过他两三次，我向他打听过，因为担心他的住处离我们经常聚会的地方太近。只要我愿意，他绝对听我的。他在阁楼里写诗，我想他还梦见过我哩。我说什么他就会做什么。就让他来给宫廷送信。"

侯爵从椅子上站起身来，鞠了一躬。"刚才您还没让我把话说完，伯爵夫人，"他说，"我本想说：你的献身非常伟大，可是你的智慧和魅力更在其上。"

当密谋者们忙于商量的时候，大卫正在润饰他"致楼梯恋人"的诗句。他听见羞怯的敲门声，打开门，看见她站在那儿，心里一惊。她气喘吁吁，好像是遇到了麻烦，无邪的眼睛睁得大大的，如同小孩一般。

"先生，"她上气不接下气，"我来找你，因为我碰到了困难。我相信你真诚善良，而我又不认识其他可以帮忙的人。我跑过了好多条街啊，碰到的都是一些爱

swaggering men! Monsieur, my mother is dying. My uncle is a captain of guards in the palace of the king. Some one must fly to bring him. May I hope – "

"Mademoiselle," interrupted Davis, his eyes shining with the desire to do her service, "your hopes shall be my wings. Tell me how I may reach him."

The lady thrust a sealed paper into his hand.

"Go to the south gate – the south gate, mind – and say to the guards there, 'The falcon has left his nest.' They will pass you, and you will go to the south entrance to the palace. Repeat the words, and give this letter to the man who will reply 'Let him strike when he will.' This is the password, monsieur, entrusted to me by my uncle, for now when the country is disturbed and men plot against the king's life, no one without it can gain entrance to the palace grounds after nightfall. If you will, monsieur, take him this letter so that my mother may see him before she closes her eyes."

"Give it me," said David, eagerly. "But shall I let you return home through the streets alone so late? I – "

"No, no – fly. Each moment is like a precious jewel. Some time," said the

吹牛皮的男人。先生，我的母亲快要不行了。我叔叔是国王宫廷里的警卫队长。我得找个人立刻捎信给他。我可以请……"

"小姐，"大卫打断她，眼里闪耀着想急切为她效劳的欲望，"你的愿望就是我的翅膀。告诉我怎样和他联系吧。"

贵妇人往他手中塞了一封封好的信。

"到南大门——记住，是南大门——然后对那儿的守卫说'猎鹰已经离巢'。他们会放你过去。接着你就到了宫廷南面的入口。重复这句口令，把信交给回答'让他出击，只要他愿意。'的人。这是口令，先生，是叔叔嘱咐我的。现在国家动荡不安，有人在密谋造反，所以在天黑之后答不出口令的人就不能进宫。请先生把这封信交给他，这样我母亲在闭眼之前能见他一面。"

"把信给我，"大卫急切地说，"可是这么晚了，怎能让你一人从街上回家去？让我……"

"不，不行——快去吧。每一秒都跟珠宝一样珍贵，"贵妇

lady, with eyes long and cozening, like a gypsy's, "I will try to thank you for your goodness."

The poet thrust the letter into his breast, and bounded down the stairway. The lady, when he was gone, returned to the room below.

The eloquent eyebrows of the marquis interrogated her.

"He is gone," she said, "as fleet and stupid as one of his own sheep, to deliver it."

The table shook again from the batter of Captain Desrolles's fist.

"Sacred name!" he cried; "I have left my pistols behind! I can trust no others."

"Take this," said the marquis, drawing from beneath his cloak a shining, great weapon, ornamented with carven silver. "There are none truer. But guard it closely, for it bears my arms and crest, and already I am suspected. Me, I must put many leagues between myself and Paris this night. To-morrow must find me in my château. After you, dear countess."

The marquis puffed out the candle. The lady, well cloaked, and the two gentlemen softly descended the stairway and flowed into the crowd that roamed along the narrow pavements of the Rue Conti.

人说，眼睛又如吉普赛人一样细长狡黠了，"我会找机会感谢你的好意的。"

诗人把信揣进胸口，三步并作两步地下楼去了。等他走后，贵妇人就回到了下面的房间。

侯爵那表情丰富的眉毛向她发出询问。

"他去了，"她说，"就跟他养的羊羔一样又快又傻地送信去了。"

桌子再一次因德罗尔斯上尉的击拳而震动。

"真见鬼！"他大叫道，"我把枪给落下了！我不敢把枪给其他人。"

"拿这支去，"侯爵说，从外套下抽出一支锃亮的大枪杆，上面镶着银饰，"没有什么枪比他更厉害了。但要小心看着它，上面有我的纹章和饰徽，我已经被怀疑了。今天夜里我得离开巴黎。明天天一亮必须赶到庄园。你先请，伯爵夫人。"

侯爵把蜡烛吹灭。贵妇人穿好外衣，同两位男士一道轻声下了楼，汇入孔第街狭窄的人行道上那四处闲荡的人潮之中。

David sped. At the south gate of the king's residence a halberd was laid to his breast, but he turned its point with the words; "The falcon has left his nest."

"Pass, brother," said the guard, "and go quickly."

On the south steps of the palace they moved to seize him, but again the mot de passe charmed the watchers. One among them stepped forward and began: "Let him strike – " but a flurry among the guards told of a surprise. A man of keen look and soldierly stride suddenly pressed through them and seized the letter which David held in his hand. "Come with me," he said, and led him inside the great hall. Then he tore open the letter and read it. He beckoned to a man uniformed as an officer of musketeers, who was passing. "Captain Tetreau, you will have the guards at the south entrance and the south gate arrested and confined. Place men known to be loyal in their places." To David he said: "Come with me."

He conducted him through a corridor and an anteroom into a spacious chamber, where a melancholy man, sombrely dressed, sat brooding in a great, leather-covered chair. To that man he

大卫急奔而去。在国王寝宫的南大门前，一支戟顶住了他的胸口，但他的一句——"猎鹰已经离巢。"就让它收回去了。

"过去吧，兄弟，"门卫说，"走快点。"

当他走到宫廷南面入口的台阶时，有几个侍卫跑来抓住他，但一听到口令就只能依判断住了手。其中一个人走上前来说："让他出击……"话还未说完，侍卫当中就起了一阵骚动。一个表情敏锐、有着军人气质的人突然从人群中挤出来,抢走了大卫手上的那封信。"跟我来，"他说，领着大卫进了大厅。他撕开信封读了一遍，然后朝路过的穿步兵军官制服的人招了招手。"泰德洛上尉，去把南面入口和南大门的侍卫抓住关起来。换上我们了解的对王室忠心的人。"他又对大卫说："跟我来。"

他带着大卫穿过走廊和接待室，来到一间宽敞的房间。屋里有个面色忧愁的人，衣服的颜色也是阴暗的，他坐在一张大皮套椅上沉思。侍卫对这个人说：

said:

"Sire, I have told you that the palace is as full of traitors and spies as a sewer is of rats. You have thought, sire, that it was my fancy. This man penetrated to your very door by their connivance. He bore a letter which I have intercepted. I have brought him here that your majesty may no longer think my zeal excessive."

"I will question him," said the king, stirring in his chair. He looked at David with heavy eyes dulled by an opaque film. The poet bent his knee.

"From where do you come?" asked the king.

"From the village of Vernoy, in the province of Eure-et-Loir, sire."

"What do you follow in Paris?"

"I – I would be a poet, sire."

"What did you in Vernoy?"

"I minded my father's flock of sheep."

The king stirred again, and the film lifted from his eyes.

"Ah! in the fields!"

"Yes, sire."

"You lived in the fields; you went out in the cool of the morning and lay among the hedges in the grass. The flock distributed itself upon the hillside; you drank of the living stream; you ate your

"陛下，我向您说过，宫廷里到处都是叛贼和内奸，就像阴沟里尽是老鼠一样。陛下认为我是在胡思乱想。可正是有了他们的默许，这个人才会一直窜到您的门前来。他带着一封信，让我给截下了。我把他带到这儿来，您也许就不会再认为我热切的操心是多余的了。"

"我来问他，"国王说，在椅子里挪了挪。他看着大卫，眼神凝重而迟缓，就像盖着一层不透明的薄膜。诗人行了个屈膝礼。

"你从哪儿来？"国王问。

"从厄尔—卢瓦尔省的维尔诺瓦村来，陛下。"

"你在巴黎做什么？"

"我……想做诗人，陛下。"

"你在维尔诺瓦干什么？"

"照看父亲的羊群。"

国王又动了一下身子，眼睛上的薄膜揭开了。

"喔！在田野里放羊？"

"是的，陛下。"

"你在田野里过日子，在清凉的早晨出门，躺在草地上的树篱之间。羊群自己分散在山坡上寻草吃；你喝的是流动的溪水，在树荫下吃甜甜的黑面包，而且

sweet, brown bread in the shade, and you listened, doubtless, to blackbirds piping in the grove. Is not that so, shepherd?"

"It is, sire," answered David, with a sigh; "and to the bees at the flowers, and, maybe, to the grape gatherers singing on the hill."

"Yes, yes," said the king, impatiently; "maybe to them; but surely to the blackbirds. They whistled often, in the grove, did they not?"

"Nowhere, sire, so sweetly as in Eure-et-Loir. I have endeavored to express their song in some verses that I have written."

"Can you repeat those verses?" asked the king, eagerly. "A long time ago I listened to the blackbirds. It would be something better than a kingdom if one could rightly construe their song. And at night you drove the sheep to the fold and then sat, in peace and tranquillity, to your pleasant bread. Can you repeat those verses, shepherd?"

"They run this way, sire," said David, with respectful ardour:

"'Lazy shepherd, see your lambkins
Skip, ecstatic, on the mead;
See the firs dance in the breezes,

你肯定还可以听见山鸟在树林里啼啭。是这样的吗，牧羊人？"

"是这样，陛下，"大卫答道，叹了口气，"我还可以看到花丛中的蜜蜂，说不定还能听见采葡萄的人在山上唱歌。"

"对，对，"国王有些不耐烦，"能否听到她们唱歌可能说不准，但肯定听得见山鸟歌唱。它们经常在林子里吹哨，对吗？"

"没有哪儿的山鸟的歌声能比得上厄尔—卢瓦尔的甜美的。我把它们唱的歌写到了我的一些诗里面。"

"你可以背一背这些诗吗？"国王问，很急切，"很久以前我也听过山鸟唱歌。要是能听懂它们唱的每一个字，那可胜过拥有一个王国呢。到了晚上，你把羊群赶回栅栏，然后坐下来愉快地吃面包，既平静又安详。你能背背你写的那些诗吗，牧羊人？"

"有一首是这样的，陛下，"大卫说，伴着崇敬的热情，

"懒惰的牧羊人，瞧你的小羊羔；
欢喜若狂，在草地上蹦跳；
看杉树在微风中舞姿悠扬，

Hear Pan blowing at his reed.

"Hear us calling from the tree-tops,

See us swoop upon your flock;

Yield us wool to make our nests warm

In the branches of the – '"

"If it please your majesty,"

interrupted a harsh voice, "I will ask a question or two of this rhymester. There is little time to spare. I crave pardon, sire, if my anxiety for your safety offends."

"The loyalty," said the king, "of the Duke d'Aumale is too well proven to give offence." He sank into his chair, and the film came again over his eyes.

"First," said the duke, "I will read you the letter he brought:

"To-night is the anniversary of the dauphin's death. If he goes, as is his custom, to midnight mass to pray for the soul of his son, the falcon will strike, at the corner of the Rue Esplanade. If this be his intention, set a red light in the upper room at the southwest corner of the palace, that the falcon may take heed."

"Peasant," said the duke, sternly, "you have heard these words. Who gave you this message to bring?"

"My lord duke," said David, sincerely,

听潘神吹奏芦笛宛转飘荡。

"听我们在树梢上呼喊,

看我们在羊背上骑玩;

给我们羊毛筑我们的暖巢,

在枝叶间,在……"

"陛下,"一个刺耳的声音打断他的背诵,"请允许我向这个打油诗人提一两个问题。快没时间了。如果我对您安全的担忧冒犯了您,只好请您原谅,陛下。"

"你的忠诚,"国王说,"多玛尔公爵,久经考验,不会让我生气。"他又缩进椅子里,眼睛上的那层薄膜又笼罩上了。

"首先,"公爵说,"我向您读一读他带来的信。"

"今晚是王太子的忌辰。如果他按习惯去做午夜弥撒,为他儿子的灵魂祷告,猎鹰就要出击,地点在伊斯普拉那德大街。如果他已定于今晚去作弥撒,就在宫廷西南角的楼上亮起红灯,以引起猎鹰的注意。"

"乡巴佬,"公爵厉声说,"你都听到这些话了。是谁让你送信的?"

"我的公爵大人,"大卫真

"I will tell you. A lady gave it me. She said her mother was ill, and that this writing would fetch her uncle to her bedside. I do not know the meaning of the letter, but I will swear that she is beautiful and good."

"Describe the woman," commanded the duke, "and how you came to be her dupe."

"Describe her!" said David with a tender smile. "You would command words to perform miracles. Well, she is made of sunshine and deep shade. She is slender, like the alders, and moves with their grace. Her eyes change while you gaze into them; now round, and then half shut as the sun peeps between two clouds. When she comes, heaven is all about her; when she leaves, there is chaos and a scent of hawthorn blossoms. She came to see me in the Rue Conti, number twenty-nine."

"It is the house," said the duke, turning to the king, "that we have been watching. Thanks to the poet's tongue, we have a picture of the infamous Countess Quebedaux."

"Sire and my lord duke," said David, earnestly, "I hope my poor words have done no injustice. I have looked into that

诚地说，"让我告诉你，是一个贵妇人让我送信的。她说她的母亲病了，要送信给她叔叔，好让他回去看她。我不懂这封信的意思，但我可以发誓，这位夫人既美丽又善良。"

"说说这个女人长什么样，"公爵命令道，"再说说你怎么中了她的计。"

"说她的长相！"大卫带着温柔的微笑说。"那就等于是让言语发挥奇迹。好吧，她既是明亮的阳光，又是阴暗的阴影。她的身材像杨柳般纤细，一举一动都充满着杨柳的优雅。当你凝视她的眼睛，它们会变幻莫测，原本是圆圆的，当太阳在两朵云彩间往外窥探时，它们又微微半闭。她来时，天堂随之降临；她去时，混乱接踵而至，留下山楂的气味。她是在孔第街 29 号来找我的。"

"正是我们一直监视的那幢房子，"公爵转过身，对国王说，"感谢这位诗人的巧舌，我们才有了幅名声败坏的库珀多伯爵夫人的画像。"

"陛下，公爵大人，"大卫急切地说，"但愿我笨拙的言语没有减损她的美貌。我仔细端详过贵妇人的双眼。我敢以性命打

lady's eyes. I will stake my life that she is an angel, letter or no letter."

The duke looked at him steadily. "I will put you to the proof," he said, slowly. "Dressed as the king, you shall, yourself, attend mass in his carriage at midnight. Do you accept the test?"

David smiled. "I have looked into her eyes," he said. "I had my proof there. Take yours how you will."

Half an hour before twelve the Duke d'Aumale, with his own hands, set a red lamp in a southwest window of the palace. At ten minutes to the hour, David, leaning on his arm, dressed as the king, from top to toe, with his head bowed in his cloak, walked slowly from the royal apartments to the waiting carriage. The duke assisted him inside and closed the door. The carriage whirled away along its route to the cathedral.

On the qui vive in a house at the corner of the Rue Esplanade was Captain Tetreau with twenty men, ready to pounce upon the conspirators when they should appear.

But it seemed that, for some reason, the plotters had slightly altered their plans. When the royal carriage had reached the Rue Christopher, one square

赌，她是一个天使，不管有没有那封信。"

公爵目不转睛地看着他。"我要用你来证实，"他不紧不慢地说，"你来穿上国王的衣服，坐上他的马车去参加午夜弥撒。你敢接受这个试验吗？"

大卫微微一笑。"我仔细端详过她的双眼，"他说，"她的眼睛已经证实了。你想怎么样都行。"

离 12 点还有半小时，多玛尔公爵带上自己的亲信，在王宫最西南角房间的一扇窗户里点亮了一盏红灯。12 点差 10 分，大卫从上到下装扮成国王的样子，用外套把头罩住，由多玛尔公爵搀扶着，慢慢从王室向等待出发的马车走去。公爵搀扶他上了车，关上门。马车朝大教堂飞驰而去。

在伊斯普拉那德大街转角处的一座房子里，泰德洛上尉带着 20 个人严阵以待，随时准备着在密谋者出现时给他们猛烈的一击。

但是，不知出于什么原因策划者们好像稍微修改了计划。王家马车驶到克利斯多夫大街，离伊斯普拉那德大街还有一个街区

nearer than the Rue Esplanade, forth from it burst Captain Desrolles, with his band of would-be regicides, and assailed the equipage. The guards upon the carriage, though surprised at the premature attack, descended and fought valiantly. The noise of conflict attracted the force of Captain Tetreau, and they came pelting down the street to the rescue. But, in the meantime, the desperate Desrolles had torn open the door of the king's carriage, thrust his weapon against the body of the dark figure inside, and fired.

Now, with loyal reinforcements at hand, the street rang with cries and the rasp of steel, but the frightened horses had dashed away. Upon the cushions lay the dead body of the poor mock king and poet, slain by a ball from the pistol of Monseigneur, the Marquis de Beaupertuys.

THE MAIN ROAD

Three leagues, then, the road ran, and turned into a puzzle. It joined with another and a larger road at right angles. David stood, uncertain, for a while, and then sat himself to rest upon its side.

Whither these roads led he knew not.

时，德罗尔斯上尉突然冲了出来，后面跟着他那帮弑君凶手，朝马车及随从们猛扑过来。车上的侍卫被这过早的袭击给吓了一大跳，但仍然下车英勇奋战。激烈的战斗声引来了泰德洛上尉那队人马。他们一路疾行，赶来援助。可是，就在同一时间，怒不可遏的德罗尔斯上尉已经砸开了国王马车的门，把枪管抵在车里黑乎乎的身体上，开了火。

这时，皇家的救兵赶到了，大街上叫喊声四起，钢枪嘎嚓嘎嚓响，但是受惊的马已经跑得不见了。坐垫上躺着可怜的假扮国王的诗人的尸体，他被从博佩杜依斯侯爵大人的手枪射出的一颗子弹击毙了。

主干道

这条路向前延伸了三英里，然后便看不清楚了。它与另一更宽的路相交成直角。大卫站立着，犹豫了一阵，然后在路边坐下休息起来。

这些路通向何处，他不得而

Either way there seemed to lie a great world full of chance and peril. And then, sitting there, his eye fell upon a bright star, one that he and Yvonne had named for theirs. That set him thinking of Yvonne, and he wondered if he had not been too hasty. Why should he leave her and his home because a few hot words had come between them? Was love so brittle a thing that jealousy, the very proof of it, could break it? Mornings always brought a cure for the little heartaches of evening. There was yet time for him to return home without any one in the sweetly sleeping village of Vernoy being the wiser. His heart was Yvonne's; there where he had lived always he could write his poems and find his happiness.

David rose, and shook off his unrest and the wild mood that had tempted him. He set his face steadfastly back along the road he had come. By the time he had re-travelled the road to Vernoy, his desire to rove was gone. He passed the sheep-fold, and the sheep scurried, with a drumming flutter, at his late footsteps, warming his heart by the homely sound. He crept without noise into his little room and lay there, thankful that his feet had

知。哪一条都好像通向一个充满机遇和危险的巨大世界。他坐在那儿,眼睛看到了一颗明亮的星星,那颗他和伊冯娜为两个人命名的星。这使他想到了伊冯娜,并开始怀疑自己是不是理智。就因为伊冯娜跟他拌了几句嘴,他就该离开她、离开家么?爱情竟然如此脆弱,甚至嫉妒——这恰恰是爱情的证明——该让它破碎吗?早晨的到来总能让前夜心中的小伤痛得到治愈的。维尔诺瓦全村的人都还在酣睡之中,他有的是时间回家,不会有人知道这事儿的。他的心属于伊冯娜,那里是他心灵所在的地方,在那儿他可以写他的诗,找到他的幸福。

大卫站起来,抖去身上的不安和那曾诱惑他的疯狂情绪。他坚定地朝着来时的路走回去。当他回到维尔诺瓦的时候,想要漂泊的欲望已经荡然无存了。他经过羊圈,羊儿们听到他晚归的步声,都急急地拥过来,冲着他咩咩地叫唤,那熟悉犹如家人的声音温暖着他的心。他轻轻地钻进自己的小房间,躺了下来,庆幸自己在那时候挣脱了踏上陌路的

escaped the distress of new roads that night.

How well he knew woman's heart! The next evening Yvonne was at the well in the road where the young congregated in order that the cure might have business. The corner of her eye was engaged in a search for David, albeit her set mouth seemed unrelenting. He saw the look; braved the mouth, drew from it a recantation and, later, a kiss as they walked homeward together.

Three months afterwards they were married. David's father was shrewd and prosperous. He gave them a wedding that was heard of three leagues away. Both the young people were favourites in the village. There was a procession in the streets, a dance on the green; they had the marionettes and a tumbler out from Dreux to delight the guests.

Then a year, and David's father died. The sheep and the cottage descended to him. He already had the seemliest wife in the village. Yvonne's milk pails and her brass kettles were bright – *ouf!* they blinded you in the sun when you passed that way. But you must keep your eyes upon her yard, for her flower beds were so neat and gay they restored to you your

苦痛。

他太懂女人的心了！第二天晚上伊冯娜去了路边的水井。年轻人经常聚在那里一起听神甫的布道。她的眼角一刻不停地寻找着大卫，尽管紧抿的嘴唇看上去仍然火气不减。他看到她的表情，勇敢地走过去，从她嘴中争取到了原谅。后来，在两人一起回家的路上，他得到了一个吻。

三个月以后他们结婚了。大卫的父亲既精明又阔绰，为他们举办了一场轰动方圆三英里的婚礼。两个年轻人都挺受村里人喜爱的。街上道喜的人排起了队，还在草地上跳起了舞。他们从德鲁克斯请来演杂技的和演木偶戏的人来招待客人。

一年后，大卫的父亲去世了，把羊群和茅舍留给了他。他已经娶到了全村最贤惠的妻子。伊冯娜把奶桶和黄铜茶壶擦得锃亮——喔，看哪！你在太阳光下经过的时候它们的亮光会刺得你看不清路。但是再看看她的庭院，花坛整洁规矩，花儿愉快绽放，于是你的视力又得到恢复了。还

sight. And you might hear her sing, aye, as far as the double chestnut tree above Pere Gruneau's blacksmith forge.

But a day came when David drew out paper from a long-shut drawer, and began to bite the end of a pencil. Spring had come again and touched his heart. Poet he must have been, for now Yvonne was well-nigh forgotten. This fine new loveliness of earth held him with its witchery and grace. The perfume from her woods and meadows stirred him strangely. Daily had he gone forth with his flock, and brought it safe at night. But now he stretched himself under the hedge and pieced words together on his bits of paper. The sheep strayed, and the wolves, perceiving that difficult poems make easy mutton, ventured from the woods and stole his lambs.

David's stock of poems grew longer and his flock smaller. Yvonne's nose and temper waxed sharp and her talk blunt. Her pans and kettles grew dull, but her eyes had caught their flash. She pointed out to the poet that his neglect was reducing the flock and bringing woe upon the household. David hired a boy to guard the sheep, locked himself in the little room at the top of the cottage, and

有她的歌声，真的，你在格鲁诺大伯铁匠铺旁的那棵重瓣板栗树下都可以听到。

但是有一天，大卫从关了很久的抽屉里取出纸，开始咬起铅笔头来了。春天又来了，这触动着他的心。他一定算是个诗人，因为现在伊冯娜差不多已经被忘掉了。清新大地的美丽和精致带着魔力和优雅把他给迷住了。树林和草地散发出的芳香，搅动着他内心奇异的感受。以前他每天带着羊群出去，到了晚上又领着它们回来，安然无恙。可是现在，他躺在灌木丛下，在纸片上拼凑着句子。羊儿们四处散落着，趁他正苦苦地写着诗句的时候，狼群大胆地从树林中窜出来，轻易地就偷走了他的羊羔。

大卫的诗写得越来越多，羊儿却变得越来越少。伊冯娜消瘦下去，脾气暴躁起来，话语也变得刻薄。她的锅碗瓢壶也变得暗淡无光了，但她的眼睛却犀利刺目。她对诗人指出，是他的疏忽导致了羊群的减少，也给家庭带来了悲哀。于是大卫雇了个男孩来放羊，把自己锁在茅舍顶上的小屋子里，写更多的诗。这小男

wrote more poems. The boy, being a poet by nature, but not furnished with an outlet in the way of writing, spent his time in slumber. The wolves lost no time in discovering that poetry and sleep are practically the same; so the flock steadily grew smaller. Yvonne's ill temper increased at an equal rate. Sometimes she would stand in the yard and rail at David through his high window. Then you could hear her as far as the double chestnut tree above Pere Gruneau's blacksmith forge.

M. Papineau, the kind, wise, meddling old notary, saw this, as he saw everything at which his nose pointed. He went to David, fortified himself with a great pinch of snuff, and said:

"Friend Mignot, I affixed the seal upon the marriage certificate of your father. It would distress me to be obliged to attest a paper signifying the bankruptcy of his son. But that is what you are coming to. I speak as an old friend. Now, listen to what I have to say. You have your heart set, I perceive, upon poetry. At Dreux, I have a friend, one Monsieur Bril – Georges Bril. He lives in a little cleared space in a houseful of books. He is a learned man; he visits Paris each year; he

孩天生就是一个诗人，但又不通过写作来宣泄他的诗情，他的时间都用来打盹儿了。狼群很快就发现诗歌和睡眠原来是一回事，于是羊群持续减少。伊冯娜的坏脾气也以同等的速度加剧。有时她站在院子中间，透过高高的窗户对着大卫破口大骂。这叫骂声，你在格鲁诺大伯铁匠铺旁的那棵重瓣板栗树下都可以听到。

帕皮诺老先生是一位心地善良、头脑睿智、好管闲事的公证人，他看到了这一切，因为凡是在他的鼻尖所指的方向发生的事情，都逃不过他的眼睛。他找到大卫，鼓足勇气，对他说：

"米尼奥朋友，我曾经在你父亲的结婚证书上盖了章。如果还不得不为他儿子破产的文件作公证的话，那会让我很痛心的。而你确实就是在走向破产。我要以一个老朋友的身份说几句。你要听好了。我能看出，你的心思都放在诗歌上了。我在德鲁克斯有个朋友，布里尔先生——乔治·布里尔。他住的地方狭小清洁，堆满了书籍。他是一个有学

himself has written books. He will tell you when the catacombs were made, how they found out the names of the stars, and why the plover has a long bill. The meaning and the form of poetry is to him as intelligent as the baa of a sheep is to you. I will give you a letter to him, and you shall take him your poems and let him read them. Then you will know if you shall write more, or give your attention to your wife and business."

"Write the letter," said David, "I am sorry you did not speak of this sooner."

At sunrise the next morning he was on the road to Dreux with the precious roll of poems under his arm. At noon he wiped the dust from his feet at the door of Monsieur Bril. That learned man broke the seal of M. Papineau's letter, and sucked up its contents through his gleaming spectacles as the sun draws water. He took David inside to his study and sat him down upon a little island beat upon by a sea of books.

Monsieur Bril had a conscience. He flinched not even at a mass of manuscript the thickness of a finger-length and rolled to an incorrigible curve. He broke the back of the roll against his knee and began to read. He slighted nothing; he

问的人，每年都要去巴黎，自己也写了一些书。他可以告诉你地下陵墓是什么时候建造的，人是怎样为星星命名的，为什么鸻鸟的嘴又细又长。他对诗的意义和形式的了解就如同你对羊儿的咩咩叫声一样多。我来写封信，你带着信去找他，把你的诗也带上让他读读。然后你会明白是该继续写诗，还是该多关注你的妻子和正事了。"

"请写信吧，"大卫说，"很可惜，你没早点儿告诉我。"

第二天早晨太阳升起时，大卫已经走在去德鲁克斯的路上了，手臂下夹着他那卷宝贵的诗集。中午，他来到布里尔先生门前，掸去脚上的灰尘。那位博学的人拆开帕皮诺先生的信，如太阳吸收水分一般，通过闪闪发光的眼镜片吸透了信的内容。他把大卫带进了书房，在书海中空出一块小岛让他坐下。

布里尔先生做事很用心。在有一手指那么厚的参差不齐卷成一团的诗稿面前，他甚至一点都没有退缩。他打开诗卷，放在膝上，开始读起来。他一个字也不疏漏，一头钻进诗稿，就像一只

bored into the lump as a worm into a nut, seeking for a kernel.

Meanwhile, David sat, marooned, trembling in the spray of so much literature. It roared in his ears. He held no chart or compass for voyaging in that sea. Half the world, he thought, must be writing books.

Monsieur Bril bored to the last page of the poems. Then he took off his spectacles, and wiped them with his handkerchief.

"My old friend, Papineau, is well?" he asked.

"In the best of health," said David.

"How many sheep have you, Monsieur Mignot?"

"Three hundred and nine, when I counted them yesterday. The flock has had ill fortune. To that number it has decreased from eight hundred and fifty."

"You have a wife and home, and lived in comfort. The sheep brought you plenty. You went into the fields with them and lived in the keen air and ate the sweet bread of contentment. You had but to be vigilant and recline there upon nature's breast, listening to the whistle of the blackbirds in the grove. Am I right thus far?"

蛀虫钻进了一颗坚果壳，探寻着果仁。

大卫坐在一旁，不知道该做些什么，如此浩瀚的书海使他禁不住颤抖。海涛在他耳边咆哮。在那片海里航行，他既没有航海图，也没有指南针。他心想，世界上肯定有一半的人都在写书。

布里尔先生一直钻到了诗的最后一页，然后他摘下眼镜，用手绢擦了擦镜片。

"我的老朋友帕皮诺身体还好吗？"他问。

"再好不过了。"大卫说。

"你有多少只羊呢，米尼先生？"

"309只，我昨天刚数过。羊群运气很差。原先有850只，一直减少到现在这个数。"

"你已经有了妻室，生活舒适。羊群带给你许多东西。你赶着羊群去田里，呼吸着清新的空气，吃着甜美的面包。你什么都不用做，只需要提高警惕，躺在大自然的怀抱里，听林子里山鸟的鸣啼就行了。是这样吗？"

"It was so," said David.

"I have read all your verses," continued Monsieur Bril, his eyes wandering about his sea of books as if he conned the horizon for a sail. "Look yonder, through that window, Monsieur Mignot; tell me what you see in that tree."

"I see a crow," said David, looking.

"There is a bird," said Monsieur Bril, "that shall assist me where I am disposed to shirk a duty. You know that bird, Monsieur Mignot; he is the philosopher of the air. He is happy through submission to his lot. None so merry or full-crawed as he with his whimsical eye and rollicking step. The fields yield him what he desires. He never grieves that his plumage is not gay, like the oriole's. And you have heard, Monsieur Mignot, the notes that nature has given him? Is the nightingale any happier, do you think?"

David rose to his feet. The crow cawed harshly from his tree.

"I thank you, Monsieur Bril," he said, slowly. "There was not, then, one nightingale among all those croaks?"

"I could not have missed it," said Monsieur Bril, with a sigh. "I read every word. Live your poetry, man; do not try to write it any more."

"是这样的。"大卫说。

"我已经读完了你的诗，"布里尔先生继续说，他的眼神游弋在书海中，似乎要在地平线上寻找一只船帆，"请看远处，透过那扇窗户，米尼奥先生，告诉我，你在那棵树上看见了什么？"

"一只乌鸦。"大卫看过去。

"这只鸟，"布里尔先生说，"在我想逃避职责的时候，它能帮我一把。你知道这鸟的，米尼奥先生。他就是自然中的哲学家。他因为顺从命运而感到幸福。没有谁有他这么欢喜开心，心满足了，它的眼里是奇思异想，脚下嬉闹自在。他想要什么，大地就为他生产什么。他从来不会为自己的羽毛没有黄鹂鸟那么漂亮而伤心。米尼奥先生，你也听到过自然赐予他的音符，对吗？你难道会觉得夜莺比他更幸福吗？"

大卫站起身来。乌鸦在树上刺耳地哇哇大叫着。

"谢谢你，布里尔先生，"他缓缓地说，"在这些聒噪声中难道没有一声夜莺的音符？"

"如果有，我不可能错过，"布里尔先生叹了口气，"每个字我都读过了。去过你充满诗意的生活吧，小伙子，不要再写诗了。"

"I thank you," said David, again. "And now I will be going back to my sheep."

"If you would dine with me," said the man of books, "and overlook the smart of it, I will give you reasons at length."

"No," said the poet, "I must be back in the fields cawing at my sheep."

Back along the road to Vernoy he trudged with his poems under his arm. When he reached his village he turned into the shop of one Zeigler, a Jew out of Armenia, who sold anything that came to his hand.

"Friend," said David, "wolves from the forest harass my sheep on the hills. I must purchase firearms to protect them. What have you?"

"A bad day, this, for me, friend Mignot," said Zeigler, spreading his hands, "for I perceive that I must sell you a weapon that will not fetch a tenth of its value. Only last I week I bought from a peddlar a wagon full of goods that he procured at a sale by a commissionaire of the crown. The sale was of the château and belongings of a great lord – I know not his title – who has been banished for conspiracy against the king. There are some choice firearms in the lot. This pistol – oh, a weapon fit for a prince! – it

"谢谢你，"大卫再次说道，"我这就回到我的羊群身边去。"

"如果你愿意和我一起吃饭，"这位读书人说，"又不计较失败的痛苦，我可以给你细讲一下原因。"

"不，"诗人说，"我得回到田野去，对着我的羊群聒噪。"

在回维尔诺瓦的路上，他步履沉重，诗夹在手臂下。到村里，他拐进一家叫齐格勒的人开的商店。他是一个从亚美尼亚来的犹太人，到手的任何东西他都卖。

"朋友，"大卫说，"森林里的狼群跑到山上来袭击我的羊群。我得买点家伙来保护它们。你有什么样的枪卖？"

"今天我生意不好，米尼奥朋友，"齐格勒说，摊了摊双手，"只好便宜些卖给你一支，它的价格连价值的十分之一都不到。上个星期我刚从一个小贩那儿买来一大车东西，他是在一次拍卖中从国王的警卫哪儿搞到的。卖的是一个大贵族的庄园和财产——我不知道他的头衔——他因密谋造反而被流放了。拍卖会上有几把上等手枪。这支手枪，噢，简直可以给王子用了！我只卖你40法郎，米尼奥朋友，就算我少

shall be only forty francs to you, friend Mignot – if I lose ten by the sale. But perhaps an arquebuse –"

"This will do," said David, throwing the money on the counter. "Is it charged?"

"I will charge it," said Zeigler. "And, for ten francs more, add a store of powder and ball."

David laid his pistol under his coat and walked to his cottage. Yvonne was not there. Of late she had taken to gadding much among the neighbours. But a fire was glowing in the kitchen stove. David opened the door of it and thrust his poems in upon the coals. As they blazed up they made a singing, harsh sound in the flue.

"The song of the crow!" said the poet.

He went up to his attic room and closed the door. So quiet was the village that a score of people heard the roar of the great pistol. They flocked thither, and up the stairs where the smoke, issuing, drew their notice.

The men laid the body of the poet upon his bed, awkwardly arranging it to conceal the torn plumage of the poor black crow. The women chattered in a luxury of zealous pity Some of them ran to tell

赚十块吧。这儿还有支火绳枪，说不定……"

"就它了，"大卫说着把40法郎甩在柜台上，"装子弹了吗？"

"我这就来装，"齐格勒说，"再多给10法郎，就可以加一包火药和子弹。"

大卫把枪放在外衣下面，走回了茅舍。伊冯娜不在家。最近，她经常到邻居家串门。但厨房的灶炉里仍生着火。大卫打开灶门，把诗稿塞进去，扔到煤炭上。它们在烈火中燃烧时，还在烟道里刺耳地唱着，尖叫着。

"这是乌鸦的歌！"诗人说。

他回到阁楼上的小屋子里，把门关上。村子里安静极了，有十几个人听到了那支大手枪发出的巨响。他们一起拥到楼上，那里冒起了烟，引起了他们的注意。

男人们把诗人的尸体平放在床上，笨拙地把它收拾干净，以遮住从这可怜的黑乌鸦身上掉下的羽毛。女人们交谈着，诉说着无限热切的怜悯之情。有几个还

Yvonne.

M. Papineau, whose nose had brought him there among the first, picked up the weapon and ran his eye over its silver mountings with a mingled air of connoisseurship and grief.

"The arms," he explained, aside, to the curé, "and crest of Monseigneur, the Marquis de Beaupertuys."

跑去给伊冯娜报了信。

帕皮诺先生好事的鼻子也嗅出了这事，他是来得最早的人之一。他捡起手枪，仔细审视镶着银饰的手把，表情中夹杂着对枪饰的鉴赏和对死者的哀悼。

"枪柄上刻的是，"他在一旁对神甫解释道，"德博佩杜依斯侯爵大人的纹章和饰徽。"

15. THE GREEN DOOR
15. 绿门

Suppose you should be walking down Broadway after dinner, with ten minutes allotted to the consummation of your cigar while you are choosing between a diverting tragedy and something serious in the way of vaudeville. Suddenly a hand is laid upon your arm. You turn to look into the thrilling eyes of a beautiful woman, wonderful in diamonds and Russian sables. She thrusts hurriedly into your hand an extremely hot buttered roll, flashes out a tiny pair of scissors, snips off the second button of your overcoat, meaningly ejaculates the one word, "parallelogram!" and swiftly flies down a cross street, looking back fearfully over her shoulder.

That would be pure adventure. Would you accept it? Not you. You would flush with embarrassment; you would sheepishly drop the roll and continue down Broadway, fumbling feebly for the missing button. This you would do unless you are one of the blessed few in whom the pure spirit of adventure is not dead.

True adventurers have never been

假设吃过晚餐以后，你要到百老汇大街逛逛，边逛边考虑着抽完雪茄以后，是去看一场赏心悦目的悲剧呢，还是去欣赏歌舞杂耍那里来点儿严肃的东西。突然，一只手搭在了你的胳膊上。你刚转过身，就看见一位美人勾魂摄魄的双眼。她身穿俄国黑貂皮大衣，满身上下珠光宝气。她匆忙地把一个热腾腾的奶油卷饼猛地塞到你手里，然后一把玲珑的小剪子银光一闪，你大衣上的第二颗纽扣便不翼而飞了。只见她意味深长地吐出一个词"平行四边形"，然后便迅速掠过十字街口而去，还惊惶地回头一瞥。

这可是实实在在的惊险啊。会有人接受它吗？至少你不会。你会烧红了脸，尴尬得很；你会羞涩不安地丢下卷饼，继续沿着百老汇大街往下走，双手虚弱地摸索着那枚丢失的纽扣。你一定会这么做，除非你是那稀有的几个有福之人——这些人纯真的冒险精神还没有消弭。

真正的探险家向来不多。像

plentiful. They who are set down in print as such have been mostly business men with newly invented methods. They have been out after the things they wanted – golden fleeces, holy grails, lady loves, treasure, crowns and fame. The true adventurer goes forth aimless and uncalculating to meet and greet unknown fate. A fine example was the Prodigal Son – when he started back home.

Half-adventurers – brave and splendid figures – have been numerous. From the Crusades to the Palisades they have enriched the arts of history and fiction and the trade of historical fiction. But each of them had a prize to win, a goal to kick, an axe to grind, a race to run, a new thrust in tierce to deliver, a name to carve, a crow to pick – so they were not followers of true adventure.

In the big city the twin spirits Romance and Adventure are always abroad seeking worthy wooers. As we roam the streets they slyly peep at us and challenge us in twenty different guises. Without knowing why, we look up suddenly to see in a window a face that seems to belong to our gallery of intimate portraits; in a sleeping thoroughfare we hear a cry of agony and fear coming from an empty

本故事里这样上了报的冒险家几乎都是利用了新发明的商人。他们出来寻找他们渴求的东西——什么金羊毛啊，圣杯啊，女人的爱情啊，财富啊，还有权利和名誉等等。而真正的探险家却是漫无目的地前行，随时邂逅和迎接未知的命运。一个不错的例子就是"回头浪子"——在他返乡时遇上的事情。

不完全的冒险家——那些英勇无畏、出类拔萃的人物——倒也不少。从十字军东征到帕利塞兹丘陵[1]，他们填充了历史，丰富了小说，也促进了历史小说这门行业的发展。但他们每个人都有目标：赢奖章，进个球，磨砺斧子，角逐赛跑，展示击剑第三式的新把式，把一个新名字刻在奖杯上，因某事与人一决高下——因此，他们不是真正的探险家。

在这个大城市里，浪漫和冒险这一对孪生子总是四处寻觅称职的追求者。当我们在街头徘徊时，他们就鬼鬼祟祟地窥视着我们，还用不下 20 次的伪装来考验我们。不知所以然地，我们蓦然举眸，就看见一扇窗里有一张脸，像极了某个老友；走到一条已熟睡的大道上，一间空荡荡的门窗紧闭的宅子

and shuttered house; instead of at our familiar curb, a cab-driver deposits us before a strange door, which one, with a smile, opens for us and bids us enter; a slip of paper, written upon, flutters down to our feet from the high lattices of Chance; we exchange glances of instantaneous hate, affection and fear with hurrying strangers in the passing crowds; a sudden douse of rain – and our umbrella may be sheltering the daughter of the Full Moon and first cousin of the Sidereal System; at every corner handkerchiefs drop, fingers beckon, eyes besiege, and the lost, the lonely, the rapturous, the mysterious, the perilous, changing clues of adventure are slipped into our fingers. But few of us are willing to hold and follow them. We are grown stiff with the ramrod of convention down our backs. We pass on; and some day we come, at the end of a very dull life, to reflect that our romance has been a pallid thing of a marriage or two, a satin rosette kept in a safe-deposit drawer, and a lifelong feud with a steam radiator.

Rudolf Steiner was a true adventurer. Few were the evenings on which he did not go forth from his hall bedchamber in search of the unexpected and the egre-

里传出了饱含痛苦和恐惧的叫喊；出租马车的车夫不是停在我们熟悉的道边，而是把我们丢在一个陌生的门前，那儿站着一个人，浅笑着为我们打开门请我们进去；一张写字的纸条自圣坛高高的隔栅上翩然落到我们脚边；我们和过往人群里匆忙赶路的陌生人对视一眼，交换着双方的憎恶，喜爱与恐惧；倾盆大雨总是突如其来——我们的雨伞大概可以给满月的女儿和恒星系的表妹遮风挡雨；在每条街道的拐弯处有手绢飘然而落，纤纤玉指在召唤着我们，一双双眸子将我们包围，然后，有关冒险的种种失意、孤独、狂欢、玄奥、艰险的万千诱饵便溜到了我们指缝间。然而我们中间极少有人愿意消受这诱饵。刻板的风俗犹如一根通条自背上直贯而下，使我们遍体僵硬。我们还得继续枯燥的人生；然后有一天，我们迎来了无趣人生的终结，才开始反省，我们的罗曼史是何等地惨白暗淡，它只不过包含了一两段姻缘和放在保险库保险匣内的一枚缎子玫瑰花饰、以及一辈子与蒸汽取暖炉无休止的斗争。

不过鲁道夫·斯坦纳算是一个真正的探险家。他经常在晚上离开他过道旁的斗室，跑出去寻

gious. The most interesting thing in life seemed to him to be what might lie just around the next corner. Sometimes his willingness to tempt fate led him into strange paths. Twice he had spent the night in a station-house; again and again he had found himself the dupe of ingenious and mercenary tricksters; his watch and money had been the price of one flattering allurement. But with undiminished ardour he picked up every glove cast before him into the merry lists of adventure.

One evening Rudolf was strolling along a cross-town street in the older central part of the city. Two streams of people filled the sidewalks – the home-hurrying, and that restless contingent that abandons home for the specious welcome of the thousand-candle-power *table d'hôte*.

The young adventurer was of pleasing presence, and moved serenely and watchfully. By daylight he was a salesman in a piano store. He wore his tie drawn through a topaz ring instead of fastened with a stick pin; and once he had written to the editor of a magazine that "Junie's Love Test" by Miss Libbey, had been the book that had most influenced

找意外事件或是离谱的事情。对他来说，人生里最大的乐事便是下一秒可能碰上的怪事。有时他自愿去冒险，结果却误入歧途。有两次他是在一个车站过的夜；好多次他发现自己沦为机灵又贪财的骗子的囊中物，别人一拍马屁，他就立刻昏了头，结果手表和钱都被洗劫一空。然而他却热情不减，一旦诱惑出现，他都会欣欣然地前往，继续闯进冒险的神奇世界。

一日傍晚，鲁道夫在一条位于老城中心横穿城区的大道上晃荡。两边人行道上的人流鱼贯而过——这群人中有匆匆赶往家中的让人，也有一些心神不宁的人，这些人不回家，他们准备去吃一千支烛光照明华而不实的公司套餐。

这位年轻的冒险家满脸愉悦，他沉着而警惕地迈着步子。白天的时候，他是一家钢琴店的推销员。他的领带不用别针固定，而是从一只黄玉石环中套过去。有一回，他写信给一家杂志编辑，说李泌小姐的《朱丽的爱情考验》极大地影响了他的生活。

his life.

During his walk a violent chattering of teeth in a glass case on the sidewalk seemed at first to draw his attention (with a qualm), to a restaurant before which it was set; but a second glance revealed the electric letters of a dentist's sign high above the next door. A giant negro, fantastically dressed in a red embroidered coat, yellow trousers and a military cap, discreetly distributed cards to those of the passing crowd who consented to take them.

This mode of dentistic advertising was a common sight to Rudolf. Usually he passed the dispenser of the dentist's cards without reducing his store; but tonight the African slipped one into his hand so deftly that he retained it there smiling a little at the successful feat.

When he had travelled a few yards further he glanced at the card indifferently. Surprised, he turned it over and looked again with interest. One side of the card was blank; on the other was written in ink three words, "The Green Door." And then Rudolf saw, three steps in front of him, a man throw down the card the negro had given him as he passed. Rudolf picked it up. It was

他行走途中，人行道上一只玻璃橱里传来牙齿道具猛烈打颤的声音，这声音一开始似乎把他的注意力转移到（带着一抹疑虑）了一家餐馆，因为玻璃橱就设在那前面。可是再一看，就发现了隔壁高高挂着的牙医的灯饰标牌。一个健硕的黑人，穿着花里胡哨的红色刺绣外套，黄裤子，头上戴着一顶军帽，正小心翼翼地把宣传卡发给过往行人中乐意收下的人。

鲁道夫早看惯了牙医的这种宣传方式。往常的话，他会径直走过去，毫不理睬；然而这天晚上，非洲黑人十分灵巧地往他手里塞了一张宣传卡，使得他对黑人的成功不禁莞尔一笑。

他又往前走了几码，并漫不经心地瞥了手中的卡片一眼。令人感到惊讶的是，他翻过卡片，兴致盎然地又看了一遍。只见宣传卡的一面是空白的；另一面用墨水笔写着"绿门"二字。这时候鲁道夫看见离他前方三步远的位置，一个男人丢掉了当他过路时黑人交给他的卡片。鲁道夫把卡片捡起来，看见上面印着牙医

printed with the dentist's name and address and the usual schedule of "plate work" and "bridge work" and "crowns," and specious promises of "painless" operations.

The adventurous piano salesman halted at the corner and considered. Then he crossed the street, walked down a block, recrossed and joined the upward current of people again. Without seeming to notice the negro as he passed the second time, he carelessly took the card that was handed him. Ten steps away he inspected it. In the same handwriting that appeared on the first card "The Green Door" was inscribed upon it. Three or four cards were tossed to the pavement by pedestrians both following and leading him. These fell blank side up. Rudolf turned them over. Every one bore the printed legend of the dental "parlours."

Rarely did the arch sprite Adventure need to beckon twice to Rudolf Steiner, his true follower. But twice it had been done, and the quest was on.

Rudolf walked slowly back to where the giant negro stood by the case of rattling teeth. This time as he passed he received no card. In spite of his gaudy and ridiculous garb, the Ethiopian dis-

的姓名、地址，以及常见的"镶假牙"，"做齿桥"和"镶齿冠"的时间表，另外还有空洞的"无痛"手术承诺等等。

这位喜爱冒险的钢琴推销员在街角踌躇不前，凝神思索着。一会儿，就见他穿过大街，走过一个街区，再穿过马路，融入返回的人流中。第二次路过玻璃橱的时候，他装作没有注意到那个黑人，只随意地接过了递到他手上的宣传卡。他往前走了10步以后，仔细的检查着这张卡片。上面有与第一张卡一样的笔迹，还有"绿门"二字。他前后的行人随手把三四张卡片丢到了人行道上，卡片落地时空白面向上。鲁道夫都把它们捡起来翻看，发现每一张卡上面都印着牙医"手术治疗室"的说明。

"冒险"这只头号小妖不需向它真正的追随者鲁道夫·斯坦纳发出两次召唤。但是，它现在已经是二度召唤鲁道夫了，而且他的要求还在继续。

鲁道夫慢慢踱回巨型黑人站着的地方，他身边是放着嘎嘎直响的牙齿的玻璃橱。这一回，他经过时没有接到卡片。那个黑人

played a natural barbaric dignity as he stood, offering the cards suavely to some, allowing others to pass unmolested. Every half minute he chanted a harsh, unintelligible phrase akin to the jabber of car conductors and grand opera. And not only did he withhold a card this time, but it seemed to Rudolf that he received from the shining and massive black countenance a look of cold, almost contemptuous disdain.

The look stung the adventurer. He read in it a silent accusation that he had been found wanting. Whatever the mysterious written words on the cards might mean, the black had selected him twice from the throng for their recipient; and now seemed to have condemned him as deficient in the wit and spirit to engage the enigma.

Standing aside from the rush, the young man made a rapid estimate of the building in which he conceived that his adventure must lie. Five stories high it rose. A small restaurant occupied the basement.

The first floor, now closed, seemed to house millinery or furs. The second floor, by the winking electric letters, was the dentist's. Above this a polyglot babel of

尽管穿得花里胡哨，荒谬可笑，可他站在那儿，仍流露出几分天然的、野蛮人的尊严，他表情温和地把宣传卡片递给一些过往行人，同时让另一些过客不受打扰地走过。每隔半分钟，他就朗声喊一句刺耳的莫名其妙的话，像极了火车车厢里列车员的吆喝和大歌剧里含糊不清的唱词。这回他不仅没他给卡片，甚至在鲁道夫看来，他那张光亮的大黑脸还朝他露出一种冷淡的、几乎是轻蔑的神情。

这个表情刺伤了探险家。使他从中看到了无声的指责，他就是缺少这种指责。不论卡片上那神秘的字到底意味着什么，黑人倒是从人流中两次相中他作为接受者；而现在，他似乎在指责他还远远没有具备揭开这个谜底的才智与热忱。

于是我们的年轻人退到一旁，避开来往的人流，迅速地扫了一眼面前这幢楼，他认定这次的冒险正是在这里。楼房共有五层，一间小餐馆占据着地下室。

楼房的第一层已经关门了，它好像是一个女帽店或者皮衣铺子。第二层外面带电的招牌明明灭灭，这就是牙医诊所了。再往

signs struggled to indicate the abodes of palmists, dressmakers, musicians and doctors. Still higher up draped curtains and milk bottles white on the window sills proclaimed the regions of domesticity.

After concluding his survey Rudolf walked briskly up the high flight of stone steps into the house. Up two flights of the carpeted stairway he continued; and at its top paused. The hallway there was dimly lighted by two pale jets of gas one – far to his right, the other nearer, to his left. He looked toward the nearer light and saw, within its wan halo, a green door. For one moment he hesitated; then he seemed to see the contumelious sneer of the African juggler of cards; and then he walked straight to the green door and knocked against it.

Moments like those that passed before his knock was answered measure the quick breath of true adventure. What might not be behind those green panels! Gamesters at play; cunning rogues baiting their traps with subtle skill; beauty in love with courage, and thus planning to be sought by it; danger, death, love, disappointment, ridicule – any of these might respond to that temerarious rap.

上便是通天塔一般的招牌，它们互相争斗着，用各种语言标示着手相术士、裁缝、乐师和医生的所在。再往上，万国旗似的尿布以及窗台上白晃晃的奶瓶说明那儿是住宅区。

经过一番观察，鲁道夫敏捷地踏上高高的石阶，走进楼房里。登上两段铺有地毯的楼梯后，他继续往上走，直到停在最高一层。走廊里点着两盏昏暗的煤气灯，右面的那盏离他很远，左边那盏离他比较近。他向近的那盏望去，在灯光暗淡苍白的晕圈中，他看见有一扇绿门。他犹疑了一下，仿佛又看见了那个戴发卡的非洲骗子脸上露出的傲慢的嘲讽。但他还是径直走过去，抬手敲了敲门。

等待是如此地漫长。知道自己面临的是真正的冒险，鲁道夫的呼吸不禁急促起来。在那扇绿色门板后面真的任何事情都可能出现！红眼的赌徒；狡猾的无赖以娴熟的技巧设下的陷阱；佳人恋上英雄并计划着把他弄到手；危险，死亡，爱情，失意，嘲笑——这些东西里，随便哪一个都有可能回应他那鲁莽的一敲。

A faint rustle was heard inside, and the door slowly opened. A girl not yet twenty stood there, white-faced and tottering. She loosed the knob and swayed weakly, groping with one hand. Rudolf caught her and laid her on a faded couch that stood against the wall. He closed the door and took a swift glance around the room by the light of a flickering gas jet. Neat, but extreme poverty was the story that he read.

The girl lay still, as if in a faint. Rudolf looked around the room excitedly for a barrel. People must be rolled upon a barrel who – no, no; that was for drowned persons. He began to fan her with his hat. That was successful, for he struck her nose with the brim of his derby and she opened her eyes. And then the young man saw that hers, indeed, was the one missing face from his heart's gallery of intimate portraits. The frank, grey eyes, the little nose, turning pertly outward; the chestnut hair, curling like the tendrils of a pea vine, seemed the right end and reward of all his wonderful adventures. But the face was woefully thin and pale.

The girl looked at him calmly, and then smiled.

"Fainted, didn't I?" she asked, weakly.

里面传来微弱的沙沙声，门慢慢地被打开了。一位不满20岁的少女站在门口，脸色煞白，步履蹒跚。她松开门把，身子孱弱地摇晃，伸出一只手摸索着。鲁道夫扶住她，把她扶到墙边的一个褪色的沙发上躺下。他关上门，借着忽明忽灭的煤气灯光快速地打量了一下屋子。他能看出的就是，房间很整洁，然而家徒四壁。

姑娘安静地卧着，她似乎昏迷了。鲁道夫激动地环视屋子想找到一只桶。那些人总要在桶上滚来滚去的，就是——不，不对，只有溺死鬼才那样做吧。他开始用自己的帽子给她扇风，这个办法不错。因为当他用圆顶礼帽帽檐儿碰到她的鼻子的时候，她睁开了双眼。然后，年轻人便看清楚了那张脸，发现那张脸正是他心目中熟悉的面孔展览里缺少的那一个。灰色的眼眸坦坦荡荡，小鼻子高傲地向上翘着，还有宛如青豆藤蔓般的栗色卷发，这正是对他惊心动魄的经历最好的归宿和回报呵。但令人伤心的是，那张脸很消瘦，很苍白。

姑娘镇静地看着他，然后轻轻笑了。

"我刚才晕过去了，是不

"Well, who wouldn't? You try going without anything to eat for three days and see!"

"Himmel!" exclaimed Rudolf, jumping up. "Wait till I come back."

He dashed out the green door and down the stairs. In twenty minutes he was back again, kicking at the door with his toe for her to open it. With both arms he hugged an array of wares from the grocery and the restaurant. On the table he laid them – bread and butter, cold meats, cakes, pies, pickles, oysters, a roasted chicken, a bottle of milk and one of red-hot tea.

"This is ridiculous," said Rudolf, blusteringly, "to go without eating. You must quit making election bets of this kind. Supper is ready." He helped her to a chair at the table and asked: "Is there a cup for the tea?" "On the shelf by the window," she answered. When he turned again with the cup he saw her, with eyes shining rapturously, beginning upon a huge Dill pickle that she had rooted out from the paper bags with a woman's unerring instinct. He took it from her, laughingly, and poured the cup full of milk. "Drink that first" he ordered, "and then you shall have some tea, and then a

是？"她虚弱地问，"唉，如果三天三夜什么也不吃，又有谁不会晕过去呢！"

"老天呐！"鲁道夫大叫着跳起来，"等我回来。"

他冲出绿门，飞奔着下楼。20分钟以后他又回来了，他用脚尖磕门板，喊她开门，他怀里抱着一大堆从食品杂货店和餐馆买来的货物。他把东西放在餐桌上——面包和黄油、冷肉、蛋糕、馅饼、泡菜、牡蛎、一只烤鸡、一瓶牛奶和一罐热乎乎的茶。

"真是荒唐，"鲁道夫怒气冲冲地说道，"你竟然不吃饭硬扛着。身体可不能押在选美的赌博上！晚饭好了。"他把她扶到餐桌前坐下，接着问："有没有杯子可以装茶？""在窗户旁的架子上。"她回答说。他端着杯子转身回来的时候，看见她双眼因为兴高采烈而发出了光亮，她开始嚼一大块莳萝腌的泡菜，那是她凭着女人精确的本能从一个个纸袋里翻出来的。他笑着从她嘴边夺走泡菜，给她满满地倒了一杯牛奶。"先喝这个，"他命令道，"然后喝点茶，再吃一只

chicken wing. If you are very good you shall have a pickle to-morrow. And now, if you'll allow me to be your guest we'll have supper."

He drew up the other chair. The tea brightened the girl's eyes and brought back some of her colour. She began to eat with a sort of dainty ferocity like some starved wild animal. She seemed to regard the young man's presence and the aid he had rendered her as a natural thing – not as though she undervalued the conventions; but as one whose great stress gave her the right to put aside the artificial for the human. But gradually, with the return of strength and comfort, came also a sense of the little conventions that belong; and she began to tell him her little story. It was one of a thousand such as the city yawns at every day – the shop girl's story of insufficient wages, further reduced by "fines" that go to swell the store's profits; of time lost through illness; and then of lost positions, lost hope, and – the knock of the adventurer upon the green door.

But to Rudolf the history sounded as big as the Iliad or the crisis in "Junie's Love Test."

"To think of you going through all

他把另外一把椅子拖过来。热茶使得姑娘眼中有了光芒,也让她的脸恢复了红润。她开始大嚼起来,像一只濒临饿死的野兽,毫不挑剔而且凶猛。看来她把年轻人的到来和对她的帮助视作是理所当然的了——好像不是她贬低习俗的价值,而是有什么人的强力给予了她权力,让她摒弃了人类矫揉造作的姿态。但是随着她的体力和舒适感的恢复,某种传统观念又浮现出来。然后她开始讲自己的小故事。那不过是每天让城市都听得打哈欠的千篇一律的故事——商店女店员薪水本来就少得可怜,又被各种克扣弄得更加微薄了,扣罚的薪水都成了商店赚得的利润。她因为生病不能上班,接着就丢了工作,当然就灰心丧气了,再然后——探险家就敲开了这个绿色的门。

不过,在鲁道夫听来,她的往事就像《伊利亚特》一样宏大壮丽,又像《朱丽的爱情考验》一样跌宕起伏。

"想不到你吃了这么多苦!"

that," he exclaimed.

"It was something fierce," said the girl, solemnly.

"And you have no relatives or friends in the city?"

"None whatever."

"I am all alone in the world, too," said Rudolf, after a pause.

"I am glad of that," said the girl, promptly; and somehow it pleased the young man to hear that she approved of his bereft condition.

Very suddenly her eyelids dropped and she sighed deeply.

"I'm awfully sleepy," she said, "and I feel so good."

Then Rudolf rose and took his hat. "I'll say good-night. A long night's sleep will be fine for you."

He held out his hand, and she took it and said "good-night." But her eyes asked a question so eloquently, so frankly and pathetically that he answered it with words.

"Oh, I'm coming back to-morrow to see how you are getting along. You can't get rid of me so easily."

Then, at the door, as though the way of his coming had been so much less important than the fact that he had come,

他长叹道。

"我确实是个苦命人。"姑娘一脸严肃地说道。

"你在这个城市里都没有什么亲戚和朋友吗?"

"我什么熟人也没有。"

"我在这个世界上也是孑然一身。"鲁道夫顿了一下说道。

"我对此感到很高兴,"姑娘快口快语;听见姑娘称许自己痛失亲人的悲惨处境,年轻人不知为何竟然觉得高兴。

很快的,她阖上了眼睛,深深地叹了口气。

"我很困,"她说,"不过也感觉好极了。"

鲁道夫站起身,取过帽子。"那么,晚安吧。好好地睡一觉,这对你有益。"

他探出手,她握住它,对他道"晚安"。但她的双眼却在明明白白地向他询问,那眼神饱含深意,凄婉动人,弄得他不得不开口回答。

"噢,我明天再来瞧瞧你恢复得怎么样了。你是不会那么轻易摆脱我的。"

接着,在门口的时候,好像他怎么找来的不如他来了这个事实更重要似的,她问道:"你怎

she asked: "How did you come to knock at my door?"

He looked at her for a moment, remembering the cards, and felt a sudden jealous pain. What if they had fallen into other hands as adventurous as his? Quickly he decided that she must never know the truth. He would never let her know that he was aware of the strange expedient to which she had been driven by her great distress.

"One of our piano tuners lives in this house," he said. "I knocked at your door by mistake."

The last thing he saw in the room before the green door closed was her smile.

At the head of the stairway he paused and looked curiously about him. And then he went along the hallway to its other end; and, coming back, ascended to the floor above and continued his puzzled explorations. Every door that he found in the house was painted green.

Wondering, he descended to the sidewalk. The fantastic African was still there. Rudolf confronted him with his two cards in his hand.

"Will you tell me why you gave me these cards and what they mean?" he asked.

么会来敲我的门呢？"

他盯着她看了一会儿，想到了那些卡片，心中猛地因嫉妒而感到了疼痛。如果那些卡片也落到别的和他一样具有冒险精神的人手里，会出现怎么样的结果呢？他迅速作出决定，不能让她知道事实的真相。他永远不打算让她知道他已然了解了事情的真相：受极度困苦所迫，她才使用了如此奇异的办法。

"我们琴行的一个钢琴调音师住在这个楼里。"他说，"我给弄错了，敲成你的门了。"

绿门关上之前，他最后看到的是她的微笑。

在楼道口，他停了下来，好奇地向四周张望着。然后，他沿着走廊走到另一头；又折回来，再爬到上一层，他迷惑地四处看了看。这才发现楼里每扇门都刷成了绿色。

他满腹狐疑地下楼，来到人行道上。那个奇异的非洲人还站在那里。鲁道夫手里抓着两张卡，当面质问他。

"能不能告诉我，为什么你要发给我这些卡？它们究竟意味着什么？"

黑人绽开一个大大的友善的

In a broad, good-natured grin the negro exhibited a splendid advertisement of his master's profession.

"Dar it is, boss," he said, pointing down the street. "But I' spect you is a little late for de fust act."

Looking the way he pointed Rudolf saw above the entrance to a theatre the blazing electric sign of its new play, "The Green Door."

"I'm informed dat it's a fust-rate show, sah," said the negro. "De agent what represents it pussented me with a dollar, sah, to distribute a few of his cards along with de doctah's. May I offer you one of de doctah's cards, sah?"

At the corner of the block in which he lived Rudolf stopped for a glass of beer and a cigar. When he had come out with his lighted weed he buttoned his coat, pushed back his hat and said, stoutly, to the lamp post on the corner:

"All the same, I believe it was the hand of Fate that doped out the way for me to find her."

Which conclusion, under the circumstances, certainly admits Rudolf Steiner to the ranks of the true followers of Romance and Adventure.

笑容，给他主人的职业作了一个绝佳的广告。

"就在诺（那）儿，老板。"他指向街的那一头道，"可是，我抢（想）您要是想砍（看）底（第）一场可是有点迟了。"

沿着他手指的方向，鲁道夫瞧见一家剧院入口上方挂着新上演的剧目闪亮的灯饰广告，那剧名就叫作《绿门》。

"他们和我说，千（先）生，这是七（一）流的演出。"黑人说，"管事的代理该（给）了我一块钱，千（先）生，让我发义（医）生的广告时顺便帮忙发几张宣传卡。您打算要一张义（医）生的广告吗，千（先）生？[2]

在住处街区拐角处的小店停下，鲁道夫喝了一杯啤酒，抽了一支雪茄。他走出小店，叼着一支燃着的雪茄，然后扣好外套的纽扣，把帽子往后脑勺一推，坚定地对着拐角处的灯柱说道：

"无论如何，我笃信这是命运之手设计，让我能够找到她。"

在这种境况下，这个推论结果当然使鲁道夫·斯坦纳成为了名副其实的浪漫和冒险的信徒。

1. 帕利塞兹丘陵(The Palisades)，位于美国纽约州东南部和新泽西州东北部。这里有公园，可以徒步旅行、露营、滑雪等。

2. 这个黑人说英语舌头不够灵便。

16. MEMOIRS OF A YELLOW DOG
16. 黄狗自传

I don't suppose it will knock any of you people off your perch to read a contribution from an animal. Mr. Kipling and a good many others have demonstrated the fact that animals can express themselves in remunerative English, and no magazine goes to press nowadays without an animal story in it, except the old-style monthlies that are still running pictures of Bryan and the Mont Pelee horror.

But you needn't look for any stuck-up literature in my piece, such as Bearoo, the bear, and Snakoo, the snake, and Tammanoo, the tiger, talk in the jungle books. A yellow dog that's spent most of his life in a cheap New York flat, sleeping in a corner on an old sateen underskirt (the one she spilled port wine on at the Lady Longshoremen's banquet), mustn't be expected to perform any tricks with the art of speech.

I was born a yellow pup; date, locality, pedigree and weight unknown. The first

我想，读一篇动物写的稿子是不会让你们人类毁掉的。吉卜林先生[1]，还有其他许多人已经证明了这个事实，那就是动物能够用英语表达自己的思想情感，因为这样可以得到回报。还有，如今拿去印刷的随便哪份杂志没有一篇动物故事呢，当然也有例外，就是那些还在连载布赖恩[2]和蒙特·佩利恐怖连环画的老式月刊。

不过，您可不要指望在我的这篇小文章里找到丛林小说的那套，什么熊卵呀、熊呀、蛇卵呀、蛇呀、坦慕卵[3]呀、老虎呀……之类神气活现的文学。一只在纽约一套廉租公寓中度过了大半生的黄狗，睡在屋子的角落里，身子下垫着一条陈旧的棉缎衬裙（就是在朗肖曼女士的宴会上被她洒上了波特酒的那条），你可别认为他会玩弄什么语言技巧。

我生下来就是只黄色的小狗仔，出生年月、地点、身世血统以

thing I can recollect, an old woman had me in a basket at Broadway and Twenty-third trying to sell me to a fat lady. Old Mother Hubbard was boosting me to beat the band as a genuine Pomera-nian-Hambletonian-Red-Irish-Cochin-China-Stoke-Pogis fox terrier. The fat lady chased a V around among the samples of gros grain flannelette in her shopping bag till she cornered it, and gave up. From that moment I was a pet – a mamma's own wootsey squidlums. Say, gentle reader, did you ever have a 200-pound woman breathing a flavour of Camembert cheese and Peau d'Espagne pick you up and wallop her nose all over you, remarking all the time in an Emma Eames tone of voice: "Oh, oo's um oodlum, doodlum, woodlum, toodlum, bitsy-witsy skoodlums?"

From a pedigreed yellow pup I grew up to be an anonymous yellow cur looking like a cross between an Angora cat and a box of lemons. But my mistress never tumbled. She thought that the two primeval pups that Noah chased into the ark were but a collateral branch of my ancestors. It took two policemen to keep her from entering me at the Madison

及几斤几两统统不知道。我能记得的头件事儿,就是一个老女人把我放到一只篮子里,到百老汇和第23街的街口,设法把我卖给一位胖妇人。哈伯德老妈妈吹得天花乱坠,夸我叫得比乐队演奏还好听,说我是货真价实的波美拉尼亚[4]—汉布尔顿[5]—红毛爱尔兰—交趾支那[6]——贪吃的波吉斯猎狐犬。胖女人在她提着的装满了罗锻棉法兰绒样品的购物袋里面使劲摸索着一张五块钱,直到把那钱逼得无处可逃方才作罢。从那时起,我成了一只宠物——妈妈的心肝宝贝。我说,儒雅的读者们,您是否有过如此经历:一个重200磅的妇人,一呼气就喷出一股卡门伯特奶酪和西班牙牛皮味儿,她把你搂在怀里,用她的鼻子在你全身上下乱拱,还一直用爱玛·埃姆斯[7]的调调说着:"哦哦,oo's um oodlum, doodlum, woodlum, toodlum, bitsy-witsy skoodlums?[8]"

我从一只有身份的黄狗仔渐渐长成一只无名黄毛杂种狗,看起来像是安哥拉猫跟柠檬交配出来的。但是我的女主人从没发现,她觉得被诺亚赶上方舟的那两只远古的狗是我祖先的旁系血亲。她还执意要带我去麦迪逊广场花

Square Garden for the Siberian blood-hound prize.

I'll tell you about that flat. The house was the ordinary thing in New York, paved with Parian marble in the entrance hall and cobblestones above the first floor. Our fiat was three – well, not flights – climbs up. My mistress rented it unfurnished, and put in the regular things – 1903 antique unholstered parlour set, oil chromo of geishas in a Harlem tea house, rubber plant and husband.

By Sirius! there was a biped I felt sorry for. He was a little man with sandy hair and whiskers a good deal like mine. Henpecked? – well, toucans and flam-ingoes and pelicans all had their bills in him. He wiped the dishes and listened to my mistress tell about the cheap, ragged things the lady with the squirrel-skin coat on the second floor hung out on her line to dry. And every evening while she was getting supper she made him take me out on the end of a string for a walk.

If men knew how women pass the time when they are alone they'd never marry. Laura Lean Jibbey, peanut brittle, a little

我给您说说我住的那套房子吧。那幢房子在纽约很普通，门廊里铺着来自帕索斯岛的大理石，一楼铺着鹅卵石。这套房子有三个房间——但没有楼梯。女主人出租这间房子时，里面没什么家具，她只在摆了几件常见的东西——1903年产的古色古香的挂毯，一幅彩色石印画，上面画着一间哈莱姆 [9] 的茶室里的日本艺妓、一棵橡胶树和一个丈夫。

老天爷！我真替一个有两只脚的动物感到难过。他个头小，头发黄棕色，还长着一脸和我很像的腮须。他是个妻管严？——唉，他身上被巨嘴鸟、火烈鸟和塘鹅啄得不成样子啦，他收拾吃饭的碟子盘子，听我的女主人喋喋不休地说她把不值钱的褴褛衣衫和松鼠皮大衣搁一块儿晾到二楼的晒衣绳上。每到夜幕降临，当她准备晚饭的时候，就交代他用一根带子拴住我出去遛遛。

要是男人知道女人单独在家的时候是如何消磨时间的，那他们肯定不愿意结婚。如劳娜·利

almond cream on the neck muscles, dishes unwashed, half an hour's talk with the iceman, reading a package of old letters, a couple of pickles and two bottles of malt extract, one hour peeking through a hole in the window shade into the flat across the air-shaft – that's about all there is to it. Twenty minutes before time for him to come home from work she straightens up the house, fixes her rat so it won't show, and gets out a lot of sewing for a ten-minute bluff.

I led a dog's life in that flat. 'Most all day I lay there in my corner watching that fat woman kill time. I slept sometimes and had pipe dreams about being out chasing cats into basements and growling at old ladies with black mittens, as a dog was intended to do. Then she would pounce upon me with a lot of that drivelling poodle palaver and kiss me on the nose – but what could I do? A dog can't chew cloves.

I began to feel sorry for Hubby, dog my cats if I didn't. We looked so much alike that people noticed it when we went out; so we shook the streets that Morgan's cab drives down, and took to

恩·吉比，她脖子上沾着花生糖，还有一点杏仁奶酪，菜碟子也不洗，就能跟卖冰的小贩聊上半个钟头，她会读一大包老掉牙的信，尝几块泡菜，吃两瓶麦芽膏，跑到窗边透过遮光帘的一个破洞再穿过天井偷窥对面的那套房子，一看就是一个小时——也就是这些事儿。离丈夫下班到家还有20分钟的时候，她马上整理好房间，戴好假发，以便不露出什么破绽，然后取出一大包针线活儿做上10分钟，这就瞒过了她的丈夫。

我就在那个房间里过着属于我的狗的生活。将近整个白天，我都躺在属于我的小地盘里，看着那个胖妇人这么消磨时间。有时候我睡着了，做些白日梦，比如把猫们赶进地下室，并朝着戴黑色连指手套的老女人咆哮，这才是一只狗应该做的。接着女主人就拿什么卷毛狗胡扯淡的无聊东西大做文章，斥责我一通，然后又亲亲我的鼻子——我能怎么做？一只狗又不能去嚼丁香叶。

我开始替哈比感到难过，如果我不能把猫赶走，他就得像条狗儿一样去撵它们。我们长得奇像无比，只要我俩一出门，人们就会注意到我们；因此，我俩经常

climbing the piles of last December's snow on the streets where cheap people live.

One evening when we were thus promenading, and I was trying to look like a prize St. Bernard, and the old man was trying to look like he wouldn't have murdered the first organ-grinder he heard play Mendelssohn's wedding-march, I looked up at him and said, in my way:

"What are you looking so sour about, you oakum trimmed lobster? She don't kiss you. You don't have to sit on her lap and listen to talk that would make the book of a musical comedy sound like the maxims of Epictetus. You ought to be thankful you're not a dog. Brace up, Benedick, and bid the blues begone."

The matrimonial mishap looked down at me with almost canine intelligence in his face.

"Why, doggie," says he, "good doggie. You almost look like you could speak. What is it, doggie – Cats?"

Cats! Could speak!

出没在摩根[10]的出租马车每天都经过的大街上，把那儿弄得鸡犬不宁。或者是去穷人居住的街区，爬去年冬天留在那里的雪堆。

一天晚上，我们就像这样在街上溜达，我一心想让自己看起来像一只得了头奖的圣贝尔纳狗[11]，而哈比这个老头子使出浑身解数，使自己看起来绝不可能是杀害第一个在街头演奏门德尔松的《婚礼进行曲》的手摇风琴师的凶手。我抬眼瞧着他，用狗语说：

"为什么你看上去闷闷不乐呢，你这个两边倒的大笨蛋？她又不会亲你，你用不着蹲在她的大腿上，强忍着听她的那些无聊话，那些话能让一部音乐喜剧听起来像埃庇克泰德[12]式的格言。你真该谢天谢地，因为你不是一只狗。打起精神来，本尼狄克，把那些烦闷丢到九霄云外去。"

这个饱受婚姻摧残的老头低头看着我，脸上几乎能看出犬类的聪明劲儿来。

"噢，小狗儿，"他说，"乖小狗儿，看起来你好像是能够张嘴讲话的嘛。你想说什么呢？小狗儿——难道你想说说猫吗？"

猫！这倒是真能说说！

But, of course, he couldn't understand. Humans were denied the speech of animals. The only common ground of communication upon which dogs and men can get together is in fiction.

In the flat across the hall from us lived a lady with a black-and-tan terrier. Her husband strung it and took it out every evening, but he always came home cheerful and whistling. One day I touched noses with the black-and-tan in the hall, and I struck him for an elucidation.

"See, here, Wiggle-and-Skip," I says, "you know that it ain't the nature of a real man to play dry nurse to a dog in public. I never saw one leashed to a bow-wow yet that didn't look like he'd like to lick every other man that looked at him. But your boss comes in every day as perky and set up as an amateur prestidigitator doing the egg trick. How does he do it? Don't tell me he likes it."

"Him?" says the black-and-tan. "Why, he uses Nature's Own Remedy. He gets spifflicated. At first when we go out he's

但是他自然不可能明白，人类被动物的语言能力拒之门外。狗与人类能交流这种事情只能出现在虚构的小说里。

我们对面的房子里住着一位女士，她养了一条杂毛狗。每到晚上，她丈夫用皮带套住狗，牵着它出去遛，当他回家时，总是愉快地吹着口哨。一天，我和那只杂毛狗在门厅碰了面，我撞撞它，要它解释一下。

"瞧，欢欢，"我说道，"你知道的，男人生来就不喜欢当着众人的面照看狗。我还没见过哪条被人牵着的狗不想去舔别的瞧他的人的。可是，你的男主人每天都得意洋洋地走回来，那神气劲活像一个变鸡蛋的业余魔术师！他是怎么做到的呢？你可别告诉我他就喜欢这个。"

"他？"杂毛狗说，"噢，他只是顺其自然罢了。他总是略带几分醉意。我们刚开始一起出

as shy as the man on the steamer who would rather play pedro when they make 'em all jackpots. By the time we've been in eight saloons he don't care whether the thing on the end of his line is a dog or a catfish. I've lost two inches of my tail trying to sidestep those swinging doors."

The pointer I got from that terrier – vaudeville please copy – set me to thinking.

One evening about 6 o'clock my mistress ordered him to get busy and do the ozone act for Lovey. I have concealed it until now, but that is what she called me. The black-and-tan was called "Tweetness." I consider that I have the bulge on him as far as you could chase a rabbit. Still "Lovey" is something of a nomenclatural tin can on the tail of one's self respect.

At a quiet place on a safe street I tightened the line of my custodian in front of an attractive, refined saloon. I made a dead-ahead scramble for the doors, whining like a dog in the press despatches that lets the family know that

去的时候，他也很害羞，就好像轮船上那个玩牌的家伙，每次别人攒起一笔特大的赌注，他都宁可出彼得牌[13]一样。等我们串了八个酒吧后，他就醉倒了，根本不在乎跟在他身后的是狗还是一条鲇鱼。过旋转门的时候，我朝前跨步，想躲开转门，结果还是给夹掉了两寸尾巴呢。"

那条狗说得我茅塞顿开——沃德维尔请记下来——我开始好好考虑。

一天傍晚，大概六点钟的样子，我的女主人交代他快点干活儿，然后带小情人出去透透气。我一直把这名儿藏着掖着，不过她就是这么叫我的。她叫杂毛狗"吱吱"。我仔细想了想，就撵兔子来说，我总算比它强点儿，不管怎么样，"小情人"也算是一个能让人卖弄卖弄的名字吧。

在一条安全的街上有个安静的地方，当我们走到一家迷人高雅的酒吧门前时，我死命地朝门口冲过去，把看护人手中的绳子拽得紧紧的，就像那只新闻电讯中发出呜呜哀鸣声的小狗，它想

little Alice is bogged while gathering lilies in the brook.

"Why, darn my eyes," says the old man, with a grin; "darn my eyes if the saffron-coloured son of a seltzer lemonade ain't asking me in to take a drink. Lemme see – how long's it been since I saved shoe leather by keeping one foot on the foot-rest? I believe I'll – "

I knew I had him. Hot Scotches he took, sitting at a table. For an hour he kept the Campbells coming. I sat by his side rapping for the waiter with my tail, and eating free lunch such as mamma in her flat never equalled with her home-made truck bought at a delicatessen store eight minutes before papa comes home.

When the products of Scotland were all exhausted except the rye bread the old man unwound me from the table leg and played me outside like a fisherman plays a salmon. Out there he took off my collar and threw it into the street.

"Poor doggie," says he; "good doggie. She shan't kiss you any more. 'S a darned shame. Good doggie, go away and get

法儿让全家知道小埃丽丝在溪边摘百合花时掉进了泥沼。

"啊呀！这眼睛真是不中用了，"老头儿咧嘴笑着说，"我那个用柠檬汁染色的黄毛狗要拖我进去喝一口呢。我想想啊，他们本来要剥下他的皮做皮鞋的，是我踩在门口踏脚板上才救了他，多久了呢？我想我要……"

我知道我成功了。他坐在一张桌前，享用着热苏格兰威士忌。一个小时左右，他不停地叫坎贝尔公司[14]的罐头食品。我蹲在他旁边，一边摇着尾巴招呼服务员，一边享受着免费午餐，妈妈在家时，用爸爸回家之前八分钟在一家熟食店买回来的半成品蔬菜做的饭菜可是远远比不上这个的。

等到苏格兰的特产被喝了个底朝天，就剩下黑面包时，老头儿把我从餐桌腿下解下来带到外面逗弄，像渔夫逗弄大马哈鱼似的。在那儿，他解下我的领圈，把它们丢到马路上。

"可怜的小狗，"他说，"好小狗。她再也不会亲你啦。呸，她可真让人害臊。乖小狗，走吧，

run over by a street car and be happy."

I refused to leave. I leaped and frisked around the old man's legs happy as a pug on a rug.

"You old flea-headed wood-chuck-chaser," I said to him – "you moon-baying, rabbit-pointing, egg-stealing old beagle, can't you see that I don't want to leave you? Can't you see that we're both Pups in the Wood and the missis is the cruel uncle after you with the dish towel and me with the flea liniment and a pink bow to tie on my tail. Why not cut that all out and be pards forever more?"

Maybe you'll say he didn't understand – maybe he didn't. But he kind of got a grip on the Hot Scotches, and stood still for a minute, thinking.

"Doggie," says he, finally, "we don't live more than a dozen lives on this earth, and very few of us live to be more than 300. If I ever see that flat any more I'm a flat, and if you do you're flatter; and that's no flattery. I'm offering 60 to 1 that Westward Ho wins out by the length of a

叫马路上的车把你碾死吧，祝你有个好心情。"

我不离开。我绕着老头儿的腿跳来跳去地撒欢儿，快活得像一条在地毯上打滚的哈巴狗。

"你这个满脑袋长虱子就爱追土拨鼠的老家伙，"我对他说，"你这个老绝户，整天异想天开，就知道追兔子、偷鸡摸蛋，难道看不出我不想离开你吗？难道你感觉不到，咱俩都是林子里的狗，女主人就是冷酷的当铺老板，成天摇着洗碗抹布撵得你到处跑。要不就是给我尾巴上绑粉红色的蝴蝶结，还硬要给我涂防虱油！干吗不快刀斩乱麻呢，这一辈子干脆就咱俩给彼此做伴儿吧？"

也许，你会说他根本听不懂——也许他是不懂。可是他却紧紧攥着热苏格兰威士忌的瓶子，静静地站着思索了一分钟。

"小狗儿，"他最终开口道，"我们这辈子可没多少命来折腾，只有极少数人才能活300年。要是我再看见那套房子，我就是个大笨蛋，要是你再回去，那么你比我还笨！这可不是奉承你。咱们打赌，俩人一块儿往西跑，

dachshund."

There was no string, but I frolicked along with my master to the Twenty-third street ferry. And the cats on the route saw reason to give thanks that prehensile claws had been given them.

On the Jersey side my master said to a stranger who stood eating a currant bun:

"Me and my doggie, we are bound for the Rocky Mountains."

But what pleased me most was when my old man pulled both of my ears until I howled, and said:

"You common, monkey-headed, rat-tailed, sulphur-coloured son of a door mat, do you know what I'm going to call you?"

I thought of "Lovey," and I whined dolefully.

"I'm going to call you 'Pete,'" says my master; and if I'd had five tails I couldn't have done enough wagging to do justice to the occasion.

我准能赢你一个达克斯猎狗那么长的距离；我赌 60 块，你赌 1 块。"

没有带子套着我，可我还是在主人腿前腿后跑着，一直跟着他来到 23 街的渡口。路上的猫儿们觉得应该表示感激，因为那四只对它们具有威胁的爪子已无用武之地了。

到了泽西一侧，我主人对一个站着吃葡萄干面包的陌生家伙说：

"我和我的小狗两个，要去洛基山。"

不过最让我高兴的是，老头儿扯着我的两只耳朵，扯得我叫唤起来，他说道：

"你这个不入眼、爱瞎闹、尾巴不长毛又黄皮瘦骨的蹭门垫的小狗崽儿，你知道我要叫你什么吗？"

我想到了"小情人"，我呜呜地哀声叫个不停。

"我就叫你皮特吧。"我的主人说。现在，我就算长五条尾巴，把它们都摇起来也不能表达出我的兴奋。

1. 约·鲁·吉卜林（Joseph Rudyard Kipling,1865~1936），英国作家，出生于印度，1907年获诺贝尔文学奖。
2. 威廉·詹宁斯·布赖恩（1860~1925），美国民主党的领袖，1895年担任《奥马哈世界先驱报》编辑。
3. 作者可能暗指纽约市的民主党组织"坦慕尼协会Tammany"，也称作"坦慕尼厅"。
4. 波美拉尼亚——是在波兰北部与德国东北，位于波罗的海南岸的地理及历史区域。
5. 汉布尔顿——美国标准种驾车赛马，是当今大多数驾车赛马的祖先。
6. 交趾支那——交趾是中国古代对越南的称呼。
7. 爱玛·埃姆斯（1865~1962），美国抒情女高音歌唱家。
8. 哈莱姆——纽约市一著名黑人聚居区。
9. J. S. 摩根（1813~1890），美国金融巨头。这里借喻富翁居住的地方。
10. 圣贝尔纳狗——瑞士的"国狗"。身体强壮，肌肉发达，头大而重。
11. 埃庇克泰德（Epictetus，约公元100年），古希腊哲学家。
12. 彼得牌——属于"全四"（高王牌、低王牌、王牌杰克或成局四种情况时可以得分）类牌戏中的王牌五。
13. 坎贝尔公司——美国1869年成立的一家罐头食品制造公司。1922年改组，成立坎贝尔羹汤公司。

17. AN UNFINISHED STORY
17. 没有结束的故事

We no longer groan and heap ashes upon our heads when the flames of Tophet are mentioned. For, even the preachers have begun to tell us that God is radium, or ether or some scientific compound, and that the worst we wicked ones may expect is a chemical reaction. This is a pleasing hypothesis; but there lingers yet some of the old, goodly terror of orthodoxy.

There are but two subjects upon which one may discourse with a free imagination, and without the possibility of being controverted. You may talk of your dreams; and you may tell what you heard a parrot say. Both Morpheus and the bird are incompetent witnesses; and your listener dare not attack your recital. The baseless fabric of a vision, then, shall furnish my theme – chosen with apologies and regrets instead of the more limited field of pretty Polly's small talk.

I had a dream that was so far removed from the higher criticism that it had to do with the ancient, respectable, and lamented bar-of-judgment theory.

提起炼狱之火，我们再也不会呻吟叹息，也不会再往自己头上堆积灰烬了。因为，就连布道士都已经开始告诉我们，上帝是镭，或是乙醚，或是其他某种化合物，因此，我们这些罪恶的人可能遭受到的惩罚最多也就是个化学反应而已。这种假设倒让人颇感兴奋；然而，正统信仰下形成的持久而巨大的恐惧感仍然萦绕在人们心头。

现在人们只能在两个话题上自由发挥想像力了，而且就算大肆讨论也不用担心会遭到辩驳。一个是说你的梦；还有一个是说从鹦鹉那儿听来的话。梦神俄尔普斯和鹦鹉都不是合格的证人，所以听众也不敢随便攻击你的言论。因此，这个故事的主题完全是无根据的幻想和虚构，比漂亮鹦鹉的饶舌来的更为随意，所以在此我深表歉意和遗憾。

我做了一个梦，与更高层次的圣经考证学没什么关系，倒是与古老陈旧、让人尊敬又悲叹的末日审判论颇有渊源。

Gabriel had played his trump; and those of us who could not follow suit were arraigned for examination. I noticed at one side a gathering of professional bondsmen in solemn black and collars that buttoned behind; but it seemed there was some trouble about their real estate titles; and they did not appear to be getting any of us out.

A fly cop – an angel policeman – flew over to me and took me by the left wing. Near at hand was a group of very prosperous-looking spirits arraigned for judgment.

"Do you belong with that bunch?" the policeman asked.

"Who are they?" was my answer.

"Why," said he, "they are – "

But this irrelevant stuff is taking up space that the story should occupy.

Dulcie worked in a department store. She sold Hamburg edging, or stuffed peppers, or automobiles, or other little trinkets such as they keep in department stores. Of what she earned, Dulcie received six dollars per week. The remainder was credited to her and debited to somebody else's account in the ledger kept by G– Oh, primal energy, you say, Reverend Doctor – Well then, in the

加百列打出了他的王牌,我们这些人中无法跟上牌的就会被安排接受审讯。我注意到有一边聚集了一群职业保荐人,身着庄严的黑色衣服,衣领是从后面扣起来的。可是好像他们的房地产所有权出了什么问题,因此我们当中似乎没人能被保出去。

一个飞警——就是天使警察——朝我飞过来,抓住我的左翅膀。近在咫尺的是一群外表华丽、被安排等待审判的精灵们。

"你们是不是一伙的?"警察问道。

"他们是谁?"我反问。

"这个,"警察说,"他们是……"

哎呀,不相干的事儿已经说的太多了,我们还是说正事吧。

达尔西在一家百货公司工作。她卖的是些汉堡花边、胡椒面、玩具汽车、或是其他百货公司经常会出售的一些小东西。达尔西每个礼拜真正能领到的薪水只有六美元,剩下的则以达尔西作为借方、另外什么人作为贷方记在上帝管理的账簿上——哦,尊敬的牧师先生,你把上帝叫做原能——那么我应该说,剩下的帐都记在原能的账簿上。

Ledger of Primal Energy.

During her first year in the store, Dulcie was paid five dollars per week. It would be instructive to know how she lived on that amount. Don't care? Very well; probably you are interested in larger amounts. Six dollars is a larger amount. I will tell you how she lived on six dollars per week.

One afternoon at six, when Dulcie was sticking her hat-pin within an eighth of an inch of her *medulla oblongata*, she said to her chum, Sadie – the girl that waits on you with her left side:

"Say, Sade, I made a date for dinner this evening with Piggy."

"You never did!" exclaimed Sadie admiringly. "Well, ain't you the lucky one? Piggy's an awful swell; and he always takes a girl to swell places. He took Blanche up to the Hoffman House one evening, where they have swell music, and you see a lot of swells. You'll have a swell time, Dulce."

Dulcie hurried homeward. Her eyes were shining, and her cheeks showed the delicate pink of life's – real life's – approaching dawn. It was Friday; and she had fifty cents left of her last week's wages.

The streets were filled with the

达尔西在百货公司工作的第一年，每星期只挣五美元。如果我们知道她是怎么拿这点儿钱来养活自己的，倒是挺有教育意义的一件事。你说没兴趣？哦，估计你只对大笔的钱才感兴趣。六美元就是更大的一笔钱。就让我告诉你，每周她是如何靠六美元来度日的。

某天下午 6 点，达尔西一边把帽针别在离她的骨髓延髓只有八分之一英寸远的位置，一边对她的密友，珊迪——一个习惯用身体左侧招呼顾客的姑娘说：

"嘿，珊，今儿晚上我和'猪仔'约好了一起吃饭。"

"真不敢想像！"珊迪艳羡地大叫，"嗬，你说你是不是挺走运的？'猪仔'可是个有钱人，老是带姑娘去高档的地方。有天晚上他把布兰奇带到霍夫曼酒家去了，在那儿听高雅的音乐，还能见到一大堆阔佬。达尔西，这回你也要风光一下了。"

达尔西匆匆往家赶。她的眼睛亮闪闪的，双颊呈现着黎明到来之前那种粉嫩的红晕，饱含着生命的——真正的生命的——气息。今天是星期五，她上星期的工资还剩下五毛钱。

rush-hour floods of people. The electric lights of Broadway were glowing – calling moths from miles, from leagues, from hundreds of leagues out of darkness around to come in and attend the singeing school. Men in accurate clothes, with faces like those carved on cherry stones by the old salts in sailors' homes, turned and stared at Dulcie as she sped, unheeding, past them. Manhattan, the night-blooming cereus, was beginning to unfold its dead-white, heavy-odoured petals.

Dulcie stopped in a store where goods were cheap and bought an imitation lace collar with her fifty cents. That money was to have been spent otherwise – fifteen cents for supper, ten cents for breakfast, ten cents for lunch. Another dime was to be added to her small store of savings; and five cents was to be squandered for licorice drops – the kind that made your cheek look like the toothache, and last as long. The licorice was an extravagance – almost a carouse – but what is life without pleasures?

Dulcie lived in a furnished room. There is this difference between a furnished room and a boarding-house. In a furnished room, other people do not

这时正是下班高峰期，街上人潮拥挤。百老汇的电灯闪烁着耀眼的光芒，把方圆几英里、几海里甚至几百海里以外的飞蛾，都引到了这所能把它们烤焦了的学校里上课。男人们穿着正装，面容就像海员之家的老水手刻在樱桃核上的小人一样。他们都转过脸盯着看大步朝前走的达尔西，可是归心似箭的她却目不斜视地从这些男人身边穿了过去。曼哈顿就像一朵在夜间盛开的仙人掌花，现在正要展开它那颜色惨白、香味浓重的花瓣。

达尔西走进一家专门卖便宜货的商店，用最后的五毛钱买了条仿丝衣领。这笔钱本来是该有其他用途的——一毛五晚饭，一毛早饭，一毛午饭，剩下一毛会加到她那微薄的积蓄里，最后五分她会浪费在甘草片上——那种酸得让你的脸抽搐得像在牙痛且持续时间也和牙痛一样久的甘草片。就算是这甘草片也是一种奢侈，差不多算得上狂欢。可是生活没有了乐趣，那还是生活吗？

达尔西租的房间是带家具的，这跟那种寄宿公寓可不一样。住在这里的话，即使你在挨饿，别人也不会知道。

know it when you go hungry.

Dulcie went up to her room – the third floor back in a West Side brownstone-front. She lit the gas. Scientists tell us that the diamond is the hardest substance known. Their mistake. Landladies know of a compound beside which the diamond is as putty. They pack it in the tips of gas-burners; and one may stand on a chair and dig at it in vain until one's fingers are pink and bruised. A hairpin will not remove it; therefore let us call it immovable.

So Dulcie lit the gas. In its one-fourth-candle-power glow we will observe the room.

Couch-bed, dresser, table, washstand, chair – of this much the landlady was guilty. The rest was Dulcie's. On the dresser were her treasures – a gilt china vase presented to her by Sadie, a calendar issued by a pickle works, a book on the divination of dreams, some rice powder in a glass dish, and a cluster of artificial cherries tied with a pink ribbon.

Against the wrinkly mirror stood pictures of General Kitchener, William Muldoon, the Duchess of Marlborough, and Benvenuto Cellini. Against one wall was a plaster of Paris plaque of an

达尔西上楼来到她的房间——位于西区一幢褐色门面大楼三层的背面。她点亮煤气灯。科学家告诉我们，在已知的物质中钻石是最坚硬的，他们可错了。房东太太们晓得一种化合物，和它比起来钻石简直像油灰一样软。她们把这东西塞在煤气灯的火眼上，就算你站在椅子上使劲撬，把手指撬肿了，也不能把这东西撬起来。用发夹去撬也一样白搭。所以我们就叫它撬不动吧。

达尔西点燃了煤气灯。借着这只有烛光亮度四分之一的光线，让我们来观察这个房间吧。

沙发床，梳妆台，桌子，洗脸架，椅子——这些大部分是房东太太提供的，剩下的东西属于达尔西自己。梳妆台上放着她的宝贝——一个烫金陶瓷花瓶，那是珊迪送她的礼物，一本腌菜作坊印发的日历，一本解梦的书，一些盛在玻璃盘里的米粉，还有一束粉红丝带系着的塑料樱花。

在那面皱皱巴巴的镜子旁放着的是基奇纳将军、威廉·马尔登、马尔伯勒公爵夫人、本威努托·切利尼的肖像。一面墙上挂的是奥卡拉汉戴着罗马头盔的石

ري

O'Callahan in a Roman helmet. Near it was a violent oleograph of a lemon-coloured child assaulting an inflammatory butterfly. This was Dulcie's final judgment in art; but it had never been upset. Her rest had never been disturbed by whispers of stolen copes; no critic had elevated his eyebrows at her infantile entomologist.

Piggy was to call for her at seven. While she swiftly makes ready, let us discreetly face the other way and gossip.

For the room, Dulcie paid two dollars per week. On week-days her breakfast cost ten cents; she made coffee and cooked an egg over the gaslight while she was dressing. On Sunday mornings she feasted royally on veal chops and pineapple fritters at "Billy's" restaurant, at a cost of twenty-five cents – and tipped the waitress ten cents. New York presents so many temptations for one to run into extravagance. She had her lunches in the department-store restaurant at a cost of sixty cents for the week; dinners were $1.05. The evening papers – show me a New Yorker going without his daily paper! – came to six cents; and two Sunday papers – one for the personal column and the other to read – were ten cents. The

膏像。旁边是一幅色彩浓郁的石板油画，画上是一个柠檬肤色的小孩正在追逐一只花哨的蝴蝶。达尔西觉得这幅画是艺术作品的最高境界，不过这种认识迄今为止也没遭到任何反对。人们悄声议论着作品的真伪，但这从来不曾打扰她的平静。也没有批评家对她的少年昆虫学家嗤之以鼻。

"猪仔"约好晚上7点钟来接她。趁她匆忙准备时，我们还是悄悄转过来随便闲聊几句吧。

每个礼拜，达尔西都要支付两美元的房租。工作日，她花一毛钱吃早饭。早上起床后，她一边穿衣服，一边用煤气灯煮一杯咖啡和一个鸡蛋。到了礼拜天的早上，她就会奢侈一下，花两毛五分钱到比利餐厅吃一顿牛仔肉和炸菠萝馅饼，还要给女招待一毛钱的小费。纽约城总是展示出过多的诱惑，让你不由得想奢侈一把。中午，她就在百货公司的餐厅吃午饭，一个礼拜花六毛；晚饭却要花上一元零五分钱。晚报——你倒是指一个走在街上不拿报纸的纽约人给我看看？——花去六分；还有两份礼拜天出的报纸——一份是关于招聘的，另一份仅供阅读——又花去一毛。

213

total amounts to $4.76. Now, one has to buy clothes, and –

I give it up. I hear of wonderful bargains in fabrics, and of miracles performed with needle and thread; but I am in doubt. I hold my pen poised in vain when I would add to Dulcie's life some of those joys that belong to woman by virtue of all the unwritten, sacred, natural, inactive ordinances of the equity of heaven. Twice she had been to Coney Island and had ridden the hobby-horses. 'Tis a weary thing to count your pleasures by summers instead of by hours.

Piggy needs but a word. When the girls named him, an undeserving stigma was cast upon the noble family of swine. The words-of-three-letters lesson in the old blue spelling book begins with Piggy's biography. He was fat; he had the soul of a rat, the habits of a bat, and the magnanimity of a cat. He wore expensive clothes; and was a connoisseur in starvation. He could look at a shop-girl and tell you to an hour how long it had been since she had eaten anything more nourishing than marshmallows and tea. He hung about the shopping districts, and prowled around in department stores with his invitations to dinner. Men who escort

这样总的开销就有四元七毛六分钱。哦，一个人总得买衣服呀，还有……

算了，我放弃了。我听说布料非常便宜，用针线就可以拼凑出奇迹来，但我对此持怀疑的态度。我本来打算给达尔西的生活添上这些女人专属的乐趣，它们是公正的上苍制定的不成文却神圣不可改变的天理，可是我只能徒然地举着笔。她去过两次科尼岛，还骑过两次木摇马。不能以钟点而是以年份来计算你享受过的乐趣，实在是让人觉得乏味。

一个词就能概括"猪仔"的一切。当姑娘们给他起了这么个名号时，神圣的猪的家族也因此背上了不该有的耻辱。"猪仔"的传记可以从那本蓝色拼写书中三个字母的单词说起。他很胖，有着跟老鼠一样的灵魂，蝙蝠一样的生活习惯，还像猫一样的博爱。他穿着华贵的衣服，在鉴别饥饿方面可是个行家。他一眼就能看出来，哪个女售货员已经有多久没有享用过比果汁软糖或茶水更有营养的东西了，误差在一小时之内。他在闹市区转悠，在百货公司里晃荡，搜寻着可以被他邀请一起吃饭的对象。在街上

dogs upon the streets at the end of a string look down upon him. He is a type; I can dwell upon him no longer; my pen is not the kind intended for him; I am no carpenter.

At ten minutes to seven Dulcie was ready. She looked at herself in the wrinkly mirror. The reflection was satisfactory. The dark blue dress, fitting without a wrinkle, the hat with its jaunty black feather, the but-slightly-soiled gloves – all representing self-denial, even of food itself – were vastly becoming.

Dulcie forgot everything else for a moment except that she was beautiful, and that life was about to lift a corner of its mysterious veil for her to observe its wonders. No gentleman had ever asked her out before. Now she was going for a brief moment into the glitter and exalted show.

The girls said that Piggy was a "spender." There would be a grand dinner, and music, and splendidly dressed ladies to look at, and things to eat that strangely twisted the girls' jaws when they tried to tell about them. No doubt she would be asked out again. There was a blue pongee suit in a window that she knew – by saving twenty cents a week

牵着绳子遛狗的男人都瞧不起他，他也算是一个另类吧。我不想再浪费笔墨说他了。我的笔可不是打算用来写他的，我也不是什么木匠。

差 10 分钟到 7 点的时候，达尔西已经准备妥当了。她在那面皱巴巴的镜子里看着自己。镜子里的样子看起来真是令人赏心悦目。深蓝色的套装十分合体，没有丝毫褶皱，圆盘帽上还插了一根挺招摇的黑色羽毛，手套也只有点儿不太干净。这些东西——虽然都是她自我克制甚至是用挨饿换来的——却非常得体。

有那么一瞬间，达尔西忘记了一切，只想到自己是如此地美丽。生活就要掀开它神秘面纱的一角，让她领略其中的奥妙。以前还没有哪位先生邀她出去过。但是现在，她马上就要站在尊贵荣耀的光环下了，即使只有片刻。

姑娘们都说"猪仔"挥金如土。一会儿肯定会有一顿盛餐和美妙的音乐，能看到穿着华丽的妇人们，能吃到姑娘们一谈论起来下巴都会抽的那些食物。毋庸置疑，她以后还会再次被邀请。她知道一个橱窗里有件蓝色丝绸套装。要是一个礼拜能攒下两毛

instead of ten, in – let's see – Oh, it would run into years! But there was a second-hand store in Seventh Avenue where –

Somebody knocked at the door. Dulcie opened it. The landlady stood there with a spurious smile, sniffing for cooking by stolen gas.

"A gentleman's downstairs to see you," she said. "Name is Mr. Wiggins."

By such epithet was Piggy known to unfortunate ones who had to take him seriously.

Dulcie turned to the dresser to get her handkerchief; and then she stopped still, and bit her underlip hard. While looking in her mirror she had seen fairyland and herself, a princess, just awakening from a long slumber. She had forgotten one that was watching her with sad, beautiful, stern eyes – the only one there was to approve or condemn what she did. Straight and slender and tall, with a look of sorrowful reproach on his handsome, melancholy face, General Kitchener fixed his wonderful eyes on her out of his gilt photograph frame on the dresser.

Dulcie turned like an automatic doll to the landlady.

"Tell him I can't go," she said dully. "Tell him I'm sick, or something. Tell

而不是一毛，多长时间才能——得多少年呢！不过，在第七大道有家二手货铺子，那儿有……

有人在敲门。达尔西开了门。女房东满脸假笑地站在那儿，鼻子拼命在闻有没有人偷用煤气在煮东西。

"楼下有位先生在等你，"她说，"他的名字是威金斯。"

有人不幸地把"猪仔"当作正人君子时，他就使用这个称号。

达尔西转身去梳妆台取她的手帕。突然，她停下了，用力地咬着下唇。刚才照镜子的时候，她看到了仙境乐园，看到自己是一位公主，才刚刚从漫长的睡眠里苏醒过来，但她完全忘了，有人在用忧郁、美丽却饱含严厉的眼睛看着她。惟一一个对她的所作所为进行褒贬的人。他身材修长笔挺，英俊而忧郁的脸上布满了悲伤的责备，正从烫金相框里用那双令人惊奇的双眼盯着梳妆台。这个人就是基奇纳将军。

达尔西转过身来面对着女房东，像个机械的洋娃娃。

"请告诉他我不能去，"她愣愣地说，"就说我病了吧，或

him I'm not going out."

After the door was closed and locked, Dulcie fell upon her bed, crushing her black tip, and cried for ten minutes. General Kitchener was her only friend. He was Dulcie's ideal of a gallant knight. He looked as if he might have a secret sorrow, and his wonderful moustache was a dream, and she was a little afraid of that stern yet tender look in his eyes. She used to have little fancies that he would call at the house sometime, and ask for her, with his sword clanking against his high boots. Once, when a boy was rattling a piece of chain against a lamp-post she had opened the window and looked out. But there was no use. She knew that General Kitchener was away over in Japan, leading his army against the savage Turks; and he would never step out of his gilt frame for her. Yet one look from him had vanquished Piggy that night. Yes, for that night.

When her cry was over Dulcie got up and took off her best dress, and put on her old blue kimono. She wanted no dinner. She sang two verses of "Sammy." Then she became intensely interested in a little red speck on the side of her nose. And after that was attended to, she drew up a

者怎么都行。告诉他我不去了。"

把门关上又锁好以后，达尔西一头栽在床上，哭了有10分钟，把帽子上的黑羽毛都压坏了。基奇纳将军是她惟一的朋友，她心中理想的英勇骑士。他看起来内心好像隐藏着什么伤心事，他那把令人惊叹的胡须更是让人痴迷。她甚至有点害怕他眼睛中流露出来的温柔却严厉的神色。从前她经常存有小小的幻想，幻想他穿着高筒靴来到这幢房子找她，向她求爱，他佩戴的长剑碰撞着靴子喀拉作响。曾经有一次，一个男孩用一条铁链在路灯杆子上弄得咔嗒响，她还打开窗子看了又看，但丝毫没用。她知道，基奇纳将军正在遥远的日本，率领着他的大军跟野蛮的土耳其人开战，他不可能从烫金像框里走出来向她求爱。但是，这天晚上他用一个眼神就击退了"猪仔"。是的，这天晚上就是这样的。

哭完以后，达尔西站起来脱下她最好的装扮，换上蓝色的旧睡衣。她什么也不想吃。她唱了两节《萨米》，然后又专注于鼻子一边的一个小粉刺。都处理完以后，她将一把椅子拉到摇晃的桌子旁，用一副旧牌给自己算命。

chair to the rickety table, and told her fortune with an old deck of cards.

"The horrid, impudent thing!" she said aloud. "And I never gave him a word or a look to make him think it!"

At nine o'clock Dulcie took a tin box of crackers and a little pot of raspberry jam out of her trunk, and had a feast. She offered General Kitchener some jam on a cracker; but he only looked at her as the sphinx would have looked at a butterfly – if there are butterflies in the desert.

"Don't eat it if you don't want to," said Dulcie. "And don't put on so many airs and scold so with your eyes. I wonder if you'd be so superior and snippy if you had to live on six dollars a week."

It was not a good sign for Dulcie to be rude to General Kitchener. And then she turned Benvenuto Cellini face downward with a severe gesture. But that was not inexcusable; for she had always thought he was Henry VIII, and she did not approve of him.

At half-past nine Dulcie took a last look at the pictures on the dresser, turned out the light, and skipped into bed. It's an awful thing to go to bed with a good-night look at General Kitchener, William Muldoon, the Duchess of

"多可怕，多厚颜无耻的人啊！"她大吼道，"我可是一个字、一个眼色都没有暗示过他，他居然认为我会跟他去吃饭！"

9点钟的时候，达尔西从箱子里取出一盒饼干和一小罐山莓酱，好好享受了一番。她用饼干蘸了些山莓酱递给基奇纳将军吃，可他只是看着她，就像狮身人面像看着蝴蝶那样——如果沙漠里有蝴蝶的话。

"不想吃就算了，"达尔西说，"别那么自视清高，拿你的眼睛责怪我。我倒要看看，要是你也一礼拜只挣6块钱，你还不会这么高高在上、傲慢无礼！"

达尔西对基奇纳将军这么粗鲁无礼，可不是什么好迹象。接着，她猛地把本韦努托·切利尼的像翻扣下来。这也是可以理解的，因为她一直觉得他就是亨利八世，而她很不赞成亨利八世。

9：30，达尔西最后看了一眼梳妆台上的画像，熄灭了灯，跳上床去。睡觉前只能用眼神跟基奇纳将军、威廉·马尔登、马尔伯勒公爵夫人以及本韦努托·切利尼道晚安真的很糟糕。实际上，

Marlborough, and Benvenuto Cellini. This story really doesn't get anywhere at all. The rest of it comes later – sometime when Piggy asks Dulcie again to dine with him, and she is feeling lonelier than usual, and General Kitchener happens to be looking the other way; and then –

As I said before, I dreamed that I was standing near a crowd of prosperous-looking angels, and a policeman took me by the wing and asked if I belonged with them.

"Who are they?" I asked.

"Why," said he, "they are the men who hired working-girls, and paid 'em five or six dollars a week to live on. Are you one of the bunch?"

"Not on your immortality," said I. "I'm only the fellow that set fire to an orphan asylum, and murdered a blind man for his pennies."

这个故事本来就没有什么结局。剩下的情节后来还是发生了——有一次，"猪仔"又请达尔西出去吃饭，她那时恰好比往常感觉更加孤独，而基奇纳将军又正好在看另一个方向，接着……

前面说过了，我梦见自己站在一群有着华丽外表的天使旁边，一个警察抓住我的翅膀，问我跟他们是不是一伙。

"他们是谁？"我问。

"噢，"他说，"他们就是雇佣打工女的那些人，每礼拜只给五六块钱让她们过活。你也是他们一伙的吗？"

"我发誓我不是，"我说，"我只不过是个放火烧了个孤儿院，还为几个便士谋害过一个瞎子的人。"

18. AN ADJUSTMENT OF NATURE
18. 艺术加工

In an art exhibition the other day I saw a painting that had been sold for $5,000. The painter was a young scrub out of the West named Kraft, who had a favourite food and a pet theory. His pabulum was an unquenchable belief in the Unerring Artistic Adjustment of Nature. His theory was fixed around corned-beef hash with poached egg. There was a story behind the picture, so I went home and let it drip out of a fountain-pen. The idea of Kraft – but that is not the beginning of the story.

Three years ago Kraft, Bill Judkins (a poet), and I took our meals at Cypher's, on Eighth Avenue. I say "took." When we had money, Cypher got it "off of" us, as he expressed it. We had no credit; we went in, called for food and ate it. We paid or we did not pay. We had confidence in Cypher's sullenness end smouldering ferocity. Deep down in his sunless soul he was either a prince, a fool or an artist. He sat at a worm-eaten desk,

前些天我在画展上看见一幅画，这幅画卖了 5 000 元。画它的年轻画家叫克拉弗特，是个从西部来的三流货色。这个人只对一种食物情有独钟，还有一套喜爱的理论。他坚信所有天然的东西必须进行艺术加工，这个理论就是他的精神食粮，他相信这它绝对正确。这个理论以一道菜为基础，即腌牛肉肉末炒土豆泥配水煮荷包蛋。这幅画背后还有个故事，于是我回家拿笔记了下来。克拉弗特的想法——不过，本故事可不是从这里开始的。

三年前，克拉弗特、比尔·贾金斯（一位诗人）和我在第八街的塞弗尔餐馆用餐。我说"用餐"，如果我们手头宽裕的话。塞弗尔把我们的钱"拿走"了，他是这么说的。我们从不赊账。我们进餐馆然后叫吃的，吃掉端上的饭菜后，我们要么付钱要么不付。我们确信塞弗尔会脸色阴郁，心里闷烧着一股狠劲。在他阴郁的灵魂深处，他或者是个王子，或

covered with files of waiters' checks so old that I was sure the bottomest one was for clams that Hendrik Hudson had eaten and paid for. Cypher had the power, in common with Napoleon III. and the goggle-eyed perch, of throwing a film over his eyes, rendering opaque the windows of his soul. Once when we left him unpaid, with egregious excuses, I looked back and saw him shaking with inaudible laughter behind his film. Now and then we paid up back scores.

But the chief thing at Cypher's was Milly. Milly was a waitress. She was a grand example of Kraft's theory of the artistic adjustment of nature. She belonged, largely, to waiting, as Minerva did to the art of scrapping, or Venus to the science of serious flirtation. Pedestalled and in bronze she might have stood with the noblest of her heroic sisters as "Liver-and-Bacon Enlivening the World." She belonged to Cypher's. You expected to see her colossal figure loom through that reeking blue cloud of smoke from frying fat just as you expect the Palisades to appear through a drifting

者是个傻瓜，抑或是个艺术家。他坐在一张被虫蛀得千疮百孔的办公桌前，桌上堆满一摞一摞的账单，这些已经是陈年老账。我敢说，最下面那张一定是亨利·哈德逊[1]吃牡蛎后付的账单。塞弗尔有拿破仑三世[2]和鼓眼鲈鱼一样的本领，他能给自己的眼睛罩上一层膜，糊上这对心灵的窗户。有一回，我们随口胡诌了一些借口没给饭钱就溜出了餐馆，出门前我回头望了他一眼，看见他正藏在那层膜后面无声地大笑，笑得全身颤颤。当然我们有时也会把以往赊欠的费用一次付清。

不过，要说塞弗尔餐馆里最主要的东西，那还得算是米丽。米丽是个女服务员，她算得上是克拉弗特艺术加工理论的极佳典范。在很大程度上来讲，她天生适合于跑堂这一行，正如密涅瓦[3]擅长于拆毁艺术，维纳斯擅长于严肃调情科学。如果用铜浇铸，装上基座，她完全可以成为一座昭示"腊肉炒猪肝使生活大放异彩"的神像，全然不会逊色于她那些英雄姊妹中最高贵的一个。她属于塞弗尔餐馆。你期待着瞧见她那健硕的身躯隐隐约约地出没于炸肥肉时腾起的臭气熏天的

Hudson River fog. There amid the steam of vegetables and the vapours of acres of "ham and," the crash of crockery, the clatter of steel, the screaming of "short orders," the cries of the hungering and all the horrid tumult of feeding man, surrounded by swarms of the buzzing winged beasts bequeathed us by Pharaoh, Milly steered her magnificent way like some great liner cleaving among the canoes of howling savages.

Our Goddess of Grub was built on lines so majestic that they could be followed only with awe. Her sleeves were always rolled above her elbows. She could have taken us three musketeers in her two hands and dropped us out of the window. She had seen fewer years than any of us, but she was of such superb Evehood and simplicity that she mothered us from the beginning. Cypher's store of eatables she poured out upon us with royal indifference to price and quantity, as from a cornucopia that knew no exhaustion. Her voice rang like a great silver bell; her smile was many-toothed

蓝色烟雾之中，正如你渴望帕利塞德出现在缓缓游移的哈德逊河的浓稠烟雾中一般。餐馆里，米丽身陷于炒菜冒出的热气、成堆的"火腿"腾起的蒸汽中，隐没在杯碟的碎裂声、金属撞击的响声、喊"快餐"的尖利吆喝声、肚子饿扁了的食客的咒骂声以及食客用餐时发出的所有让人恶心的喧嚣与嘈杂声中，四周还充斥着成群的法老遗留给我们的嗡嗡嘤嘤长了翅膀的野生动物，而她总是优雅迷人地穿梭来去，宛若一艘巨轮穿行在怒号不止的野蛮人所乘坐的独木舟中一样。

我们这些穷酸文人的女神以几行诗为支撑，这些诗行宏伟壮美，我们只得满怀敬畏地膜拜。米丽总把两只袖子高高挽起。她能用两只手把我们三个滑膛枪手提起来丢到窗外去。她比我们中的任何一个都小，可她率性自然，如夏娃一般单纯，所以她一开始就像母亲一样对我们。她把塞佛尔餐馆里能吃的东西一股脑儿端出来给我们吃，全然不顾其价格之昂贵、分量之多，仿佛餐馆是永不穷尽的科纽考皮亚[4]。她的声音银铃般动听；她总面带笑容，而且一笑便露出一大排白牙；她

and frequent; she seemed like a yellow sunrise on mountain tops. I never saw her but I thought of the Yosemite. And yet, somehow, I could never think of her as existing outside of Cypher's. There nature had placed her, and she had taken root and grown mightily. She seemed happy, and took her few poor dollars on Saturday nights with the flushed pleasure of a child that receives an unexpected donation.

It was Kraft who first voiced the fear that each of us must have held latently. It came up apropos, of course, of certain questions of art at which we were hammering. One of us compared the harmony existing between a Haydn symphony and pistache ice cream to the exquisite congruity between Milly and Cypher's.

"There is a certain fate hanging over Milly," said Kraft, "and if it overtakes her she is lost to Cypher's and to us."

"She will grow fat?" asked Judkins, fearsomely.

"She will go to night school and become refined?" I ventured anxiously.

"It is this," said Kraft, punctuating in a puddle of spilled coffee with a stiff fore-

就像刚在山顶上升起的暖黄色朝阳，一见到她我就想起约塞米蒂。不知为何，我很难想像她如果离开塞弗尔餐馆将如何生存。老天把她搁置在餐馆里，她就在那里扎根成长。她看起来倒很快活，一到周六晚上领到那几块少得可怜的工钱就乐得满脸通红，活像个意外收到红包的小孩子。

克拉弗特第一个直言指出，我们三人中每人心中都有些惴惴不安。当然，它是与我们正潜心钻研的一个艺术问题息息相关的。我们之中有个人拿存在于海顿[5]交响乐和阿月浑子果仁冰激凌之间的和谐感同米丽和塞弗尔餐馆之间的微妙和谐相比较。

"米丽无法逃脱某种宿命，"克拉弗特说，"如果她臣服于这种命运，那么塞弗尔餐馆和我们都将失去她。"

"她会长胖么？"贾金斯小心翼翼地问。

"她会去读夜校，变得优雅起来么？"我也不无忧虑地冒出一句。

"是这样的，"克拉弗特说着，边用一根僵硬的食指蘸着一

finger. "Caesar had his Brutus – the cotton has its bollworm, the chorus girl has her Pittsburger, the summer boarder has his poison ivy, the hero has his Carnegie medal, art has its Morgan, the rose has its –"

"Speak," I interrupted, much perturbed. "You do not think that Milly will begin to lace?"

"One day," concluded Kraft, solemnly, "there will come to Cypher's for a plate of beans a millionaire lumberman from Wisconsin, and he will marry Milly."

"Never!" exclaimed Judkins and I, in horror.

"A lumberman," repeated Kraft, hoarsely.

"And a millionaire lumberman!" I sighed, despairingly.

"From Wisconsin!" groaned Judkins.

We agreed that the awful fate seemed to menace her. Few things were less improbable. Milly, like some vast virgin stretch of pine woods, was made to catch the lumberman's eye. And well we knew the habits of the Badgers, once fortune

小摊溅出来的咖啡戳来戳去，"恺撒的对手是布鲁徒斯——而棉花的对手是棉铃虫，歌剧合唱队女歌手的对手是匹兹堡人，暑期寄宿学校的学生的对手是有毒的常青藤，是英雄总会获得卡内基奖章，是艺术自会有摩根巨头[6]的支持，是玫瑰就有……"

"你倒说说，"我烦躁地打断他，"你觉得米丽会结婚么？"

"会有那么一天，"克拉弗特正经八百地断定，"一个从威斯康星州来的身揣百万金元的伐木工会走进塞弗尔餐馆点一盘豆子，而这个人将娶米丽为妻。"

"不可能！"贾金斯和我惊恐万分地大吼。

"一个伐木工人啊。"克拉弗特用嘶哑的嗓音又说了一遍。

"还是一个富豪伐木工人啊！"我无比绝望地长叹。

"来自威斯康星！"贾金斯沉痛地呻吟。

我们都觉得，米丽就要大难临头了。这种事发生的可能性太大啦。米丽就像是一大片原始松树林，生来就会吸引伐木工的目光。我们都知道那些交了好运，发了横财的威斯康星人会怎

smiled upon them. Straight to New York they hie, and lay their goods at the feet of the girl who serves them beans in a beanery. Why, the alphabet itself connives. The Sunday newspaper's headliner's work is cut for him.

"Winsome Waitress Wins Wealthy Wisconsin Woodsman."

For a while we felt that Milly was on the verge of being lost to us. It was our love of the Unerring Artistic Adjustment of Nature that inspired us. We could not give her over to a lumberman, doubly accursed by wealth and provincialism. We shuddered to think of Milly, with her voice modulated and her elbows covered, pouring tea in the marble teepee of a tree murderer. No! In Cypher's she belonged – in the bacon smoke, the cabbage perfume, the grand, Wagnerian chorus of hurled ironstone china and rattling casters.

Our fears must have been prophetic, for on that same evening the wildwood discharged upon us Milly's preordained confiscator – our fee to adjustment and order. But Alaska and not Wisconsin bore the burden of the visitation.

做。他们会飞奔到纽约，找一家廉价小馆子吃豆子，随便哪个姑娘给他们上豆子，他们就会把带去的货呈现在姑娘的脚下。啊呀，事情本来就是这么开始的。纽约报纸周末版的头条可是留给他的：

"美艳招待女招得好夫婿——来自威斯康星的樵夫阔佬。"

有那么一阵，我们觉得很快就要失去米丽了。我们受到钟爱的"永远正确的艺术加工"理论的鼓励，认为不能把她交给一个伐木工，他的百万家产和满身土气使他显得更加面目可憎。一想到米丽变了声调，遮了胳膊肘，跑到一个森林杀手的大理石圆锥帐篷里去端茶送水，我们都忍不住地打寒颤。这决不能发生！她是属于塞弗尔餐馆的，她是属于熏肉的油烟，白菜的芬芳，还有混合了丢来掷去的坚质陶器声和吧嗒吧嗒的投掷者所发出的声音的瓦格纳[7]式的餐厅合唱曲的。

我们的忧虑最终变成了现实。那晚，从原始森林里跑来一个命中注定要没收米丽的家伙——就当是我们的艺术加工和整理费吧。但他不是来自威斯康星，

We were at our supper of beef stew and dried apples when he trotted in as if on the heels of a dog team, and made one of the mess at our table. With the freedom of the camps he assaulted our ears and claimed the fellowship of men lost in the wilds of a hash house. We embraced him as a specimen, and in three minutes we had all but died for one another as friends.

He was rugged and bearded and wind-dried. He had just come off the "trail," he said, at one of the North River ferries. I fancied I could see the snow dust of Chilcoot yet powdering his shoulders. And then he strewed the table with the nuggets, stuffed ptarmigans, bead work and seal pelts of the returned Klondiker, and began to prate to us of his millions.

"Bank drafts for two millions," was his summing up, "and a thousand a day piling up from my claims. And now I want some beef stew and canned peaches. I never got off the train since I mushed out of Seattle, and I'm hungry. The stuff the niggers feed you on Pullmans don't count. You gentlemen order what you

而是来自阿拉斯加。

当时我们正好在用晚餐，吃的是炖牛肉和苹果干，把桌子弄得一片狼藉，他快步踱进餐馆，就像是坐在狗拉的雪橇上一样。他那一副随随便便的像同性恋一样忸怩作态的样子，简直就是强奸我们的耳朵，他声称要加入迷失在廉价餐馆荒野中的男人队伍。我们把他当成一个怪物一样拥抱，可三分钟后，我们却已倾心如故，几乎算的上心知莫逆了。

他身材结实，蓄着一嘴络腮胡，皮肤被风吹得干燥粗糙。他说，他刚在北江一个渡口下了车。我觉得我都能瞧见奇尔库特的雪尘簌簌地飘落到他的肩头的景象。接着他在桌上堆满了从克朗代克[8]发财归来所带的金块、雪鸟标本、念珠、海豹皮，然后开始对我们吹嘘他的百万家产。

"我银行汇票有 200 万，"他总结道，"而且我的那些采矿场一天就能挣到一千块。嗯，这会儿，我想来点炖牛肉，还有罐头蜜桃。自打我坐着狗拉雪橇出了西雅图，我就没从火车上下来过，现在我可饿坏了。普尔门式列车车厢里那些黑鬼给你吃的东

want."

And then Milly loomed up with a thousand dishes on her bare arm – loomed up big and white and pink and awful as Mount Saint Elias – with a smile like day breaking in a gulch. And the Klondiker threw down his pelts and nuggets as dross, and let his jaw fall half-way, and stared at her. You could almost see the diamond tiaras on Milly's brow and the hand-embroidered silk Paris gowns that he meant to buy for her.

At last the bollworm had attacked the cotton – the poison ivy was reaching out its tendrils to entwine the summer boarder – the millionaire lumberman, thinly disguised as the Alaskan miner, was about to engulf our Milly and upset Nature's adjustment.

Kraft was the first to act. He leaped up and pounded the Klondiker's back. "Come out and drink," he shouted. "Drink first and eat afterward." Judkins seized one arm and I the other. Gaily, roaringly, irresistibly, in jolly-good-fellow style, we dragged him from the restaurant to a cafe, stuffing his pockets with his embalmed birds and indigestible

西什么事也顶不了，你们几位先生想吃什么就自己叫吧。"

然后，米丽隐隐约约地出现了，一只裸着的胳膊上堆满了一层层地盘子——如同圣伊莱尔斯峰一样伟岸洁白，艳若桃花，她就令人肃然起敬地现身——带着像产金地的冲沟山洪暴发般的粲然笑容。只见克朗代克人像丢废品般抛开那堆海豹皮和金块，半张着嘴，一动不动地盯着她。你几乎都能看见米丽头上的钻石首饰和手工刺绣的巴黎真丝睡袍，那都是他计划要买给她的东西。

终于，棉铃虫开始进攻棉花——毒青藤伸长了藤蔓缠住了寄宿学校的暑期学生——身揣百万的伐木工人披着薄薄的阿拉斯加采矿人的伪装，就要一口吞噬掉我们的米丽，把这位天生丽质的姑娘搅得心神不宁。

克拉弗特第一个采取行动。他一下子跳起来，拍着克朗代克人的背大叫："走，我们去干一杯。""先喝酒，再吃饭。"贾金斯和我各自抓住他一只胳膊，往他兜里填满涂着防腐油的雪鸟标本和不能当饭吃的金块，嬉笑着，喊叫着，像几个欢快的哥儿们一样，不由分说地把他拖出了

nuggets.

There he rumbled a roughly good-humoured protest. "That's the girl for my money," he declared. "She can eat out of my skillet the rest of her life. Why, I never see such a fine girl. I'm going back there and ask her to marry me. I guess she won't want to sling hash any more when she sees the pile of dust I've got."

"You'll take another whiskey and milk now," Kraft persuaded, with Satan's smile. "I thought you up-country fellows were better sports."

Kraft spent his puny store of coin at the bar and then gave Judkins and me such an appealing look that we went down to the last dime we had in toasting our guest.

Then, when our ammunition was gone and the Klondiker, still somewhat sober, began to babble again of Milly, Kraft whispered into his ear such a polite, barbed insult relating to people who were miserly with their funds, that the miner crashed down handful after handful of silver and notes, calling for all the fluids in the world to drown the imputation.

Thus the work was accomplished. With his own guns we drove him from

餐馆，带进一家咖啡馆。

在那儿，他嘟嘟囔囔地抗议着，不过情绪蛮好："她就是为我的钱而生的小妞儿。"他宣布道，"她一辈子都可以吃我碗里的饭。啊呀，我从来没见过这么美的妞儿，我要回到那儿去，求她嫁给我。我估计她要是瞧见我的那些金粉，就再也不想在一家小饭馆里做女堂倌了吧。"

"再喝点威士忌和牛奶吧！"克拉弗特劝说着，脸上挂着撒旦一般的微笑，"我觉得你们这些北方来的家伙很能喝酒呢！"

克拉弗特把他那微薄的积蓄扔在了酒吧，之后用极富魅力的眼神瞥了贾金斯和我一眼，结果我俩把所有钱也花了个精光，用来同我们的客人干杯。

最后，我们都已经粮绝弹尽了，可克朗代克人仍有些清醒，他又开始喋喋不休地讲米丽，克拉弗特凑近他，给他耳朵里彬彬有礼地灌输着令人羞辱的话，他说富人都一毛不拔，异常吝啬，弄得那个采矿人丢下大把大把的银子和钞票，叫来全世界的酒，似乎要将那污名溺死。

就这样，大功告成。借了他的武器，我们把他赶出了战场。

the field. And then we had him carted to a distant small hotel and put to bed with his nuggets and baby seal-skins stuffed around him.

"He will never find Cypher's again," said Kraft. "He will propose to the first white apron he sees in a dairy restaurant to-morrow. And Milly – I mean the Natural Adjustment – is saved!"

And back to Cypher's went we three, and, finding customers scarce, we joined hands and did an Indian dance with Milly in the centre.

This, I say, happened three years ago. And about that time a little luck descended upon us three, and we were enabled to buy costlier and less wholesome food than Cypher's. Our paths separated, and I saw Kraft no more and Judkins seldom.

But, as I said, I saw a painting the other day that was sold for $5,000. The title was "Boadicea," and the figure seemed to fill all out-of-doors. But of all the picture's admirers who stood before it, I believe I was the only one who longed for Boadicea to stalk from her frame, bringing me corned-beef hash with poached egg.

I hurried away to see Kraft. His satanic

然后我们叫了一辆出租车，把他扔到一个偏僻的小旅社，弄上床，四周给他堆满金块和小海豹皮。

"他再也找不着塞弗尔餐馆啰。"克拉弗特说，"明儿他就会向他看见的奶品店第一位女招待求婚啦。而米丽——我指的是天生丽质的那位——就得救了！"

接着我们三人回到塞弗尔餐馆，看见餐馆里只有稀稀拉拉的顾客，于是我们手拉手围住米丽，跳起一支印第安舞。

这事，嗨，就是三年前发生的。差不多那时候，有点小运气降临到了我们头上，我们可以买到比塞弗尔餐馆价钱贵的食品，尽管不那么有利健康。再然后我们就各奔东西了，我再没见过克拉弗特，也很少见到贾金斯。

然而，我先前提过了，前几天我看见了一幅售价 5000 元的画，名叫《勃蒂希亚》，这位勃蒂希亚的外形看起来似乎想撑破画框。不过，我相信，在那些站在画前满怀崇拜观赏画作的人里面，我是惟一渴望勃蒂希亚昂然走出画框，给我上一道腌牛肉肉末炒土豆泥配水煮荷包蛋的。

我匆忙离开，去探望克拉弗

eyes were the same, his hair was worse tangled, but his clothes had been made by a tailor.

"I didn't know," I said to him.

"We've bought a cottage in the Bronx with the money," said he. "Any evening at 7."

"Then," said I, "when you led us against the lumberman – the – Klondiker – it wasn't altogether on account of the Unerring Artistic Adjustment of Nature?"

"Well, not altogether," said Kraft, with a grin.

特。他依旧是那双撒旦般的眼睛，头发也是蓬乱的，只是更糟了，不过他穿的倒是裁缝做的衣服。

"我以前不知道。"我对他说。

"我和她用那些钱在布朗克斯[9]买了一幢小别墅，"他说，"随便哪天晚上7点，过来看看吧。"

"那么，"我说，"你带我们跟那个伐木工对着干——对，就是那个——克朗代克人——并不全是为了永远正确的艺术加工原则啦？"

"呃，不全是吧。"克拉弗特答道，并且咧嘴一笑。

1. 哈德逊（约 1550~1661），英国探险家，曾经到哈德逊河探险。
2. 拿破仑三世（1803~1873），拿破仑一世的侄子，原名路易·拿破仑，法国皇帝（1852~1870）。
3. 密涅瓦（Minerva），罗马神话中的艺术、技艺和智慧女神，即希腊神话中的雅芙娜。
4. 科纽考皮亚（Cornucopia），希腊神话中象征丰饶的羊角。
5. 费约·海顿（1732~1809），奥地利著名作曲家。
6. 安德鲁·卡内基（1835~1919），美国钢铁巨头；
   裘尼·斯宾塞·摩根（1813~1890），美国金融巨头。
7. 瓦格纳（Richard Wagner, 1813~1883），德国作曲家。
8. 克朗代克，位于加拿大育空地区西部，1896 年此地掀起黄金浪潮。
9. 布朗克斯，隶属于纽约市的区。

19. THE WHIRLIGIG OF LIFE
19. 生活的陀螺

Justice-of-the-Peace Benaja Widdup sat in the door of his office smoking his elder-stem pipe. Half-way to the zenith the Cumberland range rose blue-gray in the afternoon haze. A speckled hen swaggered down the main street of the "settlement," cackling foolishly.

Up the road came a sound of creaking axles, and then a slow cloud of dust, and then a bull-cart bearing Ransie Bilbro and his wife. The cart stopped at the Justice's door, and the two climbed down. Ransie was a narrow six feet of sallow brown skin and yellow hair. The imperturbability of the mountains hung upon him like a suit of armour. The woman was calicoed, angled, snuff-brushed, and weary with unknown desires. Through it all gleamed a faint protest of cheated youth unconscious of its loss.

The Justice of the Peace slipped his feet into his shoes, for the sake of dignity, and moved to let them enter.

"We-all," said the woman, in a voice like the wind blowing through pine

治安法官贝内加·威德普坐在办公室门口,抽着接骨木做的烟斗。坎伯兰山脉的半山腰处被午后的雾霭笼罩着,显得有点暗蓝,又有点灰白。一只花斑母鸡在"殖民地"大街上大摇大摆地走着,咯咯地傻叫个不停。

路的一头传来车轴的吱吱声,接着是缓慢飞扬的尘土,像云一样,然后出现了一辆牛车,车上坐着兰西·比尔布罗和他的妻子。牛车在治安官的门边停下,两人爬下车。兰西很瘦,大约有六英尺高,长着褐色的皮肤和黄头发。他像一座山一样沉默不语,使他看上去像是穿上了一件盔甲的外衣。女人身穿白棉布衣服,背有点驼,牙齿上有残留的烟草粉末,同时带着一种由于前途未卜而造成的不耐烦。这一切都透露出一种模糊的反抗,抗议青春遭到了欺骗,抗议青春在不知不觉中悄悄流逝。

治安法官的双脚滑进了鞋子,以此来维持自己的尊严。他挪开身子,让他们俩走进办公室。

boughs, "wants a divo'ce." She looked at Ransie to see if he noted any flaw or ambiguity or evasion or partiality or self-partisanship in her statement of their business.

"A divo'ce," repeated Ransie, with a solemn nod. "We-all can't git along together nohow. It's lonesome enough fur to live in the mount'ins when a man and a woman keers fur one another. But when she's a-spittin' like a wildcat or a-sullenin' like a hoot-owl in the cabin, a man ain't got no call to live with her."

"When he's a no-'count varmint," said the woman, "without any especial warmth, a-traipsin' along of scalawags and moonshiners and a-layin' on his back pizen 'ith co'n whiskey, and a-pesterin' folks with a pack o' hungry, triflin' houn's to feed!"

"When she keeps a-throwin' skillet lids," came Ransie's antiphony, "and slings b'ilin' water on the best coon-dog in the Cumberlands, and sets herself agin' cookin' a man's victuals, and keeps him awake o' nights accusin' him of a sight of doin's!"

"When he's al'ays a-fightin' the revenues, and gits a hard name in the mount'ins fur a mean man, who's gwine

"我们俩，"女人说，声音就像风吹过松树枝，"想离婚。"她眼瞅着兰西，看他是否要批评她所陈述的事情有什么缺陷、模糊、隐瞒、偏袒、或者自我偏袒。

"离婚！"兰西边重复道，边严肃庄重地点点头。"我们两个现在是没办法一起过了。即使一个男人和一个女人和和气气地在山里生活，那也已经够让人无聊寂寞的了。更何况在小木屋里的时候，她不是像野猫那么凶就是像号枭一样赌气，凭什么男人要和这样一个人一起过。"

"他是个无能的家伙，"女人冷冷地说，"只知道和一群流氓地痞还有违法酒贩东游西逛，一灌玉米酒就不省人事，丢下一群烦人的饿狗闹食！"

"她老是摔锅盖，"轮到兰西数落起来，"她把滚烫的开水倒在坎伯兰地区最好的猎浣熊的狗身上，宁肯在那里闲坐着也不给男人做饭，男人做什么都不对，每天晚上她都吵得人没法睡觉！"

"他总是和收税的人打架，山区里的人都知道他是个恶人，晚上谁还能睡得着觉？"

to be able fur to sleep o' nights?"

The Justice of the Peace stirred deliberately to his duties. He placed his one chair and a wooden stool for his petitioners. He opened his book of statutes on the table and scanned the index. Presently he wiped his spectacles and shifted his inkstand.

"The law and the statutes," said he, "air silent on the subjeck of divo'ce as fur as the jurisdiction of this co't air concerned. But, accordin' to equity and the Constitution and the golden rule, it's a bad barg'in that can't run both ways. If a justice of the peace can marry a couple, it's plain that he is bound to be able to divo'ce 'em. This here office will issue a decree of divo'ce and abide by the decision of the Supreme Co't to hold it good."

Ransie Bilbro drew a small tobacco-bag from his trousers pocket. Out of this he shook upon the table a five-dollar note. "Sold a b'arskin and two foxes fur that," he remarked. "It's all the money we got."

"The regular price of a divo'ce in this co't," said the Justice, "air five dollars." He stuffed the bill into the pocket of his homespun vest with a deceptive air of indifference. With much bodily toil and mental travail he wrote the decree upon

治安法官缓慢而又谨慎地开始履行公务。他把一张椅子和一个木凳放在两位离婚申请人旁边，打开桌上的《法规条例》，开始浏览索引。不久，他擦了擦眼镜，挪了挪墨水瓶。

"法律和法规，"他说，"就本庭的司法权而论，没有关于离婚的条例。但是，根据衡平法、宪法和为人准则，生意应该有来有去。如果治安官能为两口子证婚，很明显，那他也就能让他们离婚。本庭将要颁布离婚法令，并且遵循最高法院的规定，来保证它的有效性。"

兰西·比尔布罗从裤兜里掏出一个小烟草袋，从里面抖出一张五美元的钞票放到桌上。"这是卖一张熊皮和两张狐皮所得的钱，"他解释道，"这是我们全部的财产。"

"本庭办理离婚的固定价格，"治安法官说，"是五美元。"他假装满不在乎地把钞票塞进土布马甲上的口袋里。在经历了身体和头脑的辛苦工作后，他才在

half a sheet of foolscap, and then copied it upon the other. Ransie Bilbro and his wife listened to his reading of the document that was to give them freedom:

"Know all men by these presents that Ransie Bilbro and his wife, Ariela Bilbro, this day personally appeared before me and promises that hereinafter they will neither love, honour, nor obey each other, neither for better nor worse, being of sound mind and body, and accept summons for divorce according to the peace and dignity of the State. Herein fail not, so help you God. Benaja Widdup, justice of the peace in and for the county of Piedmont, State of Tennessee."

The Justice was about to hand one of the documents to Ransie. The voice of Ariela delayed the transfer. Both men looked at her. Their dull masculinity was confronted by something sudden and unexpected in the woman.

"Judge, don't you give him that air paper yit. 'Tain't all settled, nohow. I got to have my rights first. I got to have my ali-money. 'Tain't no kind of a way to do fur a man to divo'ce his wife 'thout her havin' a cent fur to do with. I'm a-layin' off to be a-goin' up to brother Ed's up on Hogback Mount'in. I'm bound fur to hev

半页纸上写完离婚判决,然后又在另外半页上抄了一遍。兰西·比尔布罗和他的妻子听着他宣读将会给他们带来自由的文件:

"本判决的当事人兰西·比尔布罗及其妻阿里娜·比尔布罗,今天亲自来到本官这里,经双方协议,决定如下:无论福与祸,他们不再互敬互爱,不再彼此听从。当事人神志清醒,身体健康,根据本州的治安和尊严,准予其离婚请求。今后两人不再是夫妻关系,请上帝明证。田纳西州比德蒙特县治安法官贝内加·威德普"

治安法官正要把一张离婚证书递给兰西的时候,阿里娜说的话延迟了他递交的动作。两个男人都盯着她看,他们作为男人愚钝的本性被女人突如其来、始料不及的天性打了个措手不及。

"法官,你先别给他离婚协议书。再怎么说,事情还没彻底结束呢。我必须先得到我的权利,他得付给我赡养费。没有男人把老婆休了,而不给她一分钱生活费的。我打算到霍格巴克山去投靠我的兄弟埃德。我必须得有双鞋子,一些鼻烟还有其他东西。

a pa'r of shoes and some snuff and things besides. Ef Rance kin affo'd a divo'ce, let him pay me ali-money."

Ransie Bilbro was stricken to dumb perplexity. There had been no previous hint of alimony. Women were always bringing up startling and unlooked-for issues.

Justice Benaja Widdup felt that the point demanded judicial decision. The authorities were also silent on the subject of alimony. But the woman's feet were bare. The trail to Hogback Mountain was steep and flinty.

"Ariela Bilbro," he asked, in official tones, "how much did you 'low would be good and sufficient ali-money in the case befo' the co't."

"I 'lowed," she answered, "fur the shoes and all, to say five dollars. That ain't much fur ali-money, but I reckon that'll git me to up brother Ed's."

"The amount," said the Justice, "air not onreasonable. Ransie Bilbro, you air ordered by the co't to pay the plaintiff the sum of five dollars befo' the decree of divo'ce air issued."

"I hain't no mo' money," breathed Ransie, heavily. "I done paid you all I had."

兰西既然有钱付离婚的费用，他就得付给我赡养费。"

兰西·比尔布罗大吃一惊，他几乎愣住了。这个女人从前根本就没提过赡养费这回事。女人总是能提出些令人震惊、做梦也想不到的话题来。

治安法官贝内加·威德普觉得这个问题有必要让法庭来判决。但《法规条例》上也没有提赡养费这回事。可是，这女人光着两只脚，没有穿鞋。而且去霍格巴克山的小道非常陡峭，上面布满了燧石。

"阿里娜·比尔布罗，"他用公事公办的语气说道，"你认为多少赡养费是合理的？请在法庭上讲出来。"

"我觉得，"她答道，"鞋再加上别的一些必需的东西，就五美元吧。这不算多，但我想这笔钱可以让我到达埃德兄弟家。"

"这个数目，"治安官说，"不能算不合理。兰西·比尔布罗，本庭命令你付给原告赡养费五美元，然后才能把离婚证发给你。"

"我一分钱也没有了，"兰西重重地喘息道。"我把所有的钱都给你了。"

"Otherwise," said the Justice, looking severely over his spectacles, "you air in contempt of co't."

"I reckon if you gimme till to-morrow," pleaded the husband, "I mout be able to rake or scrape it up somewhars. I never looked for to be a-payin' no ali-money."

"The case air adjourned," said Benaja Widdup, "till to-morrow, when you-all will present yo'selves and obey the order of the co't. Followin' of which the decrees of divo'ce will be delivered." He sat down in the door and began to loosen a shoestring.

"We mout as well go down to Uncle Ziah's," decided Ransie, "and spend the night." He climbed into the cart on one side, and Ariela climbed in on the other. Obeying the flap of his rope, the little red bull slowly came around on a tack, and the cart crawled away in the nimbus arising from its wheels.

Justice-of-the-peace Benaja Widdup smoked his elder-stem pipe. Late in the afternoon he got his weekly paper, and read it until the twilight dimmed its lines. Then he lit the tallow candle on his table, and read until the moon rose, marking the time for supper. He lived in the double

"如果你拒绝支付的话，"治安法官从眼镜上方严厉地盯着兰西，"你就是藐视法庭。"

"我想你能不能让我等到明天，"这位丈夫请求道，"我也许能借到一些钱，凑齐五美元。因为我从没想到要付什么赡养费。"

"本案休庭，"贝内加·威德普说，"明天继续。你们俩明天到庭听候判决。判决宣判之后，离婚证会发给你们的。"他在门口坐下，开始解鞋带。

"我们还是可以去齐亚叔叔家，"兰西决定道，"在他家过一夜。"他从一侧爬上牛车，阿里娜从另一侧爬上去。他一抖缰绳，小红牛缓缓地按照缰绳的指引转了个弯，牛车在车轮带起的飞扬的尘土中慢慢地驶走了。

治安法官贝内加·威德普抽起了他的接骨木烟斗。傍晚，他定的周报送过来之后他就一直读，直到夜幕降临字迹无法辨认时，他点起桌子上的蜡烛，继续读，直到月亮都升起来了——通常这个时候他就会去吃晚饭了。

log cabin on the slope near the girdled poplar. Going home to supper he crossed a little branch darkened by a laurel thicket. The dark figure of a man stepped from the laurels and pointed a rifle at his breast. His hat was pulled down low, and something covered most of his face.

"I want yo' money," said the figure, "'thout any talk. I'm gettin' nervous, and my finger's a-wabblin' on this here trigger."

"I've only got f-f-five dollars," said the Justice, producing it from his vest pocket.

"Roll it up," came the order, "and stick it in the end of this here gun-bar'l."

The bill was crisp and new. Even fingers that were clumsy and trembling found little difficulty in making a spill of it and inserting (this with less ease) into the muzzle of the rifle.

"Now I reckon you kin be goin' along," said the robber.

The Justice lingered not on his way.

The next day came the little red bull, drawing the cart to the office door. Justice Benaja Widdup had his shoes on, for he was expecting the visit. In his presence Ransie Bilbro handed to his wife a five-dollar bill. The official's eye sharply

他住在山坡上的一间双层原木的小屋里，靠近一棵剥皮杨树。他回家吃晚饭必须经过一条小岔道，而月桂树丛把小道遮蔽得阴森森的。这时一个黑咕隆咚的身影从月桂树中迈出来，用步枪对准了他的胸膛。那人的帽子拉得很低，大半张脸都被遮住了。

"我要你的钱，"那人说道，"别说话。我现在很是紧张，我的手指就在扳机上颤动呢。"

"我只有五——五——五美元。"治安法官说着，从马甲口袋里把钱掏出来。

"卷起来，"对方命令道，"塞进枪口里。"

这张新票子非常脆。尽管手指不灵活，并且在发抖，但要把它卷起来也不会太难，可要是把它塞进枪口里就不那么容易了。

"现在我想你可以走了，"强盗说。

治安法官一秒都没有耽搁就赶紧跑掉了。

第二天，小红牛拉着牛车又来到办公室门口。治安法官贝内加·威德普知道他们会来，所以鞋子一直穿在脚上。当着他的面，兰西·比尔布罗把一张五美元的票子递给了他的妻子。治安法官

viewed it. It seemed to curl up as though it had been rolled and inserted into the end of a gun-barrel. But the Justice refrained from comment. It is true that other bills might be inclined to curl. He handed each one a decree of divorce. Each stood awkwardly silent, slowly folding the guarantee of freedom. The woman cast a shy glance full of constraint at Ransie.

"I reckon you'll be goin' back up to the cabin," she said, along 'ith the bull-cart. There's bread in the tin box settin' on the shelf. I put the bacon in the b'ilin'-pot to keep the hounds from gittin' it. Don't forget to wind the clock to-night."

"You air a-goin' to your brother Ed's?" asked Ransie, with fine unconcern.

"I was 'lowin' to get along up thar afore night. I ain't sayin' as they'll pester theyselves any to make me welcome, but I hain't nowhar else fur to go. It's a right smart ways, and I reckon I better be goin'. I'll be a-sayin' good-bye, Ranse – that is, if you keer fur to say so."

"I don't know as anybody's a hound dog," said Ransie, in a martyr's voice, "fur to not want to say good-bye – 'less you air so anxious to git away that you

目光锐利地盯着票子。它看起来被人卷过，就像有人曾经把它卷起来塞进枪口里一样。但治安法官尽力克制着自己，没有说什么。说真的，别的票子也可能会被人卷过呀。他发给每人一份离婚证。两人尴尬地站在那，谁都不说话，只是慢慢地把那保证他们自由的证书折了起来。女人羞怯的看了看兰西，表情十分的拘束。

"我想你要坐牛车回木屋。"她说，"架子上的罐头盒里有面包。我把咸肉搁在锅里了，省得被狗吃掉。今晚别忘了给钟上发条。"

"你去你兄弟埃德家？"兰西特意漫不经心地问道。

"我是打算天黑前赶到那儿。我没说他们会非常欢迎我，但除此以外，我没有别的地方可以去。还有好长一段路呢，我想我最好马上上路。就是说，该说再见了，兰西——要是你也愿意说的话。"

"如果有谁连再见都不肯说，那简直连头畜生都不如，"兰西就像一个殉难者一样说道，"除非你急着赶路，不想听我

don't want me to say it."

Ariela was silent. She folded the five-dollar bill and her decree carefully, and placed them in the bosom of her dress. Benaja Widdup watched the money disappear with mournful eyes behind his spectacles.

And then with his next words he achieved rank (as his thoughts ran) with either the great crowd of the world's sympathizers or the little crowd of its great financiers.

"Be kind o' lonesome in the old cabin to-night, Ranse," he said.

Ransie Bilbro stared out at the Cumberlands, clear blue now in the sunlight. He did not look at Ariela.

"I 'low it might be lonesome," he said; "but when folks gits mad and wants a divo'ce, you can't make folks stay."

"There's others wanted a divo'ce," said Ariela, speaking to the wooden stool. "Besides, nobody don't want nobody to stay."

"Nobody never said they didn't."

"Nobody never said they did. I reckon I better start on now to brother Ed's."

"Nobody can't wind that old clock."

"Want me to go back along 'ith you in the cart and wind it fur you, Ranse?"

说。"

阿里娜没再说什么。她小心翼翼地把五美元钞票和离婚证折好，放进怀里。贝内加·威德普眼镜下面的眼睛悲伤地望着钞票一点点消失了。

他即将说出的话（他脑海里思绪翻腾），让他要么是世上一大群富有同情心的人们中的一员，要么就是剩余的一小部分的金融家们中的一员。

"今晚的小屋将相当孤独难熬，兰西，"他说。

兰西·比尔布罗抬头眺望着坎伯兰山脉，阳光下，群山一片蔚蓝。他没有看阿里娜。

"我知道会很孤独难熬的，"他说，"但有人发疯般地要求离婚，你也不能强留人家啊。"

"是有个人人要离婚，"阿里娜对着木凳说。"而且，也没人要我留下。"

"没人说过不让你留下。"

"可也没人说过让我留下。我想我最好马上赶路，到埃德兄弟家去。"

"再没人给旧钟上发条了。"

"你要我跟你坐牛车回去帮你给钟上发条吗，兰西？"

The mountaineer's countenance was proof against emotion. But he reached out a big hand and enclosed Ariela's thin brown one. Her soul peeped out once through her impassive face, hallowing it.

"Them hounds shan't pester you no more," said Ransie. "I reckon I been mean and low down. You wind that clock, Ariela."

"My heart hit's in that cabin, Ranse," she whispered, "along 'ith you. I ai'nt a-goin' to git mad no more. Le's be startin', Ranse, so's we kin git home by sundown."

Justice-of-the-peace Benaja Widdup interposed as they started for the door, forgetting his presence.

"In the name of the State of Tennessee," he said, "I forbid you-all to be a-defyin' of its laws and statutes. This co't is mo' than willin' and full of joy to see the clouds of discord and misunderstandin' rollin' away from two lovin' hearts, but it air the duty of the co't to p'eserve the morals and integrity of the State. The co't reminds you that you air no longer man and wife, but air divo'ced by regular decree, and as such air not entitled to the benefits and 'purtenances of the mattermonal estate."

山里人的脸上没有流露出任何情感。但他伸出一只大手，紧握住阿里娜那褐色的小手。她神情麻木的脸上突然有了灵魂，使这张脸变得神圣起来。

"那些狗再不会给你添麻烦了，"兰西说。"我想我过去真的很自私，没什么本事还不上进。阿里娜，你回来给钟上发条吧。"

"我的心一直都在那间木屋里，兰西，"她轻轻说道，"她和你在一起。我再也不会发脾气了兰西，我们走吧，我想我们能赶在太阳落山前到家。"

治安法官贝内加·威德普阻止了他们朝门前走去的脚步。这对小两口竟忘记了他的存在。

"凭田纳西州的名义，"他说，"我不允许你们俩公然蔑视本州的法律和法令。本法庭很愿意也很高兴看到两颗相爱的心上不再有争吵与误会的乌云。但是，本法庭的职责是维护州政府的道德和正义。本法庭提醒你们，你们现在已经不再是夫妻，离婚已经正式判决。因此，你们不再享有婚姻状况下的一切权益。"

Ariela caught Ransie's arm. Did those words mean that she must lose him now when they had just learned the lesson of life?"But the co't air prepared," went on the Justice, "fur to remove the disabilities set up by the decree of divo'ce. The co't air on hand to perform the solemn ceremony of marri'ge, thus fixin' things up and enablin' the parties in the case to resume the honour'ble and elevatin' state of mattermony which they desires. The fee fur performin' said ceremony will be, in this case, to wit, five dollars."Ariela caught the gleam of promise in his words. Swiftly her hand went to her bosom. Freely as an alighting dove the bill fluttered to the Justice's table. Her sallow cheek coloured as she stood hand in hand with Ransie and listened to the reuniting words.Ransie helped her into the cart, and climbed in beside her. The little red bull turned once more, and they set out, hand-clasped, for the mountains. Justice-of-the-peace Benaja Widdup sat in his door and took off his shoes. Once again he fingered the bill tucked down in his vest pocket. Once again he smoked his elder-stem pipe. Once again the speckled hen swaggered down the main street of the "settlement," cackling foolishly.

阿里娜紧紧抓住兰西的胳膊。他们刚刚汲取了生活的教训，难道这些话意味着她此刻必须失去他吗？"不过，"治安法官继续说道，"本法庭可以消除离婚判决造成的障碍。本法庭可以随时承办婚礼的庄重仪式，从而使本案的双方能够恢复他们渴望的光荣高尚的婚姻状况。仪式的承办费，将会是，就本案来说吧，是五美元。"阿里娜抓住了他话中的希望。她的手迅速地伸进怀里。那张钞票就像一只飞落的鸽子一样拍打着翅膀，自由地落在了治安法官的桌子上。当她同兰西手牵手站着，听着重新结合的结婚誓言时，她那苍白的脸庞有了些许颜色。兰西先扶她上了牛车，才爬上去坐在她身边。小红牛再一次转过弯，他们的手紧紧地握在一起，向着群山进发了。治安法官贝内加·威德普在门口坐下，把鞋子脱掉。他再一次把手伸进背心的口袋里去抚摸钞票，并抽起那只接骨木的烟斗。那只花斑母鸡也再一次在"殖民地"大街上大摇大摆地走着，咯咯地傻叫个不停。

20. THE PENDULUM
20. 钟摆

"Eighty-first street – let 'em out, please," yelled the shepherd in blue.

A flock of citizen sheep scrambled out and another flock scrambled aboard. Ding-ding! The cattle cars of the Manhattan Elevated rattled away, and John Perkins drifted down the stairway of the station with the released flock.

John walked slowly toward his flat. Slowly, because in the lexicon of his daily life there was no such word as "perhaps." There are no surprises awaiting a man who has been married two years and lives in a flat. As he walked John Perkins prophesied to himself with gloomy and downtrodden cynicism the foregone conclusions of the monotonous day.

Katy would meet him at the door with a kiss flavored with cold cream and butter-scotch. He would remove his coat, sit upon a macadamized lounge and read, in the evening paper, of Russians and Japs slaughtered by the deadly linotype. For

"到第八十一号大街啦,让他们下车,"身穿蓝色衣服的牧羊人大声喊道。

一群市民像绵羊似的乱哄哄地挤下车,另一群又你争我抢的挤上去。叮——叮!曼哈顿运送高架牲口的公交车横冲直撞的开走了。在车站的阶梯上,约翰·帕金斯和下车的人群一起,在人流中挪动着脚步。

约翰慢悠悠地挪向他的公寓。之所以慢悠悠地,是因为在他日常生活的词典里,已经没有"可能"这样的词汇了。对于一个已经结婚两年,住在公寓里的男人来说,不会有什么惊喜和意外在等着他。约翰·帕金斯走着,情绪低沉,心情压抑,还有些愤世嫉俗,心里料定这单调的生活将枯燥乏味,一成不变的继续。

凯蒂总会在家门口等着他,给他一个带有冷乳酪和奶油糖果味道的吻。他则总是脱掉外套,坐在像铺着碎石子的沙发上,阅读晚报上关于致命的莱诺整行铸排机屠杀俄罗斯人和日本人的消

dinner there would be pot roast, a salad flavored with a dressing warranted not to crack or injure the leather, stewed rhubarb and the bottle of strawberry marmalade blushing at the certificate of chemical purity on its label. After dinner Katy would show him the new patch in her crazy quilt that the iceman had cut for her off the end of his four-in-hand. At half-past seven they would spread newspapers over the furniture to catch the pieces of plastering that fell when the fat man in the flat overhead began to take his physical culture exercises. Exactly at eight Hickey & Mooney, of the vaudeville team (unbooked) in the flat across the hall, would yield to the gentle influence of delirium tremens and begin to overturn chairs under the delusion that Hammerstein was pursuing them with a five-hundred-dollar-a-week contract. Then the gent at the window across the air-shaft would get out his flute; the nightly gas leak would steal forth to frolic in the highways; the dumbwaiter would slip off its trolley; the janitor would drive Mrs. Zanowitski's five children once more across the Yalu, the lady with the champagne shoes and the Skye terrier would trip downstairs and paste her

息。晚饭总是炖好的肉块，一盘用"保证无损皮革"的调味酱拌好的沙拉，焖的烂熟的大黄和一瓶看到自己身上贴的证明化学纯度的商标之后羞红了脸的草莓果酱。吃完晚饭后，凯蒂总又会让他看百衲被上的新补丁，打补丁的料子是那个卖冰的人把他的活结领带尖剪下来送给她的。7：30整，公寓楼上的那个胖子就开始锻炼身体，他们总是摊开报纸铺在家具上，用来接震下来的泥灰。到了 8 点，住在走廊那边，（未预约的）希基和穆尼的歌舞杂耍队，总会屈服在他们那震颤性谵妄的温柔影响之下，因为痴心妄想哈默斯坦[1]会带着一周500美元报酬的合约紧追在他们两个之后而打翻椅子。然后，住在通风井对面的、靠在窗边的那位绅士又会拿出长笛；夜间泄漏的煤气总会偷偷地溜到大马路上面去玩耍；楼上与楼下之间送饭菜的小型升降机又会脱离轨道；看门人会再次把柴诺维茨基夫人的五个孩子赶过鸭绿江去；而那位穿着浅褐黄色鞋子的太太，会带着斯凯狗步伐轻快地跑下楼，把她星期四用的名字贴在电铃和信箱上——弗罗格摩尔公寓的夜生活就

Thursday name over her bell and letter-box – and the evening routine of the Frogmore flats would be under way.

John Perkins knew these things would happen. And he knew that at a quarter past eight he would summon his nerve and reach for his hat, and that his wife would deliver this speech in a querulous tone:

"Now, where are you going, I'd like to know, John Perkins?"

"Thought I'd drop up to McCloskey's," he would answer, "and play a game or two of pool with the fellows."

Of late such had been John Perkins's habit. At ten or eleven he would return. Sometimes Katy would be asleep; sometimes waiting up, ready to melt in the crucible of her ire a little more gold plating from the wrought steel chains of matrimony. For these things Cupid will have to answer when he stands at the bar of justice with his victims from the Frogmore flats.

To-night John Perkins encountered a tremendous upheaval of the commonplace when he reached his door. No Katy was there with her affectionate, confectionate kiss. The three rooms seemed in porten-

照例正式开始了。

约翰·帕金斯心想这些事一定会发生的。他还明白，一到8：15，他一定会鼓起勇气伸手去取帽子，而他妻子就会满腹牢骚地说道：

"我想知道你现在要去哪儿，约翰·帕金斯？"

"我到麦克洛斯基那里看看，"他总是如此回答，"去和他们玩一两盘台球。"

这已经成了约翰·帕金斯最近的习惯。不到10点或11点他是不会回来的。凯蒂有时已经睡着了，有时还会等着他，准备用她那盛怒的坩埚把锻好的婚姻钢链上镀有的那一层金再多融化掉一点。当他站在被告席上被公开审问，面对这个来自弗罗格摩尔公被他伤害的人时，丘比特将不得不为这些事做辩护。

而今天晚上，当约翰·帕金斯走到家门口时，却遭遇到了单调生活里突发的一个巨大变化。没有凯蒂那充满深情和奶油味道的吻在门口等着他，三间屋子像

tous disorder. All about lay her things in confusion. Shoes in the middle of the floor, curling tongs, hair bows, kimonos, powder box, jumbled together on dresser and chairs – this was not Katy's way. With a sinking heart John saw the comb with a curling cloud of her brown hair among its teeth. Some unusual hurry and perturbation must have possessed her, for she always carefully placed these comb-ings in the little blue vase on the mantel to be some day formed into the coveted feminine "rat."

Hanging conspicuously to the gas jet by a string was a folded paper. John seized it. It was a note from his wife running thus:

"Dear John: I just had a telegram saying mother is very sick. I am going to take the 4.30 train. Brother Sam is going to meet me at the depot there. There is cold mutton in the ice box. I hope it isn't her quinsy again. Pay the milkman 50 cents. She   had it bad last spring. Don't forget to write to the company about the gas meter, and your good socks are in the top drawer. I will write to-morrow. 'Hastily, 'KATY."

遭到抢劫似的一片狼藉，她的所有东西都乱七八糟，堆得到处都是。地板正中央是胡乱摊放的鞋子，卷发钳、发结、睡衣和香粉盒在梳妆台和椅子上乱成一团——这可不是凯蒂的习惯。看见一团凯蒂的褐色头发缠在梳子上，约翰的心情变得很低沉。肯定有什么不同寻常的让人焦虑不安的急事发生了，否则的话她总是会小心谨慎把梳掉的头发放到壁炉架上一个小小的蓝色花瓶里，想着有一天要用它做一个适合女孩子用的"发套"。

一张折好的纸很醒目地用小细绳挂在煤气喷嘴上。约翰一把抓住纸片，那是他妻子写给他的便条，内容如下：

"亲爱的约翰：我刚刚收到一份电报，说母亲病得很严重。我要搭四点半的火车回家，我的哥哥山姆会在那边的火车站把我接回去。冷羊肉放在冰箱里。希望妈妈不是扁桃腺炎复发。记得给送牛奶的人 50 美分。可是去年春天她病得非常严重。别忘了给公司写信说一说煤气表的事，顶格抽屉里有洗好的袜子。明天我会给你写信，现在时间不多了。凯蒂"

Never during their two years of matrimony had he and Katy been separated for a night. John read the note over and over in a dumbfounded way. Here was a break in a routine that had never varied, and it left him dazed.

There on the back of a chair hung, pathetically empty and formless, the red wrapper with black dots that she always wore while getting the meals. Her week-day clothes had been tossed here and there in her haste. A little paper bag of her favorite butter-scotch lay with its string yet unwound. A daily paper sprawled on the floor, gaping rectangularly where a railroad time-table had been clipped from it. Everything in the room spoke of a loss, of an essence gone, of its soul and life departed. John Perkins stood among the dead remains with a queer feeling of desolation in his heart.

He began to set the rooms tidy as well as he could. When he touched her clothes a thrill of something like terror went through him. He had never thought what existence would be without Katy. She had become so thoroughly annealed into his life that she was like the air he breathed – necessary but scarcely no-

结婚整整两年，他没有一晚上是和凯蒂分开度过的。约翰傻傻地一遍又一遍地读那张便条。一成不变的生活被打乱了，这让他感到头晕眼花。

一个椅子背后挂着她的围裙，红色的底子上有黑黑的小圆点，以前她做饭时总爱穿着，而现在它空空的不成形状，实在惹人爱怜。她急匆匆的离开，连平日里穿的衣服也扔得到处都是，也没来得及解开她最爱吃的奶油糖果纸袋上的细绳。一张日报散落在地板上，一个长方形的口子张着大嘴，原来上面的火车时刻表已经被她剪下来了。房间里，每一样东西都在讲述着一种残缺，讲述失落的精华，诉说着灵魂和生命的远离。站在一堆死气沉沉的衣物旁边，约翰·帕金斯感到异乎寻常的孤寂。

他开始着手整理房间，尽可能收拾得整齐一些。可是一碰到她的衣服，一股恐惧的电流就会袭击他的全身。他从来也没有想过，没有凯蒂的生活会是什么样子。她已经彻底融入到他的生活中去，就像他呼吸的空气一样——必不可少却一点也不引人注

ticed. Now, without warning, she was gone, vanished, as completely absent as if she had never existed. Of course it would be only for a few days, or at most a week or two, but it seemed to him as if the very hand of death had pointed a finger at his secure and uneventful home.

John dragged the cold mutton from the ice-box, made coffee and sat down to a lonely meal face to face with the strawberry marmalade's shameless certificate of purity. Bright among withdrawn blessings now appeared to him the ghosts of pot roasts and the salad with tan polish dressing. His home was dismantled. A quinsied mother-in-law had knocked his lares and penates sky-high. After his solitary meal John sat at a front window.

He did not care to smoke. Outside the city roared to him to come join in its dance of folly and pleasure. The night was his. He might go forth unquestioned and thrum the strings of jollity as free as any gay bachelor there. He might carouse and wander and have his fling until dawn if he liked; and there would be no wrathful Katy waiting for him, bearing the chalice that held the dregs of his joy. He

意。而现在，连个招呼也不打，她就离开了，消失了，还消失地无影无踪，就好像她从来没有来过一样。当然，也许只要几天或者最多一两个星期她就会回来了，但这对他来说，仿佛死亡之神的手指头已经伸向了他安静祥和的家。

约翰从冰箱里拿出冷羊肉，煮好咖啡，坐下来一个人孤零零地吃饭，面对着他的是草莓果酱瓶上那不知羞耻的纯度证明。再也没有炖肉块和用棕黄色、亮晶晶的色拉油拌好的凉菜，这些东西就像是上帝的祝福，而现在这些祝福却都被收回了，只剩下幻想中的影子。他的家被拆散了。家庭的守护神被这个患扁桃腺炎的老丈母娘赶到了天外。孤独的晚饭过后，他坐到了窗前。

他不想抽烟。窗外，城市在大声地呼唤他：来吧，一起疯狂，一起跳舞，一起狂欢。夜晚现在完全属于他了。再也没人追问他去要哪里，他可以无拘无束地去任何地方，像任何快乐的单身汉一样，恣意狂欢。只要他愿意，他就可以随处晃荡，肆意寻欢直到天亮；再也不会有盛怒的凯蒂在等他，强忍他的酩酊大醉。只

might play pool at McCloskey's with his roistering friends until Aurora dimmed the electric bulbs if he chose. The hymeneal strings that had curbed him always when the Frogmore flats had palled upon him were loosened. Katy was gone.

John Perkins was not accustomed to analyzing his emotions. But as he sat in his Katy-bereft 10x12 parlor he hit unerringly upon the keynote of his discomfort. He knew now that Katy was necessary to his happiness. His feeling for her, lulled into unconsciousness by the dull round of domesticity, had been sharply stirred by the loss of her presence. Has it not been dinned into us by proverb and sermon and fable that we never prize the music till the sweet-voiced bird has flown – or in other no less florid and true utterances?

"I'm a double-dyed dub," mused John Perkins, "the way I've been treating Katy. Off every night playing pool and bumming with the boys instead of staying home with her. The poor girl here all alone with nothing to amuse her, and me acting that way! John Perkins, you're the worst kind of a shine. I'm going to make it up for the little girl. I'll take her out and let her see some amusement. And I'll cut

要他喜欢，他就可以在麦克洛斯基那儿同那帮吵吵闹闹的朋友打台球，直到黎明女神欧若拉让电灯黯然失色。当他正腻烦了弗罗格摩尔公寓时，一直捆着他的婚姻缰绳却突然松开了。凯蒂走了。

约翰·帕金斯没有分析自我情感的习惯。但是，坐在那间宽10英尺、长12英尺的客厅里，他准确地找到了他苦恼的主要根源。他终于明白了，对于他的幸福来说，凯蒂是必不可少的。他对她的爱情早已被枯燥无味的家庭生活催入梦乡，毫无意识了，而现在却被她的突然离开所唤醒。难道谚语、布道和寓言，还有一些同样真诚和华丽的词藻不是一遍遍告诫过我们说，在歌喉甜美的鸟儿飞走之前，我们是不会珍视音乐的？

"我是个彻头彻尾的傻瓜，"约翰·帕金斯沉思道，"我一直那样对待凯蒂。每天晚上我都和朋友们玩台球、闲逛，从来没有留在家里陪过她。这个可怜的姑娘孤单的地待在家里，没有任何乐趣，而我还那样对待她！约翰·帕金斯，你真是个王八蛋。我要好好地补偿她，带她出去玩玩。现在，我要同麦克洛斯基那

out the McCloskey gang right from this minute."

Yes, there was the city roaring outside for John Perkins to come dance in the train of Momus. And at McCloskey's the boys were knocking the balls idly into the pockets against the hour for the nightly game. But no primrose way nor clicking cue could woo the remorseful soul of Perkins the bereft. The thing that was his, lightly held and half scorned, had been taken away from him, and he wanted it. Backward to a certain man named Adam, whom the cherubim bounced from the orchard, could Perkins, the remorseful, trace his descent.

Near the right hand of John Perkins stood a chair. On the back of it stood Katy's blue shirtwaist. It still retained something of her contour. Midway of the sleeves were fine, individual wrinkles made by the movements of her arms in working for his comfort and pleasure. A delicate but impelling odor of bluebells came from it. John took it and looked long and soberly at the unresponsive grenadine. Katy had never been unresponsive. Tears: – yes, tears – came into John Perkins's eyes. When she came back things would be different. He would

伙人断绝来往。"

是的，外边的城市在大声呼唤约翰·金斯到莫摩斯的队伍中去跳舞。而在麦克洛斯基那儿，伙伴们正悠闲地把球打进球袋，打发时间。然而，凯蒂走了，寻欢作乐也好，咔嗒响的球杆也好，都再也不能蛊惑帕金斯那懊悔的灵魂。曾经属于他的，曾经遭到他轻视和嘲讽的，都被她从他的身边带走了。而他现在是多么的需要她！回想那个名叫亚当的男人——他是被天使们撵出伊甸园的，这个懊悔的帕金斯或许正在步他的后尘。

约翰·帕金斯的右手边有一把椅子，上面搭着凯蒂的蓝色衬衣式连衣裙，还保留着她身体线条的痕迹。袖管的中间部分有几条独特的纤细皱痕，那是她为了他的舒适和快乐而挥动手臂辛苦劳作时留下的。衣服散发出一股雅致的清香，沁人心脾，有着圆叶风铃草般的香气。约翰拿着它，久久地冷峻地盯着这条紧捻纱罗织裙，而裙子却毫无反应。而凯蒂从来不会毫无反应。泪水——是啊，泪水——涌入了约翰·帕金斯的双眼。当她回来的时候，

make up for all his neglect. What was life without her?

The door opened. Katy walked in carrying a little hand satchel. John stared at her stupidly.

"My! I'm glad to get back," said Katy. "Ma wasn't sick to amount to anything. Sam was at the depot, and said she just had a little spell, and got all right soon after they telegraphed. So I took the next train back. I'm just dying for a cup of coffee."

Nobody heard the click and rattle of the cog-wheels as the third-floor front of the Frogmore flats buzzed its machinery back into the Order of Things. A band slipped, a spring was touched, the gear was adjusted and the wheels revolve in their old orbit.

John Perkins looked at the clock. It was 8.15. He reached for his hat and walked to the door.

"Now, where are you going, I'd like to know, John Perkins?" asked Katy, in a querulous tone.

"Thought I'd drop up to McCloskey's," said John, "and play a game or two of pool with the fellows."

一切都会不一样了。他要弥补他之前对她的全部冷落。没有她，生活会成什么样？

门突然开了。凯蒂拎着小小的手提包走了进来。约翰傻傻地盯着她。

"哎！我很高兴这么快就回来了，"凯蒂说，"妈妈病得不严重。山姆在火车站等着我，说她的病只发作了一会，他们刚把电报发出去，妈妈就没事了。然后我就马上搭下一班火车回来了。我真想喝一杯咖啡。"

没有人会听见嵌齿轮发出的喀嚓和格格的声响，弗罗格摩尔公寓三楼前面的机械装置悄无声息的迅速回到正轨。传运带在滑行，发条活动起来，齿轮校准了位，轮子又朝着原来的轨迹驶去。

约翰·帕金斯看了看表，正好 8：15。他伸手取下帽子，向门口走去。

"喂，我想知道你现在要去哪里啊，约翰·帕金斯？"凯蒂怨声怨气地问道。

"我会到麦克洛斯基那儿看看，"约翰答道，"和他们玩一两盘台球。"

21. THE MAKING OF A NEW YORKER
21. 一个纽约人的成长

Besides many other things, Raggles was a poet. He was called a tramp; but that was only an elliptical way of saying that he was a philosopher, an artist, a traveller, a naturalist and a discoverer. But most of all he was a poet. In all his life he never wrote a line of verse; he lived his poetry. His Odyssey would have been a Limerick, had it been written. But, to linger with the primary proposition, Raggles was a poet.

Raggles's specialty, had he been driven to ink and paper, would have been sonnets to the cities. He studied cities as women study their reflections in mirrors; as children study the glue and sawdust of a dislocated doll; as the men who write about wild animals study the cages in the zoo. A city to Raggles was not merely a pile of bricks and mortar, peopled by a certain number of inhabitants; it was a thing with a soul characteristic and distinct; an individual conglomeration of life, with its own peculiar essence, flavor and feeling.

除了懂得很多事情之外，拉格斯还是个诗人。他被人们称作流浪汉，可这只是在隐晦地说他是一位哲学家，一位艺术家，一个旅行者，一个博物学家和发现者。但最重要的，他还是个诗人。他这辈子没写过一句诗，但是他的生活本身就是诗。要是让他写荷马史诗《奥德赛》，那将会是一首五行打油诗。但是，如果说起他的第一事业，那他一定是个诗人。

要是强逼拉格斯写点什么的话，他的特长会是写关于城市的十四行诗。他研究城市的劲头，就像女人研究自己在镜子中的影子、像孩子们研究被大卸八块的玩具里面的粘胶和锯末、像描写野生动物的人来研究动物园里的笼子一样。城市在拉格斯的眼中，不仅仅是一定数量的居民住的那些房屋，它有着独特的与众不同的灵魂；它是一盘独一无二的生活大杂烩，有自己特有的精华、滋味和情感。从南到北，由西向

Two thousand miles to the north and south, east and west, Raggles wandered in poetic fervor, taking the cities to his breast. He footed it on dusty roads, or sped magnificently in freight cars, counting time as of no account. And when he had found the heart of a city and listened to its secret confession, he strayed on, restless, to another. Fickle Raggles! – but perhaps he had not met the civic corporation that could engage and hold his critical fancy.

Through the ancient poets we have learned that the cities are feminine. So they were to poet Raggles; and his mind carried a concrete and clear conception of the figure that symbolized and typified each one that he had wooed.

Chicago seemed to swoop down upon him with a breezy suggestion of Mrs. Partington, plumes and patchouli, and to disturb his rest with a soaring and beautiful song of future promise. But Raggles would awake to a sense of shivering cold and a haunting impression of ideals lost in a depressing aura of potato salad and fish.

Thus Chicago affected him. Perhaps there is a vagueness and inaccuracy in the

东，拉格斯怀着诗人的热情，游遍了大江南北的每一座城市。他不管什么时间，要么在尘土飞扬的道路行走；要么采取高贵一点的方式：搭顺风车，坐在运输货车上飞速行进。一但他找到一座城市的心脏，听到了它秘密的告白，他就毫不停留，立即奔赴下一个城市。菲克尔·拉格斯！也许他还没遇到能吸引住他、能承受住他的批判、能勾起他无穷幻想的城市。

古典诗人告诉我们城市具有女性的气质。诗人拉格斯也是这样认为的。他的脑海中有一个个具体清晰的典型化形象，象征着他所追求过的每一个城市。

听到帕廷顿夫人轻松愉快的建议，看到羽毛饰品和闻到广藿香，他就觉得芝加哥好像要倾倒在自己身上了。一首关于未来希望的高亢激昂的美妙歌曲也会打扰他的休息。但当拉格斯醒来时，会感到让他瑟瑟发抖的寒冷，想起萦绕心头的理想已经逝去，只剩下土豆色拉和鱼的气味，这好不令人懊恼。

这就是芝加哥给他的感觉。也许这段描写含糊不清，不够准

description; but that is Raggles's fault. He should have recorded his sensations in magazine poems.

Pittsburg impressed him as the play of "Othello" performed in the Russian language in a railroad station by Dockstader's minstrels. A royal and generous lady this Pittsburg, though – homely, hearty, with flushed face, washing the dishes in a silk dress and white kid slippers, and bidding Raggles sit before the roaring fireplace and drink champagne with his pigs' feet and fried potatoes.

New Orleans had simply gazed down upon him from a balcony. He could see her pensive, starry eyes and catch the flutter of her fan, and that was all. Only once he came face to face with her. It was at dawn, when she was flushing the red bricks of the banquette with a pail of water. She laughed and hummed a chansonette and filled Raggles's shoes with ice-cold water. Allons!

Boston construed herself to the poetic Raggles in an erratic and singular way. It seemed to him that he had drunk cold tea and that the city was a white, cold cloth that had been bound tightly around his brow to spur him to some unknown but tremendous mental effort. And, after all,

确，但这是拉格斯的错误。他应该把他的感觉写成一首诗，登在诗刊里。

匹兹堡给他的印象就像是在一个火车站里，一群多克斯塔德的吟游歌手用俄语演出的戏剧《奥赛罗》。匹兹堡就是一位出身皇室，慷慨大方的女士——却也朴素、亲切，有着红彤彤的面颊，穿着丝绸衣服和白色的小山羊皮拖鞋清洗餐具，并让拉格斯坐在火热的壁炉前，喝香槟，啃猪脚，吃炸土豆。

新奥尔良只是坐在高高的阳台上，朝下盯着他看。他能看见她正在沉思的星眸，看见她轻轻扇动的扇子，也就是这些。只有一次与她面对面。那是拂晓时分，她正用一桶水冲洗人行道上铺的红砖。她笑着，哼着小调，把冰冷的水灌进了拉格斯的鞋子。并粗鲁的让拉格斯走开！

波士顿则用稀奇古怪却卓越非凡的方式把她与诗意的拉格斯结合在一起。就像是他喝了冷茶，而城市这块冰冷的白布紧紧地缠在他的额头上，刺激着他，让他盲目地做出巨大的精神努力。之后，他为了谋生开始铲雪；而白

he came to shovel snow for a livelihood; and the cloth, becoming wet, tightened its knots and could not be removed.

Indefinite and unintelligible ideas, you will say; but your disapprobation should be tempered with gratitude, for these are poets' fancies – and suppose you had come upon them in verse!

One day Raggles came and laid siege to the heart of the great city of Manhattan. She was the greatest of all; and he wanted to learn her note in the scale; to taste and appraise and classify and solve and label her and arrange her with the other cities that had given him up the secret of their individuality. And here we cease to be Raggles's translator and become his chronicler.

Raggles landed from a ferry-boat one morning and walked into the core of the town with the blase air of a cosmopolite. He was dressed with care to play the role of an "unidentified man." No country, race, class, clique, union, party clan or bowling association could have claimed him. His clothing, which had been donated to him piece-meal by citizens of different height, but same number of inches around the heart, was not yet as uncomfortable to his figure as those

布变得越来越湿，打的结也越来越紧，无法解开。

模糊不明，无法理解的鬼想法，你会这样说。但你的谴责应该用感激之情来调和，因为这全是诗人的幻想——想像一下你自己正在感受诗歌！

一天，拉格斯来到了曼哈顿，他千方百计想要赢取这座大城市的芳心。她是所有城市中最伟大的。他想知道她的个性之音，领略她，评估她，给她分类，理解她，给她贴上标签，把她和那些把个性秘密全部泄漏给他的城市归为一类。现在，我们不再是拉格斯的翻译，而是他的记录人。

一天上午，拉格斯带着世界公民那副厌烦享乐的神气从渡船上下来，步行到市中心。他细心装扮成为一位"无法识别身份的人"。他不属于任何国家、种族、阶级、集团、工会、党派，也不属于任何一个保龄球协会。他的衣服是与他身高不同，但胸围相同的公民们捐赠给他的，但是这样穿可比穿那些横贯大陆的裁缝们为他量身定做的衣服，手里拿着提箱，身穿背带裤，拿着丝手

speciments of raiment, self-measured, that are railroaded to you by transcontinental tailors with a suit case, suspenders, silk handkerchief and pearl studs as a bonus. Without money – as a poet should be – but with the ardor of an astronomer discovering a new star in the chorus of the milky way, or a man who has seen ink suddenly flow from his fountain pen, Raggles wandered into the great city.

Late in the afternoon he drew out of the roar and commotion with a look of dumb terror on his countenance. He was defeated, puzzled, discomfited, frightened. Other cities had been to him as long primer to read; as country maidens quickly to fathom; assend price of subscription with answer rebuses to solve; as oyster cocktails to swallow; but here was one as cold, glittering, serene, impossible as a four-carat diamond in a window to a lover outside fingering damply in his pocket his ribbon-counter salary.

The greetings of the other cities he had known – their homespun kindliness, their human gamut of rough charity, friendly curses, garrulous curiosity and easily estimated credulity or indifference. This city of Manhattan gave him no clue; it

帕，别着珍珠领扣舒服得多了。不值一文——一个诗人就应该如此——带着天文学家在银河合唱队中发现了一颗新星的热情，或是有着一个人看见墨水突然从他的钢笔里流出的激情，拉格斯漫步走入了这座伟大的城市。

到了傍晚时分，他从喧闹嘈杂的环境里溜走，脸上露出一副被吓傻了的恐惧表情。他被打败了，迷惑了，沮丧了，害怕了。其他城市对他而言，就像是阅读识字课本，像很容易被看穿的农村姑娘，像只需在价格栏上画一笔的征订单，像吞下牡蛎鸡尾酒；但这座城市却是冷冰冰的，亮晶晶的，宁静的，像橱窗里一颗四克拉的钻石，窗外的情人只能可望而不可及地眼睁睁地看着它，手放在兜里捏着卷成一沓的工资，都快捏出汗来了。

他了解其他城市的问候——朴实的亲切，粗犷的善意，友好的诅咒，喋喋不休的好奇的追问，容易被看穿的轻信或冷漠。而曼哈顿这座城市没有给他线索。它像是被围墙围了起来，而他却在

was walled against him. Like a river of adamant it flowed past him in the streets. Never an eye was turned upon him; no voice spoke to him. His heart yearned for the clap of Pittsburg's sooty hand on his shoulder; for Chicago's menacing but social yawp in his ear; for the pale and eleemosynary stare through the Bostonian eyeglass – even for the precipitate but unmalicious boot-toe of Louisville or St. Louis.

On Broadway Raggles, successful suitor of many cities, stood, bashful, like any country swain. For the first time he experienced the poignant humiliation of being ignored. And when he tried to reduce this brilliant, swiftly changing, ice-cold city to a formula he failed utterly. Poet though he was, it offered him no color similes, no points of comparison, no flaw in its polished facets, no handle by which he could hold it up and view its shape and structure, as he familiarly and often contemptuously had done with other towns. The houses were interminable ramparts loopholed for defense; the people were bright but bloodless spectres passing in sinister and selfish array.

The thing that weighed heaviest on

墙外。它像一条滔滔奔流的大河,沿着街道从他身边流过。没有一只眼睛转去看他;也没有人和他说话。他心里怀念匹兹堡那被煤炭熏黑的手掌拍打在他的肩上;怀念芝加哥在他耳边气势汹汹但不排外的喧闹;怀念波士顿人透过镜片那黯然无光但却充满善意的注视——甚至怀念路易斯维尔或圣路易斯那猛然而来但不含恶意的皮鞋尖。

成功追求过许多城市的拉格斯,站在百老汇前局促不安,就像一个刚从农村来的求爱者。他第一次尝到了被忽视的心酸和耻辱。当他尝试着把这座漂亮耀眼,水性杨花,冰冷刺骨的城市变成一个公式时,他彻底失败了。尽管他是个诗人,但这座城市没有给他彩色的明喻,也没有让他任何可以比较的地方,在它光滑的表面上面,没有任何瑕疵,没给他任何机会让他放肆的打量,以便他批评它的形状和结构,他无法再像以前轻蔑的对待其他的城市一样对待它。这儿的房子就像堡垒,布满了防御的枪眼;而市民则是欢快且冰冷的幽灵,随着阴险而自私的人群流动。

最压制拉格斯的灵魂,阻碍

Raggles's soul and clogged his poet's fancy was the spirit of absolute egotism that seemed to saturate the people as toys are saturated with paint. Each one that he considered appeared a monster of abominable and insolent conceit. Humanity was gone from them; they were toddling idols of stone and varnish, worshipping themselves and greedy for though oblivious of worship from their fellow graven images. Frozen, cruel, implacable, impervious, cut to an identical pattern, they hurried on their ways like statues brought by some miracles to motion, while soul and feeling lay unaroused in the reluctant marble.

Gradually Raggles became conscious of certain types. One was an elderly gentleman with a snow-white, short beard, pink, unwrinkled face and stony, sharp blue eyes, attired in the fashion of a gilded youth, who seemed to personify the city's wealth, ripeness and frigid unconcern. Another type was a woman, tall, beautiful, clear as a steel engraving, goddess-like, calm, clothed like the princesses of old, with eyes as coldly blue as the reflection of sunlight on a glacier. And another was a by-product of this town of marionettes – a broad, swaggering, grim,

他发挥诗人的想像力的东西则是这儿的人绝对以自我为中心的那种精神，这种精神浸透了人们的全身，就像是给玩具染上了颜色。在他看来，每个人都像是令人讨厌的傲慢自负的怪物。他们没有人性，他们是石头和清漆的正在蹒跚行走的偶像，他们崇拜自己，他们急切地渴望却又没有察觉到同胞们对他们的崇拜。他们冷酷无情，残忍麻木，全被雕刻成一个样子匆匆而过，就像在奇迹的作用下运动的大理石雕塑一样，而它们的灵魂和感觉却在这大理石里面休眠。

拉格斯逐渐认识到了一些典型人物。一种是位老绅士，有着雪白的胡须，红润而且没有任何皱纹的脸庞，和一双像石头一般冷漠尖锐的蓝眼睛，他打扮的像镀金青年一样的时髦，好像是这城市里财富、成熟和冷漠的化身。另一种典型人物是位妇女，像刻在钢雕版上的人物一样高大，美丽，清晰，像女神一样，镇定冷酷，浑身的打扮则像是前朝的公主，冷冷的蓝眼睛，就像冰川上反射的阳光。第三种类型是这座木偶城市的副产品——一个无所

threateningly sedate fellow, with a jowl as large as a harvested wheat field, the complexion of a baptized infant and the knuckles of a prize-fighter. This type leaned against cigar signs and viewed the world with frapped contumely.

A poet is a sensitive creature, and Raggles soon shrivelled in the bleak embrace of the undecipherable. The chill, sphinx-like, ironical, illegible, unnatural, ruthless expression of the city left him downcast and bewildered. Had it no heart? Better the woodpile, the scolding of vinegar-faced housewives at back doors, the kindly spleen of bartenders behind provincial free-lunch counters, the amiable truculence of rural constables, the kicks, arrests and happy-go-lucky chances of the other vulgar, loud, crude cities than this freezing heartlessness.

Raggles summoned his courage and sought alms from the populace. Unheeding, regardless, they passed on without the wink of an eyelash to testify that they were conscious of his existence. And then he said to himself that this fair but pitiless city of Manhattan was with-

顾忌，洋洋得意，冷酷无情，严肃地吓人的人，他的面颊肥硕得像块丰收的麦田，面色像受过洗礼的婴儿，长着职业拳击手那样的指关节。这样的一位典型人物靠着雪茄广告牌，用轻蔑的冷眼观察着世界。

诗人是个敏感的生物，在这种令人无法辨认的陌生冷酷的环境里，拉格斯枯萎了。这座城市表现出的冷酷残忍，嘲讽挖苦，不近人情，让他情绪低落；这座城市又像斯芬克斯之谜一样让人难以理解，使他困惑茫然。难道他是没有心的吗？就算一堆木柴、黄脸婆在后门面的咒骂、在免费午餐柜台后面站着的外地来打工的酒保所露出的善意的怒气、乡下警官友好的粗暴、被人踢打，关进蹲监，或者其他庸俗、热闹、粗俗的城市，一切的一切都比这冷酷麻木无情无义的城市要好的多。

拉格斯鼓起勇气，从平民百姓手里乞讨施舍。但他们根本不看他，毫不在意他，他们匆匆走过，连眼皮也不眨一下，根本没有意识到他的存在。于是他对自己说，这美丽却无情的曼哈顿没有灵魂；它的居民只是金属线和

out a soul; that its inhabitants were manikins moved by wires and springs, and that he was alone in a great wilderness.

Raggles started to cross the street. There was a blast, a roar, a hissing and a crash as something struck him and hurled him over and over six yards from where he had been. As he was coming down like the stick of a rocket the earth and all the cities thereof turned to a fractured dream.

Raggles opened his eyes. First an odor made itself known to him – an odor of the earliest spring flowers of Paradise. And then a hand soft as a falling petal touched his brow. Bending over him was the woman clothed like the princess of old, with blue eyes, now soft and humid with human sympathy. Under his head on the pavement were silks and furs. With Raggles's hat in his hand and with his face pinker than ever from a vehement burst of oratory against reckless driving, stood the elderly gentleman who personified the city's wealth and ripeness. From a nearby cafe hurried the by-product with the vast jowl and baby complexion, bearing a glass full of a crimson fluid that suggested delightful possibilities.

"Drink dis, sport," said the by-product,

弹簧控制的牵线木偶，他告诉自己，在这片广阔的荒原上，只有他一个活生生的人。

拉格斯开始穿越街道。在一阵爆炸声、吼叫声、嘶嘶声中，什么东西撞倒了他，把他抛到了六码以外的地方。当他像火箭筒一样撞落在地时，地球和所有的城市随之变成了一个破碎的梦。

拉格斯睁开眼睛。一阵香气扑面而来——天堂里早春时节的花香。然后是一只软软的手轻轻地触碰到他的额头，就像一片花瓣落在上面。一位穿得像前朝公主似的女人俯身看着他，她那双蓝眼睛此刻因为富含着人类的同情心而温柔湿润。他躺在人行道上，头下枕着丝手帕和毛皮衣服。他的身边站着一位老绅士，简直就是这座城市财富和成熟的化身。他手里拿着拉格斯的帽子，脸由于慷慨激昂地训斥鲁莽的司机涨得更红了。有着肥硕面颊和婴儿肤色的副产品，从附近的咖啡厅急匆匆端来满满的一杯深红色的液体，勾起了他愉悦的联想。

"喝了它，朋友，"副产品

holding the glass to Raggles's lips.

Hundreds of people huddled around in a moment, their faces wearing the deepest concern. Two flattering and gorgeous policemen got into the circle and pressed back the overplus of Samaritans. An old lady in a black shawl spoke loudly of camphor; a newsboy slipped one of his papers beneath Raggles's elbow, where it lay on the muddy pavement. A brisk young man with a notebook was asking for names.

A bell clanged importantly, and the ambulance cleaned a lane through the crowd. A cool surgeon slipped into the midst of affairs.

"How do you feel, old man?" asked the surgeon, stooping easily to his task. The princess of silks and satins wiped a red drop or two from Raggles's brow with a fragrant cobweb.

"Me?" said Raggles, with a seraphic smile, "I feel fine."

He had found the heart of his new city.

In three days they let him leave his cot for the convalescent ward in the hospital. He had been in there an hour when the attendants heard sounds of conflict. Upon investigation they found that Raggles had

说，把杯子举到拉格斯唇边。

一会儿，就有几百人挤在了他的周围，他们的脸上都露出深深的关切之情。两位讨人喜欢的英俊警察挤进人群，把过多热心助人的人赶到后面去。一位披着黑披肩的老太太大声谈论着樟脑的事情；一个报童把一份报纸悄悄地塞在了拉格斯的胳膊肘下，因为它正好落在了泥泞的人行道上。一位生气勃勃的年轻人正拿着笔记本打听姓名。

铃声叮当响起，救护车从人群中开出了一条道。一位冷静的外科医生悄悄溜到了人群的中心。

"感觉怎么样，老兄？"外科医生问，弯下腰着手工作。身穿绸缎的公主用香喷喷的丝巾擦去了拉格斯额头上冒出的一两滴红红的血珠。

"我？"拉格斯说，脸上带着天使般纯洁的微笑，"我感觉很好。"

他终于找到了新城市的心。

三天后，他们才让他从特护病床移到康复病房。他到那儿还没一小时，护士就听见了争吵声。他们过去询问，结果发现拉格斯殴打并打伤了康复病房里的一个

assaulted and damaged a brother conva-lescent – a glowering transient whom a freight train collision had sent in to be patched up.

"What's all this about?" inquired the head nurse.

"He was runnin' down me town," said Raggles.

"What town?" asked the nurse.

"Noo York," said Raggles.

病人——一位眼冒怒火的在那短暂停留的过客,他是因为货物列车碰撞事件而被送来包扎的。

"这到底是怎么回事?"护士长问。

"他辱骂我的家乡。"拉格斯说。

"你家在哪儿?"护士问。

"纽约!"拉格斯回答。

22. A MIDSUMMER KNIGHT'S DREAM
22. 仲夏骑士梦

"The knights are dead;

Their swords are rust.

Except a few who have to hustle

all the time

To raise the dust."

"骑士已死；

剑已锈钝。

存活的一些只能，

匆度岁月

去扬起灰尘。"

Dear Reader: It was summertime. The sun glared down upon the city with pitiless ferocity. It is difficult for the sun to be ferocious and exhibit compunction simultaneously. The heat was – oh, bother thermometers! – who cares for standard measures, anyhow? It was so hot that –

亲爱的读者：现在正值夏天。太阳俯瞰着这座城市，凶相穷尽，毫无怜悯之情。太阳在凶相毕露的同时还得表现自己饱受良心的谴责，这真是不太容易情。气温是——哦，去它的温度计！——不管怎么说，谁又在乎标准的计量呢？天这么热，以至于——

The roof gardens put on so many extra waiters that you could hope to get your gin fizz now – as soon as all the other people got theirs. The hospitals were putting in extra cots for bystanders. For when little, woolly dogs loll their tongues out and say "woof, woof!" at the fleas that bite 'em, and nervous old black bombazine ladies screech "Mad dog!" and policemen begin to shoot, somebody is going to get hurt. The man from

屋顶花园的餐厅用上了这么多的临时服务员，以便让你能够期盼马上就能得到你的杜松子汽酒——只要其他人都拿到了他们的那份。医院在为看热闹的人们加病床。这是因为，当毛茸茸的小狗伸出舌头冲着在叮它们的跳蚤"汪，汪！"乱叫时，身穿黑色细斜纹衣服的神经质老太太便尖叫起来说："疯狗！"，警察则拔枪射击，而这时，就会有人

Pompton, N.J., who always wears an overcoat in July, had turned up in a Broadway hotel drinking hot Scotches and enjoying his annual ray from the calcium. Philanthropists were petitioning the Legislature to pass a bill requiring builders to make tenement fire-escapes more commodious, so that families might die all together of the heat instead of one or two at a time. So many men were telling you about the number of baths they took each day that you wondered how they got along after the real lessee of the apartment came back to town and thanked 'em for taking such good care of it. The young man who called loudly for cold beef and beer in the restaurant, protesting that roast pullet and Burgundy was really too heavy for such weather, blushed when he met your eye, for you had heard him all winter calling, in modest tones, for the same ascetic viands. Soup, pocketbooks, shirt waists, actors and baseball excuses grew thinner. Yes, it was summertime.

A man stood at Thirty-fourth street waiting for a downtown car. A man of forty, gray-haired, pink-faced, keen, nervous, plainly dressed, with a harassed

受伤了。一个从新泽西州庞波顿来的男人，在这个 7 月里老穿着外套。他曾出现在百老汇的一家酒店里，一面品着热的苏格兰威士忌，一面享受着一年一次的钙辐射。慈善家们正在请求立法机关通过一个法案，要求建筑商把经济公寓的安全梯改建得更宽敞一些，这样的话，全家人就会有可能一起死于中暑，而不是一次只死掉一两个了。当租房子的人回到城里，谢过费心照料房子的人之后，好多人会跟你讲他们每天洗澡的次数，于是你便会很想知道他们是怎样挺过来的。餐馆里那位年轻人真的受不了这天气了，他扯着嗓子点了冷牛肉和冰镇啤酒，拒绝为烤仔鸡和勃艮第红酒买单。一见你的眼睛，他就会脸红，因为整个冬天你都听到过他用不高不低的嗓音，点只有禁欲者才吃的饭菜，一模一样的，从来没有变化。汤淡了，钱夹瘪了，衬衫的腰身细了，演员瘦了，打棒球的少了。没错，现在正值夏天。

一个男人站在第三十四大街上，等着开往市区的车。他已年过四十，头发灰白，面色红润，敏感并容易感到不安。他穿着朴

look around the eyes. He wiped his forehead and laughed loudly when a fat man with an outing look stopped and spoke with him.

"No, siree," he shouted with defiance and scorn. "None of your old mosquito-haunted swamps and skyscraper mountains without elevators for me. When I want to get away from hot weather I know how to do it. New York, sir, is the finest summer resort in the country. Keep in the shade and watch your diet, and don't get too far away from an electric fan. Talk about your Adirondacks and your Catskills! There's more solid comfort in the borough of Manhattan than in all the rest of the country together. No, siree! No tramping up perpendicular cliffs and being waked up at 4 in the morning by a million flies, and eating canned goods straight from the city for me. Little old New York will take a few select summer boarders; comforts and conveniences of homes – that's the ad. that I answer every time."

"You need a vacation," said the fat man, looking closely at the other. "You haven't been away from town in years. Better come with me for two weeks, anyhow. The trout in the Beaverkill are

素的衣裳，眼睛里透着厌倦。一个像是出门在外的胖男人停下同他说话时，这个等车的男人擦了擦额头，大声地笑起来。

"不，先生，"他不屑一顾地叫喊着。"你们那些布满蚊虫的沼泽和像没有电梯的摩天大楼一样的高山，都和我没有关系。当我想躲开炎热的天气时我知道该怎么办。先生，纽约可是这个国家里最好的避暑地。呆在阴凉的地方，注意你的饮食，别离电风扇太远。然后尽管吹嘘你们的阿迪朗达克和卡茨基尔群山吧！曼哈顿比全国所有的其他地区加在一起还要舒服些。不，先生！我不会去爬陡峭的山崖，不想在大清早 4 点钟就被上百万只苍蝇弄醒，吃的还是直接从这座城市运来的罐头。年迈的纽约愿意挑几个夏天来做客的人，使他们感觉宾至如归——广告就是这么说的，我每次也这样回答。"

"你需要放放假了，"胖子说，并仔细打量着这个人，"你有好些年没有走出过这个城市了。不管怎样，你最好跟我出去玩两周。这个时候，比弗基尔的

jumping at anything now that looks like a fly. Harding writes me that he landed a three-pound brown last week."

"Nonsense!" cried the other man. "Go ahead, if you like, and boggle around in rubber boots wearing yourself out trying to catch fish. When I want one I go to a cool restaurant and order it. I laugh at you fellows whenever I think of you hustling around in the heat in the country thinking you are having a good time. For me Father Knickerbocker's little improved farm with the big shady lane running through the middle of it."

The fat man sighed over his friend and went his way. The man who thought New York was the greatest summer resort in the country boarded a car and went buzzing down to his office. On the way he threw away his newspaper and looked up at a ragged patch of sky above the housetops.

"Three pounds!" he muttered, absently. "And Harding isn't a liar. I believe, if I could – but it's impossible – they've got to have another month – another month at least."

In his office the upholder of urban

鳟鱼正活蹦乱跳地朝那些苍蝇一样的虫子扑过去。哈丁写信说，上周他钓到了一条三磅重的褐色鳟鱼。"

"你说这个有什么用呢！"对方嚷道，"如果你乐意那么做你就去呀！穿上橡胶靴子，累死累活地去抓鱼呀。我什么时候想吃鱼了，去一家凉快的饭馆点一条就行了。想到你们这号人在这个国家的热气中马不停蹄地到处转，还自以为过得很好，我就觉得好笑。我呢，就待在这农场了，宽大的林荫道穿过了它的中间，纽约的祖先把它建成后就没怎么变过。"

胖子对这位朋友叹了口气，自己走了。这位认为纽约是全国最棒的避暑胜地的人上了一辆轿车，嗡嗡地驶向他的办公室。路上，他扔掉报纸，抬头看着屋顶上面参差不齐的天空。

"三磅重！"他不经意地嘀咕道。"哈丁不会说谎。我相信，要是我能——但这是不可能的事——他们得再呆一个月——至少再待一个月。"

在办公室里，这位力挺在城

midsummer joys dived, headforemost, into the swimming pool of business. Adkins, his clerk, came and added a spray of letters, memoranda and tele-grams.

At 5 o'clock in the afternoon the busy man leaned back in his office chair, put his feet on the desk and mused aloud:

"I wonder what kind of bait Harding used."

She was all in white that day; and thereby Compton lost a bet to Gaines. Compton had wagered she would wear light blue, for she knew that was his fa-vorite color, and Compton was a mil-lionaire's son, and that almost laid him open to the charge of betting on a sure thing. But white was her choice, and Gaines held up his head with twenty-five's lordly air.

The little summer hotel in the moun-tains had a lively crowd that year. There were two or three young college men and a couple of artists and a young naval officer on one side. On the other there were enough beauties among the young ladies for the correspondent of a society paper to refer to them as a "bevy." But the moon among the stars was Mary Sewell. Each one of the young men

市享受仲夏之乐的人一头扎进公务这个游泳池里。他的秘书阿德金斯拿着一叠信件、备忘录和电报走进来。

下午 5 点，这位大忙人仰面靠在办公室的椅子上，双脚放到桌上，若有所思地说：

"我在想哈丁用的是什么诱饵呢。"

那天她一身洁白，康普顿也就因此输给了盖恩斯。康普顿曾打赌说她会穿一身淡蓝，因为她知道那是他最喜欢的颜色，康普顿是位百万富翁的儿子，这差点让他公开了这场他有把握的赌注的价码。然而，她选择了白色。盖恩斯昂着头，带着他那 25 岁特有的高傲神气。

那一年，山里消夏的小旅馆迎来了一群活跃的客人。一边是两三个年轻的男大学生，几位艺术家，和一位年轻的海军军官。另一边都是年轻的女士，她们中间有足够多的美女，完全可以匹配社会上任何一家报纸给她们的"美女帮"的美称。而玛莉·休厄尔则是那群星托起的月亮。每一位年轻男士都迫不及待地和她

greatly desired to arrange matters so that he could pay her millinery bills, and fix the furnace, and have her do away with the "Sewell" part of her name forever. Those who could stay only a week or two went away hinting at pistols and blighted hearts. But Compton stayed like the mountains themselves, for he could afford it. And Gaines stayed because he was a fighter and wasn't afraid of millionaire's sons, and – well, he adored the country.

"What do you think, Miss Mary?" he said once. "I knew a duffer in New York who claimed to like it in the summer time. Said you could keep cooler there than you could in the woods. Wasn't he an awful silly? I don't think I could breathe on Broadway after the 1st of June."

"Mamma was thinking of going back week after next," said Miss Mary with a lovely frown.

"But when you think of it," said Gaines, "there are lots of jolly places in town in the summer. The roof gardens, you know, and the – er – the roof gardens."

Deepest blue was the lake that day – the day when they had the mock tournament, and the men rode clumsy farm

生出事端，这样就可以为她支付头饰用品的账单了。他们想给火炉加足燃料，使她把名字中的"休厄尔"永远熔化掉。那些只能待一两周的人，暗施小计之后，便黯然神伤地离去。可是，康普顿像一座山那样驻留了下来，因为他付得起钱。盖恩斯也留了下来，因为他是个勇士，不惧怕百万富翁的儿子，还有——嗯，他崇拜乡村生活。

"你感觉怎样，玛莉小姐？"有一次他说道，"我认识一个纽约的笨蛋说他喜欢那儿的夏天。还说你在那儿能比在森林里更凉快。他是不是忒糊涂了？我觉得，6月1号以后，我在百老汇那儿连呼吸都不顺畅了。"

"妈妈想过完下周就回去，"玛莉小姐边说边可爱地皱了皱眉。

"不过，你再想一想，"盖恩斯说，"会发现夏天城里还是有很多好玩的地方的。比如屋顶花园，你知道的，还有——呃——屋顶花园。"

那天，湖水湛蓝无比——他们在林中的空地上模拟了一场骑士比武，男士们骑着农场里笨拙

horses around in a glade in the woods and caught curtain rings on the end of a lance. Such fun!

Cool and dry as the finest wine came the breath of the shadowed forest. The valley below was a vision seen through an opal haze. A white mist from hidden falls blurred the green of a hand's breadth of tree tops half-way down the gorge. Youth made merry hand-in-hand with young summer. Nothing on Broadway like that.

The villagers gathered to see the city folks pursue their mad drollery. The woods rang with the laughter of pixies and naiads and sprites. Gaines caught most of the rings. His was the privilege to crown the queen of the tournament. He was the conquering knight – as far as the rings went. On his arm he wore a white scarf. Compton wore light blue. She had declared her preference for blue, but she wore white that day.

Gaines looked about for the queen to crown her. He heard her merry laugh, as if from the clouds. She had slipped away and climbed Chimney Rock, a little granite bluff, and stood there, a white fairy among the laurels, fifty feet above their heads.

的马争抢挂在长矛尖上的响铃。真是太有意思了!

绿树成荫的森林散发着美酒般凉爽而干燥的气息。透过乳白色的云雾,森林下边可以看见一道峡谷。在峡谷的半山腰,一片白雾从隐约的瀑布中升起,巴掌宽的绿树梢若隐若现。年轻人和年轻的夏天快乐地牵着手。在百老汇不会有这样的事情。

村民们聚在一起,看着城里人疯狂的追逐打闹。树林中响遍了仙子精灵和水泉女神的笑声。盖恩斯抢到的响铃最多,他因此获得了给比武大会的女王加冕的特权。他是获胜的骑士——就抢到的响铃数量而言。他的手臂上缠着一条白围巾,而康普顿缠的是浅蓝色的。她曾说过她偏爱蓝色,可是那天她穿的是白色。

盖恩斯四下寻找着女王,要给她加冕。他听到了她欢快的笑声,那笑声好似来自云端。她悄悄溜走了,爬上了希姆尼巨石——那是一个小小的花岗岩峭壁。她站在那儿,宛若月桂丛中的一位白衣仙子,比众人都高出15英尺来。

Instantly he and Compton accepted the implied challenge. The bluff was easily mounted at the rear, but the front offered small hold to hand or foot. Each man quickly selected his route and began to climb, A crevice, a bush, a slight projection, a vine or tree branch – all of these were aids that counted in the race. It was all foolery – there was no stake; but there was youth in it, cross reader, and light hearts, and something else that Miss Clay writes so charmingly about.

Gaines gave a great tug at the root of a laurel and pulled himself to Miss Mary's feet. On his arm he carried the wreath of roses; and while the villagers and summer boarders screamed and applauded below he placed it on the queen's brow.

"You are a gallant knight," said Miss Mary.

"If I could be your true knight always," began Gaines, but Miss Mary laughed him dumb, for Compton scrambled over the edge of the rock one minute behind time.

What a twilight that was when they drove back to the hotel! The opal of the valley turned slowly to purple, the dark woods framed the lake as a mirror, the tonic air stirred the very soul in one. The

他和康普顿立刻接受了这不言而喻的挑战。峭壁从后面上是很容易的，但是正面很少有支撑点能让手脚攀踏。两人很快就选好了各自的线路，开始往上爬。一条裂缝，一丛灌木，凸出一点的石壁，一根藤条或树枝——所有这些都算是比赛中的援助。这真是蠢事——没有奖金，但有青春，有一争高下的对手，有轻松的心，还有克莱小姐写的什么东西，如此迷人。

盖恩斯用力抓住一条月桂树的树根，使劲一拉，就到了玛丽小姐的脚下。他的手臂上挎着玫瑰花环；下面村民们和来消夏的客人们欢呼着鼓掌，他把花环戴到了女王的头上。

"你是一位英勇的骑士，"玛莉小姐说。

"要是我永远是你真正的骑士该有多好，"盖恩斯说，可是玛莉小姐笑他天真，因为一分钟以后康普顿就爬到了岩石边。

当他们驾车回旅馆的时候，暮色是如此的迷人！笼罩峡谷的乳白色烟雾慢慢变成了紫色，幽暗的树林环绕着镜子一般的湖面，充满激励的空气让人感到兴奋，搅得人心神荡漾。最早在群

first pale stars came out over the mountain tops where yet a faint glow of –

"I beg your pardon, Mr. Gaines," said Adkins.

The man who believed New York to be the finest summer resort in the world opened his eyes and kicked over the mucilage bottle on his desk.

"I – I believe I was asleep," he said.

"It's the heat," said Adkins. "It's something awful in the city these" –

"Nonsense!" said the other. "The city beats the country ten to one in summer. Fools go out tramping in muddy brooks and wear themselves out trying to catch little fish as long as your finger. Stay in town and keep comfortable – that's my idea."

"Some letters just came," said Adkins. "I thought you might like to glance at them before you go."

Let us look over his shoulder and read just a few lines of one of them:

MY DEAR, DEAR HUSBAND: Just received your letter ordering us to stay another month...Rita's cough is almost gone...Johnny has simply gone wild like a little Indian ... Will

峰上空升起的星星闪烁着微弱的光芒，天空还有一丝隐约的光亮——

"很抱歉，盖恩斯先生，"阿德金斯说。

这个认为纽约是世界上最好的避暑胜地的人，睁开眼睛，并踢倒了桌上的胶水瓶。

"我——我想我是睡着了，"他说。

"因为天气热嘛，"阿德金斯说，"这时候呆在城里真糟糕——"

"荒唐！"对方说，"夏天，城里可胜过乡下十倍呢。只有傻瓜才会淌在泥泞的溪水中，累死累活地去抓只有你手指头那么点长的小鱼。待在城里，舒舒服服的——这就是我的观点。"

"刚收到几封信，"阿德金斯说，"我想你可能想在下班前看一眼。"

让我们越过他的肩头去，看一下其中一封信上的几行字吧：

我亲爱的、亲爱的丈夫：

刚收到你命令我们多待一个月的信……丽塔不怎么咳嗽了……约翰尼简直变野了，像个印第安族的小孩……

be the making of both children... work so hard, and I know that your business can hardly afford to keep us here so long...best man that ever...you always pretend that you like the city in summer...trout fishing that you used to be so fond of...and all to keep us well and happy...come to you if it were   not doing the babies so much good...I stood last evening on Chimney Rock in exactly the same spot where I was when you put the wreath of roses on my head...through all the world...when you said you would be my true knight...fifteen years ago, dear, just think!...have always been that to me...ever and ever,

MARY.

The man who said he thought New York the finest summer resort in the country dropped into a cafe on his way home and had a glass of beer under an electric fan.

"Wonder what kind of a fly old Harding used," he said to himself.

这会把两个孩子都变野的……工作很艰辛，我知道你的生意难以担负让我们在这儿待这么久的开销……你真是我见过的最好的男人……你总是装着喜欢城里的夏天……以前你是多么喜欢钓鳟鱼啊……都是为了让我们过得好，过得幸福……如果不是怕影响孩子们的话我一定会回到你的身边陪伴你……昨晚我站在希姆尼巨石上面，恰好就站在你把玫瑰花环戴在我头上的那个地方……经历了世间的一切……当你说你将是我真正的骑士……15 年前，亲爱的，想想吧！……一直那样待我吧……永远永远。

玛莉

说他觉得纽约是全国最好的避暑胜地的这个人，在回家的路上进了一家咖啡馆，吹着电扇喝了一杯啤酒。

"真想知道，哈丁用的是哪一种钓鱼钩，"他自言自语地说道。

23. THE COUNT AND THE WEDDING GUEST
23. 伯爵与婚礼上的来客

One evening when Andy Donovan went to dinner at his Second Avenue boarding-house, Mrs. Scott introduced him to a new boarder, a young lady, Miss Conway. Miss Conway was small and unobtrusive. She wore a plain, snuffy-brown dress, and bestowed her interest, which seemed languid, upon her plate. She lifted her diffident eyelids and shot one perspicuous, judicial glance at Mr. Donovan, politely murmured his name, and returned to her mutton. Mr. Donovan bowed with the grace and beaming smile that were rapidly winning for him social, business and political advancement, and erased the snuffy-brown one from the tablets of his consideration.

Two weeks later Andy was sitting on the front steps enjoying his cigar. There was a soft rustle behind and above him, and Andy turned his head – and had his head turned.

Just coming out the door was Miss Conway. She wore a night-black dress of crêpe de – crêpe de – oh, this thin black

一天晚上，安迪·多诺万在他寄宿的第二大街的公寓里进餐的时候，司各特夫人给他介绍了一位新来的寄宿者。她是个年轻的姑娘，名字叫康韦。康韦个头不高，长得也不是很显眼。她穿着一套朴素的棕黄色衣服，兴致不高，只是盯着自己的菜盘。她羞怯地抬起头，朝多诺万先生投去清楚而又审视的一瞥。她十分礼貌地小声地重复着他的名字。之后她又埋头吃自己的羊肉。多诺万先生优雅地点点头，脸上露出愉快的微笑。这一举动立即抬高了他的社会、政治和经济上的地位，而那位穿棕黄色套服的姑娘根本不在他的考虑之列。

两个星期后，安迪正坐在门前的台阶上悠然自得地抽着香烟。在他身后，从高处传来一阵柔和的沙沙声，安迪回头看了一下——随后彻底把头转了过去。

正要出门的是康韦小姐。她身着黑色的晚装——薄薄的黑纱。帽子也是黑色的，一块乌黑

goods. Her hat was black, and from it drooped and fluttered an ebon veil, filmy as a spider's web. She stood on the top step and drew on black silk gloves. Not a speck of white or a spot of color about her dress anywhere. Her rich golden hair was drawn, with scarcely a ripple, into a shining, smooth knot low on her neck. Her face was plain rather than pretty, but it was now illuminated and made almost beautiful by her large gray eyes that gazed above the houses across the street into the sky with an expression of the most appealing sadness and melancholy.

Gather the idea, girls – all black, you know, with the preference for *crêpe de* – oh, *crêpe de Chine* – that's it. All black, and that sad, faraway look, and the hair shining under the black veil (you have to be a blonde, of course), and try to look as if, although your young life had been blighted just as it was about to give a hop-skip-and-a-jump over the threshold of life, a walk in the park might do you good, and be sure to happen out the door at the right moment, and – oh, it'll fetch 'em every time. But it's fierce, now, how cynical I am, ain't it? – to talk about mourning costumes this way.

Mr. Donovan suddenly reinscribed

的面纱搭在帽子上，像蜘蛛网一样轻薄，随风飘动。她站在最高一层台阶上，正在戴一双黑丝手套。她的衣服上没有一点白色或其他颜色。她那浓密的金发直披下来，没有一丝波痕，只在脖子后绾了个光滑发亮的发髻。她相貌一般并不十分美丽。可当她那双大眼睛凝望着街对面房子上的天空，脸上呈现出了感人的哀伤时，那张面孔就变得迷人起来，使她几乎算的上是美丽动人了。

总的印象就是，姑娘们——穿一身黑纱，你知道，她们喜欢黑色——噢，黑纱——就是这样。穿一身黑衣，还有那忧郁悲伤、恍惚出神的表情；还有那黑色面纱下发亮的头发（当然必须是位金发女郎啰）；似乎在尽力地给人一种感觉，尽管你年轻的生命已经饱受挫折，正准备像三级跳远一样跃入生命之门。那么去公园里散散步会对你会有好处的，而且要在合适的时间出门随便走一走，还有——噢，对她们而言，随时这样做都有好处的。然而这未免太残忍了，看我，多么地庸俗世故，竟然这样谈论服丧。

多诺万先生突然间又把康韦

Miss Conway upon the tablets of his consideration. He threw away the remaining inch-and-a-quarter of his cigar, that would have been good for eight minutes yet, and quickly shifted his center of gravity to his low cut patent leathers.

"It's a fine, clear evening, Miss Conway," he said; and if the Weather Bureau could have heard the confident emphasis of his tones it would have hoisted the square white signal, and nailed it to the mast.

"To them that has the heart to enjoy it, it is, Mr. Donovan," said Miss Conway, with a sigh.

Mr. Donovan, in his heart, cursed fair weather. Heartless weather! It should hail and blow and snow to be consonant with the mood of Miss Conway.

"I hope none of your relatives – I hope you haven't sustained a loss?" ventured Mr. Donovan.

"Death has claimed," said Miss Conway, hesitating – "not a relative, but one who – but I will not intrude my grief upon you, Mr. Donovan."

"Intrude?" protested Mr. Donovan. "Why, say, Miss Conway, I'd be de-

小姐列入了他的考虑之列。他扔掉手上仅剩的四分之一英寸的香烟,这截烟本来还可供他享受上八分钟。他迅速地把注视的焦点转移到他的低开口的膝皮鞋上。

"真是一个可爱、晴朗的傍晚,康韦小姐。"他说,而且假若气象局能听到他那信心十足的强调语气,恐怕会收起那块白色的正方形的信号旗,并把它钉到旗杆上去。

"对于那些有心情欣赏的人而言,确实如此。多诺万先生。"康韦小姐说着轻轻叹了一口气。

多诺万先生在心里暗暗咒骂着这个好天气。多么无情的天气呵!应该下冰雹、刮大风、下雪、下雨,这样才能与康韦小姐的心情产生共鸣啊!

"我希望你的亲戚没有——我希望你没有遭遇任何不幸?"多诺万鼓起勇气问道。

"死神已降临,"康韦小姐说,有些踌躇——"不是亲戚,而是个——但我不愿让我的悲伤来打扰你的生活,多诺万先生。"

"打扰?"多诺万抗议道,"为什么这样说呢?康韦小姐,

lighted, that is, I'd be sorry – I mean I'm sure nobody could sympathize with you truer than I would."

Miss Conway smiled a little smile. And oh, it was sadder than her expression in repose.

"'Laugh, and the world laughs with you; weep, and they give you the laugh,'" she quoted. "I have learned that, Mr. Donovan. I have no friends or acquaintances in this city. But you have been kind to me. I appreciate it highly."

He had passed her the pepper twice at the table.

"It's tough to be alone in New York – that's a cinch," said Mr. Donovan. "But, say – whenever this little old town does loosen up and get friendly it goes the limit. Say you took a little stroll in the park, Miss Conway – don't you think it might chase away some of your mullygrubs? And if you'd allow me –"

"Thanks, Mr. Donovan. I'd be pleased to accept of your escort if you think the company of one whose heart is filled with gloom could be anyways agreeable to you."

Through the open gates of the iron-railed, old, downtown park, where the elect once took the air, they strolled,

我会很高兴的，我意思是，我将会很难过——我是想说，没有任何人会比我更真心地同情你了。"

康韦小姐脸上微微浮出一丝笑意。哦，这笑比她的沉默更加令人悲伤，令人可怜。

"笑吧，世界会与你同笑；哭吧，世界也会给你笑声。"她引用了一句名言。"我明白这道理，多诺万先生。在这个城市，我没有朋友也没有熟人，但你对我真好。我非常感激你。"

吃饭时，他曾两次递给她胡椒粉。

"一个人在纽约生活很艰难——这是肯定的。"多诺万先生说，"但要是这个古老的小城不那么冷酷，变得友善起来，这个城市也就走到尽头了。你要去公园散散步，康韦小姐——难道你不认为去散散步可以驱散你心头的忧伤吗？假如你允许我——"

"谢谢你，多诺万先生。我很高兴接受您的陪伴，如果你认为一个心情忧郁悲伤的人还能给你带来一点愉快的话。"

穿过敞开的大门，他们步入铁栏杆围起来的古老的市中央的公园。这里曾是特权集团的游玩

and found a quiet bench.

There is this difference between the grief of youth and that of old age: youth's burden is lightened by as much of it as another shares; old age may give and give, but the sorrow remains the same.

"He was my fiance," confided Miss Conway, at the end of an hour. "We were going to be married next spring. I don't want you to think that I am stringing you, Mr. Donovan, but he was a real Count. He had an estate and a castle in Italy. Count Fernando Mazzini was his name. I never saw the beat of him for elegance. Papa objected, of course, and once we eloped, but papa overtook us, and took us back. I thought sure papa and Fernando would fight a duel. Papa has a livery business – in P'kipsee, you know."

"Finally, papa came 'round, all right, and said we might be married next spring. Fernando showed him proofs of his title and wealth, and then went over to Italy to get the castle fixed up for us. Papa's very proud, and when Fernando wanted to give me several thousand dollars for my trousseau he called him down something awful. He wouldn't even let

之处。在公园里,他们找到了一处幽静的地方,坐在一条长凳上。

青年人的忧伤与老年人的忧伤不同。青年人的忧伤会因别人的分享而减少,而老年人的忧伤不管有多少人来分享,都不会有丝毫的减少。

"他是我的未婚夫,"一小时后,康韦终于把心中秘密告诉了他。"我们本来打算明年春天结婚。我不想让你认为我在欺骗你。可是多诺万先生,他是一位真正的伯爵。他在意大利有地产和一座城堡。他的名字叫弗兰多·马齐尼伯爵。他身上贵族的优雅是那般完美。当然了,因为父亲的反对,我们私奔了,但父亲追上了我们,把我们带了回来。我心想,父亲肯定会和弗兰多决斗。父亲是做服装生意的——在蒲基比,你应该知道这个地方。"

"最终,父亲终于同意了,他说我们可以在明年结婚。弗兰多给父亲看了他的头衔证明和财产证明后,就去意大利修缮城堡,好为将来的生活做准备。父亲是个非常骄傲的人。当弗兰多想给我几千美金买嫁妆时,父亲狠狠地骂了他一顿。他甚至不允许我接受弗兰多送的一枚戒指或其他

me take a ring or any presents from him. And when Fernando sailed I came to the city and got a position as cashier in a candy store."

"Three days ago I got a letter from Italy, forwarded from P'kipsee, saying that Fernando had been killed in a gondola accident."

"That is why I am in mourning. My heart, Mr. Donovan, will remain forever in his grave. I guess I am poor company, Mr. Donovan, but I cannot take any interest in no one. I should not care to keep you from gayety and your friends who can smile and entertain you. Perhaps you would prefer to walk back to the house?"

Now, girls, if you want to observe a young man hustle out after a pick and shovel, just tell him that your heart is in some other fellow's grave. Young men are grave-robbers by nature. Ask any widow. Something must be done to restore that missing organ to weeping angels in *crêpe de Chine*. Dead men certainly get the worst of it from all sides.

"I'm awfully sorry," said Mr. Donovan, gently. "No, we won't walk back to the house just yet. And don't say you haven't no friends in this city, Miss

任何礼物。当他坐船回意大利后，我便来到这个城市，找到了一份在糖果店干出纳的工作。"

"三天前，我收到一封来自意大利的信，是由蒲基比转来的。信中说，弗兰多在一次沉船事故中遇难了。"

"这便是我穿丧服的原因。我的心，多诺万先生，将永远在他的坟墓里伴随着他。我知道自己不是一个好伴侣，可我不会再对任何人感兴趣了。我不应该阻止你和你的那些心情愉快、可以给你带来欢乐的朋友在一起。也许你宁愿回到住处去了吧？"

好吧，年轻的女孩子们，如果你想观察一个青年男子是如何冲到铁镐铁铲面前去的话，请告诉他你的心已经在另一个男人的坟墓里了。年轻男人是天生的"盗墓者"，随便哪一个寡妇都会告诉你这一真理。必须得想办法帮助那位穿黑丧衣的天使恢复那失去的感官才行。不管怎么说，死人必然是最倒霉的。

"我真为你感到难过。"多诺万先生温柔地说。"不，我们现在先别回住处。康韦小姐，千万别再说你在这个城市没有任何

Conway. I'm awful sorry, and I want you to believe I'm your friend, and that I'm awful sorry."

"I've got his picture here in my locket," said Miss Conway, after wiping her eyes with her handkerchief. "I never showed it to anybody; but I will to you, Mr. Donovan, because I believe you to be a true friend."

Mr. Donovan gazed long and with much interest at the photograph in the locket that Miss Conway opened for him. The face of Count Mazzini was one to command interest. It was a smooth, intelligent, bright, almost a handsome face – the face of a strong, cheerful man who might well be a leader among his fellows.

"I have a larger one, framed, in my room," said Miss Conway. "When we return I will show you that. They are all I have to remind me of Fernando. But he ever will be present in my heart, that's a sure thing."

A subtle task confronted Mr. Donovan, – that of supplanting the unfortunate Count in the heart of Miss Conway. This his admiration for her determined him to do. But the magnitude of the undertaking did not seem to weigh upon his spirits. The sympathetic but cheerful friend was

朋友。我非常同情你。希望你相信，我就是你的朋友，我真的很同情你的遭遇。"

"在我项链的金属盒里有他的照片。"用手帕擦了擦眼睛后，康韦小姐说。"我从未给任何人看过，但我想给你看，多诺万先生。因为我相信你是个真正的朋友。"

康韦打开盒子，多诺万先生怀着极大的兴趣久久地望着那张照片。马齐尼伯爵的脸庞很有魅力，干净、机智、聪明，是个英俊的男子———一张霸气的开朗的男人的面孔。在朋友当中他也应该是个带头大哥之类的人物。

"我还有一张更大的，镶着镜框，在我的房间里。"康韦小姐说，"我们回去后，我会拿给你看的。这便是我所拥有的会让我想起他的全部东西。但是，毫无疑问，他将会永远在我心里。"

一个微妙的任务摆在了多诺万的面前——那便是取代不幸的伯爵在康韦小姐心中的位置。决定这么做，是出自他对康韦小姐的倾慕。但这项浩大的工程并未使他感到沉重。他要扮演的角色是一个充满同情心而又让人心情

the role he essayed; and he played it so successfully that the next half-hour found them conversing pensively across two plates of ice-cream, though yet there was no diminution of the sadness in Miss Conway's large gray eyes.

Before they parted in the hall that evening she ran upstairs and brought down the framed photograph wrapped lovingly in a white silk scarf. Mr. Donovan surveyed it with inscrutable eyes.

"He gave me this the night he left for Italy," said Miss Conway. "I had the one for the locket made from this."

"A fine-looking man," said Mr. Donovan, heartily. "How would it suit you, Miss Conway, to give me the pleasure of your company to Coney next Sunday afternoon?"

A month later they announced their engagement to Mrs. Scott and the other boarders. Miss Conway continued to wear black.

A week after the announcement the two sat on the same bench in the down-town park, while the fluttering leaves of the trees made a dim kinetoscopic picture of them in the moonlight. But Donovan had worn a look of abstracted gloom all day. He was so silent to-night that love's

愉快的朋友；而且他又扮演得如此成功，以至于半小时后他们已经面对面地坐着，吃着两盒冰淇淋，深情地互相倾诉心里话了，虽然康韦小姐那双灰褐色大眼睛里面的忧郁还没有消减。

那晚，当他们在大厅里分手之前，她迅速地跑上楼去把那幅更大的照片抱了下来。照片镶在镜框里，用一条白色的丝绸围巾精心地包裹着；多诺万先生仔细地看着这照片，神情神秘莫测。

"这是他去意大利之前那天晚上给我的。"康韦小姐说，"金盒子里的那张是缩洗出来的。"

"一位英俊的男子汉。"多诺万亲切地说道，"康韦小姐，不知你愿不愿意下星期天的下午陪我去趟康莱？"

一个月之后，他们向司各特太太和其他寄宿者宣布了他们订婚的消息。康韦小姐仍然穿着一身黑色衣服。

他们宣布订婚一周后，两人又坐在市中心公园的那一条长凳上。月光下，摇曳的树叶在地上的影子显得昏暗不清。一整天，多诺万脸上都是一副莫名其妙的沮丧神情。晚上更是一句话也不说，弄得他的情人实在憋不住涌

lips could not keep back any longer the questions that love's heart propounded.

"What's the matter, Andy, you are so solemn and grouchy to-night?"

"Nothing, Maggie."

"I know better. Can't I tell? You never acted this way before. What is it?"

"It's nothing much, Maggie."

"Yes it is; and I want to know. I'll bet it's some other girl you are thinking about. All right. Why don't you go get her if you want her? Take your arm away, if you please."

"I'll tell you then," said Andy, wisely, "but I guess you won't understand it exactly. You've heard of Mike Sullivan, haven't you? 'Big Mike' Sullivan, everybody calls him."

"No, I haven't," said Maggie. "And I don't want to, if he makes you act like this. Who is he?"

"He's the biggest man in New York," said Andy, almost reverently. "He can about do anything he wants to with Tammany or any other old thing in the political line. He's a mile high and as broad as East River. You say anything against Big Mike, and you'll have a mil-

上心头的疑问：

"发生什么事了，安迪？你今晚为什么这么严肃忧郁呢？"

"没事儿，玛吉。"

"别骗我了，我难道连这都看不出来吗？你以前从来都不会这样的。到底怎么了？"

"不是什么大事，玛吉。"

"是大事，而且我很想知道发生了什么。我敢打赌你一定是在想别的女孩子。不过没关系，如果你想她，你为什么不去找她呢？请把手臂拿开吧。"

"那我就告诉你吧。"安迪灵机一动说道，"但我猜你是不会完全明白的。你一定听说过麦克·萨利万，是吗？'大麦克'·萨利万。大家都这样叫他。"

"没，我没听说过，"玛吉说，"我也不愿意听到这个名字，如果你是因为他才变成这个样子的话。他是谁？"

"他是整个纽约的老大。"安迪说道，口气几乎可以算恭敬了。他和坦慕尼协会或政界的任何一个古老势力都联系密切，他想干什么就干什么。他身材高大，肩膀像伊斯特河一样宽。如果你说了他的坏话，不到两秒钟就会

lion men on your collarbone in about two seconds. Why, he made a visit over to the old country awhile back, and the kings took to their holes like rabbits.

"Well, Big Mike's a friend of mine. I ain't more than deuce-high in the district as far as influence goes, but Mike's as good a friend to a little man, or a poor man as he is to a big one. I met him to-day on the Bowery, and what do you think he does? Comes up and shakes hands. 'Andy,' says he, 'I've been keeping cases on you. You've been putting in some good licks over on your side of the street, and I'm proud of you. What'll you take to drink?" He takes a cigar, and I take a highball. I told him I was going to get married in two weeks. 'Andy,' says he, 'send me an invitation, so I'll keep in mind of it, and I'll come to the wedding.' That's what Big Mike says to me; and he always does what he says.

"You don't understand it, Maggie, but I'd have one of my hands cut off to have Big Mike Sullivan at our wedding. It would be the proudest day of my life. When he goes to a man's wedding, there's a guy being married that's made for life. Now, that's why I'm maybe looking sore to-night."

有数百万人来攻击你。他刚刚访问了一个古老的国家，那里的首领们像兔子一样乖乖地躲进了自己的洞里。

"告诉你吧，大麦克是我的一个朋友。虽然我个头不高，也没什么影响力，但麦克对小人物或穷人与对大人物或富人是完全一样的。今天我在波法立碰见他。你猜他是怎么作的？他走过来和我握手！'安迪'，他说，'我一直都在打听你的消息，你现在已经有些影响力了，我真为你感到骄傲。你想喝点什么吗？'他掏出一支雪茄，我要了一杯威士忌。我告诉他再过两周我就要结婚了。""安迪，"他说，"送一份请柬给我吧，这样我才不会忘记。我会去参加你的婚礼的。"这是大麦克和我说的，而他是个一诺千金的人。

"你不明白的，玛吉，为了麦克能来参加我的婚礼，我情愿砍下自己的一只手。这将会是我这辈子最骄傲的日子。如果麦克去参加一个男人的婚礼，就意味着这个男人结婚成家后能享受平静的生活。哦，这就是为什么今晚我可能显得有些沮丧的原因。"

"Why don't you invite him, then, if he's so much to the mustard?" said Maggie, lightly.

"There's a reason why I can't," said Andy, sadly. "There's a reason why he mustn't be there. Don't ask me what it is, for I can't tell you."

"Oh, I don't care," said Maggie. "It's something about politics, of course. But it's no reason why you can't smile at me."

"Maggie," said Andy, presently, "do you think as much of me as you did of your – as you did of the Count Mazzini?"

He waited a long time, but Maggie did not reply. And then, suddenly she leaned against his shoulder and began to cry – to cry and shake with sobs, holding his arm tightly, and wetting the *crêpe de Chine* with tears.

"There, there, there!" soothed Andy, putting aside his own trouble. "And what is it, now?"

"Andy," sobbed Maggie. "I've lied to you, and you'll never marry me, or love me any more. But I feel that I've got to tell. Andy, there never was so much as the little finger of a count. I never had a beau in my life. But all the other girls had; and they talked about 'em; and that

"那你为什么不邀请他呢？如果他对于今后的家庭生活是这么重要的话。"玛吉轻轻地说。

"我不请他是有原因的。"安迪难过地说，"他绝对不能参加我们的婚礼是有原因的，别再问我了，我不能告诉你。"

"噢，没关系，"玛吉说，"那是些与政治有关的事。但这不能解释为何你一直对我绷着脸。"

"玛吉"，安迪立即问道，"在你的心目中，我和你的——和马齐尼伯爵同样重要吗？"

他等了好长一段时间。然而，玛吉一直没有回答。突然，她靠在他的肩膀上大哭起来——哭得整个身体都在抽搐。她不停地颤抖，紧紧地抓住他的胳膊，她的泪水流下来，打湿了她的黑丧服。

"好啦！好啦！别哭了。"安迪安慰道，把自己的苦恼先放在一边。"现在好些了吗？"

"安迪，"玛吉还在抽泣，"我欺骗了你，你再也不会娶我了，再也不会爱我了。但是，我想我必须告诉你真相。其实，安迪，根本没有伯爵这个人。我也从没有过任何男朋友，而其他女孩子都有过。而且她们都常常把那些事挂在嘴边，仿佛这样就能

seemed to make the fellows like 'em more. And, Andy, I look swell in black – you know I do. So I went out to a photograph store and bought that picture, and had a little one made for my locket, and made up all that story about the Count, and about his being killed, so I could wear black. And nobody can love a liar, and you'll shake me, Andy, and I'll die for shame. Oh, there never was anybody I liked but you – and that's all."

But instead of being pushed away, she found Andy's arm folding her closer. She looked up and saw his face cleared and smiling.

"Could you – could you forgive me, Andy?"

"Sure," said Andy. "It's all right about that. Back to the cemetery for the Count. You've straightened everything out, Maggie. I was in hopes you would before the wedding-day. Bully girl!"

"Andy," said Maggie, with a somewhat shy smile, after she had been thoroughly assured of forgiveness, "did you believe all that story about the Count?"

"Well, not to any large extent," said

使男人们更加爱她们。还有，安迪，我穿黑衣服很有气质——这你是知道的。所以我去了一家照相馆，买了那张照片；又专门为了小金盒缩印了那张小照片。我还编造了关于一位伯爵以及他怎样遇难的故事，这样我才可以全身穿黑色衣服。我知道，没有人会爱撒谎的人，你一定会离开我。安迪，我也会因为羞耻而死去。在这个世上，我没有爱过任何人，只爱过你——我想说的就这些。"

但是，她发现自己不但没有被推开，反而被安迪的手臂搂得更紧了。她抬起头来，望着他。只见他脸上的愁云已经散去，并且脸上堆满了笑容。

"你，你能原谅我吗，安迪？"

"当然，"安迪肯定地说。"我可以理解你为什么这样做。去公墓看看伯爵吧，你已经解决了一切问题，玛吉。我本来就对你充满信心，知道你会在婚礼前把一切都处理好，亲爱的宝贝。"

"安迪，"玛吉说，她彻底相信他已经原谅了她，她羞怯地笑了笑。"你以前完全相信那个关于伯爵的故事吗？"

"噢，并不是太相信。"安

Andy, reaching for his cigar case, "because it's Big Mike Sullivan's picture you've got in that locket of yours."

迪边说边伸手去掏雪茄，"因为你那小金盒子里的照片正是大麦克·萨利万。"

24. THE MARRY MONTH OF MAY
24. 快乐五月

Prithee, smite the poet in the eye when he would sing to you praises of the month of May. It is a month presided over by the spirits of mischief and madness. Pixies and flibbertigibbets haunt the budding woods: Puck and his train of midgets are busy in town and country.

In May nature holds up at us a chiding finger, bidding us remember that we are not gods, but overconceited members of her own great family. She reminds us that we are brothers to the chowder-doomed clam and the donkey; lineal scions of the pansy and the chimpanzee, and but cousins-german to the cooing doves, the quacking ducks and the housemaids and policemen in the parks.

In May Cupid shoots blindfolded – millionaires marry stenographers; wise professors woo white-aproned gum-chewers behind quick-lunch counters; schoolma'ams make big bad boys remain after school; lads with ladders steal lightly over lawns where Juliet waits in her trellissed window with her telescope

当诗人向你歌颂五月的时候，请您瞄准他的眼睛用力地打下去。这个月份被爱捣蛋和疯狂的精灵所主宰，小淘气和轻浮之徒常常出没于刚刚抽出嫩牙的树林中；帕克和他的侏儒队伍也在城市和乡村之间忙忙碌碌。

五月里，大自然向我们竖起一根手指头来责备我们，它要我们记住，我们不是神，而只是她的大家庭中一名过于自高自大的成员。她提醒我们，我们是命中注定做海鲜杂烩汤的蛤蜊还有驴子的兄弟，同性恋男子和黑猩猩的直系后代，是咕咕叫的鸽子，呱呱叫的鸭子，女仆和公园里的警察的堂表兄弟或姐妹。

五月，丘比特闭上眼睛胡乱放箭——百万富翁娶了速记员；睿智的教授向快餐柜台后面系着白色围裙嚼着口香糖的女人求婚；学校的女教师吸引了年龄较大的坏孩子，使得他们放了学也不愿意回家；情人悄悄带着梯子穿越草坪，而朱丽叶正等在格子

packed; young couples out for a walk come home married; old chaps put on white spats and promenade near the Normal School; even married men, grown unwontedly tender and sentimental, whack their spouses on the back and growl: "How goes it, old girl:"

This May, who is no goddess, but Circe, masquerading at the dance given in honour of the fair debutante, Summer, puts the kibosh on us all.

Old Mr. Coulson groaned a little, and then sat up straight in his invalid's chair. He had the gout very bad in one foot, a house near Gramercy Park, half a million dollars and a daughter. And he had a housekeeper, Mrs. Widdup. The fact and the name deserve a sentence each. They have it.

When May poked Mr. Coulson he became elder brother to the turtle-dove. In the window near which he sat were boxes of jonquils, of hyacinths, geraniums and pansies. The breeze brought their odour into the room. Immediately there was a well-contested round between the breath of the flowers and the

窗里边，做好了私奔的准备；年轻的情侣们外出散步，还没回家就结了婚；老家伙们穿着白罩鞋，在师范学校附近转悠；甚至已婚的男人，也变得反常地温柔和多愁善感起来，一边狠狠地捶打其配偶的后背，一边咆哮道："感觉怎么样？老姑娘？"

这个五月，不是女神，而是老妖婆喀耳刻。就像在夏天为首次进入社交界的青年女子举办的盛大庆祝舞会上，妖婆戴着面具，就是为了把我们吓退。

库尔森先生在轻声地呻吟，然后在轮椅上挺直了身子。他的一只脚患有严重的痛风。他在格兰梅塞公园旁有幢房子，还有百万美元的一半的财产和一个女儿。他还有个女管家，叫威德普夫人。这个女管家和她的名字绝对值得各用一整个句子来描述，它们确实是有深远意义的。

当五月戏弄着库尔森先生时，他变成了斑鸠的大哥。他靠窗坐着，旁边是一盆盆长寿花，风信子，天竺葵花和圆三色堇花。微风把花香送进屋里，顿时，花的香味和痛风药水散发出的刺鼻臭气展开了一场激烈的竞争。臭气轻而易举地赢得了胜利。但是

able and active effluvium from gout liniment. The liniment won easily; but not before the flowers got an uppercut to old Mr. Coulson's nose. The deadly work of the implacable, false enchantress May was done.

Across the park to the olfactories of Mr. Coulson came other unmistakable, characteristic, copyrighted smells of spring that belong to the-big-city-above-the-Subway, alone. The smells of hot asphalt, underground caverns, gasoline, patchouli, orange peel, sewer gas, Albany grabs, Egyptian cigarettes, mortar and the undried ink on newspapers. The in-blowing air was sweet and mild. Sparrows wrangled happily everywhere outdoors. Never trust May.

Mr. Coulson twisted the ends of his white mustache, cursed his foot, and pounded a bell on the table by his side.

In came Mrs. Widdup. She was comely to the eye, fair, flustered, forty and foxy.

"Higgins is out, sir," she said, with a smile suggestive of vibratory massage. "He went to post a letter. Can I do anything for you, sir?"

"It's time for my aconite," said old Mr. Coulson. "Drop it for me. The bottle's

花儿还是给库尔森老先生的鼻子带来了一阵芬芳。虚伪的五月妖婆，给了他难以平息的致命一击。

另一些明确的，典型的，春天专有的气息——单单属于地铁之上的大都市——穿越公园，涌入了库尔森先生的嗅觉器官，诸如热沥青、地洞、汽油、广藿香、橙皮、下水道排出的气体、奥尔巴尼的大商店、埃及卷烟、砂浆和油墨未干的报纸等等之类的气味。但吹进房间的空气又甜又暖，处处都有麻雀喳喳地在窗外欢叫。绝对不能信任五月。

库尔森先生捻了捻雪白的胡子，大声诅咒着他的脚，然后重重地按了按身边桌子上的铃。

威德普夫人走进来。她长得很养眼，体态优美，虽然已经 40 岁，但还是非常的性感。

"希金斯出去了，先生，"她笑着说，让人想起被按摩时的舒服感觉。"他去邮局寄信了。我能为你做些什么吗，先生？"

"到我吃乌头的时间了，"库尔森老先生说。"给我把药倒

there. Three drops. In water. D – that is, confound Higgins! There's nobody in this house cares if I die here in this chair for want of attention."

Mrs. Widdup sighed deeply.

"Don't be saying that, sir," she said. "There's them that would care more than any one knows. Thirteen drops, you said, sir?"

"Three," said old man Coulson.

He took his dose and then Mrs. Widdup's hand. She blushed. Oh, yes, it can be done. Just hold your breath and compress the diaphragm.

"Mrs. Widdup," said Mr. Coulson, "the springtime's full upon us."

"Ain't that right?" said Mrs. Widdup. "The air's real warm. And there's bock-beer signs on every corner. And the park's all yaller and pink and blue with flowers; and I have such shooting pains up my legs and body."

"'In the spring,'" quoted Mr. Coulson, curling his mustache, "'a y – that is, a man's – fancy lightly turns to thoughts of love.'"

"Lawsy, now!" exclaimed Mrs. Widdup; "ain't that right? Seems like it's in the air."

出来。瓶子就在那儿。三滴,兑水。倒——就是说,该死的希金斯!我需要人照顾,就算是我因为无人关心而死在这张椅子上,也不会有人在意。"

威德普夫人深深叹了口气。

"别这么说,先生,"她说。"有些人会好好地照顾你,比任何人都更尽心地照顾你。是13滴吗,先生?"

"3滴,"老库尔森先生说。

吃过药之后,他握住了威德普夫人的手,她脸红了。嗯,是的,没问题,只要你屏住呼吸,压紧隔膜就可以了。

"威德普夫人,"库尔森先生说,"春天就在我们身边。"

"难道这不好吗?"威德普夫人说道。"天气真的暖和了。每个街角都有卖啤酒的人。公园里到处鲜花盛开,一片姹紫嫣红;我的双腿和身体也疼痛起来。"

"在春天,"库尔森先生吟诵道,同时用手卷着胡子,"一个年轻——我是说,一个男人的——幻想悄悄转向了爱情。"

"天哪!现在!"威德普夫人喊道;"你说的对!我感觉爱情似乎就在空气中似的。"

"'In the spring,'" continued old Mr. Coulson, "'a livelier iris shines upon the burnished dove.'"

"They do be lively, the Irish," sighed Mrs. Widdup pensively.

"Mrs. Widdup," said Mr. Coulson, making a face at a twinge of his gouty foot, "this would be a lonesome house without you. I'm an – that is, I'm an elderly man – but I'm worth a comfortable lot of money. If half a million dollars' worth of Government bonds and the true affection of a heart that, though no longer beating with the first ardour of youth, can still throb with genuine –"

The loud noise of an overturned chair near the portieres of the adjoining room interrupted the venerable and scarcely suspecting victim of May.

In stalked Miss Van Meeker Constantia Coulson, bony, durable, tall, high-nosed, frigid, well-bred, thirty-five, in-the-neighbourhood-of- Gramercy-Parkish. She put up a lorgnette. Mrs. Widdup hastily stooped and arranged the bandages on Mr. Coulson's gouty foot.

"I thought Higgins was with you," said Miss Van Meeker Constantia.

"在春天，"库尔森先生继续说道，"绚丽的彩虹照耀着闪闪发亮的白鸽。"

"他们的确很有活力，那些爱尔兰人，"威德普夫人若有所思地叹道。

"威德普夫人，"库尔森先生说，痛风的脚的阵痛使他皱起了眉头，"如果没有你，这房子就是孤独寂寞的。我是个——也就是说，我是个老人——但我有很多钱。如果说价值百万美元一半的政府债券，再加上一颗饱含真情的心，尽管它不再有青年人初恋的激情，可是仍然在跳动，为了真心的——"

隔壁房间的门帘旁边，传来了椅子打翻的响声，恰好阻止了五月妖婆去伤害值得尊敬却几乎没有察觉到的受害者。

范·米克·康斯坦蒂亚·库尔森小姐昂首阔步地走了进来。她瘦削，结实，高高的个子和鼻子，冷漠，戴着副长柄眼镜，受过良好教育，她35岁了，是典型的格兰梅塞公园附近的居民。威德普夫人赶紧弯下腰，给库尔森先生痛风的脚缠上绷带。

"我本以为希金斯会在你身边，"范·米克·康斯坦蒂亚小

"Higgins went out," explained her father, "and Mrs. Widdup answered the bell. That is better now, Mrs. Widdup, thank you. No; there is nothing else I require."

The housekeeper retired, pink under the cool, inquiring stare of Miss Coulson.

"This spring weather is lovely, isn't it, daughter?" said the old man, consciously conscious.

"That's just it," replied Miss Van Meeker Constantia Coulson, somewhat obscurely. "When does Mrs. Widdup start on her vacation, papa?"

"I believe she said a week from to-day," said Mr. Coulson.

Miss Van Meeker Constantia stood for a minute at the window gazing, toward the little park, flooded with the mellow afternoon sunlight. With the eye of a botanist she viewed the flowers – most potent weapons of insidious May. With the cool pulses of a virgin of Cologne she withstood the attack of the ethereal mildness. The arrows of the pleasant sunshine fell back, frostbitten, from the cold panoply of her unthrilled bosom. The odour of the flowers waked no soft sentiments in the unexplored recesses of her dormant heart. The chirp of the spar-

"希金斯出去了，"她父亲解释说，"威德普夫人是应铃过来。我现在好多了，威德普夫人，谢谢。不，没事了，没别的事了。"

在库尔森小姐冷冷的追究目光直射下，女管家红着脸走开了。

"春天的天气很可爱，不是吗，女儿？"老人特意装作不经意地问道。

"也就那样，"范·米克·康斯坦蒂亚·库尔森小姐的回答令人有些晦涩难懂。"爸爸，威德普夫人什么时候开始休假？"

"我记得她说一周之后，"库尔森先生说。

下午，范·米克·康斯坦蒂亚小姐在窗边站了有一分钟的时间，她凝视着洒满温暖阳光的小公园，用植物学家的目光观察着鲜花——阴险的五月里最具威力的武器。她有着圣洁贞女般的冷静，这让她抵制住了缥缈虚幻的温和的进攻。令人愉快的阳光根本射不进她的心里去，她那死一般平静的心，被冰冷的盔甲包裹着，阳光在这里都遭遇了霜冻。花香不能唤醒她内心深处的温柔感情，因为她的心正在休眠。麻雀的叽叽喳喳只能给她带来痛

rows gave her a pain. She mocked at May.

But although Miss Coulson was proof against the season, she was keen enough to estimate its power. She knew that elderly men and thick-waisted women jumped as educated fleas in the ridiculous train of May, the merry mocker of the months. She had heard of foolish old gentlemen marrying their housekeepers before. What a humiliating thing, after all, was this feeling called love!

The next morning at 8 o'clock, when the iceman called, the cook told him that Miss Coulson wanted to see him in the basement.

"Well, ain't I the Olcott and Depew; not mentioning the first name at all?" said the iceman, admiringly, of himself.

As a concession he rolled his sleeves down, dropped his icehooks on a syringa and went back. When Miss Van Meeker Constantia Coulson addressed him he took off his hat.

"There is a rear entrance to this basement," said Miss Coulson, "which can be reached by driving into the vacant lot next door, where they are excavating for a building. I want you to bring in that way within two hours 1,000 pounds of ice.

苦。她嘲笑五月。

尽管库尔森小姐反对这个季节，但她还是很敏锐地去估价它的能量。她，这个嘲笑季节的人，清楚地知道，上了年纪的男人们和有着水桶腰的女人们就像可笑的五月列车上受过训练的跳蚤一样不安分。她以前听说过一些关于愚蠢的老绅士娶了女管家的事情。总之，把这种感情叫做爱情是件多么丢人的事！

第二天早晨 8 点，卖冰的人来了，厨子告诉他库尔森小姐想在地下室见他。

"哎，我又不是奥尔科特和迪普，怎么都不提我的名字呢？"卖冰人自我欣赏地说道。

最后他还是让步了，他把袖子捋下来，把冰钩放在一株山梅花上，然后朝回走。当范·米克·康斯坦蒂亚·库尔森小姐向他讲话时，他就向她脱帽行礼。

"地下室有个后门，"库尔森小姐说，"从隔壁的空地就可以进来，他们正在空地上挖地基盖房子。我要你两小时之内从那道门搬 1 000 磅冰进来。你可以找一两个人帮你。我会告诉你把冰

You may have to bring another man or two to help you. I will show you where I want it placed. I also want 1,000 pounds a day delivered the same way for the next four days. Your company may charge the ice on our regular bill. This is for your extra trouble."

Miss Coulson tendered a ten-dollar bill. The iceman bowed, and held his hat in his two hands behind him.

"Not if you'll excuse me, lady. It'll be a pleasure to fix things up for you any way you please."

Alas for May!

About noon Mr. Coulson knocked two glasses off his table, broke the spring of his bell and yelled for Higgins at the same time.

"Bring an axe," commanded Mr. Coulson, sardonically, "or send out for a quart of prussic acid, or have a policeman come in and shoot me. I'd rather that than be frozen to death."

"It does seem to be getting cool, Sir," said Higgins. "I hadn't noticed it before. I'll close the window, Sir."

"Do," said Mr. Coulson. "They call this spring, do they? If it keeps up long I'll go back to Palm Beach. House feels

放在什么地方。此外，我每天还要 1 000 磅冰，从同一条道运进来，从明天算起，连续送四天。你的公司可以把冰钱记在我们定期支付的账单上。这是给你额外辛苦的报酬。"

库尔森小姐给了他一张 10 美元的钞票。卖冰人点头鞠躬，双手拿着帽子放在身后。

"嗯，要是你能原谅我就好了，小姐。为您效力是我的荣幸，不管干什么，只要能让您高兴，那就太好了。"

哎呀，为了五月！

大约中午的时候，库尔森先生打翻了桌上的两只玻璃杯，拽坏了铃的弹簧，他大声叫喊着希金斯。

"去拿把斧子来，"库尔森先生语带嘲讽地命令道，"或去找人弄一夸脱氢氰酸来，或者让警察来枪毙我吧。我宁愿这样也不愿意被冻死。"

"好像的确是冷起来了，先生，"希金斯说。"我以前没有注意到。我马上关窗户，先生。"

"快去，"库尔森先生说。"他们还把这种天气叫春天，是不是？如果还是这么冷，我就回

like a morgue."

Later Miss Coulson dutifully came in to inquire how the gout was progressing.

"Stantia," said the old man, "how is the weather outdoors?"

"Bright," answered Miss Coulson, "but chilly."

"Feels like the dead of winter to me," said Mr. Coulson.

"An instance," said Constantia, gazing abstractedly out the window, "of 'winter lingering in the lap of spring,' though the metaphor is not in the most refined taste."

A little later she walked down by the side of the little park and on westward to Broadway to accomplish a little shopping.

A little later than that Mrs. Widdup entered the invalid's room.

"Did you ring, Sir?" she asked, dimpling in many places. "I asked Higgins to go to the drug store, and I thought I heard your bell."

"I did not," said Mr. Coulson.

"I'm afraid," said Mrs. Widdup, "I interrupted you sir, yesterday when you were about to say something."

"How comes it, Mrs. Widdup," said

棕榈滩去。这房子给人的感觉就像太平间。"

过了一会儿，库尔森小姐恪尽本分地进来问他的痛风好点了没有。

"斯坦蒂亚，"老人问，"外面天气怎么样？"

"晴朗，"库尔森小姐答道，"但是很冷。"

"我觉得这简直就是冻死人的冬天，"库尔森先生说。

"这的确是个特例，"康斯坦蒂亚说，眼睛茫然地盯着窗外，"'冬天在春的大腿上逗留，'尽管这么比喻有些粗俗。"

不久，她从小花园旁边走过，向西走向百老汇，她要去逛街购物了。

又过了一会儿，威德普夫人走进了病人的房间。

"你按铃了吗，先生？"她问，脸上洋溢着笑容。"我让希金斯去药店了，我以为听到了你的铃声。"

"我没按铃，"库尔森先生说。

"我恐怕，"威德普夫人说，"我打断了你，先生，昨天当你要说什么的时候。"

"这是怎么回事，威德普

old man Coulson sternly, "that I find it so cold in this house?"

"Cold, Sir?" said the housekeeper, "why, now, since you speak of it it do seem cold in this room. But, outdoors it's as warm and fine as June, sir. And how this weather do seem to make one's heart jump out of one's shirt waist, sir. And the ivy all leaved out on the side of the house, and the hand-organs playing, and the children dancing on the sidewalk – 'tis a great time for speaking out what's in the heart. You were saying yesterday, sir – "

"Woman!" roared Mr. Coulson; "you are a fool. I pay you to take care of this house. I am freezing to death in my own room, and you come in and drivel to me about ivy and hand-organs. Get me an overcoat at once. See that all doors and windows are closed below. An old, fat, irresponsible, one-sided object like you prating about springtime and flowers in the middle of winter! When Higgins comes back, tell him to bring me a hot rum punch. And now get out!"

But who shall shame the bright face of May? Rogue though she be and disturber of sane men's peace, no wise virgins cunning nor cold storage shall make her bow her head in the bright galaxy of

夫，"库尔森老人严肃地问道，"房间怎么这么冷？"

"冷？先生？"女管家说，"你问为什么？嗯，你说冷，这房间里确实有些冷。但是门外就像 6 月一样暖和晴朗，先生。这天气好得几乎让人的心就要跳出衬衣了，先生。房子一面墙上的常春藤都长叶子了，大人们在玩手摇风琴，孩子们在人行道上跳舞——现在是把心里话说出来的最佳时刻。昨天你要说的是，先生。"

"女人！"库尔森先生吼道；"你这个笨蛋。我出工钱让你看管这房子，我在房间里快被冻死了，而你却进来给我胡言乱语地唠叨什么常春藤和手摇风琴。赶紧给我披件大衣。看看下边的门窗关好了没有。你这个又老又肥，又没责任心的家伙，还敢大放厥词，在冬天说什么春天和花儿！希金斯一回来，就叫他给我送杯热的朗姆潘趣酒来。现在，你马上给我出去！"

谁会让五月明媚的脸庞蒙羞呢？尽管她淘气，扰乱了理智男人的宁静，但是，无论是明智的贞女还是冷冻室，都无法让她在 12 月份的明亮星系中低头认输。

months.

Oh, yes, the story was not quite finished. A night passed, and Higgins helped old man Coulson in the morning to his chair by the window. The cold of the room was gone. Heavenly odours and fragrant mildness entered. In hurried Mrs. Widdup, and stood by his chair. Mr. Coulson reached his bony hand and grasped her plump one. "Mrs. Widdup," he said, "this house would be no home without you. I have half a million dollars. If that and the true affection of a heart no longer in its youthful prime, but still not cold, could – ""I found out what made it cold," said Mrs. Widdup, leanin' against his chair. "'Twas ice – tons of it – in the basement and in the furnace room, everywhere. I shut off the registers that it was coming through into your room, Mr. Coulson, poor soul! And now it's Maytime again."

"A true heart," went on old man Coulson, a little wanderingly, "that the springtime has brought to life again, and – but what will my daughter say, Mrs. Widdup?""Never fear, sir," said Mrs. Widdup, cheerfully. "Miss Coulson, she ran away with the iceman last night, sir!"

啊，是的，故事还远没有结束。一个夜晚过去了，早晨时候，希金斯帮老库尔森坐到窗边的椅子上。房间里的寒冷消失了。令人愉快的花香和甜蜜的温柔又涌入了房间。威德普夫人匆匆进来，站在他的椅子旁。库尔森先生伸出瘦骨嶙峋的手，抓住了她丰满圆润的手。"威德普夫人，"他说，"没有你，这房子就不会是个家。我有百万美元的一半。如果连这再加上一颗充满了真情的心，尽管这颗心不再年轻，但它还没有冷，它将——""我知道为什么房间会这么冷了，"威德普夫人边说，边靠在他的椅子上。"是冰——好多吨的冰——在地下室里，在暖气炉间里，到处都有。我把传送寒冷到你房间里来的暖气片关掉了，库尔森先生，可怜的人！现在又是五月了。"

"一颗真心，"库尔森先生接着说，他有些走神，"春天又让我活过来了，还有——可是，我女儿会说些什么呢，威德普夫人？""别怕，先生，"威德普夫人高兴地说，"库尔森小姐昨晚和卖冰人一起私奔了，先生！"

25. THE TRIMMED LAMP
25. 被剪亮的灯

Of course there are two sides to the question. Let us look at the other. We often hear "shop-girls" spoken of. No such persons exist. There are girls who work in shops. They make their living that way. But why turn their occupation into an adjective? Let us be fair. We do not refer to the girls who live on Fifth Avenue as "marriage-girls."

Lou and Nancy were chums. They came to the big city to find work because there was not enough to eat at their homes to go around. Nancy was nineteen; Lou was twenty. Both were pretty, active, country girls who had no ambition to go on the stage.

The little cherub that sits up aloft guided them to a cheap and respectable boarding-house. Both found positions and became wage-earners. They remained chums. It is at the end of six months that I would beg you to step forward and be introduced to them. Meddlesome Reader: My Lady friends, Miss Nancy and Miss Lou. While you are shaking hands please

自然，这个问题是有两个方面的。让我们看看另一个方面吧。我们常会听人谈起"商店姑娘"，其实上并没有这样的人。商店里只有售货女郎，她们靠着这份工作维持生存。为什么要把她们的工作变成个形容词呢？让我们公正一点吧。我们就不会称住在第五大道的姑娘们为"婚姻姑娘"。

卢和南茜是一对好朋友。家里揭不开锅了，她们就来到这个城市找活养活自己。南茜19岁，卢20岁，她们都很活泼漂亮，但并没有雄心壮志去登台表演。

天上的小天使领着她们找到了一幢便宜又体面的公寓。然后两个人都找到了工作，靠工资过活。他们仍然是好朋友，已经在一起待了快六个月了。所以，亲爱的读者，请你走上前来，让我把她们介绍给你吧。爱管闲事的读者：这两位是我的女性朋友，南茜小姐和卢小姐。和她们握手

take notice – cautiously – of their attire. Yes, cautiously; for they are as quick to resent a stare as a lady in a box at the horse show is.

Lou is a piece-work ironer in a hand laundry. She is clothed in a badly-fitting purple dress, and her hat plume is four inches too long; but her ermine muff and scarf cost $25, and its fellow beasts will be ticketed in the windows at $7.98 before the season is over. Her cheeks are pink, and her light blue eyes bright. Contentment radiates from her.

Nancy you would call a shop-girl – because you have the habit. There is no type; but a perverse generation is always seeking a type; so this is what the type should be. She has the high-ratted pompadour, and the exaggerated straightfront. Her skirt is shoddy, but has the correct flare. No furs protect her against the bitter spring air, but she wears her short broadcloth jacket as jauntily as though it were Persian lamb! On her face and in her eyes, remorseless type-seeker, is the typical shop-girl expression. It is a look of silent but contemptuous revolt against cheated womanhood; of sad

的时候，请谨慎留意他们的盛装。对，谨慎些；因为如果她们被人注视，就会像坐在马匹展览会包厢里的贵妇人一样，愤怒地把那些不知趣的人瞪回去。

卢在一家手工洗衣店做熨衣工，领计件工资。她穿的紫色衣服很不合身，帽子上的羽毛饰品也比正常的长了四英寸。但她的白貂手笼和披肩价值 25 美元，在这个季节快结束之前，同类的商品在橱窗里的标价也就是 7.98 美元。她的脸蛋红扑扑的，淡蓝色的眼睛亮晶晶的，满脸写着心满意足的神情。

因为你们已经养成了这样的习惯，因此你们可以把南茜称作商店姑娘。其实本来没有什么类型可言，可固执的一代总是要找一个类型，那么她就属于这个类型。她的头发高高地向后梳起，前面整齐的有些夸张。她的裙子很劣质，但却是绝对标准的喇叭形。她没有毛皮大衣来抵御春天的冷风，但她高高兴兴地穿着细平布的短夹克，就当那是波斯羔羊皮装一样。那些孜孜不倦的类型寻找者，会发现她的脸上和眼睛里，有着典型的商店姑娘的表情。这种无声的表情，透露着对

prophecy of the vengeance to come.
When she laughs her loudest the look is
still there. The same look can be seen in
the eyes of Russian peasants; and those of
us left will see it some day on Gabriel's
face when he comes to blow us up. It is a
look that should wither and abash man;
but he has been known to smirk at it and
offer flowers – with a string tied to them.

Now lift your hat and come away,
while you receive Lou's cheery "See you
again," and the sardonic, sweet smile of
Nancy that seems, somehow, to miss you
and go fluttering like a white moth up
over the housetops to the stars.

The two waited on the corner for Dan.
Dan was Lou's steady company. Faithful? Well, he was on hand when Mary
would have had to hire a dozen subpoena
servers to find her lamb.

"Ain't you cold, Nance?" said Lou.
"Say, what a chump you are for working
in that old store for $8. a week! I made
$18.50 last week. Of course ironing ain't
as swell work as selling lace behind a
counter, but it pays. None of us ironers
make less than $10. And I don't know

哄骗女子行为的轻蔑和反抗，和
即将到来的报复的伤心预言。即
使她笑得最响亮的时候，她的脸
上眼里仍带有这种表情。俄罗斯
农民的眼睛里也有同样的表情；
加百列下凡训斥我们的时候，我
们中的那些活下去的人，也将在
他的脸上看到这种表情。这是一
种可以震慑男人，让他们感到羞
愧的表情；他们以对此报以傻笑
而闻名，并且还送上鲜花——用
丝带缠好的花束。

卢会欢快地对你说再见，南
茜则露出嘲讽甜蜜的微笑，请你
拿起你的帽子，立即走开。不过，
南茜的嘲笑似乎与你擦肩而过，
就像白蛾掠过屋顶，飞向星空。

两人站在街角等丹。丹和卢
已经确定了关系。这个人可靠
吗？是的，要是玛丽的羔羊丢了，
需要雇佣一群人去送寻找的时
候，丹总会去跑腿。

"南茜，你不冷吗？"卢问。
"我说，你这个小傻瓜，还在那
家老店里干，一周只挣 8 美元。
上周我挣了 18.5 元呢。当然，熨
衣服不如在柜台后卖蕾丝那么有
气派，可是挣得多啊。我们这些
熨衣工，没有一个工资一周少于

that it's any less respectful work, either."

"You can have it," said Nancy, with uplifted nose. "I'll take my eight a week and hall bedroom. I like to be among nice things and swell people. And look what a chance I've got! Why, one of our glove girls married a Pittsburg – steel maker, or blacksmith or something – the other day worth a million dollars. I'll catch a swell myself some time. I ain't bragging on my looks or anything; but I'll take my chances where there's big prizes offered. What show would a girl have in a laundry?"

"Why, that's where I met Dan," said Lou, triumphantly. "He came in for his Sunday shirt and collars and saw me at the first board, ironing. We all try to get to work at the first board. Ella Maginnis was sick that day, and I had her place. He said he noticed my arms first, how round and white they was. I had my sleeves rolled up. Some nice fellows come into laundries. You can tell 'em by their bringing their clothes in suit cases; and turning in the door sharp and sudden."

"How can you wear a waist like that,

10 元的。而且我也不认为这份工作低贱。"

"你干就好了，"南茜说，她鼻子翘得高高的。"我就愿意一周挣八美元，住走廊里的小卧室。我喜欢和漂亮的东西还有气派的有钱人呆在一起。看看我有怎样的机会！瞧，我们中一个卖手套的姑娘嫁给了一位匹兹堡人——一位钢铁商，或铁匠什么的——只用了几天时间，她的身价就值 100 万美元了。总有一天我也会钓到一个金龟婿。我不是在吹嘘我有多漂亮，但我总要在机会多的地方碰碰运气吧。一个姑娘待在洗衣店里能秀给谁看？"

"那怎么了，我就是在洗衣店里遇到丹的，"卢不无炫耀地说，"他来取他星期天穿的衬衫和领子，看见我在第一张桌子旁熨衣服。我们都争着在那张桌子上干活。那天埃拉·麦金尼斯生病了，我就站在了她的位置上。他说第一眼看到的是我的胳膊，感觉又丰满又白皙。因为我把袖管卷了起来。一些还不错的小伙子会来洗衣店。要是有人把衣服放进手提箱里，冷不防的把门推开，你就知道是他们来了。"

"你怎么能穿这样的上衣外

Lou?" said Nancy, gazing down at the offending article with sweet scorn in her heavy-lidded eyes. "It shows fierce taste."

"This waist?" cried Lou, with wide-eyed indignation. "Why, I paid $16 for this waist. It's worth twenty-five. A woman left it to be laundered, and never called for it. The boss sold it to me. It's got yards and yards of hand embroidery on it. Better talk about that ugly, plain thing you've got on."

"This ugly, plain thing," said Nancy, calmly, "was copied from one that Mrs. Van Alstyne Fisher was wearing. The girls say her bill in the store last year was $12,000. I made mine, myself. It cost me $1.50. Ten feet away you couldn't tell it from hers."

"Oh, well," said Lou, good-naturedly, "if you want to starve and put on airs, go ahead. But I'll take my job and good wages; and after hours give me something as fancy and attractive to wear as I am able to buy."

But just then Dan came – a serious young man with a ready-made necktie, who had escaped the city's brand of frivolity – an electrician earning 30 dollars

套呢，卢？"南茜娇嗔道，并睁大眼睛看着那件扎眼的上衣。"你的眼光真让人难以置信。"

"你说这件上衣吗？"卢说，眼睛因愤怒而瞪得大大的，"怎么啦，这衣服花了我16美元呢。它本来值25美元。一个女人拿来洗熨，后来一直没取走，于是老板就把它卖给我了。这上面的有成码的手工刺绣。还是谈谈你身上那件又丑又普通的东西吧。"

"这件丑陋普通的东西，"南茜平静地说，"是按照范·阿尔斯泰林·费希尔夫人身上穿的那件缝制出来的。姑娘们说她去年在店里花了12 000元买衣服。这是我为自己做的，只花了 1.5元。如果站在10英尺远的地方，你不会发现这两件有什么不同。"

"哦，好吧，"卢和善地说，"如果你喜欢受穷挨饿装气派，那就随你吧。但是我喜欢我的工作和高工资；下班之后，我会买能买得起的高档别致、诱人眼球的衣服来穿。"

恰好在这个时候，丹来了——他是个严肃认真的年轻人，打着活扣领带，但没有被打上城市里特有的轻浮的烙印——他是

per week who looked upon Lou with the sad eyes of Romeo, and thought her embroidered waist a web in which any fly should delight to be caught.

"My friend, Mr. Owens – shake hands with Miss Danforth," said Lou.

"I'm mighty glad to know you, Miss Danforth," said Dan, with outstretched hand. "I've heard Lou speak of you so often."

"Thanks," said Nancy, touching his fingers with the tips of her cool ones, "I've heard her mention you – a few times."

Lou giggled.

"Did you get that handshake from Mrs. Van Alstyne Fisher, Nance?" she asked.

"If I did, you can feel safe in copying it," said Nancy.

"Oh, I couldn't use it, at all. It's too stylish for me. It's intended to set off diamond rings, that high shake is. Wait till I get a few and then I'll try it."

"Learn it first," said Nancy wisely, "and you'll be more likely to get the rings."

"Now, to settle this argument," said

个电工，一周能挣 30 美元。他的眼睛透露出罗密欧一样的悲伤，他凝视着卢，心里想着，她的刺绣上衣简直就是蜘蛛网，任何苍蝇都愿意陷进去。

"欧文斯先生，我的朋友——和丹福斯小姐握握手吧"卢说。

"很高兴认识你，丹福斯小姐，"丹一边说一边伸出手，"我常听卢提到你。"

"谢谢，"南茜说，边用冷冰的指尖碰了碰他的手指，"我也听她提起过你——几次。"

卢咯咯地笑了。

"你是从范·阿尔斯泰林·费希尔夫人那儿学的怎这样握手吗，南茜？"她问。

"如果我学了，那么你就可以跟我学，"南茜答道。

"哦，我是不会那样握手的，那样太气派了。手抬得那么高，是用来炫耀钻石戒指的。等我有几枚钻戒之后，我再试试吧。"

"先学会再说，"南茜明智地说，"那样你才更有机会得到戒指。"

"现在，为了调停你们的争

Dan, with his ready, cheerful smile, "let me make a proposition. As I can't take both of you up to Tiffany's and do the right thing, what do you say to a little vaudeville? I've got the rickets. How about looking at stage diamonds since we can't shake hands with the real spar-klers?"

The faithful squire took his place close to the curb; Lou next, a little peacocky in her bright and pretty clothes; Nancy on the inside, slender, and soberly clothed as the sparrow, but with the true Van Alstyne Fisher walk – thus they set out for their evening's moderate diversion.

I do not suppose that many look upon a great department store as an educational institution. But the one in which Nancy worked was something like that to her. She was surrounded by beautiful things that breathed of taste and refinement. If you live in an atmosphere of luxury, luxury is yours whether your money pays for it, or another's.

The people she served were mostly women whose dress, manners, and posi-tion in the social world were quoted as criterions. From them Nancy began to take toll – the best from each according to

执，"丹说，脸上挂着时刻准备好的欢快微笑，"请允许我提个建议，既然我不能送你们到蒂芬尼珠宝店来解决此事，那么去看一场小小的歌舞杂耍表演怎么样？我有入场券。如果我们不能与钻石握手，那么就去欣赏舞台上的钻石，如何？"

这位忠诚的护卫沿着路边走；卢靠在他身边，穿着鲜艳靓丽的衣服，像只小孔雀；南茜在最里面，身材苗条，衣着素净，像只小麻雀，但她走起路来，有着范·阿尔斯泰林·费希尔式的风度——他们就这样出发了，去适度享受一下晚间的娱乐。

我不认为会有很多人把大百货商店当作教育机构。但是，南茜就把她工作的地方当成了受教育的地方。她被精美的事物包围着，一切都是那么的精致典雅。如果你生活在豪华的氛围当中，豪华就是你的，不管是你花钱还是别人花钱。

她的顾客大多是社交圈里衣着、风度和地位被拿来作为评判标准的女士。南茜开始依照自己的想法从她们身上博采精华。

her view.

From one she would copy and practice a gesture, from another an eloquent lifting of an eyebrow, from others, a manner of walking, of carrying a purse, of smiling, of greeting a friend, of addressing "inferiors in station." From her best beloved model, Mrs. Van Alstyne Fisher, she made requisition for that excellent thing, a soft, low voice as clear as silver and as perfect in articulation as the notes of a thrush. Suffused in the aura of this high social refinement and good breeding, it was impossible for her to escape a deeper effect of it. As good habits are said to be better than good principles, so, perhaps, good manners are better than good habits. The teachings of your parents may not keep alive your New England conscience; but if you sit on a straight-back chair and repeat the words "prisms and pilgrims" forty times the devil will flee from you. And when Nancy spoke in the Van Alstyne Fisher tones she felt the thrill of *noblesse oblige* to her very bones.

There was another source of learning in the great departmental school. Whenever you see three or four shop-girls gather in a bunch and jingle

从这个人那里学习一个手势，并加以练习；从另外一人那里学习怎样优雅流畅的高挑眉毛；从其余的人那儿模仿怎样走路、怎样拿钱包、怎样微笑、怎样与朋友打招呼、怎样居高临下的同"身份更低一等"的人说话。范·阿尔斯泰林·费希尔夫人是她最好的模特，从她身上她学到了最棒的东西，那就是如银铃般软软的，低低的，清晰的声音，像画眉鸟的歌喉一样完美。四处都是高贵气质和良好教养的氛围，摆脱其这样深的影响，对她来说是不可能的。既然都说好习惯胜过好准则，那么也许，好举止也能胜过好习惯。父母的教诲不一定能让你对新英格兰的良心刻骨铭心；可是如果你坐在直背椅上，把"棱镜和朝圣者"重复念上40遍，那么磨鬼也会逃走离的你远远的。南茜用范·阿尔斯泰林·费希尔式的腔调说话时，她感到"贵族阶级"带给他的震颤传遍了她全身的每一根骨头。

在大百货学校里还有另一个学问的来源。一但你看到三四个商店姑娘凑在一起，叽叽咕咕的在扯些愚蠢的话题，金属丝的手

their wire bracelets as an accompaniment to apparently frivolous conversation, do not think that they are there for the purpose of criticizing the way Ethel does her back hair. The meeting may lack the dignity of the deliberative bodies of man; but it has all the importance of the occasion on which Eve and her first daughter first put their heads together to make Adam understand his proper place in the household. It is Woman's Conference for Common Defense and Exchange of Strategical Theories of Attack and Repulse upon and against the World, which is a Stage, and Man, its Audience who Persists in Throwing Bouquets Thereupon. Woman, the most helpless of the young of any animal – with the fawn's grace but without its fleetness; with the bird's beauty but without its power of flight; with the honey-bee's burden of sweetness but without its – Oh, let's drop that simile – some of us may have been stung.

During this council of war they pass weapons one to another, and exchange stratagems that each has devised and formulated out of the tactics of life.

"I says to 'im," says Sadie, "ain't you the fresh thing! Who do you suppose I am, to be addressing such a remark to

镯叮当作响，不要以为她们是在那儿七嘴八舌的讨论埃塞尔的发型。这种聚会也许没有男人审议机构的庄重，但却与夏娃同她大女儿第一次召开的家庭会议同样的重要。那次会议，她们使亚当明白了他在家庭中的位置。这就是女人的会议，为了沟通交流攻守世界的战略理论以及组织共同防御。世界是个舞台，男人就是观众，他们连续不断地向台上扔花束。在所有幼小的动物之中，女人是最需要保护的——她们如同幼鹿般的优美，却没有它的敏捷；有鸟儿般的美丽，却不会飞翔；有蜜蜂般甜蜜的负担，却没有它的——哦，不提这个比喻了——说不定我们中有些人曾经被蜜蜂蛰过呢。

在这次战争理事会上，她们相互交换武器，交流各自利用生活策略构思发明的花招。

"我对他说，"赛迪说，"你这个无礼的东西！你把我当成什么人了，竟敢这样跟我说话？你

me? And what do you think he says back
to me?"

The heads, brown, black, flaxen, red,
and yellow bob together; the answer is
given; and the parry to the thrust is decided upon, to be used by each thereafter
in passages-at-arms with the common
enemy, man.

Thus Nancy learned the art of defense;
and to women successful defense means
victory.

The curriculum of a department store
is a wide one. Perhaps no other college
could have fitted her as well for her life's
ambition – the drawing of a matrimonial
prize.

Her station in the store was a favored
one. The music room was near enough
for her to hear and become familiar with
the works of the best composers – at least
to acquire the familiarity that passed for
appreciation in the social world in which
she was vaguely trying to set a tentative
and aspiring foot. She absorbed the edu-
cating influence of art wares, of costly and
dainty fabrics, of adornments that are almost culture to women.

The other girls soon became aware of
Nancy's ambition. "Here comes your

们想想，他会怎么回答我？"

一个个小脑袋瓜，褐色的，黑色的，红色的，亚麻色的，黄色的，聚在一起晃来晃去，答案就出来了；躲避攻击的策略确定了以后，每个人都会在与她们共同的敌人——男人——交战时使用它。

南茜就此学会了防御的艺术；对女人而言，成功的防御就是胜利。

百货店里的课程很广泛。也许没有别的大学适合她，能实现她的人生抱负——中婚姻大奖的渴望。

她在店里的位置对她是很有利的。音乐店离她很近，近得足以让她听到和熟悉最好的作曲家的作品——至少要努力地去熟悉它，社交界误以为熟悉就是欣赏，而她正隐隐约约迈着志向远大的脚步试探着走入社交界。她还从艺术品、昂贵精美的布料、装饰品这些几乎是女人必须具备的修养中学习，教化自己。

其他姑娘很快就意识到了南茜的雄心壮志。"南茜，你的百

millionaire, Nancy," they would call to her whenever any man who looked the role approached her counter. It got to be a habit of men, who were hanging about while their women folk were shopping, to stroll over to the handkerchief counter and dawdle over the cambric squares. Nancy's imitation high-bred air and genuine dainty beauty was what attracted. Many men thus came to display their graces before her. Some of them may have been millionaires; others were certainly no more than their sedulous apes. Nancy learned to discriminate. There was a window at the end of the handkerchief counter; and she could see the rows of vehicles waiting for the shoppers in the street below. She looked and perceived that automobiles differ as well as do their owners.

Once a fascinating gentleman bought four dozen handkerchiefs, and wooed her across the counter with a King Cophetua air. When he had gone one of the girls said:

"What's wrong, Nance, that you didn't warm up to that fellow. He looks the swell article, all right, to me."

"Him?" said Nancy, with her coolest, sweetest, most impersonal, Van Alstyne

万富翁来了，"只要有一个看上去像有钱人的男人走进南希的柜台，姑娘们就会这么说。这已经是男人们的习惯了：当他们所陪同的女人们去选购商品的时候，他们就四处溜达，闲逛到手帕柜台，在麻纱方巾上消磨时间。南希通过模仿得来的高贵神态还有真正的优雅美丽吸引了他们。于是，不少男人来到她面前展示他们的风度。他们有的可能是百万富翁；而有一些不过是精心模仿有钱人的人。南希知道该怎样去分辨。手帕柜台一边有扇窗户，她能看见街上有一排排汽车，等候着买东西的人。她看到车就明白了，车同人一样，是有区别的。

曾经有一位的风度翩翩的绅士买了四打手帕，带着科斐图亚国王般的神气隔着柜台向她求婚。他走了之后，其中一个姑娘问道：

"怎么了，南茜，你对他一点都不热情。他看上去就是个有钱人啊，依我看，他真的很好啊。"

"他？"南茜说，脸上带着范·阿尔斯泰林·费希尔式的微

Fisher smile; "not for mine. I saw him drive up outside. A 12 H. P. machine and an Irish chauffeur! And you saw what kind of handkerchiefs he bought – silk! And he's got dactylis on him. Give me the real thing or nothing, if you please."

Two of the most "refined" women in the store – a forelady and a cashier – had a few "swell gentlemen friends" with whom they now and then dined. Once they included Nancy in an invitation. The dinner took place in a spectacular cafe whose tables are engaged for New Year's eve a year in advance. There were two "gentlemen friends" – one without any hair on his head – high living ungrew it; and we can prove it – the other a young man whose worth and sophistication he impressed upon you in two convincing ways – he swore that all the wine was corked; and he wore diamond cuff buttons. This young man perceived irresistible excellencies in Nancy. His taste ran to shop-girls; and here was one that added the voice and manners of his high social world to the franker charms of her own caste. So, on the following day, he appeared in the store and made her a

笑，最冷酷、最甜美、也不带任何的感情色彩。"我可不这样认为，他坐车来的时候被我看见了。一辆12马力的车，一个爱尔兰司机！再看看他买的是什么手帕——丝绸的！而且，他还有指炎。如果你愿意，要么就给我个真货，要么就什么也别给。"

店里两个最"优雅"的女人——领班和出纳——有几个"阔绰的绅士朋友"，时不时会请她们吃顿饭。有一次也邀请了南茜。他们是在一家富丽堂皇的咖啡馆里吃的晚餐，那儿除夕夜的桌子得提前一年预订。共有两位"绅士朋友"——一位头上没有任何毛发——高贵的生活会让人不长头发，我们可以证明这一点。——另一位还年轻，他用两种方式来说服你，让你相信他很有钱，很世故。他发誓说，所有的酒都塞着软木瓶塞；并且他的衣服袖子上镶有钻石纽扣。这个年轻男人察觉到了南茜身上散发出来的令人无法抗拒的诱惑力。于是他的口味变了，开始喜欢上了商店姑娘；而她不仅有自己那个社会等级显而易见的魅力，也有他所在的上流社会的谈吐和风度。于是，第二天，他就出现在商店里，隔

serious proposal of marriage over a box of hem-stitched, grass-bleached Irish linens. Nancy declined. A brown pompadour ten feet away had been using her eyes and ears. When the rejected suitor had gone she heaped carboys of upbraidings and horror upon Nancy's head.

"What a terrible little fool you are! That fellow's a millionaire – he's a nephew of old Van Skittles himself. And he was talking on the level, too. Have you gone crazy, Nance?"

"Have I?" said Nancy. "I didn't take him, did I? He isn't a millionaire so hard that you could notice it, anyhow. His family only allows him $20,000 a year to spend. The bald-headed fellow was guying him about it the other night at supper."

The brown pompadour came nearer and narrowed her eyes.

"Say, what do you want?" she inquired, in a voice hoarse for lack of chewing-gum. "Ain't that enough for you? Do you want to be a Mormon, and marry Rockefeller and Gladstone Dowie and the King of Spain and the whole bunch? Ain't $20,000 a year good enough for you?"

着一盒用土法漂白的爱尔兰抽丝刺绣麻纱手帕，郑重地向她求婚。可南茜拒绝了。十英尺外，有一个褐色头发，梳成高卷式发型的姑娘一直在仔细观察，并用心倾听。等到那个遭到拒绝的求婚者走了以后，她把南茜骂了个狗血喷头。

"你这个傻瓜！你真是傻到家了，那人可是个百万富翁——他是范·斯基特尔斯老先生的侄子呀！还有，他态度是多么的真诚。你疯了吗，南茜？"

"我疯了吗？"南茜说。"我可不能答应他！不管怎么说，他还算不上真正的百万富翁，你会明白这一点的。他家每年只给他两万美元而已。那天晚上吃饭的时候，那个秃老头还为这件事笑话他呢。"

褐色头发，梳着高卷式发型的姑娘走近一些，眯起了眼睛。

"说，你到底想要什么样的人呢？"她追问道，因为没嚼口香糖，所以她的声音有些嘶哑。"这样的人还不能让你满意吗？你想做摩门教徒，嫁给洛克菲勒、格拉斯通·道伊和西班牙国王这样的人吗？一年两万元对你来说还不够吗？"

Nancy flushed a little under the level gaze of the black, shallow eyes.

"It wasn't altogether the money, Carrie," she explained. "His friend caught him in a rank lie the other night at dinner. It was about some girl he said he hadn't been to the theater with. Well, I can't stand a liar. Put everything together – I don't like him; and that settles it. When I sell out it's not going to be on any bargain day. I've got to have something that sits up in a chair like a man, anyhow. Yes, I'm looking out for a catch; but it's got to be able to do something more than make a noise like a toy bank."

"The physiopathic ward for yours!" said the brown pompadour, walking away.

These high ideas, if not ideals – Nancy continued to cultivate on $8. per week. She bivouacked on the trail of the great unknown "catch," eating her dry bread and tightening her belt day by day. On her face was the faint, soldierly, sweet, grim smile of the preordained man-hunter. The store was her forest; and many times she raised her rifle at game that seemed broad-antlered and big; but

南茜被那双肤浅的黑眼睛瞪得有些脸红。

"这并不全是因为钱的关系，卡丽，"她解释道。"那天晚上吃饭时，他公然撒谎，还被他的朋友给揭穿了。是关于一个姑娘的事，他说他没有陪她去过电影院。哼，我可受不了爱说谎的人。所有的事加起来，结果就是——我不喜欢他，这事就这么定了。我要把自己卖掉的时候，可不会随随便便地打折。无论如何我都得找个坐在椅子上像个男子汉的人。我现在是在寻找猎物，但他不能像个只会发出声音的玩具银行，他必须有点真本事才行。"

"精神病院就是为你这种人开的！"褐色头发卷说完就走开了。

这些崇高的想法，如果算不上理想的话——得继续依靠南茜每星期的八美元来滋养。她啃着干面包，勒紧裤腰带，日复一日不知疲倦地追踪着那个未知的大"猎物"。她就像天生注定是捕获男人的猎手那样微笑着，淡漠而英勇、甜蜜而又严酷。商店是她的森林；有好多次，她举起步枪瞄准了似乎长着鹿角的大猎

always some deep unerring instinct – perhaps of the huntress, perhaps of the woman – made her hold her fire and take up the trail again.

Lou flourished in the laundry. Out of her $18.50 per week she paid $6. for her room and board. The rest went mainly for clothes. Her opportunities for bettering her taste and manners were few compared with Nancy's. In the steaming laundry there was nothing but work, work and her thoughts of the evening pleasures to come. Many costly and showy fabrics passed under her iron; and it may be that her growing fondness for dress was thus transmitted to her through the conducting metal.

When the day's work was over Dan awaited her outside, her faithful shadow in whatever light she stood.

Sometimes he cast an honest and troubled glance at Lou's clothes that increased in conspicuity rather than in style; but this was no disloyalty; he deprecated the attention they called to her in the streets.

And Lou was no less faithful to her chum. There was a law that Nancy should go with them on whatsoever outings they might take. Dan bore the extra burden

物；但是，内心深处不会出错的本能——也许是女猎手的本能，也许是女性的本能——总是阻止她开枪，而让她继续追踪下去。

卢在洗衣店里的工作干得还不错。每周18.5美元的工钱。六美元用来支付房租伙食，剩下的钱主要花在衣服上。和南希比起来，她要提高品味和风度的机会似乎少了很多。在蒸气笼罩的洗衣店里，只有工作、工作和对即将到来的夜晚娱乐的遐想。她的熨斗熨过一件件昂贵绚丽的衣服，也许就是那个导热的金属把对服装的热爱传导给了她。

一天的工作结束了，丹就在外边等她。无论她被哪束光线照射，他都是她忠实的影子。

有时，他会老实而且不安地看着卢穿的衣服，这些衣服越来越亮眼，格调却没有提高。但这不代表不忠。只是他不赞成她这样穿，因为走在街上，这总会让她引人注意。

卢对南茜这个老朋友还是像以前一样忠诚。不管他俩去哪儿，南茜总和他们在一块，这已经成了习惯。丹开心地承受着额外的

heartily and in good cheer. It might be said that Lou furnished the color, Nancy the tone, and Dan the weight of the distraction-seeking trio. The escort, in his neat but obviously ready-made suit, his ready-made tie and unfailing, genial, ready-made wit never startled or clashed. He was of that good kind that you are likely to forget while they are present, but remember distinctly after they are gone.

To Nancy's superior taste the flavor of these ready-made pleasures was sometimes a little bitter: but she was young; and youth is a gourmand, when it cannot be a gourmet.

"Dan is always wanting me to marry him right away," Lou told her once. "But why should I? I'm independent. I can do as I please with the money I earn; and he never would agree for me to keep on working afterward. And say, Nance, what do you want to stick to that old store for, and half starve and half dress yourself? I could get you a place in the laundry right now if you'd come. It seems to me that you could afford to be a little less stuck-up if you could make a good deal more money."

"I don't think I'm stuck-up, Lou," said Nancy, "but I'd rather live on half rations

负担。可以这么说，在这个寻找娱乐的三人小组中，卢提供了色彩，南茜提供了情调，而丹提供的是力量。这个穿着整齐的成衣的护卫，打着活扣领带，有着无穷无尽温和友好的、挥洒自如的风趣，他永远不会与人起冲突。他就是那样一种人，当他在你面前时你不会在意，但是他一但离去，你就会非常清楚地想起他。

对南茜较高的品味而言，这些廉价的娱乐有时显得有点苦涩：可她毕竟还年轻。年轻人不会是美食家，但是年轻人可以开心的大吃大喝。

"丹老是要我马上嫁给他，"卢有次告诉她说。"可是我为什么要那样做呢？我现在很独立，赚的钱想怎么花就怎么花；可是如果结婚了，他绝对不会同意我继续工作。我说，南茜，你还一直待在那个商店里干什么呢？饿得半死，穿得也不好看。要是你想来洗衣店工作，我马上可以在洗衣店里给你找个位置。我隐约觉得，要是你的钱挣多了，你就不会那么傲气了。"

"我不认为我傲气，卢，"南茜说，"我宁愿待在这个地方，

and stay where I am. I suppose I've got the habit. It's the chance that I want. I don't expect to be always behind a counter. I'm learning something new every day. I'm right up against refined and rich people all the time – even if I do only wait on them; and I'm not missing any pointers that I see passing around."

"Caught your millionaire yet?" asked Lou with her teasing laugh.

"I haven't selected one yet," answered Nancy. "I've been looking them over."

"Goodness! the idea of picking over 'em! Don't you ever let one get by you Nance – even if he's a few dollars shy. But of course you're joking – millionaires don't think about working girls like us."

"It might be better for them if they did," said Nancy, with cool wisdom. "Some of us could teach them how to take care of their money."

"If one was to speak to me," laughed Lou, "I know I'd have a duck-fit."

"That's because you don't know any. The only difference between swells and other people is you have to watch 'em closer. Don't you think that red silk lining is just a little bit too bright for that

拿着只有你一半的薪水。我想我已经习惯了，这是我想要的机会。我不愿意老站在柜台后面。每天我都在学习新的东西。我一直和举止优雅的有钱人接触——尽管我只是在侍候他们；但只要猎物一露面，我就不会放过任何一个机会。"

"捕获到你的百万富翁了吗？"卢揶揄地笑着问。

"我还没选好，"南茜答道。"我一直在观察他们。"

"天哪！你竟然想在他们中筛选！千万别放过任何一个，南茜——即使他的财产少个一两块也没关系。不过当然，你是在开玩笑——百万富翁是不会看上我们这样的职业女性的。"

"如果他们看上了我们，那是他们的福气，"南茜冷静而明智地说道，"我们中的一些人能教他们如何照看好自己的财产。"

"要是有一个百万富翁同我说句话，"卢笑起来，"我肯定会晕倒的。"

"那是因为你一个也不认识。有钱人和一般人之间惟一的区别就是，你必须深入仔细的观察他们。你不认为你那件外套的红缎子衬里有点太鲜艳了吗，

coat, Lou?"

Lou looked at the plain, dull olive jacket of her friend.

"Well, no I don't – but it may seem so beside that faded-looking thing you've got on."

"This jacket," said Nancy, complacently, "has exactly the cut and fit of one that Mrs. Van Alstyne Fisher was wearing the other day. The material cost me $3.98. I suppose hers cost about $100. more."

"Oh, well," said Lou lightly, "it don't strike me as millionaire bait. Shouldn't wonder if I catch one before you do, anyway."

Truly it would have taken a philosopher to decide upon the values of the theories held by the two friends. Lou, lacking that certain pride and fastidiousness that keeps stores and desks filled with girls working for the barest living, thumped away gaily with her iron in the noisy and stifling laundry. Her wages supported her even beyond the point of comfort; so that her dress profited until sometimes she cast a sidelong glance of impatience at the neat but inelegant apparel of Dan – Dan the constant, the immutable, the undeviating.

卢？"

卢看了看她朋友穿的那件朴素的暗橄榄色夹克。

"嗯，不，我不这样认为——不过，和你穿的那件看上去褪了色的东西一比，是鲜艳了点。"

"这件夹克，"南茜沾沾自喜地说，"同范·阿尔斯泰林·费希尔夫人那天穿的在剪裁和尺寸上一模一样。布料花了我3.98元。我估计她的那件大概要花100多块。"

"哦，好啊，"卢轻快地说，"我可不认为这是钓金龟婿的诱饵。要是我在你之前钓到一个，你可别吃惊哦。"

说真的，只有哲学家才能判断这两个朋友所持观点的价值所在。商店里的柜台旁，全是那些心高气傲口味挑剔的姑娘，靠着微薄的薪水勉强度日。卢没有这种傲气和挑剔，她在透不过气的嘈杂的洗衣店里，心情愉快地挥舞着熨斗。她的工资可以让她过得很舒服，甚至还会有结余，于是她的衣服也因此更绚丽起来，直到有时她会不耐烦地瞥一眼丹整齐但不体面的衣着——丹，始终如一，毫无二心，忠贞不渝。

As for Nancy, her case was one of tens of thousands. Silk and jewels and laces and ornaments and the perfume and music of the fine world of good-breeding and taste – these were made for woman; they are her equitable portion. Let her keep near them if they are a part of life to her, and if she will. She is no traitor to herself, as Esau was; for she keeps he birthright and the pottage she earns is often very scant.

In this atmosphere Nancy belonged; and she throve in it and ate her frugal meals and schemed over her cheap dresses with a determined and contented mind. She already knew woman; and she was studying man, the animal, both as to his habits and eligibility. Some day she would bring down the game that she wanted; but she promised herself it would be what seemed to her the biggest and the best, and nothing smaller.

Thus she kept her lamp trimmed and burning to receive the bridegroom when he should come.

But, another lesson she learned, perhaps unconsciously. Her standard of values began to shift and change. Sometimes the dollar-mark grew blurred in her mind's eye, and shaped itself into letters

至于南茜，她同千千万万的人一样。教养良好、格调高雅的上流社会里的绸缎、珠宝、蕾丝、装饰品、香水和音乐——就是专门为女人制造的，其中也有她的一份。如果它们是她生命的一部分，她又愿意这样的话，就让她靠近它们吧。她不会像以前那样背叛自己；虽然她挣的稀饭钱常常少得可怜，她却没有放弃与生俱来的权利。

南茜现在就处在这样的环境中。她意志坚定，心满意足地呆在洗衣店里边，边省吃俭用，边为买廉价的衣服精打细算。她已经了解了女人；她正在研究男人这种动物，研究他们的习惯，判断他们是否合格。总有一天，她会捕获到她想要的猎物。不过，她向自己承诺，这个猎物必须在她看来是最大最好的，小一点都不行。

因此，她不停地剪亮自己的灯，让它一直燃着，随时准备迎接新郎。

不过，她还学到了另外一些课程，也许是在无意中学到的。她的价值标准开始转变。有时候，美元符号在她心中变得模糊不清，缩小成了一个个字母，而这

that spelled such words as "truth" and "honor" and now and then just "kindness." Let us make a likeness of one who hunts the moose or elk in some mighty wood. He sees a little dell, mossy and embowered, where a rill trickles, babbling to him of rest and comfort. At these times the spear of Nimrod himself grows blunt.

So, Nancy wondered sometimes if Persian lamb was always quoted at its market value by the hearts that it covered.

One Thursday evening Nancy left the store and turned across Sixth Avenue westward to the laundry. She was expected to go with Lou and Dan to a musical comedy.

Dan was just coming out of the laundry when she arrived. There was a queer, strained look on his face.

"I thought I would drop around to see if they had heard from her," he said.

"Heard from who?" asked Nancy. "Isn't Lou there?"

"I thought you knew," said Dan. "She hasn't been here or at the house where she lived since Monday. She moved all her things from there. She told one of the

一个个字母又组成了"真理"和"荣誉"之类的单词，有时会是"善良"。让我们拿一个在大森林里打猎的人来打个比方吧。他本来是要去打美洲麋或美洲赤鹿的，结果他看见一个小幽谷，长满了苔藓，绿荫掩映，一条小溪细水流长，潺潺的水声仿佛在向他诉说安宁和舒适。每逢此时，宁录[1]的长矛也会变钝的。

因此，有时南茜自己也不明白，穿着波斯羔皮大衣的人，她们的心里是否只想着波斯羔羊的市场价值。

一个星期四的傍晚，南茜离开商店，穿过第六大街，朝西往洗衣店走去。她跟卢和丹约好了一起去看音乐喜剧。

当她到达的时候，丹正好从洗衣店里出来。他的神色十分古怪和不自然。

"我想我应该来这里转转，看他们是否有她的消息，"他说。

"谁的消息？"南茜问。"卢不在洗衣店里吗？"

"我原以为你已经知道了，"丹说，"从这个星期一开始，她就没来过这儿，谁也不知道她住在什么地方，她把所有的东西都

girls in the laundry she might be going to Europe."

"Hasn't anybody seen her anywhere?" asked Nancy.

Dan looked at her with his jaws set grimly, and a steely gleam in his steady gray eyes.

"They told me in the laundry," he said, harshly, "that they saw her pass yesterday – in an automobile. With one of the millionaires, I suppose, that you and Lou were forever busying your brains about."

For the first time Nancy quailed before a man. She laid her hand that trembled slightly on Dan's sleeve.

"You've no right to say such a thing to me, Dan – as if I had anything to do with it!"

"I didn't mean it that way," said Dan, softening. He fumbled in his vest pocket.

"I've got the tickets for the show to-night," he said, with a gallant show of lightness. "If you – "

Nancy admired pluck whenever she saw it.

"I'll go with you, Dan," she said.

Three months went by before Nancy

搬走了。她和洗衣店里的一个姑娘说她可能要去欧洲了。"

"有人在什么地方见过她吗?"南茜问。

丹盯着她,忧郁地低着下巴,两只阴沉的眼睛射出钢铁般冷酷的光芒。

"洗衣店里的人告诉我,"他严厉地说,"昨天,他们看见她从这儿经过——坐在一辆汽车里,和一个百万富翁在一起。我想,就是你和卢一直绞尽脑汁想要抓住的那种人。"

这是南茜第一次在一个男人面前发抖,她把微微颤抖的手放到丹的衣袖上。

"你没有权利跟我说这种话,丹——我与这件事毫无关系!"

"我不是那个意思,"丹说话的口气缓和了一些,并在背心的口袋里摸索着什么。

"我有今晚的戏票,"他说,并尽量显得轻松一些。"如果你——"

无论何时,南茜都非常欣赏别人表现出来的勇气。

"我和你一起去,丹,"她说。

南茜再次见到卢,已经是三

saw Lou again.

At twilight one evening the shop-girl was hurrying home along the border of a little quiet park. She heard her name called, and wheeled about in time to catch Lou rushing into her arms.

After the first embrace they drew their heads back as serpents do, ready to attack or to charm, with a thousand questions trembling on their swift tongues. And then Nancy noticed that prosperity had descended upon Lou, manifesting itself in costly furs, flashing gems, and creations of the tailors' art.

"You little fool!" cried Lou, loudly and affectionately. "I see you are still working in that store, and as shabby as ever. And how about that big catch you were going to make – nothing doing yet, I suppose?"

And then Lou looked, and saw that something better than prosperity had descended upon Nancy – something that shone brighter than gems in her eyes and redder than a rose in her cheeks, and that danced like electricity anxious to be loosed from the tip of her tongue.

"Yes, I'm still in the store," said Nancy, "but I'm going to leave it next week. I've made my catch – the biggest

个月之后的事了。

一天傍晚，这个商店姑娘正沿着静悄悄的小公园急匆匆地往家赶，她听到有人喊她，刚一转身，卢飞奔过来扑进了她的怀抱。

拥抱之后，她们的头就像蛇的头那样缩回去，准备着攻击或吸引对方，千百个问题在迅速转动的舌尖上颤动着。之后，南茜发现，富贵已经降临到了卢的身上，她身上穿着昂贵的毛皮大衣，戴着闪闪发光的珠宝，还有裁缝们精工制作的时装。

"你这个小傻瓜，"卢叫到，声音很响亮很亲热，"我看你还在那家商店里干活，还像以前那么寒酸。你要打的大猎物怎么样啦——我猜，还没有到手吧！"

卢上下打量着她，却看见了有比富贵更好的东西已经降临到了南茜的身上——那样东西让她的眼睛比宝石更明亮，脸颊比玫瑰更红润，就像有电流在跳动，急着要挣脱她舌尖的束缚。

"我现在仍在商店工作，"南茜说，"不过下周就要离开那儿了。我已经捕获到了猎物——

catch in the world. You won't mind now Lou, will you? – I'm going to be married to Dan – to Dan! – he's my Dan now – why, Lou!"

Around the corner of the park strolled one of those new-crop, smooth-faced young policemen that are making the force more endurable – at least to the eye. He saw a woman with an expensive fur coat, and diamond-ringed hands crouching down against the iron fence of the park sobbing turbulently, while a slender, plainly-dressed working girl leaned close, trying to console her. But the Gibsonian cop, being of the new order, passed on, pretending not to notice, for he was wise enough to know that these matters are beyond help so far as the power he represents is concerned, though he rap the pavement with his night-stick till the sound goes up to the furthermost stars.

世界上最大的猎物。卢，现在你不会介意了，是不是？我要嫁给丹了——嫁给他！——他现在是我的丹了——你怎么啦，卢！"

一位刚刚穿上制服，面容清秀的年轻警察在公园的角落里溜达，正是这些年轻的警察让警察这支队伍更能让人忍受一些——至少看起来更顺眼些。他看见一个穿着昂贵的皮大衣，戴着钻石戒指的女人伏在公园的铁栏杆上，呜呜哭泣，旁边一个身材苗条，衣着朴素的职业女性正俯下身竭力地安慰她。但是这个吉布森[2]式的警察，由于新入行，所以只顾着走路，装做什么也没看见。他足够聪明，能够明白在这类事情上，他所代表的权力是帮不上忙的，尽管他用警棍敲打人行道，那响声能够传到最遥远的星辰。

1. 宁录：基督教《圣经》里人物，是一名英勇的猎手。
2. 吉布森(1867~1944)，美国插图画家，他曾用自己的妻子当模特画的《吉布森少女》代表了19世纪90年代美国妇女的典型形象。

26. A TECHNICAL ERROR
26. 技术误差

I never cared especially for feuds, believing them to be even more overrated products of our country than grapefruit, scrapple, or honeymoons. Nevertheless, if I may be allowed, I will tell you of an Indian Territory feud of which I was press-agent, camp-follower, and inaccessory during the fact.

I was on a visit to Sam Durkee's ranch, where I had a great time falling off unmanicured ponies and waving my bare hand at the lower jaws of wolves about two miles away. Sam was a hardened person of about twenty-five, with a reputation for going home in the dark with perfect equanimity, though often with reluctance.

Over in the Creek Nation was a family bearing the name of Tatum. I was told that the Durkees and Tatums had been feuding for years. Several of each family had bitten the grass, and it was expected that more Nebuchadnezzars would follow. A younger generation of each family

我从来不会太过计较家族世仇之类的事情，相信在我们国家，有人把这些事情的价值看得比葡萄柚、碎肉玉米炸饼或是蜜月要高。不过，如果各位允许的话，我将向你们讲述一个发生在印第安淮州[1]的世仇故事，当时我是这起事件的新闻宣传员，并随队报道，但是我并没有从中推波助澜。

当时我正在参观萨姆·德基的牧场，在那儿我玩得非常开心：从还没驯化的小马驹上摔下来，空手冲着远在两英里之外的野狼下颌挥动。萨姆大约25岁，是个性格坚毅的人，曾经因为完全镇定自若地摸黑回家而出了名，尽管他总是不情愿做这种事情的。

在克里克印第安部落里有一户姓塔特姆的家族。有人跟我说，德基家族和塔特姆家族已经结怨多年了。两个家族里都有一些人在争斗中被打死，而且可以预计会有更多的家族保卫者前赴后继。家族中的年轻一代正在慢慢

was growing up, and the grass was keeping pace with them. But I gathered that they had fought fairly; that they had not lain in cornfields and aimed at the division of their enemies' suspenders in the back – partly, perhaps, because there were no cornfields, and nobody wore more than one suspender. Nor had any woman or child of either house ever been harmed. In those days – and you will find it so yet – their women were safe.

Sam Durkee had a girl. (If it were an all-fiction magazine that I expect to sell this story to, I should say, "Mr. Durkee rejoiced in a fiancee.") Her name was Ella Baynes. They appeared to be devoted to each other, and to have perfect confidence in each other, as all couples do who are and have or aren't and haven't. She was tolerably pretty, with a heavy mass of brown hair that helped her along. He introduced me to her, which seemed not to lessen her preference for him; so I reasoned that they were surely soul-mates.

Miss Baynes lived in Kingfisher, twenty miles from the ranch. Sam lived on a gallop between the two places.

One day there came to Kingfisher a

长大成人，这种家族之间的争斗也紧随其后。不过我发现，他们之间的斗争是光明正大的。他们不会躲在玉米地里，从背后瞄准他们仇敌的背带，这其中有一部分原因可能是那里根本没有玉米地，而且也没有人穿背带裤。两个家族中从没有妇女或是孩童受到过伤害。在那个时期，家族中的妇女们都是安全的，而且将来情况依旧会如此。

萨姆·德基有个女朋友。（如果我想把这篇小说刊登在一家完全虚构的杂志上，那我想我会这么写："德基先生深爱着自己的未婚妻。"）她的名字是埃拉·贝恩斯。他们俩好像都深爱着对方，并且完全信任着对方，就跟所有彼此相爱、彼此信任或是彼此并不相爱、也并不信任的男男女女一样。她的长相还算漂亮，一头浓密的棕色长发更为他增添了几分妩媚。他介绍我们两个人认识，但这并没有丝毫减轻她对他的爱恋；因此我猜测，他们俩的的确确是一对心心相印的恩爱情侣。

贝恩斯小姐住在金费希尔，距离牧场有 20 英里远。萨姆总是在两地之间来回奔波忙碌着。

有一天，金费希尔来了位胆

courageous young man, rather small, with smooth face and regular features. He made many inquiries about the business of the town, and especially of the inhabitants cognominally. He said he was from Muscogee, and he looked it, with his yellow shoes and crocheted four-in-hand. I met him once when I rode in for the mail. He said his name was Beverly Travers, which seemed rather improbable.

There were active times on the ranch, just then, and Sam was too busy to go to town often. As an incompetent and generally worthless guest, it devolved upon me to ride in for little things such as post cards, barrels of flour, baking-powder, smoking-tobacco, and – letters from Ella.

One day, when I was messenger for half a gross of cigarette papers and a couple of wagon tires, I saw the alleged Beverly Travers in a yellow-wheeled buggy with Ella Baynes, driving about town as ostentatiously as the black, waxy mud would permit. I knew that this information would bring no balm of Gilead to Sam's soul, so I refrained from including it in the news of the city that I retailed on my return. But on the next

识过人的年轻人，他个子非常矮小，面色光滑，五官端正。他打听了许多关于这个镇子的事情，尤其是那些同姓居民的情况。他说他来自马斯科基，样子看上去应该错不了：他的脚上穿着双黄色的鞋，打着用针织成的活节领带。在我骑马去邮局的时候曾经见过他一次。他说他叫贝弗利·特拉弗斯，听起来似乎有点可疑。

当时正是牧场上的农忙时节，萨姆经常忙得没时间去镇里。作为一个没什么能力又派不上什么用场的客人，我便揽下了许多零碎的小事情，像是骑马去镇上寄明信片，买几桶面粉、发酵粉、烟草，还有取回埃拉寄来的信等等诸如此类的小事。

有一天，在我去买半摞卷烟纸和几个马车轮胎的时候，看到所谓的贝弗利·特拉弗斯和埃拉·贝恩斯一起坐在一辆黄色轮子的轻便马车上，往镇里驶去了，他们犹如黑得发亮的泥浆一样引人注目。我知道，这个消息并不会给萨姆的灵魂带来多少安慰，因此在我回去的时候，并没有把这个消息加在市镇新闻里头告诉他。但到了第二天下午，一个名

afternoon an elongated ex-cowboy of the name of Simmons, an old-time pal of Sam's, who kept a feed store in Kingfisher, rode out to the ranch and rolled and burned many cigarettes before he would talk. When he did make oration, his words were these:

"Say, Sam, there's been a description of a galoot miscallin' himself Beveledged Travels impairing the atmospheric air of Kingfisher for the past two weeks. You know who he was? He was not otherwise than Ben Tatum, from the Creek Nation, son of old Gopher Tatum that your Uncle Newt shot last February. You know what he done this morning? He killed your brother Lester – shot him in the co't-house yard."

I wondered if Sam had heard. He pulled a twig from a mesquite bush, chewed it gravely, and said:

"He did, did he? He killed Lester?"

"The same," said Simmons. "And he did more. He run away with your girl, the same as to say Miss Ella Baynes. I thought you might like to know, so I rode out to impart the information."

叫西蒙斯的高大男子骑着马来到了牧场。他是萨姆的老朋友，以前当过牛仔，如今在金费希尔开了家饲料店。他抽了不少卷烟之后才开口说话。他述说的措辞是这样的：

"我说，萨姆，在过去的两个星期里流传着关于某个谎称自己是贝弗尔·埃奇·特拉弗斯的怪人的事情，这扰乱了金费希尔的氛围。你知道那个人是谁吗？他不是别人，正是来自克里克印第安部落的本·塔特姆，在去年2月份，你的叔叔纽特打死了他的父亲老戈弗·塔特姆。你知道今天上午他都干了些什么吗？他杀死了你的兄弟莱斯特，就在院子里开枪打死了他。"

我不知道萨姆有没有听见这番话。只见他从牧豆树丛里摘了一根嫩枝，放进嘴里嚼着，面色凝重地说：

"他真的这么做了吗？他杀了莱斯特？"

"千真万确，"西蒙斯说，"而且还不止些，他还挟持了你的女朋友，就是埃拉·贝恩斯小姐。我猜你应该想知道这些消息，所以就跑来通知你了。"

"I am much obliged, Jim," said Sam, taking the chewed twig from his mouth. "Yes, I'm glad you rode Out. Yes, I'm right glad."

"Well, I'll be ridin' back, I reckon. That boy I left in the feed store don't know hay from oats. He shot Lester in the back."

"Shot him in the back?"

"Yes, while he was hitchin' his hoss."

"I'm much obliged, Jim."

"I kind of thought you'd like to know as soon as you could."

"Come in and have some coffee before you ride back, Jim?"

"Why, no, I reckon not; I must get back to the store."

"And you say –"

"Yes, Sam. Everybody seen 'em drive away together in a buckboard, with a big bundle, like clothes, tied up in the back of it. He was drivin' the team he brought over with him from Muscogee. They'll be hard to overtake right away."

"And which –"

"I was goin' on to tell you. They left on the Guthrie road; but there's no tellin' which forks they'll take – you know

"真是太感谢你了,吉姆,"萨姆一边说着,一边把口里嚼着的嫩枝吐出来,"是的,我很高兴你能骑马过来告诉我这一切,我真的非常高兴。"

"那好,我想我也该回去了。留在饲料店里看店的那个小孩连干草和燕麦都分不清楚。他是从背后向莱斯特开的枪。"

"从背后开的枪?"

"是的,当时莱斯特正在套马。"

"真是非常感谢,吉姆。"

"我猜你应该想要尽快了解这些事情。"

"先进去喝杯咖啡再回去吧,吉姆?"

"哎呀,不用了,我想还是算了;我必须得回去喽。"

"你说——"

"是的,萨姆。大伙儿都看见他们一起赶着一辆四轮马车走了,车后面还绑着个大包袱,里面好像是衣物。他赶着从马斯科基带过来的马队走了,一时半会儿是很难赶上喽。"

"那——"

"我正要告诉你呢,他们往古恩里路那里去了;但是,没听说他们要往哪条岔路走,你知道

that."

"All right, Jim; much obliged."

"You're welcome, Sam."

Simmons rolled a cigarette and stabbed his pony with both heels. Twenty yards away he reined up and called back:

"You don't want no – assistance, as you might say?"

"Not any, thanks."

"I didn't think you would. Well, so long!"

Sam took out and opened a bone-handled pocket-knife and scraped a dried piece of mud from his left boot. I thought at first he was going to swear a vendetta on the blade of it, or recite "The Gipsy's Curse." The few feuds I had ever seen or read about usually opened that way. This one seemed to be presented with a new treatment. Thus offered on the stage, it would have been hissed off, and one of Belasco's thrilling melodramas demanded instead.

"I wonder," said Sam, with a profoundly thoughtful expression, "if the cook has any cold beans left over!"

He called Wash, the Negro cook, and finding that he had some, ordered him to heat up the pot and make some strong

这的确是个问题。"

"好的，吉姆。谢谢你。"

"不客气，萨姆。"

西蒙斯卷了一支烟，用他的两个脚后跟踹了一下他的小马驹，在跑出 20 码之后他又放慢了速度，回过头来喊道：

"难道，你不想有人来帮你的忙吗？"

"不用了，谢谢。"

"我认为你也不需要。那么再见了！"

萨姆掏出一把随身携带的骨头手柄的小折刀，打开之后刮掉了粘在左脚鞋底上的一块干泥。刚开始我还以为他会对着刀刃发誓要报仇雪恨，或是背诵一段《吉卜赛的诅咒》。我曾经看见或是读到的少数几个世仇故事的开头通常都是这样的。这一次似乎要换个方式开始演出了。舞台上俗套的剧目将被轰下台，贝拉斯科[2]扣人心弦的传奇剧将取而代之。

萨姆一脸深思熟虑地说："不知道厨子有没有剩下些冷豆子！"

他召唤着黑人厨子沃什，发现还有一些豆子，于是吩咐厨子把罐子热一下，再煮些浓咖啡。

coffee. Then we went into Sam's private room, where he slept, and kept his armoury, dogs, and the saddles of his favourite mounts. He took three or four six-shooters out of a bookcase and began to look them over, whistling "The Cowboy's Lament" abstractedly. Afterward he ordered the two best horses on the ranch saddled and tied to the hitching-post.

Now, in the feud business, in all sections of the country, I have observed that in one particular there is a delicate but strict etiquette belonging. You must not mention the word or refer to the subject in the presence of a feudist. It would be more reprehensible than commenting upon the mole on the chin of your rich aunt. I found, later on, that there is another unwritten rule, but I think that belongs solely to the West.

It yet lacked two hours to supper-time; but in twenty minutes Sam and I were plunging deep into the reheated beans, hot coffee, and cold beef.

"Nothing like a good meal before a long ride," said Sam. "Eat hearty."

I had a sudden suspicion.

"Why did you have two horses sad-

然后我们来到萨姆的私人房间，他就睡在这个地方，同时这里也存放着他的武器，养着几条狗，放着他最心爱的马匹专用的马鞍。他从一个书架上取出三四把六发式的左轮手枪，仔细检查了一番，心不在焉地吹着《牛仔的挽歌》这首的曲子。接着，他又吩咐给牧场里最好的两匹马备好鞍，拴在马桩上。

这时，我发现在这个国家的每一地区里，这些世仇故事中都存在着一种特殊的习俗，虽然非常细微却都严格遵守着。在一个结下世仇的人面前，你最好不要提及他的对手，要不然，这会比谈论你那富态的姑妈下巴上那块胎记更受人指责。后来我又发现了另外一条不成文的规矩，但我觉得这应该是西部地区特有的。

虽然离晚饭时间还有两个小时，但是萨姆和我在20分钟之后，就狼吞虎咽地开始吃热好的豆子、煮好的咖啡和冷牛肉了。

"在长途跋涉之前，没什么能比这顿大餐更美味的了，"萨姆说，"真好吃。"

我突然起了疑心。

"为什么你要备了两匹

dled?" I asked.

"One, two – one, two," said Sam. "You can count, can't you?"

His mathematics carried with it a momentary qualm and a lesson. The thought had not occurred to him that the thought could possibly occur to me not to ride at his side on that red road to revenge and justice. It was the higher calculus. I was booked for the trail. I began to eat more beans.

In an hour we set forth at a steady gallop eastward. Our horses were Kentucky-bred, strengthened by the mesquite grass of the west. Ben Tatum's steeds may have been swifter, and he had a good lead; but if he had heard the punctual thuds of the hoofs of those trailers of ours, born in the heart of feudland, he might have felt that retribution was creeping up on the hoof-prints of his dapper nags.

I knew that Ben Tatum's card to play was flight – flight until he came within the safer territory of his own henchmen and supporters. He knew that the man pursuing him would follow the trail to any end where it might lead.·

During the ride Sam talked of the prospect for rain, of the price of beef, and

马？"我问道。

"一、二，一、二，"萨姆说，"你会数数的啊，不是吗？"

他的算数中包含着瞬间的疑虑和训斥。他没有想到，我并不愿意陪着他一起踏上这条复仇和正义的道路。这是更高级的微积分，我被拉进了跟踪者的行列，于是我就吃了更多的豆子。

一小时之后，我们沿着一条平坦的道路快速地向东行进。我们的马都是肯塔基种马，西部的牧豆草让它们变得更加强壮有力了。本·塔特姆的马可能会跑得更快些，况且他的骑马技术也相当精湛；但是，如果他听到我们这些追踪者的马匹在他仇敌腹地之中发出的阵阵急促的马蹄声，他或许会感到惩罚正沿着他矫健的马匹留下的蹄印在慢慢靠近。

我知道，本·塔特姆的把戏就是逃跑，他会一直跑到他的追随者和支持者们所占领的更加安全的领土范围内。他知道，无论他跑到哪里，追赶他的人都会寻踪而来。

在追赶途中，萨姆说希望能下场雨，他还说起牛肉价格和玻

of the musical glasses. You would have thought he had never had a brother or a sweetheart or an enemy on earth. There are some subjects too big even for the words in the "Unabridged." Knowing this phase of the feud code, but not having practised it sufficiently, I overdid the thing by telling some slightly funny an-ecdotes. Sam laughed at exactly the right place – laughed with his mouth. When I caught sight of his mouth, I wished I had been blessed with enough sense of hu-mour to have suppressed those anec-dotes.

Our first sight of them we had in Guthrie. Tired and hungry, we stumbled, unwashed, into a little yellow-pine hotel and sat at a table. In the opposite corner we saw the fugitives. They were bent upon their meal, but looked around at times uneasily.

The girl was dressed in brown – one of these smooth, half-shiny, silky-looking affairs with lace collar and cuffs, and what I believe they call an accor-dion-plaited skirt. She wore a thick brown veil down to her nose, and a broad-brimmed straw hat with some kind of feathers adorning it. The man wore

璃杯琴[3]。你会以为他根本不曾在这世上拥有过任何一个兄弟，或是一位爱人，亦或是一个敌人。即便说这是"完整版"，这个主题也显得太过庞大了。我知道有世仇规矩这么一说，但是并没有亲身经历过。我漫无边际地说了些微不足道而又滑稽可笑的奇闻轶事。到了可笑之处，萨姆就放声大笑起来。当我看见他的嘴时，真希望自己能有幸拥有足够多的幽默感来压倒这些奇闻轶事。

我们在古寺里第一次遇见了他们。我们当时又累又饿，磕磕绊绊、风尘仆仆地走进一家很小的黄松旅店，在一张桌子旁边坐了下来。我们发现那两个逃亡者就坐在对面的角落里。他们正在俯着身子吃饭，只不过时不时就不安地四处张望。

那姑娘穿着一身棕色衣服，那种布料手感很光滑，表面富有光泽，看上去像是丝绸之类的，领子和袖口都绣着花边，我想这就是人们所说的百褶裙吧。她的脸上蒙着厚实的棕色面纱，一直到盖住她的鼻子上，头上戴着一顶装饰着羽毛的宽边草帽。那个

plain, dark clothes, and his hair was trimmed very short. He was such a man as you might see anywhere.

There they were – the murderer and the woman he had stolen. There we were – the rightful avenger, according to the code, and the supernumerary who writes these words.

For one time, at least, in the heart of the supernumerary there rose the killing instinct. For one moment he joined the force of combatants – orally.

"What are you waiting for, Sam?" I said in a whisper. "Let him have it now!"

Sam gave a melancholy sigh.

"You don't understand; but *he* does," he said. "*he* knows. Mr. Tenderfoot, there's a rule out here among white men in the Nation that you can't shoot a man when he's with a woman. I never knew it to be broke yet. You *can't* do it. You've got to get him in a gang of men or by himself. That's why. He knows it, too. We all know. So, that's Mr. Ben Tatum! One of the 'pretty men'! I'll cut him out of the herd before they leave the hotel, and regulate his account!"

男人穿着朴素的深色外套，剪着一头短发，就是一个随便在哪儿都能遇见的男人。

他们就在那儿——杀人犯和被他挟持的女人。我们也在那儿——依照世仇规矩来说算是合法的复仇者，以及写下这篇文章的小配角。

在这个小配角的心中，至少有那么一次涌动着杀人的冲动。有那么一会儿，他已经加入战斗的队伍之中——不过只是用嘴巴上说说而已。

"你在等什么，萨姆？"我跟他耳语道，"快让他接受惩罚！"

萨姆无可奈何地叹了口气。

"你不了解，但他是知道的。"他说，"他知道你没有经验，先生，在这个国家的白人中流传着一条规矩，当一个男人身边陪伴着一个女人的时候，你不能冲着他开枪。我从没听说有人打破过这条规矩，你也不能。你得在他们一伙人待在一起或是他单独一个人的时候才能收拾他。这就是我迟迟没有动手的原因。这些他都知道。我们都知道，本·塔特姆就是这种人！一个'聪明的男人'！在他们离开这家旅店之前，我要把他从这群禽兽中

After supper the flying pair disappeared quickly. Although Sam haunted lobby and stairway and halls half the night, in some mysterious way the fugitives eluded him; and in the morning the veiled lady in the brown dress with the accordion-plaited skirt and the dapper young man with the close-clipped hair, and the buckboard with the prancing nags, were gone.

It is a monotonous story, that of the ride; so it shall be curtailed. Once again we overtook them on a road. We were about fifty yards behind. They turned in the buckboard and looked at us; then drove on without whipping up their horses. Their safety no longer lay in speed. Ben Tatum knew. He knew that the only rock of safety left to him was the code. There is no doubt that, had he been alone, the matter would have been settled quickly with Sam Durkee in the usual way; but he had something at his side that kept still the trigger-finger of both. It seemed likely that he was no coward.

So, you may perceive that woman, on occasions, may postpone instead of precipitating conflict between man and man.

剔除出去，了结他所欠下的债！"

吃过晚饭之后，这对亡命天涯的男女迅速消失了。虽然萨姆在旅店的大厅、楼梯和走廊上一直反复地搜寻直到半夜三更，但是这对逃亡者就这样离奇地逃脱了。到了第二天早上，那位蒙着面纱、穿着棕色百褶裙的女人和那个剪着短发、个子矮小的年轻男子，连同那辆套着几匹快马的四轮马车，全都消失不见了。

行进的过程显得非常单调而令人厌倦，因此这里就不再赘述。我们又一次在路上追到了他们，在差不多落后他们50码的距离。他们坐在四轮马车上转过头来看了看我们；然后接着赶车，并没有快马加鞭。他们并不指望速度能给他们带来安全。本·塔特姆知道这一点。他知道，留给他的惟一庇佑就是规矩。如果他单独一个人，萨姆·德基早就用寻常的方法迅速把事情给解决掉了，这是毋庸置疑的；但是如今他身边有个女人，使得双方都没有机会扣动扳机。他看起来似乎并不是个胆小鬼。

因此你可能会认识到，有时候女人可能会推迟男人之间的冲突，而不是加速这种冲突。但她

But not willingly or consciously. She is oblivious of codes.

Five miles farther, we came upon the future great Western city of Chandler. The horses of pursuers and pursued were starved and weary. There was one hotel that offered danger to man and entertainment to beast; so the four of us met again in the dining room at the ringing of a bell so resonant and large that it had cracked the welkin long ago. The dining room was not as large as the one at Guthrie.

Just as we were eating apple pie – how Ben Davises and tragedy impinge upon each other! – I noticed Sam looking with keen intentness at our quarry where they were seated at a table across the room. The girl still wore the brown dress with lace collar and cuffs, and the veil drawn down to her nose. The man bent over his plate, with his close cropped head held low.

"There's a code," I heard Sam say, either to me or to himself, "that won't let you shoot a man in the company of a woman; but, by thunder, there ain't one to keep you from killing a woman in the company of a man!"

And, quicker than my mind could

并不是自愿或是有意的。她根本就没有注意到规矩这种东西。

又赶了五英里路，我们来到了前景光明的西部城市钱德勒。追赶者和被追赶者的马都已经筋疲力尽、饥饿难耐了。那里有家旅馆，可以给牲畜提供食物，却让男人充满危机感；因此伴随着一阵清脆的钟声，我们四人又在餐厅里见面了。这钟声如此深沉洪亮，震动了这片古老的苍穹。而这餐厅不如古思里那家大。

正在我们吃着苹果派的时候，本·戴维塞斯的悲剧就这么发生了！我注意到萨姆正热切地注视着我们的猎物，此时他们就坐在餐厅另一边的桌子旁边。那姑娘仍旧穿着花边领子和袖口的棕色衣服，脸上的面纱盖住了她的鼻子。那男子弯着腰对着他的盘子，那颗剪着短发的头低垂着。

"有条规矩，"我听萨姆说道，好像是对我说的，又像在自言自语，"规定你不能向有女人陪伴的男人开枪；但并没规定你不能向有男人陪伴的女人开枪！"

我的脑子还没来得及反应他

follow his argument, he whipped a Colt's automatic from under his left arm and pumped six bullets into the body that the brown dress covered – the brown dress with the lace collar and cuffs and the accordion-plaited skirt.

The young person in the dark sack suit, from whose head and from whose life a woman's glory had been clipped, laid her head on her arms stretched upon the table; while people came running to raise Ben Tatum from the floor in his feminine masquerade that had given Sam the opportunity to set aside, technically, the obligations of the code.

说的是什么意思，他就已经从左臂下拔出了一把科尔特自动手枪，一口气朝那个穿着棕色衣服（就是那件有花边领子和袖口的百褶裙）的身躯射了 6 发子弹。

那个身穿着朴素的深色西装的年轻人双手伸开摊在桌上，头枕在手臂上，一个女人引以为荣的秀发彻底地被人从她的头上和她的生活中给剪掉了；与此同时，人们纷纷跑过去扶起倒在地上、伪装成女人的本·塔特姆，从技术上说，这给了萨姆摆脱规矩束缚的机会。

1. 印第安准州：美国历史上中南部的一片区域，主要是如今的俄克拉荷马州。政府把这块地区划给印第安人，并在 1834 年强迫印第安土著人迁徙进去。1889 年，这块地区的西部开放，任何人都可以在此安家立业；1890 年，西部成为俄克拉荷马准州。1907 年，西部和东部合并，成立了俄克拉荷马州。
2. 大卫·贝拉斯科：美国舞台监督，以布景逼真闻名。
3. 玻璃杯琴：在玻璃杯中加水，敲击的乐器。

27. "FOX-IN-THE-MORNING"
27. 狐狸把戏

Coralio reclined, in the mid-day heat, like some vacuous beauty lounging in a guarded harem. The town lay at the sea's edge on a strip of alluvial coast. It was set like a little pearl in an emerald band. Behind it, and seeming almost to topple, imminent, above it, rose the sea-following range of the Cordilleras. In front the sea was spread, a smiling jailer, but even more incorruptible than the frowning mountains. The waves swished along the smooth beach; the parrots screamed in the orange and ceiba-trees; the palms waved their limber fronds foolishly like an awkward chorus at the prima donna's cue to enter.

Suddenly the town was full of excitement. A native boy dashed down a grass-grown street, shrieking: "*Busca el Senor Goodwin. Ha venido un telegrafo por el!*"

The word passed quickly. Telegrams do not often come to anyone in Coralio. The cry for Senor Goodwin was taken up by a dozen officious voices. The main

赤日炎炎正午时分，科拉里奥像个无所事事的美人一样躺在守卫森严的闺房里。这个小镇位于海岸冲积带上，就像一颗镶嵌在翡翠带上的小珍珠。它的后背是与海岸线一致的科迪勒拉山脉，高高在上，层峦叠嶂，好像要倾倒一般。前面是平展的大海，像个微笑的狱吏，却比那皱着眉头的大山更为刚正不阿。浪花瑟瑟地拍打着平滑的沙滩；鹦鹉在橘树和木棉树上尖叫；棕榈树像一支拙劣的合唱队，傻兮兮地舞动着它们的枝叶暗示着歌剧女主角的进场。

小镇突然间沸腾了。一个当地的男孩沿着长草的街道一边快跑，一边尖声叫喊："去叫古德温先生。他有封电报！"

这个消息传得很快。住在科拉里奥的人很少收到电报。呼喊古德温先生的声音被十几个好事者的声音打断，沙滩平行的主街

street running parallel to the beach became populated with those who desired to expedite the delivery of the despatch. Knots of women with complexions varying from palest olive to deepest brown gathered at street corners and plaintively carolled: "*Un telegrafo por Senor Goodwin!*" The *comandante*, Don Senor el Coronel Encarnacion Rios, who was loyal to the Ins and suspected Goodwin's devotion to the Outs, hissed: "Aha!" and wrote in his secret memorandum book the accusive fact that Senor Goodwin had on that momentous date received a telegram.

In the midst of the hullabaloo a man stepped to the door of a small wooden building and looked out. Above the door was a sign that read "Keogh and Clancy" – a nomenclature that seemed not to be indigenous to that tropical soil. The man in the door was Billy Keogh, scout of fortune and progress and latter-day rover of the Spanish Main.Tintypes and photographs were the weapons with which Keogh and Clancy were at that time assailing the hopeless shores. Outside the shop were set two large frames filled with specimens of their art and skill.

Keogh leaned in the doorway, his bold

道上挤满了想尽快传递消息的人。一群群肤色各异的女人积聚在街角，有的是暗橄榄色，有的是深棕色，她们高声喊唱："有古德温先生的一封电报！"忠实于执政党的司令官恩卡纳齐昂·里约斯上校先生，怀疑古德温效忠于在野党，他"啊哈"地嘘了一声，然后在自己的秘密备忘本上记下这可以作为今后指控证据的事实：古德温先生在这个重大日子里收到了一封电报。

喧哗之中，一个男人走出一座小木房向外张望。门上方有块写着"基奥—克兰希"的招牌——好像不是热带地区地道的名称。门里的这个男人是比利·基奥，他是个到处寻求财富和追求进步的人，是西班牙大陆美洲上的近代流浪者。锡版照相机和照片是"基奥—克兰希"当时用来进攻这些无助的海岸的武器。商店外面就有两个装满了展示它们艺术和技巧样品的画框。

基奥靠在门口，他那醒目的、

and humorous countenance wearing a look of interest at the unusual influx of life and sound into the street. When the meaning of the disturbance became clear to him he placed a hand beside his mouth and shouted: "Hey! Frank!" in such a robustious voice that the feeble clamour of the natives was drowned and silenced.

Fifty yards away, on the seaward side of the street, stood the abode of the consul for the United States. Out from the door of this building tumbled Goodwin at the call. He had been smoking with Willard Geddie, the consul, on the back porch of the consulate, which was conceded to be the coolest spot in Coralio.

"Hurry up," shouted Keogh. "There's a riot in town on account of a telegram that's come for you. You want to be careful about these things, my boy. It won't do to trifle with the feelings of the public this way. You'll be getting a pink note some day with violet scent on it; and then the country'll be steeped in the throes of a revolution."

Goodwin had strolled up the street and met the boy with the message.The ox-eyed women gazed at him with shy admiration, for his type drew them. He was big, blonde, and jauntily dressed in white

富有幽默感的面容上表现出了对这街上难得的生气与喧闹的兴趣。等他弄明白这场喧闹的原因以后，他把一只手放在嘴边，喊道："嘿，弗兰克！"。这喊声如此粗犷，那些本地人微弱的声音立刻被淹没，随之安静下来。

美国领事馆坐落在50码外的街道朝海的那一面。古德温听到叫声后匆匆地从门里走出。他和威拉德·格迪领事一直在领事馆的后走廊上吸烟，那被认作是科拉里奥最凉爽的地方。

"快一点，"基奥叫道，"镇上因为给你的一封电报而轰动了。伙计，对这种事你可要小心。这样戏弄公众感情可是不行的。将来某一天你会得到一个带着紫罗兰香气的红纸条，那时候，整个国家就会陷入一场革命的阵痛之中了。"

古德温沿着街道漫步到送信的男孩的身边。眼睛瞪得像牛眼睛般大小的女人们羞涩而又爱慕地看着他，因为这一类型的男人对她们有吸引力。他身材高大、

linen, with buckskin *zapatos*. His manner was courtly, with a sort of kindly truculence in it, tempered by a merciful eye. When the telegram had been delivered, and the bearer of it dismissed with a gratuity, the relieved populace returned to the contiguities of shade from which curiosity had drawn it – the women to their baking in the mud oven sunder the orange-trees, or to the interminable combing of their long, straight hair; the men to their cigarettes and gossip in the cantinas.

Goodwin sat on Keogh's doorstep, and read his telegram. It was from Bob Englehart, an American, who lived in San Mateo, the capital city of Anchuria, eighty miles in the interior. Englehart was a goldminer, an ardent revolutionist and "good people." That he was a man of resource and imagination was proven by the telegram he had sent. It had been his task to send a confidential message to his friend in Coralio. This could not have been accomplished in either Spanish or English, for the eye politic in Anchuria was an active one. The Insand the Outs were perpetually on their guard. But Englehart was a diplomatist. There existed but one code upon which he might make requisition with promise of safety –

金发碧眼，身着白色亚麻布，脚蹬鹿革皮鞋，显得朝气蓬勃。他风度翩翩，略有些粗野之气，却因为眼中的怜爱之情而显得缓和了许多。他拿了电报以后，给了送信的一些赏钱，刚才被好奇心驱使出来的人们便放心地又回到他们原来所在的附近的荫凉处——女人们回到橘树下的泥炉烘烤食品，或无休止地梳理她们长长的直发；男人们则回到小酒吧里抽烟闲聊。

古德温坐在基奥的门阶上读电报。这封电报来自一个叫鲍布·恩格尔哈特的美国人。他住在离海岸线 80 英里外的内陆城市，安楚里亚首府圣马提奥。恩格尔哈特是一名金矿工人，一个热情的革命者和一位"好人"。从寄来的电报可以看出他是个聪明机智、富有想像力的人。他的任务是送一份秘密情报给他在科拉里奥的朋友，但他既不能用西班牙语也不能用英语写这封情报，因为安楚里亚的政治眼线极其活跃。执政党和在野党始终都保持着高度地警惕。但恩格尔哈特是个外交高手。有一种密码他可以安全地使用，那就是伟大有效的俚语密码。他的这份情报就

the great and potent code of Slang. So, here is the message that slipped, unconstrued, through the fingers of curious officials, and came to the eye of Goodwin:

His Nibs skedaddled yesterday per jack-rabbit line with all the coin in the kitty and the bundle of muslin he's spoony about. The boodle is six figures short. Our crowd in good shape, but we need the spondulicks. You collar it. The main guy and the dry goods are headed for the briny. You know what to do.

BOB.

This screed, remarkable as it was, had no mystery for Goodwin. He was the most successful of the small advance-guard of speculative Americans that had invaded Anchuria, and he had not reached that enviable pinnacle without having well exercised the arts of foresight and deduction. He had taken up political intrigue as a matter of business. He was acute enough to wield a certain influence among the leading schemers, and he was prosperous enough to be able to purchase the respect of the petty office-holders. There was always a revolutionary party; and to it he had always

从富有好奇心的官员们的手指缝里漏掉了，未经破译就展现在古德温眼前：

他的上司昨天经由长腿大野兔路线逃走了，带着小猫里面的所有硬币和那捆薄纱布。那笔款是六位数。我们的人马毫发无伤，不过，我们需要票子。这票子由你去弄。那个主要人物和干货朝海边去了。你知道怎么做。

鲍布

这封冗长的电文尽管不同寻常，但对于古德温来说并不神秘。他是入侵安楚里亚的先遣队中最成功的美国投机分子之一。要是没有预见与推理的才能，他怎么能攀上令人嫉妒的顶峰呢。他已经把政治阴谋当成生意来做了。精明过人的他足以对上层决策者施加影响，发达后也赢得了小官员们的敬重。革命党总会存在，他也就总是与之结盟，与新政权结盟又总会有所回报。现在就有一个自由党想要推翻米拉弗洛尔总统。如果革命的车轮能够成功推进，古德温就会得到内地三万

allied himself; for the adherents of a new administration received the rewards of their labours. There was now a Liberal party seeking to overturn President Miraflores. If the wheel successfully revolved, Goodwin stood to win a concession to 30,000 manzanas of the finest coffee lands in the interior. Certain incidents in the recent career of President Miraflores had excited a shrewd suspicion in Goodwin's mind that the government was near a dissolution from another cause than that of a revolution, and now Englehart's telegram had come as a corroboration of his wisdom.

The telegram, which had remained unintelligible to the Anchurian linguists who had applied to it in vain their knowledge of Spanish and elemental English, conveyed a stimulating piece of news to Goodwin's understanding. It informed him that the president of the republic had decamped from the capital city with the contents of the treasury. Furthermore, that he was accompanied in his flight by that winning adventuress Isabel Guilbert, the opera singer, whose troupe of performers had been entertained by the president at San Mateo during the past month on a scale less

曼扎纳最好的咖啡种植场。最近，米拉弗洛尔总统在任期间发生时的几件内部确定的事件使精明的古德温产生怀疑：政府即将解散了，但不是因为革命而是其他原因。此刻，恩格尔哈特来的这封电报证实了他的智慧。

尽管安楚里亚的语言学家们曾经试图用他们那点西班牙语和基础的英语知识来破解这封电报，却始终徒劳无益。但它却给古德温带来一则振奋人心的消息：共和国的总统携带所有财宝从首都秘密逃亡了。此外，陪同他逃亡的还有那位成功的女冒险家伊莎贝尔·吉尔伯特。她还是位歌剧家，她的演出团上个月在圣马提奥受到总统足以让皇室来访者感到满意的规格的款待。电报中所说的"长腿大野兔路线"不过是指科拉里奥与首都之间流行的那条骡背上的运输体系。提

modest than that with which royal visitors are often content. The reference to the "jackrabbit line" could mean nothing else than the mule-back system of transport that prevailed between Coralio and the capital. The hint that the "boodle" was "six figures short" made the condition of the national treasury lamentably clear. Also it was convincingly true that the ingoing party – its way now made a pacific one – would need the "spondulicks." Unless its pledges should be fulfilled, and the spoils held for the delectation of the victors, precarious indeed, would be the position of the new government. Therefore it was exceeding necessary to "collar the main guy," and recapture the sinews of war and government.

Goodwin handed the message to Keogh.

"Read that, Billy," he said. "It's from Bob Englehart. Can you manage the cipher?"

Keogh sat in the other half of the doorway, and carefully perused the telegram.

"Tis not a cipher," he said, finally. "Tis what they call literature, and that's a system of language put in the mouths of

到的那笔"六位数"的"那笔款"暴露出国家财富的可怜处境。还有一点可以确信的事实是，新上台的政党（它的路线是和平的）需要"票子"。除非新政府能够实现它的誓言让败者向胜者进贡，否则，它将来的地位实在是岌岌可危。因此它及其有必要"抓住大人物的领子"，重新获得逃亡政府的经费。

古德温把情报递给基奥。

"比利，你看看这个，"他说。"是鲍布·恩格尔哈特寄来的。你能解开密码吗？"

基奥坐在门口的另一边，仔细读着电报。

"这不是什么密码，"他终于开口道，"这是人们称之为文学的东西，是人们挂在嘴边上的

people that they've never been intro-duced to by writers of imagination. The magazines invented it, but I never knew before that President Norvin Green had stamped it with the seal of his approval. 'Tis now no longer literature, but language. The dictionaries tried, but they couldn't make it go for anything but dialect. Sure, now that the Western Union indorses it, it won't be long till a race of people will spring up that speaks it."

"You're running too much to philol-ogy, Billy," said Goodwin. "Do you make out the meaning of it?"

"Sure," replied the philosopher of Fortune. "All languages come easy to the man who must know 'em. I've even failed to misunderstand an order to evacuate in classical Chinese when it was backed up by the muzzle of a breech-loader. This little literary essay I hold in my hands means a game of Fox-in-the-Morning. Ever play that, Frank, when you was a kid?"

"I think so," said Goodwin, laughing. "You join hands all 'round, and –"

"You do not," interrupted Keogh. "You've got a fine sporting game mixed up in your head with 'All Around the Rosebush.' The spirit of 'Fox-in-the-

一套语言系统，而富有想像力的作家们却从来不知道。杂志发明了它，不过在诺文·格林局长盖章批准之前我一直都不知道。现在它已经不再是文学了，它只是语言。词典努力过，但也只能把它归为方言。现在美国西部已经认可了它，相信在不久的将来，一种说这种话的人民就会涌现。"

"比利，你都扯到哲学了，跑题太远了，"古德温说，"你看出来它的意思了吗？"

"当然，"这位预测命运的哲学家回答道，"如果必须要学的话，任何语言都会变得容易。如果在后膛炮炮口的威逼下，即使是用中国古文命令撤退，我也决不会误解。我现在手上拿的这个文学短文指的是一种叫做'早晨的狐狸'的游戏。弗兰克，你小时候曾经玩过这个游戏吗？"

"我想是的，"古德温大笑着说，"手拉手成一圈，然后——"

"不是你这样的，"基奥打断他，"你脑子把'环绕蔷薇'和它混在一起变成了一种好玩的运动游戏。'早晨的狐狸'的精神

Morning' is opposed to the holding of hands. I'll tell you how it's played. This president man and his companion in play, they stand up over in San Mateo, ready for the run, and shout: 'Fox-in-the-Morning!' Me and you, standing here, we say: 'Goose and the Gander!' They say: 'How many miles is it to London town?' We say: 'Only a few, if your legs are long enough. How many comes out?' They say: 'More than you're able to catch.' And then the game commences."

"I catch the idea," said Goodwin. "It won't do to let the goose and gander slip through our fingers, Billy; their feathers are too valuable. Our crowd is prepared and able to step into the shoes of the government at once; but with the treasury empty we'd stay in power about as long as a tender foot would stick on an untamed bronco.We must play the fox on every foot of the coast to prevent their getting out of the country."

"By the mule-back schedule," said Keogh, "it's five days down from San Mateo. We've got plenty of time to set our outposts. There's only three places on the coast where they can hope to sail from – here and Solitas and Alazan. They're the only points we'll have to

是反对手牵手的。我来告诉你它是怎么玩的。那位总统大人和同他游戏的伙伴们,他们在圣马提奥边站立着,随时准备逃跑,他们叫道:'早晨的狐狸!'而我和你站在这里,我们说:'母鹅和公鹅!'他们说:'从这里到伦敦有多少英里路?'我们说:'如果你们的腿够长的话,只有几里路而已。有多少只跑出来了?'他们说:'多得你们抓不完。'然后,这个游戏就开始了。"

"我知道这个意思了,"古德温说,"让那些母鹅公鹅从我们的手指缝里溜走是不行的,比利。它们的羽毛太贵重了。我们的人有能力,也已准备好立刻取代政府,但是国库空了,我们在位的时间可能跟一位新手骑在一匹桀骜不驯的野马上的时间一样短。我们必须像狐狸一样盯住海岸上的每一点,不让他们溜出这个国家。"

"走那条骡背上的小道,"基奥说,"从圣马提奥出发需要五天时间。我们有充足的时间设前哨。海岸线上只有三个地方他们有希望出海——这里、索里塔斯和阿拉赞。它们是我们惟一需要守住的几个点。这就像下国际

guard. It's as easy as a chess problem – fox to play, and mate in three moves. Oh, goosey, goosey, gander, whither do you wander? By the blessing of the literary telegraph the boodle of this benighted fatherland shall be preserved to the honest political party that is seeking to overthrow it."

The situation had been justly outlined by Keogh. The down trail from the capital was at all times a weary road to travel. A jiggety-joggety journey it was; ice-cold and hot, wet and dry. The trail climbed appalling mountains, wound like a rotten string about the brows of breathless precipices, plunged through chilling snow-fed streams, and wriggled like a snake through sunless forests teeming with menacing insect and animal life. After descending to the foothills it turned to a trident, the central prong ending at Alazan. Another branched off to Coralio; the third penetrated to Solitas. Between the sea and the foothills stretched the five miles breadth of alluvial coast. Here was the flora of the tropics in its rankest and most prodigal growth. Spaces here and there had been wrested from the jungle and planted with bananas and cane and orange groves. The

象棋一样简单——耍狐狸把戏，三步就将军。呵呵，笨蛋，笨蛋，大笨蛋，你们想往哪里跑？多亏有了这封像文学作品一样的电报，这个愚昧国家的财富才得以由那个一直试图推翻它的正直的政党来保存。"

基奥把地形的轮廓勾勒出来。从首都蔓延来的那条小道无论任何时候都是一条艰险的道路。那是一条崎岖不平的路，一会冰冷一会炎热，一会潮湿一会干燥。这条小道沿着陡峭的山峰往上爬，像一根烂绳子一样蜿蜒在令人窒息的悬崖上，穿过寒冷的、冰雪覆盖的小溪；像一条蛇蠕动着穿过遮天蔽日的、充满危险昆虫和动物的森林。下到山脚下之后，它便转向一个三岔路口，中间那一条目的地是阿拉赞，另一条分叉到科拉里奥，那第三条直穿至索里塔斯。在大海与山脚之间是宽达五英里的冲积海岸，这里是热带植物最葳蕤的地方。人们在丛林中抢出空地到处种香蕉、甘蔗和橘树。其余部分杂乱生长着野生植物，那是猴子、貘、美洲虎、短吻鳄鱼和大型爬行动物及昆虫的家。在路没有被开辟

rest was a riot of wild vegetation, the home of monkeys, tapirs, jaguars, alligators and prodigious reptiles and insects. Where no road was cut a serpent could scarcely make its way through the tangle of vines and creepers. Across the treacherous mangrove swamps few things without wings could safely pass. Therefore the fugitives could hope to reach the coast only by one of the routes named.

"Keep the matter quiet, Billy," advised Goodwin. "We don't want the Ins to know that the president is in flight. I suppose Bob's information is something of a scoop in the capital as yet. Otherwise he would not have tried to make his message a confidential one; and besides, everybody would have heard the news. I'm going around now to see Dr. Zavalla, and start a man up the trail to cut the telegraph wire."As Goodwin rose, Keogh threw his hat upon the grass by the door and expelled a tremendous sigh.

"What's the trouble, Billy?" asked Goodwin, pausing. "That's the first time I ever heard you sigh."

"'Tis the last," said Keogh. "With that sorrowful puff of wind I resign myself to a life of praiseworthy but harassing hon-

出来的地方，来一条蛇也难以穿过交织在一起的藤本植物和匍匐植物。凡是不长翅膀的东西几乎都难以安全通过那危机四伏的红树林。因此，逃亡者只有选择上面所提到过的其中的一条路才有希望到达海岸线。

"这件事要保密，比利，"古德温建议说，"我们不想让执政党知道总统在逃。我猜想鲍布的情报在首都也还是条独家消息。否则，他不会把这条信息写成密码；另外，每个人都有可能都听到过这个消息了。我现在就要去看看扎瓦拉医生，然后打发一个人到那条小道上去切断电报线。"古德温站起来的时候，基奥把帽子扔到门边的草地上，长长地叹了一口气。

"比利，有什么问题？"古德温停下来问道，"这是我第一次听到你叹气。"

"也是最后一次，"基奥说，"因为那阵伤感的风，我让自己过着一种值得称颂但却恼人的诚

esty. What are tintypes, if you please, to the opportunities of the great and hilarious class of ganders and geese? Not that I would be a president, Frank – and the boodle he's got is too big for me to handle – but in some ways I feel my conscience hurting me for addicting myself to photograph-ing a nation instead of running away with it. Frank, did you ever see the 'bundle of muslin' that His Excellency has wrapped up and carried off?"

"Isabel Guilbert?" said Goodwin, laughing. "No, I never did. From what I've heard of her, though, I imagine that she wouldn't stick at anything to carry her point. Don't get romantic, Billy. Sometimes I begin to fear that there's Irish blood in your ancestry."

"I never saw her either," went on Ke-ogh; "but they say she's got all the ladies of mythology, sculpture, and fiction re-duced to chromos. They say she can look at a man once, and he'll turn monkey and climb trees to pick cocoanuts for her. Think of that president man with Lord knows how many hundreds of thousands of dollars in one hand, and this muslin siren in the other, galloping down hill on a sympathetic mule amid songbirds and flowers! And here is Billy Keogh, because

实的生活。如果你愿意，与那群日日狂欢的伟大的公鹅母鹅们的机遇相比，锡版照相又算得了什么？并不是我想当总统，弗兰克——他携带的那笔款的数目对于我来说太大了，吃不消——而是在某些方面，我总有些觉得我的良心在责备我太沉湎于为一个国家照相而没能得到她。弗兰克，你曾见到过总统阁下裹起来带走的'那捆薄纱布'吗？"

"伊莎贝尔·吉尔伯特？"古德温大笑着，"不，我从没见过。不过，据我听说过的关于她的传闻，我想她为了达到目的会不择手段的。不要太过浪漫了，比利。有时候我开始怀疑你的祖先有爱尔兰血统。"

"我也从未见过她，"基奥继续说，"但人们都说她让神话、雕塑以及小说中的所有女性黯然失色。人们说她只要看男人一眼，男人们就会变成猴子，爬上树去为她摘可可豆。想想看，那位总统大人，上帝啊，他一只手里拿着不计其数的钱，另一只手抓住这个戴着白纱的海妖，骑在一头可怜的骡子上在鸟语花香中奔驰下山！而比利·基奥在这儿，因为善良、想过诚实的生活而被诅

he is virtuous, condemned to the unprofit-able swindle of slandering the faces of missing links on tin for an honest living! 'Tis an injustice of nature."

"Cheer up," said Goodwin. "You are a pretty poor fox to be envying a gander. Maybe the enchanting Guilbert will take a fancy to you and your tintypes after we impoverish her royal escort."

"She could do worse," reflected Keogh; "but she won't. 'Tis not a tintype gallery, but the gallery of the gods that she's fitted to adorn. She's a very wicked lady, and the president man is in luck. But I hear Clancy swearing in the back room for having to do all the work." And Keogh plunged for the rear of the "gallery," whistling gaily in a spontaneous way that belied his recent sigh over the questionable good luck of the flying president. Goodwin turned from the main street into a much narrower one that intersected it at a right angle. These side streets were covered by a growth of thick, rank grass, which was kept to a navigable shortness by the machetes of the police. Stone sidewalks, little more than a ledge in width, ran along the base of the mean and monotonous adobe houses. At the outskirts of the village these streets

咒去做无利可图的骗人勾当！这是上苍的不公。"

"振作起来，"古德温说。"你是一个非常精明的人，根本不用嫉妒一个大傻瓜。也许等我们把她的皇家护卫变成穷光蛋后，那个迷人的吉尔伯特会对你和你的锡铁版照相着迷。"

"那她的境遇可能会更糟，"基奥反思道，"但她不会爱上我的。适合她去喜爱的不是锡版照相画廊而是神仙画廊。她是个非常不道德的女人，那位总统大人交了好运。但是我现在听见克兰希在暗室里咒骂说什么事都是他干的。"基奥冲到"画廊"后边，一边自发地吹起欢快的口哨，掩盖了刚才他对那位逃亡总统能否交上好运的叹息。古德温转身走进一条与主干道成直角的非常狭窄的小巷里。这些偏僻的小巷遍生着高高密密的杂草，足以让警察的弯刀在这儿大显身手。石头的人行道只比壁架稍宽一些，沿着清一色简陋的土砖房的墙根向前延伸。这些街道逐渐消逝在村庄的边界，这里全都是加勒比人以及更穷苦的土著人用棕榈叶搭

dwindled to nothing; and here were set the palm-thatched huts of the Caribs and the poorer natives, and the shabby cabins of negroes from Jamaica and the West India islands. A few structures raised their heads above the red-tiled roofs of the one-story houses – the bell tower of the *Calaboza*, the Hotel de losE stran-jeros, the residence of the Vesuvius Fruit Company's agent, the store and resi-dence of Bernard Brannigan, a ruined cathedral in which Columbus had once set foot, and, most imposing of all, the Casa Morena – the summer "White House" of the President of Anchuria. On the principal street running along the beach – the Broad-wayof Coralio – were the larger stores, the government *bodega* and post-office, the *cuartel*, the rum-shops and the market place.

On his way Goodwin passed the house of Bernard Brannigan. It was a modern wooden building, two stories in height. The ground floor was occupied by Brannigan's store, the upper one con-tained the living apartments. A wide cool porch ran around the house half way up its outer walls. A handsome, vivacious girl neatly dressed in flowing white leaned over the railing and smiled down upon Goodwin. She was no darker than

建的棚屋，还有牙买加和西印度群岛来的黑人们的破烂小屋。有几幢建筑高出那红瓦平房的房顶——监狱的钟楼，"外国人"旅店，维苏威水果公司代理商的住宅，伯纳德·布朗尼根的商店和他的住宅，以及一座哥伦布曾经走进去过的大教堂，现在已经荒废了。而这中间最壮观的当数"海鳗之家"，也就是安楚里亚总统的避暑时住的"白宫"。在与海滩平行的那条主干道上——科拉里奥的百老汇大街——是更大的商铺、政府的仓库和邮局、兵营、酒吧和市场。

古德温在路上经过了伯纳德·布朗尼根家的那房子。这是幢两层高的现代木结构楼房，底层是布朗尼根商店，二层是住宅。一条宽宽的凉棚走廊沿着外墙绕房子半周。一个活泼美丽的姑娘，身着洁白飘逸的衣裳，靠在栏杆上俯身冲着古德温微笑。她并不比那些出身高贵的安达卢西亚人更黑，像热带地区的月光一般闪烁着光辉。"晚上好，保拉小姐，"

many an Andalusian of high descent; and she sparkled and glowed like a tropical moonlight. "Good evening, Miss Paula," said Goodwin, taking off his hat, with his ready smile. There was little difference in his manner whether he addressed women or men. Everybody in Coralio liked to receive the salutation of the big American. "Is there any news, Mr. Goodwin? Please don't say no. Isn't it warm? I feel just like Mariana in her moated grange – or was it a range? – it's hot enough."

"No, there's no news to tell, I believe," said Goodwin, with a mischievous look in his eye, "except that old Geddie is getting grumpier and crosser every day. If something doesn't happen to relieve his mind I'll have to quit smoking on his back porch – and there's no other place available that is cool enough.""He isn't grumpy," said Paula Brannigan, impulsively, "when he –" But she ceased suddenly, and drew back with a deepening colour; for her mother had been a *mestizo* lady, and the Spanish blood had brought to Paula a certain shyness that was an adornment to the other half of her demonstrative nature.

古德温脱下帽子，露出一贯的笑容。不管是跟女人还是男人打招呼，他的言谈举止都没什么差别。科拉里奥的每一个人都很乐意接受这位大个子美国人的问候。"有什么新闻吗，古德温先生？千万不要回答说没有。那还不让人激动吗？我觉得自己就像是住在被壕沟环绕的农庄里的玛丽安娜一样——或者是田庄？——足够热门了吧！"

"不，我觉得没有什么新闻可说的，"古德温回答，眼睛里闪烁着些许恶作剧的神态，"除了老格迪的脾气变得越来越乖戾和暴躁。如果没什么事情能使他心情放松的话，我就不会再在他家的后门走廊里抽烟了。不过，再也找不到这么凉快的地方了。""他并不乖戾，"保拉·布朗尼根脱口而出，"当他——"但她突然停下，脸色凝重地回屋去了。她的母亲是一个混血儿，那部分来自西班牙的血统让保拉有那么一点害羞，而这恰恰修饰了她另一半张扬的个性。

28. THE LOTUS AND THE BOTTLE
28. 莲与瓶

Willard Geddie, consul for the United States in Coralio, was working leisurely on his yearly report. Goodwin, who had strolled in as he did daily for a smoke on the much coveted porch, had found him so absorbed in his work that he departed after roundly abusing the consul for his lack of hospitality.

"I shall complain to the civil service department," said Goodwin; – "or is it a department? – perhaps it's only a theory. One gets neither civility nor service from you. You won't talk; and you won't set out anything to drink. What kind of a way is that of representing your government?"

Goodwin strolled out and across to the hotel to see if he could bully the quarantine doctor into a game on Coralio's solitary billiard table. His plans were completed for the interception of the fugitives from the capital; and now it was but a waiting game that he had to play.

The consul was interested in his report. He was only twenty-four; and he had not

美国驻科拉里奥领事威拉德·格迪正不慌不忙地在写他的年度报告。古德温像平时一样悠闲地走了进来,站在可爱的门廊里抽上一支香烟。这时他发现领事一心一意地沉浸在工作中,完全冷落了他,便在离去之前拐弯抹角地责备了他几句。

"我会向民政部投诉的,"古德温说。"这还算是个部门吗?也许只在理论上还说得过去。没有人能得到你礼貌的招待和服务。你既不说话,也不提供任何可以喝的东西。你就是这样代表你的国家形象的?"

古德温闲逛出来,溜达到街对面的旅馆,看看是不是能把那位检疫医生拐到科拉里奥惟一的台球桌上玩一局。关于中途截获从首都逃跑的亡命之徒的计划已经完成,他现在只需要伺机而动而已。

领事完全沉浸在自己的报告里。他只有24岁,在科拉里奥待

been in Coralio long enough for his enthusiasm to cool in the heat of the tropics – a paradox that may be allowed between Cancer and Capricorn.

So many thousand bunches of bananas, so many thousand oranges and cocoanuts, so many ounces of gold dust, pounds of rubber, coffee, indigo and sarsaparilla – actually, exports were twenty per cent. greater than for the previous year!

A little thrill of satisfaction ran through the consul. Perhaps, he thought, the State Department, upon reading his introduction, would notice – and then he leaned back in his chair and laughed. He was getting as bad as the others. For the moment he had forgotten that Coralio was an insignificant town in an insignificant republic lying along the by-ways of a second-rate sea. He thought of Gregg, the quarantine doctor, who subscribed for the London *Lancet*, expecting to find it quoting his reports to the home Board of Health concerning the yellow fever germ. The consul knew that not one in fifty of his acquaintances in the States had ever heard of Coralio. He knew that two men, at any rate, would have to read his report – some underling in the State

的时间还没有长到让他的热情在热带的火热天气里冷却下来——这种似是而非的怪事要是发生在南、北回归线之间倒还可以理解。

成千上万串的香蕉，数不清的柑橘和椰果，无数的砂金，橡胶、咖啡、染料和由撒尔沙根中提炼的药——出口竟然比上一年多了百分之二十！

一种兴奋得意的感觉在领事的心头蔓延。他想，国务院在看他的介绍时，也许会注意到——他向后仰靠在椅背上，开心地笑了。他干得和其他人一样差劲。此刻他居然忘了科拉里奥不过是位于次要海域的一条无关紧要的航海线旁边的一个不重要的共和国里的一个不起眼的小乡镇。他想起了格里格，就是那位检疫医生，他订阅了伦敦的《兰斯特》杂志，并期望着能从上面发现有人引用了他写给国内卫生部的有关黄热病细菌的报告。领事知道，从50个自己在美国认识的人里都挑不出一个曾经听说过科拉里奥的人。他知道不管怎样，一定会有两个人看他写的报告——国务院里的某个地位低下的职员和公

Department and a compositor in the Public Printing Office. Perhaps the typesticker would note the increase of commerce in Coralio, and speak of it, over the cheese and beer, to a friend.

He had just written: "Most unaccountable is the supineness of the large exporters in the United States in permitting the French and German houses to practically control the trade interests of this rich and productive country" – when he heard the hoarse notes of a steamer's siren.

Geddie laid down his pen and gathered his Panama hat and umbrella. By the sound he knew it to be the *Valhalla*, one of the line of fruit vessels plying for the Vesuvius Company. Down to *ninos* of five years, everyone in Coralio could name you each incoming steamer by the note of her siren.

The consul sauntered by a roundabout, shaded way to the beach. By reason of long practice he gauged his stroll so accurately that by the time he arrived on the sandy shore the boat of the customs officials was rowing back from the steamer, which had been boarded and inspected according to the laws of Anchuria.

There is no harbour at Coralio. Vessels

文印刷所的某个排字工。也许，排字工会注意到科拉里奥的贸易增长情况，然后在吃奶酪喝啤酒的时候向一位朋友提起。

当他正好写到"不能理解的是，美国的大出口商们竟然如此消极被动，让法国和德国的商业机构几乎完全控制了这个富饶多产的国家的贸易利益"时——他听到了大轮船粗哑的汽笛声。

格迪把笔放下，拿上他的巴拿马帽子和伞。只听声音他就知道是英烈祠船队开过来了，这是为维苏威公司服务的一支水果运输船队中的一艘。要是回到五年前，生活在科拉里奥的每一个人都能只凭鸣笛声就能给你说出每一艘靠岸的轮船的名字。

领事溜达着走过一条幽回曲折的林荫小道，悠闲地逛到海滩。因为长期练习的原因，他对自己的步伐掌握得非常精准，当他到达海滩时，海关工作人员的小艇正从轮船那儿往回驶向海岸。他们按照安楚里亚的法律登船进行了检查。

科拉里奥没有港口。英烈祠

of the draught of the *Valhalla* must ride at anchor a mile from shore. When they take on fruit it is conveyed on lighters and freighter sloops. At Solitas, where there was a fine harbour, ships of many kinds were to be seen, but in the road-stead off Coralio scarcely any save the fruiters paused. Now and then a tramp coaster, or a mysterious brig from Spain, or a saucy French barque would hang innocently for a few days in the offing. Then the custom-house crew would become doubly vigilant and wary. At night a sloop or two would be making strange trips in and out along the shore; and in the morning the stock of Three-Star Hennessey, wines and drygoods in Coralio would be found vastly increased. It has also been said that the customs officials jingled more silver in the pockets of their red-striped trousers, and that the record books showed no increase in import duties received.

The customs boat and the *Valhalla* gig reached the shore at the same time. When they grounded in the shallow water there was still five yards of rolling surf between them and dry sand. Then half-clothed Caribs dashed into the water, and brought in on their backs the

船队里吃水较深的轮船必须在离海岸一英里远的位置下锚。用驳船和单桅小货船来把水果运到这些轮船上。索里塔斯那里有一个很好的海港,在那可以看到各种各样的船来回穿梭,但在小镇科拉里奥的海边,除了运送水果的船只,很少有其他船只靠岸。时不时地会有一艘远途的沿海贸易船,或是一艘来自西班牙的神秘的方帆双桅船,或是一艘漂亮的法国三桅帆船,在未经许可的情况下,在远处海面上停留几天。这时,海关的工作人员会变得加倍地警惕和谨慎。晚上的时候,一两只单桅纵帆船会莫名其妙地沿着海岸进进出出。而到了早上,人们会发现三星汉尼塞公司仓库里的酒和纺织品大大增加了。还听见有人说,海关官员们的红色条纹裤子口袋里的银币叮当作响,而他们的账本上并未显示出任何增加的进口税。

海关的小艇和英烈祠号上的小艇同时到达岸边。当它们在浅水处靠岸后,还要在拍岸的水浪里走上五码才能到达干燥的沙滩。这时,半裸的加勒比人冲进水里,把英烈祠号的事务长和身穿棉布衬衫、饰有红色条纹的蓝

Valhalla's purser and the little native officials in their cotton undershirts, blue trousers with red stripes, and flapping straw hats.

At college Geddie had been a treasure as a first-baseman. He now closed his umbrella, stuck it upright in the sand, and stooped, with his hands resting upon his knees. The purser, burlesquing the pitcher's contortions, hurled at the consul the heavy roll of newspapers, tied with a string, that the steamer always brought for him. Geddie leaped high and caught the roll with a sounding "thwack." The loungers on the beach – about a third of the population of the town – laughed and applauded delightedly. Every week they expected to see that roll of papers delivered and received in that same manner, and they were never disappointed. Innovations did not flourish in Coralio.

The consul re-hoisted his umbrella and walked back to the consulate.

This home of a great nation's representative was a wooden structure of two rooms, with a native-built gallery of poles, bamboo and nipa palm running on three sides of it. One room was the official apartment, furnished chastely with a flat-top desk, a hammock, and three uncomfortable

裤子，头上戴着大草帽的小个头当地官员们背上了岸。

大学时，格迪因为是一位棒球手而成为不可多得的人才。如今他收好伞，把它垂直地插进沙子里，弯下腰曲着身，把双手放在膝盖上。那位事务长会模仿这位棒球投手的弯曲姿势，把那捆沉重的用绳拴紧的报纸猛然投向领事。报纸通常都是由这艘轮船带过来的。格迪一跃而起。只听"嘭"的一声响，报纸被接住了。海滩上闲游的人群——大约是小镇三分之一的居民——开怀大笑，鼓掌称赞。他们每个星期都期待看到那捆报纸被这样传送接收，从来都没有厌倦过。在科拉里奥，创新改革可不流行。

领事把伞从沙里拿出来，朝领事馆走去。

这个住着一个大国的代表的屋宅是一座有两间屋子的木制建筑，它的三边是用木头柱子、竹竿和棕榈叶建成的具有本地特色的走廊。其中一间屋子是办公厅，房间布置得简单朴素，只有一张平板桌子、一张吊床、三把坐起

cane-seated chairs. Engravings of the first and latest president of the country represented hung against the wall. The other room was the consul's living apartment.

It was eleven o'clock when he returned from the beach, and therefore breakfast time. Chanca, the Carib woman who cooked for him, was just serving the meal on the side of the gallery facing the sea – a spot famous as the coolest in Coralio. The breakfast consisted of shark's fin soup, stew of land crabs, breadfruit, a boiled iguana steak, aguacates, a freshly cut pineapple, claret and coffee.

Geddie took his seat, and unrolled with luxurious laziness his bundle of newspapers. Here in Coralio for two days or longer he would read of goings-on in the world very much as we of the world read those whimsical contributions to inexact science that assume to portray the doings of the Martians. After he had finished with the papers they would be sent on the rounds of the other English-speaking residents of the town.

The paper that came first to his hand was one of those bulky mattresses of printed stuff upon which the readers of certain New York journals are supposed to take their

来不舒服的藤条椅。墙上悬挂着驻在国的第一任和现任总统的雕版图肖像。另一间屋子是领事的起居室。

他从海滩上回来时已经 11 点了，正是该吃早饭的时候。湘佳，给他做饭的那个加勒比妇女，正在靠海那边的走廊上摆放早餐。那是科拉里奥有名的凉快地方。早餐有鱼翅汤、焖河蟹、面包果、烤鬣蜥肉、白嫩鳄梨、新切的菠萝、红葡萄酒和咖啡。

格迪坐在椅子上，悠闲懒散地打开那捆报纸。在科拉里奥，他每隔一天或更长时间总会读读报纸，看看这个世界在干什么，就像这个世界的我们读到的那些对火星人行为这类不精确科学的天马行空的描述。当他读完后，报纸就会被送到镇上其他说英语的居民那儿，让他们传着看。

他手里拿的第一张报纸是那种内容庞杂、体积庞大的报纸里的一张，这种报纸是给那些在安息日上教堂时打盹，读特定的纽

Sabbath literary nap. Opening this the consul rested it upon the table, supporting its weight with the aid of the back of a chair. Then he partook of his meal deliberately, turning the leaves from time to time and glancing half idly at the contents.

Presently he was struck by something familiar to him in a picture – a half-page, badly printed reproduction of a photograph of a vessel. Languidly interested, he leaned for a nearer scrutiny and a view of the florid headlines of the column next to the picture.

Yes; he was not mistaken. The engraving was of the eight-hundred-ton yacht *Idalia*, belonging to "that prince of good fellows, Midas of the money market, and society's pink of perfection, J. Ward Tolliver."

Slowly sipping his black coffee, Geddie read the column of print. Following a listed statement of Mr. Tolliver's real estate and bonds, came a description of the yacht's furnishings, and then the grain of news no bigger than a mustard seed. Mr. Tolliver, with a party of favoured guests, would sail the next day on a six weeks' cruise along the Central American

约期刊杂志的读者们准备的。领事打开报纸，把它平放在桌上，一把椅子的靠背支撑着它，让它稍稍翘起。然后，他开始享受他的早餐，时不时地翻阅着报纸，悠闲地扫一眼上面的内容。

突然，一张看上去挺熟悉的图片吸引住了他的目光。这张图片占了半个版面，复制效果不好，是一艘船的照片。他打起精神，向前倾身仔细一看，才看清照片旁边有一行文辞华丽的标题。

是的，他没看错。那幅雕版画就是 800 吨位的游艇艾达丽亚号，它的主人是"交际场上的王子、金融市场上的迈达斯、上流社会的完美典型，丁·沃德·托列弗。"

格迪一边啜饮着咖啡，一边读着那篇文章。文章先是列出了托列弗先生的不动产和债券，然后描述了这艘游艇的装置，之后就是那条比芥菜种子还要小的不重要的新闻。托列弗先生和一些尊贵的客人将于次日沿着中美洲、南美洲海岸和巴哈马群岛间进行为期六周的航海旅行。来自

and South American coasts and among the Bahama Islands. Among the guests were Mrs. Cumberland Payne and Miss Ida Payne, of Norfolk.

The writer, with the fatuous presumption that was demanded of him by his readers, had concocted a romance suited to their palates. He bracketed the names of Miss Payne and Mr. Tolliver until he had well-nigh read the marriage ceremony over them. He played coyly and insinuatingly upon the strings of "*on dit*" and "Madame Rumour" and "a little bird" and "no one would be surprised," and ended with congratulations.

Geddie, having finished his breakfast, took his papers to the edge of the gallery, and sat there in his favourite steamer chair with his feet on the bamboo railing. He lighted a cigar, and looked out upon the sea. He felt a glow of satisfaction at finding he was so little disturbed by what he had read. He told himself that he had conquered the distress that had sent him, a voluntary exile, to this far land of the lotus. He could never forget Ida, of course; but there was no longer any pain in thinking about her. When they had had that misunderstanding and quarrel he had impulsively sought this consulship, with

诺福克的坎伯兰·佩恩夫人及艾达·佩恩小姐就在这批客人的名单里。

读者总是喜欢妄加猜测，基于此需求，这位作者就捏造了一套适合他们口味的风流韵事。他把佩恩小姐和托列弗先生的名字一直放在一起，就好像他已经给他们举行了婚礼似的。他故意遮遮掩掩地却又含沙射影地玩弄着"有人说"、"谣言夫人"、"一只小鸟"、"没人会觉得惊讶的"这样的文字，最后以祝贺告终。

吃完早餐，格迪拿着报纸来到走廊边上，坐在他最喜爱的那把折叠帆布躺椅上，翘起双脚放在竹栏杆上。他点燃了一支雪茄，遥望着大海，心里泛起一阵得意之情，因为他发现自己的心情并没有被刚刚读过的报上刊登的那些事搞坏。他告诉自己，他已经不再感到忧伤了。正是这种忧伤让他当初自愿离开家乡来到这个遥远的莲之乡。当然，他永远也忘不了艾达，可是每当想起她时，他已经不再感到痛苦了。那次误会和争吵之后，他便一怒之下冲动地找到领事这一差使，想要通

the desire to retaliate upon her by detaching himself from her world and presence. He had succeeded thoroughly in that. During the twelve months of his life in Coralio no word had passed between them, though he had sometimes heard of her through the dilatory correspondence with the few friends to whom he still wrote. Still he could not repress a little thrill of satisfaction at knowing that she had not yet married Tolliver or anyone else. But evidently Tolliver had not yet abandoned hope.

Well, it made no difference to him now. He had eaten of the lotus. He was happy and content in this land of perpetual afternoon. Those old days of life in the States seemed like an irritating dream. He hoped Ida would be as happy as he was. The climate as balmy as that of distant Avalon; the fetterless, idyllic round of enchanted days; the life among this indolent, romantic people – a life full of music, flowers, and low laughter; the influence of the imminent sea and mountains, and the many shapes of love and magic and beauty that bloomed in the white tropic nights – with all he was more than content. Also, there was Paula Brannigan.

过离开她的世界、不再见她来报复她。从这方面来说,他已经彻底成功了。在科拉里奥工作的 12 个月期间,他俩之间从未有过任何联系,尽管有时他会通过仍在断断续续写信联系的几位朋友那儿了解到她的情况。当他知道她还没有嫁给托列弗或别的什么人时,还是抑制不住一丝得意之情。但是很明显,托列弗还没有放弃希望。

可是,这已经与他无关了。他已经尝到莲的滋味了。他在这片永远是下午的土地上,感到了幸福和满足。那段在美国的旧时光就像一场惹人愤怒的梦。他希望艾达现在同他一样幸福。这儿的气候像远处阿瓦隆(凯尔特传说中的西方乐土岛)那样温暖;在这个懒散、浪漫的民族中的生活充满了音乐、鲜花和低俗的笑声;近在眼前的大海和高山;五彩斑斓的爱情、魔法和漂亮姑娘盛开在热带的不眠之夜里——所有的一切,都让他满足得无以复加。而且,还有保拉·布朗尼根呢。

Geddie intended to marry Paula – if, of course, she would consent; but he felt rather sure that she would do that. Somehow, he kept postponing his proposal. Several times he had been quite near to it; but a mysterious something always held him back. Perhaps it was only the unconscious, instinctive conviction that the act would sever the last tie that bound him to his old world.

He could be very happy with Paula. Few of the native girls could be compared with her. She had attended a convent school in New Orleans for two years; and when she chose to display her accomplishments no one could detect any difference between her and the girls of Norfolk and Manhattan. But it was delicious to see her at home dressed, as she sometimes was, in the native costume, with bare shoulders and flowing sleeves.

Bernard Brannigan was the great merchant of Coralio. Besides his store, he maintained a train of pack mules, and carried on a lively trade with the interior towns and villages. He had married a native lady of high Castilian descent, but with a tinge of Indian brown showing

格迪计划与保拉结婚——当然，如果她答应的话；不过他非常自信她会同意的。不知出于什么原因，他老是推迟求婚。有好几次，他差点就要说出口了，但某种神秘的东西总是阻止了他。也许仅仅是因为那种无意识的本能的直觉使他觉得，这样做会切断他与他的过去之间那条最后的纽带。

他和保拉在一起的生活会非常的幸福。当地的女孩子中很少有能和她媲美的。她曾在新奥尔良一所修道院学校上过两年的学，只要她想要表现她的才艺的时候，没人能看出她和诺福克或曼哈顿的姑娘们之间有什么不一样。但真正秀色可餐的还是她有时候在家里的装扮：穿着当地人的服饰，裸露着双肩，衣袖随风飘舞……

伯纳德·布朗尼根是科拉里奥的大商人。他拥有自己的店铺，除此之外他还拥有一支载货的骡队，与内地的村庄乡镇进行着频繁的贸易。他娶了当地一位有高贵的卡斯蒂利亚[1]血统的女士，她橄榄色的脸颊微微透出一点印第

through her olive cheek. The union of the Irish and the Spanish had produced, as it so often has, an offshoot of rare beauty and variety. They were very excellent people indeed, and the upper story of their house was ready to be placed at the service of Geddie and Paula as soon as he should make up his mind to speak about it.

By the time two hours were whiled away the consul tired of reading. The papers lay scattered about him on the gallery. Reclining there, he gazed dreamily out upon an Eden. A clump of banana plants interposed their broad shields between him and the sun. The gentle slope from the consulate to the sea was covered with the dark-green foliage of lemon-trees and orange-trees just bursting into bloom. A lagoon pierced the land like a dark, jagged crystal, and above it a pale ceiba-tree rose almost to the clouds. The waving cocoanut palms on the beach flared their decorative green leaves against the slate of an almost quiescent sea. His senses were cognizant of brilliant scarlet and ochres amid the vert of the coppice, of odours of fruit and bloom and the smoke from Chanca's clay oven under the calabash-tree; of the treble

安人的红棕肤色。爱尔兰血统和西班牙血统的结合通常会造就出天生丽质、超凡脱俗的下一代。他们的确是非常优秀杰出的人，而且只要格迪拿定主意开口求婚，他们那座房子的上面一层，就会随时准备迎接他和保拉。

看了两个小时的报纸，领事也有些不耐烦了。在他的周围，报纸散落在走廊的地面上。他斜躺在那儿，朦胧中仿佛看到了一座伊甸园。一簇香蕉树，就像一个大盾牌一样，挡在他和太阳之间。从领事馆到海岸的那段平缓的坡地被一片含苞待放的橘树和柠檬树的茂密的深绿色树叶覆盖着。一块环礁湖深入陆地，就像一块不规则的深色水晶，它的上空有一棵淡色的木棉树，几乎高入云端。海滩上的椰子树随风摇曳，绿色的树叶在闪闪发光，背后则是那片深蓝色的几乎凝滞了的大海。他感觉到了那片绿色灌木林中掺杂的鲜红色和赭色，觉察到了水果和花朵的芳香还有一阵烟雾，湘佳正在那棵葫芦树下的黄泥火炉上做饭；他还觉察到了那些当地妇女在小棚屋里尖锐

laughter of the native women in their huts, the song of the robin, the salt taste of the breeze, the diminuendo of the faint surf running along the shore – and, gradually, of a white speck, growing to a blur, that intruded itself upon the drab prospect of the sea.

Lazily interested, he watched this blur increase until it became the *Idalia* steaming at full speed, coming down the coast. Without changing his position he kept his eyes upon the beautiful white yacht as she drew swiftly near, and came opposite to Coralio. Then, sitting upright, he saw her float steadily past and on. Scarcely a mile of sea had separated her from the shore. He had seen the frequent flash of her polished brass work and the stripes of her deck-awnings – so much, and no more. Like a ship on a magic lantern slide the *Idalia* had crossed the illuminated circle of the consul's little world, and was gone. Save for the tiny cloud of smoke that was left hanging over the brim of the sea, she might have been an immaterial thing, a chimera of his idle brain.

Geddie went into his office and sat down to dawdle over his report. If the reading of the article in the paper had left

的笑声，知更鸟的歌声，咸咸的海风，渐渐变弱的轻轻拍打海岸的浪花声——除此之外，他也觉察到了一个变得越来越模糊的白色小点，闯入了这片单调乏味的海域。

他懒洋洋地注视着那片模糊的东西逐渐扩大，直到它变成了正全速驶向海岸的艾达丽亚号。他没有改变姿势，但双眼紧紧盯着那艘漂亮的白色游艇，游艇正从科拉里奥的对面快速驶近。然后，他上身坐直，看到它从眼前平稳地驶过，继续向前。这艘游艇离海岸差不多有一英里之远。他看到游艇上不断闪着光泽的黄色铜管和甲板遮篷上的条纹——只是这些，别的就看不到了。就像幻灯片上的一只魔法轮船，艾达丽亚经过领事馆这一个明亮的小世界后就远去了。要不是海面上空还有一团烟雾，这游艇就像一个无形的东西，只是他空白脑子里的一个幻觉而已。

格迪走进办公室，坐下来翻看报告以打发时间。如果说看了报上那篇文章后，他的心没有荡

him unshaken, this silent passing of the *Idalia* had done for him still more. It had brought the calm and peace of a situation from which all uncertainty had been erased. He knew that men sometimes hope without being aware of it. Now, since she had come two thousand miles and had passed without a sign, not even his unconscious self need cling to the past any longer.

After dinner, when the sun was low behind the mountains, Geddie walked on the little strip of beach under the cocoa-nuts. The wind was blowing mildly landward, and the surface of the sea was rippled by tiny wavelets.

A miniature breaker, spreading with a soft "swish" upon the sand brought with it something round and shiny that rolled back again as the wave receded. The next influx beached it clear, and Geddie picked it up. The thing was a long-necked wine bottle of colourless glass. The cork had been driven in tightly to the level of the mouth, and the end covered with dark-red sealing-wax. The bottle contained only what seemed to be a sheet of paper, much curled from the manipulation it had undergone while being inserted. In the sealing-wax was the im-

起一丝涟漪的话，平静驶过的艾达丽亚号更是没有扰乱他的心情。它给他带来了平静安宁，让他的一切不安都消失殆尽。他明白，人有时候不会意识到自己仍然抱有希望。现在，既然这游艇悄无声息地从 2 000 英里以外而来，又悄悄经过，那么他无意识中的自我也不需要再留恋过去了。

晚饭过后，太阳落到山后了。格迪在椰树下的那片小沙滩上散步。微风轻轻吹向海岸，海面上荡起层层涟漪。

一阵碎浪随着一阵温柔的"沙沙"声，冲向沙滩，中间夹带着一个圆而发光的东西。这东西随着退去的潮水滚了回去，但当潮水再次涌向沙滩时，它又被冲上了岸。格迪拾起了它。那是一个透明玻璃制成的长颈酒瓶。瓶塞紧紧地卡在瓶嘴里面，末端封了一层深红色的蜡。瓶里只有一个看上去像纸的东西，皱巴巴的，在塞进去前应该经过了一些处理。封蜡里面有封印，似乎是一只图章戒指的印记，上面有几个连缀的首字母；但那印记做得

pression of a seal – probably of a signet-ring, bearing the initials of a monogram; but the impression had been hastily made, and the letters were past anything more certain than a shrewd conjecture. Ida Payne had always worn a signet-ring in preference to any other finger decoration. Geddie thought he could make out the familiar "IP"; and a queer sensation of disquietude went over him. More personal and intimate was this reminder of her than had been the sight of the vessel she was doubtless on. He walked back to his house, and set the bottle on his desk.

Throwing off his hat and coat, and lighting a lamp – for the night had crowded precipitately upon the brief twilight – he began to examine his piece of sea salvage.

By holding the bottle near the light and turning it judiciously, he made out that it contained a double sheet of note-paper filled with close writing; further, that the paper was of the same size and shade as that always used by Ida; and that, to the best of his belief, the handwriting was hers. The imperfect glass of the bottle so distorted the rays of light that he could read no word of the writing; but certain

太仓促潦草了，以至于那几个字母根本无法辨认，成了一个奇妙的字谜。艾达·佩恩总戴着一只图章戒指，她不是很喜欢其他的首饰饰品。格迪认为自己能够拼出"IP"[2]这两个熟悉的字母，他因此感到全身不安。毫无疑问，她就在他刚才看到的那艘船上。而这件东西比看见那艘船更能勾起他对她亲密的私人的回忆。他走回屋里，把瓶子放在桌子上。

他扔下帽子和外套，点上灯——因为黄昏逝去夜幕猛然降临笼罩了大地——便开始仔细研究起他打捞起的这件东西。

他把瓶子拿到灯的旁边，一边翻动着一边仔细地琢磨着它的来历。他辨认出里面有一张双面便笺，密密麻麻写满了字；除此之外，纸的大小和颜色都与艾达经常用的是一样；而且，他最能确定的是，笔迹是她的。玻璃瓶子的质地不太好使得光线扭曲变形，他一个字也看不清楚；但是某些大写的字母他还是看得一清

capital letters, of which he caught comprehensive glimpses, were Ida's, he felt sure.

There was a little smile both of perplexity and amusement in Geddie's eyes as he set the bottle down, and laid three cigars side by side on his desk. He fetched his steamer chair from the gallery, and stretched himself comfortably. He would smoke those three cigars while considering the problem.

For it amounted to a problem. He almost wished that he had not found the bottle; but the bottle was there. Why should it have drifted in from the sea, whence come so many disquieting things, to disturb his peace?

In this dreamy land, where time seemed so redundant, he had fallen into the habit of bestowing much thought upon even trifling matters.

He began to speculate upon many fanciful theories concerning the story of the bottle, rejecting each in turn.

Ships in danger of wreck or disablement sometimes cast forth such precarious messengers calling for aid. But he

二楚。他敢肯定这就是艾达的笔迹。

他的眼睛里流露出一丝既迷惑又高兴的笑意。他把瓶子放在桌子上，并在桌上并排摆了三支雪茄。他把他的躺椅从走廊上搬进来，舒舒服服地伸了个懒腰。他要一边抽这三支雪茄，一边思考这个问题。

因为这已经成了一个问题。他几乎祈盼自己没有发现这个瓶子。但是瓶子就在那里。为什么它会从海上漂过来？又是从哪儿来的这么多让人烦心的事，打扰了他的安宁？

在这块充满梦幻的土地上，时间总是显得非常的漫长。他已经养成了即便是芝麻大的小事也要想上半天的习惯。

他开始推测这个瓶子背后的故事，他想到了许多奇怪的可能，又一一否决了。

船只在遇难或是无法运行的危险时刻，有时候人们会利用这类不太靠得住的信使去求救。可

had seen the *Idalia* not three hours before, safe and speeding. Suppose the crew had mutinied and imprisoned the passengers below, and the message was one begging for succour! But, premising such an improbable outrage, would the agitated captives have taken the pains to fill four pages of note-paper with carefully penned arguments to their rescue.

Thus by elimination he soon rid the matter of the more unlikely theories, and was reduced – though aversely – to the less assailable one that the bottle contained a message to himself. Ida knew he was in Coralio; she must have launched the bottle while the yacht was passing and the wind blowing fairly toward the shore.

As soon as Geddie reached this conclusion a wrinkle came between his brows and a stubborn look settled around his mouth. He sat looking out through the doorway at the gigantic fire-flies traversing the quiet streets.

If this was a message to him from Ida, what could it mean save an overture toward a reconciliation? And if that, why had she not used the same methods of the

是不到三小时前，他还看到艾达丽亚号安全又快速地行驶着。假使船员叛变，把下面的旅客关了起来，那这就是来乞求援助的！可是，假定真是这样一种不太可能的骇人听闻的事件的话，那些心急火燎的俘虏们会不辞辛苦地用上四页篇幅仔细地列出一条条论据来说服别人去营救他们吗？

就这样，通过排除法，他很快摈弃了那些更不可能的设想，只剩下——尽管不大乐意——那个不那么离谱的推论，那就是，这瓶子里装着一条给他本人的消息。艾达知道他在科拉里奥；她一定是在游艇正好驶过这片海域、风向岸边吹的时候抛下了这个瓶子。

格迪一得出这个结论，双眉便皱了起来，双唇也随之僵硬起来。他坐着，向门口望去，只见成群结队的萤火虫在宁静的街道上飞过。

如果这是来自艾达的信息，除了是她主动妥协想要和好，还能意味着什么？如果是这样，那她为什么不用邮递的方式而采取

post instead of this uncertain and even flippant means of communication? A note in an empty bottle, cast into the sea! There was something light and frivolous about it, if not actually contemptuous.

The thought stirred his pride and subdued whatever emotions had been resurrected by the finding of the bottle.

Geddie put on his coat and hat and walked out. He followed a street that led him along the border of the little plaza where a band was playing and people were rambling, care-free and indolent. Some timorous *senoritas* scurrying past with fire-flies tangled in the jetty braids of their hair glanced at him with shy, flattering eyes. The air was languorous with the scent of jasmin and or-ange-blossoms.

The consul stayed his steps at the house of Bernard Brannigan. Paula was swinging in a hammock on the gallery. She rose from it like a bird from its nest. The colour came to her cheek at the sound of Geddie's voice.

He was charmed at the sight of her costume – a flounced muslin dress, with a little jacket of white flannel, all made

这种不确定、甚至是轻率的联系方式？把纸条装进空瓶子，扔进大海！这事儿显得有些轻浮愚蠢，如果它不被蔑视鄙夷的话。

这一想法刺痛了他的自尊心，并压制了他刚才因发现瓶子而复苏的情感。

格迪穿上外套，戴上帽子，走了出去。他沿着一条街来到小广场旁边，那儿有一支乐队正在演奏，人们欢快舒畅，懒洋洋地溜达着。几个胆怯的未婚姑娘，因为萤火虫骚扰她们乌黑发亮的辫子而急得团团乱转，但又用害羞而讨好的眼神看着他。空气中充满了菊花和香橙花的味道，因而显得特别沉闷。

领事在伯纳德·布朗尼根的家门口停住了脚步。保拉正在挂在走廊里的一张吊床上来回悠荡着。一听见格迪的声音，她就像小鸟出巢一样马上站了起来，脸蛋也顿时红了起来。

看到她的装束他顿时着了迷——她穿了一件缀着荷叶边的平纹薄衣，外面套了一件小巧的白

with neatness and style. He suggested a stroll, and they walked out to the old Indian well on the hill road. They sat on the curb, and there Geddie made the expected but long-deferred speech. Certain though he had been that she would not say him nay, he was thrilled with joy at the completeness and sweetness of her surrender. Here was surely a heart made for love and steadfastness. Here was no caprice or questionings or captious standards of convention.

When Geddie kissed Paula at her door that night he was happier than he had ever been before. "Here in this hollow lotus land, ever to live and lie reclined" seemed to him, as it has seemed to many mariners, the best as well as the easiest. His future would be an ideal one. He had attained a Paradise without a serpent. His Eve would be indeed a part of him, unbeguiled, and therefore more beguiling. He had made his decision to-night, and his heart was full of serene, assured content.

Geddie went back to his house whistling that finest and saddest love song, "La Golondrina." At the door his tame

色法兰绒上衣，剪裁合体款式新颖。他建议出去走一走，于是他俩走到山坡小路附近的一口印第安人的古井旁边。他们坐在井栏上，就在这里，格迪说出了早就想说却又迟迟未动口的话。尽管他十分确定她不会说不，可是看到她完全彻底地甜蜜幸福地投降了他，他仍然觉得万分喜悦。她的心毫无疑问是充满爱意忠贞不渝的。这儿没有见异思迁，没有怀疑，也没有那套吹毛求疵的陈规旧俗。

那天晚上，格迪在保拉的门口吻了她。他从来没有感到这么的幸福。"在这块空幻的莲之乡，只要住下就躺着不走了，"这样的生活对他来说，如同对许多水手一样，既是最简单的，也是最幸福的。他的未来将会是幸福美满的。他得到了一个没有毒蛇诱惑的"伊甸园"。他的夏娃将真正是他身体的一部分，从未受过诱惑，因而更加让人着迷。他今晚把这事定了下来，心里充满了宁静和满足。

格迪一路吹着口哨，吹着《燕子》这首最美最伤感的爱情之歌，回到了住所。一进门，他养的那

monkey leaped down from his shelf, chattering briskly. The consul turned to his desk to get him some nuts he usually kept there. Reaching in the half-darkness, his hand struck against the bottle. He started as if he had touched the cold rotundity of a serpent.

He had forgotten that the bottle was there.

He lighted the lamp and fed the monkey. Then, very deliberately, he lighted a cigar, and took the bottle in his hand, and walked down the path to the beach.

There was a moon, and the sea was glorious. The breeze had shifted, as it did each evening, and was now rushing steadily seaward.

Stepping to the water's edge, Geddie hurled the unopened bottle far out into the sea. It disappeared for a moment, and then shot upward twice its length. Geddie stood still, watching it. The moonlight was so bright that he could see it bobbing up and down with the little waves. Slowly it receded from the shore, flashing and turning as it went. The wind was carrying it out to sea. Soon it became a mere speck, doubtfully discerned at irregular intervals; and then the mystery of it was swallowed up by the greater mys-

只温顺的猴子就跳下书架，欢快活泼地吱吱叫着。领事走到桌边，想拿几颗他平时放在那儿的干果。他的手在昏暗的房间里摸索，正好碰到了那个瓶子。他哆嗦了一下，就像碰着了一条冰冷的毒蛇。

他早已忘记了那个瓶子还在那儿。

他点上灯，喂了猴子点吃的。然后，他不慌不忙地点上一支雪茄，拿起那个瓶子，沿小路向海滩走去。

月亮挂在夜空中。大海真是壮丽极了。轻风一到晚上便会改变方向，而此时，正稳稳地朝海面吹着。

走到海边，格迪使劲把那个没被打开的瓶子向远处扔去。它消失了一会，接着又浮出海面，好像有原来的两倍之长。格迪呆呆地站在那里，凝视着它。月光很明亮，他能看见它随着波浪上下起伏。瓶子逐渐远离了海岸，一边转动一边闪着光芒。风正把它推向大海深处。没一会儿，它就变成了一个小小的斑点，时不时地会隐隐约约地露一下面；随即，它的秘密便被大洋更大的秘密吞噬了。格迪傻傻地站在海滩

tery of the ocean. Geddie stood still upon the beach, smoking and looking out upon the water.

"Simon! – Oh, Simon! – wake up there, Simon!" bawled a sonorous voice at the edge of the water.

Old Simon Cruz was a half-breed fisherman and smuggler who lived in a hut on the beach. Out of his earliest nap Simon was thus awakened.

He slipped on his shoes and went outside. Just landing from one of the *Valhalla's* boats was the third mate of that vessel, who was an acquaintance of Simon's, and three sailors from the fruiter.

"Go up, Simon," called the mate, "and find Dr. Gregg or Mr. Goodwin or anybody that's a friend to Mr. Geddie, and bring 'em here at once."

"Saints of the skies!" said Simon, sleepily, "nothing has happened to Mr. Geddie?"

"He's under that tarpauling," said the mate, pointing to the boat, "and he's rather more than half drowned. We seen him from the steamer nearly a mile out from shore, swimmin' like mad after a bottle that was floatin' in the water, outward bound. We lowered the gig and

上，抽着烟，遥望着远处的水面。

"西蒙！——喂，西蒙！——快醒醒，西蒙！"一个洪亮的声音在海边喊道。

老西蒙·克鲁兹是个混血儿，他既打渔又走私货物，就住在海滩上一个小棚屋里。他刚睡着就被叫醒了。

他趿拉上鞋子，走了出来。刚刚从英烈祠号的一艘船下来的人有船上的三副，西蒙的一位熟人，还有水果运输船上来的三位水手。

"快上岸，西蒙，"那位三副喊道，"去找格里格医生或古德温先生，或任何格迪先生的朋友。立即把他们带到这儿来。"

"我的老天爷啊！"西蒙还没有睡醒。"格迪先生没出什么事吧？"

"他现在在那张油布下。"三副指着那只小船说道。"他差点儿就被淹死了。我们在船上看到他的时候，他正在离岸将近一英里的水面上发了疯似的拼命游着，追着一只漂流的瓶子。我们把快艇放下去，赶紧追他。他几

started for him. He nearly had his hand on the bottle, when he gave out and went under. We pulled him out in time to save him, maybe; but the doctor is the one to decide that."

"A bottle?" said the old man, rubbing his eyes. He was not yet fully awake. "Where is the bottle?"

"Driftin' along out there some'eres," said the mate, jerking his thumb toward the sea. "Get on with you, Simon."

乎快要抓到那个瓶子了，但就在那时，他耗尽了全身的力气，沉下去了。我们及时把他从水里救出来，也许他能被救活吧，但要看医生怎么说了。"

"一只瓶子？"老头问道，揉了揉眼睛。他还没有完全醒过来。"瓶子在哪里？"

"还在远处什么地方漂着呢。"三副指着大海说道。"赶紧去吧，西蒙。"

1. 卡斯蒂利亚,位于西班牙中部，是省级行政区。
2. "ＩＰ",艾达·佩恩小姐名字的首字母缩写。

29. SHOES

29. 鞋

John De Graffenreid Atwood ate of the lotus, root, stem, and flower. The tropics gobbled him up. He plunged enthusiastically into his work, which was to try to forget Rosine.

Now, they who dine on the lotus rarely consume it plain. There is a sauce *au diable* that goes with it; and the distillers are the chefs who prepare it. And on Johnny's menu card it read "brandy." With a bottle between them, he and Billy Keogh would sit on the porch of the little consulate at night and roar out great, indecorous songs, until the natives, slipping hastily past, would shrug a shoulder and mutter things to themselves about the "*Americanos diablos.*"

One day Johnny's *mozo* brought the mail and dumped it on the table. Johnny leaned from his hammock, and fingered the four or five letters dejectedly. Keogh was sitting on the edge of the table chopping lazily with a paper knife at the legs of a centipede that was crawling

约翰·德·格拉芬里德·阿特伍德吃荷的时候会把荷茎、莲藕跟荷花都一起吃掉。热带天气总是让他狼吞虎咽的。他带着一股狂热劲埋头工作,为的是能够把罗西娜忘掉。

现在,他们吃荷的时候很少干巴巴地只吃荷了;他们会配上一种只有魔鬼才会喝的烈酒;酒是厨子自己酿的,约翰尼把它称作"白兰地"。黑夜来临时,他就和比利·基奥坐在小小领事馆的门廊边上,两人中间摆一瓶酒,吼上几声提神带劲的曲子,却不怎么合时宜,直吼得本地人慌慌张张地溜过去,一边耸肩,一边咕哝着"这些个魔鬼美国佬"之类的话。

一天,约翰尼的听差送来了邮件,他一下把信都堆在了桌上。约翰尼从他的吊床上侧过身子来,灰心丧气地用手指拨弄着那四五封信。基奥坐在桌沿儿上,看见一只蜈蚣缓缓地爬过桌上的文具,就懒洋洋地用一把切纸刀

among the stationery. Johnny was in that phase of lotus-eating when all the world tastes bitter in one's mouth.

"Same old thing!" he complained. "Fool people writing for information about the country. They want to know all about raising fruit, and how to make a fortune without work. Half of 'em don't even send stamps for a reply. They think a consul hasn't anything to do but write letters. Slit those envelopes for me, old man, and see what they want. I'm feeling too rocky to move."

Keogh, acclimated beyond all possibility of ill-humour, drew his chair to the table with smiling compliance on his rose-pink countenance, and began to slit open the letters. Four of them were from citizens in various parts of the United States who seemed to regard the consul at Coralio as a cyclopaedia of information. They asked long lists of questions, numerically arranged, about the climate, products, possibilities, laws, business chances, and statistics of the country in which the consul had the honour of representing his own government.

"Write 'em, please, Billy," said that inert official, "just a line, referring them to the latest consular report. Tell 'em the

切去了蜈蚣的腿。当下,约翰尼是百无聊赖,无所事事,不知道干什么才好。

"还是老一套!"他抱怨道。"一群傻冒写信来问有关这个国家的事。他们想知道种果树的事,想知道怎么样不干活儿就能发财——简直是什么都想知道!有一半人居然不附上回信的邮票。他们认为领事馆除了写信就什么也不干了吗。伙计,帮我把那些信都拆了,看看他们想要些什么。我现在头晕,一点也不想动。"

基奥已经跟这里的水土相服了,因此也就不存在产生任何恶劣情绪的可能性。他把椅子拖到桌旁开始拆信,淡粉色的脸庞上始终洋溢着温顺的笑容。其中有四封信是合众国各地的公民写来的,看来他们把科拉里奥城的领事馆当成资讯百科全书了。他们提了一长串的问题,还把问题都编了号,什么气候啊,产品啊,可能性啊,法律啊,生意机会啊,还有领事馆所在国的统计数字啦等等。

"请回信给他们,比利,"那位怠惰的领事说道,"就写一句,让他们去找本领事馆最新的

State Department will be delighted to furnish the literary gems. Sign my name. Don't let your pen scratch, Billy; it'll keep me awake."

"Don't snore," said Keogh, amiably, "and I'll do your work for you. You need a corps of assistants, anyhow. Don't see how you ever get out a report. Wake up a minute! – here's one more letter – it's from your own town, too – Dalesburg."

"That so?" murmured Johnny showing a mild and obligatory interest. "What's it about?"

"Postmaster writes," explained Keogh. "Says a citizen of the town wants some facts and advice from you. Says the citizen has an idea in his head of coming down where you are and opening a shoe store. Wants to know if you think the business would pay. Says he's heard of the boom along this coast, and wants to get in on the ground floor."

In spite of the heat and his bad temper, Johnny's hammock swayed with his laughter. Keogh laughed too; and the pet monkey on the top shelf of the bookcase chattered in shrill sympathy with the ironical reception of the letter from Dalesburg.

那份报告。跟他们说,国务院很乐意提供珍贵的文字资料。最后署上我的名字。比利,千万别让你的笔把纸划得沙沙响,那样会弄得我睡不着觉。"

"别打呼噜,"基奥柔声细语地说,"我来帮你打理吧。总之,你得有一个军团的助手才够哩。真是难以想像你是怎么写出报告的。先别睡,就一分钟!——这儿还有一封信——是从你家乡——戴尔斯堡寄来的!"

"是吗?"约翰尼嘟囔着,尽义务似的表现出适度的兴趣。"信里都说了些什么?"

"是邮局局长写来的,"基奥解释说,"说镇里有个人想请你提供点实际情况和意见,说这个人想来你这儿开一家鞋店。想知道你认为做这个生意是否可行。这个人听说这个沿海地区经济欣欣向荣,因此想来抢占有利地位呢。"

尽管天气很热,肝火很旺,约翰尼还是禁不住哈哈大笑起来,弄得吊床都摇摇晃晃的。基奥也放声大笑;放在书柜顶层的那只宠物猴子也吱吱地叫个不停,对那封戴城来的信受到如此

"Great bunions!" exclaimed the consul. "Shoe store! What'll they ask about next, I wonder? Overcoat factory, I reckon. Say, Billy – of our 3,000 citizens, how many do you suppose ever had on a pair of shoes?"

Keogh reflected judicially.

"Let's see – there's you and me and – "

"Not me," said Johnny, promptly and incorrectly, holding up a foot encased in a disreputable deerskin *zapato*. "I haven't been a victim to shoes in months."

"But you've got 'em, though," went on Keogh. "And there's Goodwin and Blanchard and Geddie and old Lutz and Doc Gregg and that Italian that's agent for the banana company, and there's old Delgado – no; he wears sandals. And, oh, yes; there's Madama Ortiz, 'what kapes the hotel' – she had on a pair of red slippers at the *baile* the other night. And Miss Pasa, her daughter, that went to school in the States – she brought back some civilized notions in the way of footgear. And there's the *comandante's* sister that dresses up her feet on feast-days – and Mrs. Geddie, who wears

的嘲笑表示它的同情。

"这是什么事！"领事大叫道，"鞋店！我想知道接下来他们还要问什么？估计是裘衣厂吧。说说看，比利，咱们这儿的三千个居民里头，有多少人曾经穿过鞋呀？"

基奥像模像样地考虑着。

"我想想——有你，我，还有——"

"我可不算。"约翰尼立刻纠正他，尽管不是那么回事。他抬起一只脚，脚上穿着破烂不堪的鹿皮鞋，"我可是有好几个月不受穿鞋之苦啰。"

"可你也算是有鞋的人呀。"基奥继续说，"还有古德温、布良沙尔、格迪、老卢兹和多克·格雷格，还有那个给香蕉公司做代理的意大利人，还有老德尔加多——不对，他穿的是凉鞋。还有，噢，对了，还有沃里滋女士，就是总说'靠什么来管理饭店哪'的那个，前几天晚上在舞会上，她穿了一双红拖鞋。还有她女儿帕萨小姐，她在美国上学，在鞋袜方面还是带回来不少文明开化的东西。另外还有少校的妹妹，一过节她就会装扮一下她的脚丫子，格迪太太也穿着一双卡斯蒂

a two with a Castilian instep – and that's about all the ladies. Let's see – don't some of the soldiers at the *cuartel* – no: that's so; they're allowed shoes only when on the march. In barracks they turn their little toeses out to grass."

"'Bout right," agreed the consul. "Not over twenty out of the three thousand ever felt leather on their walking arrangements. Oh, yes; Coralio is just the town for an enterprising shoe store – that doesn't want to part with its goods. Wonder if old Patterson is trying to jolly me! He always was full of things he called jokes. Write him a letter, Billy. I'll dictate it. We'll jolly him back a few."

Keogh dipped his pen, and wrote at Johnny's dictation. With many pauses, filled in with smoke and sundry travellings of the bottle and glasses, the following reply to the Dalesburg communication was perpetrated:

MR. OBADIAH PATTERSON,
Dalesburg, Ala.

Dear Sir:

In reply to your favour of July 2d, I have the honour to inform you that, according to my

利亚式样的鞋——穿鞋的女士们估计就这些啦。我们再想想——兵营里驻扎的士兵中是不是也有些人——不对，不是这样；只有在行军的时候他们才被允许穿鞋。在兵营里，他们都把小小的脚趾头放出来吃草。"

"差不多了，"领事表示同意，"3000个人里，走路的时候脚上穿过皮东西的人不到20个。哦，没错，在科拉里奥城开一家有胆识的鞋店倒是挺合适的——一家不想卖鞋的鞋店。真不知道老帕特森是不是想拿我寻开心！他总是有很多他称之为玩笑的玩意儿。给他回封信，比利。我说你写。咱们也逗逗他。"

基奥蘸了蘸墨水，约翰尼一边说他一边写。中途停下来不知道多少次，期间烟雾缭绕和酒瓶酒杯来回传递。最终寄给戴尔斯堡的恶作剧出炉了：

奥巴代亚·帕特森先生
亚拉巴马，戴尔斯堡

亲爱的先生：

7月2日收到您的来信，感到无比荣幸。谨此回复。请允许我向您报告：

opinion, there is no place on the habitable globe that presents to the eye stronger evidence of the need of a first-class shoe store than does the town of Coralio. There are 3,000 inhabitants in the place, and not a single shoe store! The situation speaks for itself. This coast is rapidly becoming the goal of enterprising business men, but the shoe business is one that has been sadly overlooked or neglected. In fact, there are a considerable number of our citizens actually without shoes at present.

Besides the want above mentioned, there is also a crying need for a brewery, a college of higher mathematics, a coal yard, and a clean and intellectual Punch and Judy show. I have the honour to be, sir,

Your Obt. Servant,

JOHN DE GRAFFENREID ATWOOD, U. S. Consul at Coralio.

P.S. – Hello! Uncle Obadiah. How's the old burg racking along? What would the government do without you and me? Look out for a green-headed parrot and a bunch of bananas soon, from your old friend

JOHNNY.

"I throw in that postscript," explained the consul, "so Uncle Obadiah won't take offence at the official tone of the letter! Now, Billy, you get that correspondence fixed up, and send Pancho to the post-office

世上凡是有人居住的地方，再没有比科拉里奥城更有必要开一家一流的鞋店了。本地有 3000 居民，却没有一间鞋店！情势不言而喻。这一海岸地区正受到越来越多有魄力的商人的垂青，但鞋这方面的生意却很可惜地被忽视了。其实，目前，本地没有穿鞋的居民的数量十分可观。

除了上面所提到的，本地还急需一家酿酒厂，一所高等数学学院，一间煤场以及一个干净、高品位滑稽木偶剧演出剧场。

您谦卑的仆人

美国驻科拉里奥领事

约翰·德·格拉芬里德·阿特伍德顿首

附言：嗨！奥巴代亚大叔。咱们的老城最近咋样啦？戴城政府要是没有了你跟我可咋办呢？注意了，你很快就会收到一只绿头鹦鹉和一串香蕉，它们是你的老伙计寄去的——约翰尼

"我随手添上的那个附言，"领事解释说，"这样奥巴代亚大叔就不会因为这封信打官腔而生气了。好啦，比利，把信封上，让潘乔送到邮局去。如果他们今

with it. The *Ariadne* takes the mail out to-morrow if they make up that load of fruit to-day."

The night programme in Coralio never varied. The recreations of the people were soporific and flat. They wandered about, barefoot and aimless, speaking lowly and smoking cigar or cigarette. Looking down on the dimly lighted ways one seemed to see a threading maze of brunette ghosts tangled with a procession of insane fireflies. In some houses the thrumming of lugubrious guitars added to the depression of the *triste* night. Giant tree-frogs rattled in the foliage as loudly as the end man's "bones" in a minstrel troupe. By nine o'clock the streets were almost deserted.

Nor at the consulate was there often a change of bill. Keogh would come there nightly, for Coralio's one cool place was the little seaward porch of that official residence.

The brandy would be kept moving; and before midnight sentiment would begin to stir in the heart of the self-exiled consul. Then he would relate to Keogh the story of his ended romance. Each night Keogh would listen patiently to the tale, and be

天把水果装船的话,阿里亚德号明天就会把这封信带走了。"

科拉里奥城的夜生活总是一成不变。当地人的消遣总是无聊乏味,让人昏昏欲睡。他们光着两只脚,毫无目标地四处游荡,慢慢吞吞地谈话,抽抽雪茄或者香烟。俯视镇上灯火昏暗的街道,就像看着缠搅着一个浅黑肤色女人的鬼魂们和神志不清的萤火虫所组成的迷魂阵。一些房子里传出胡乱敲打着吉它故作悲伤而发出的音调,给这悲伤的夜晚又添加了些许沉闷。硕大的树蛙躲在一簇簇叶子里尽力发出格格的声响,仿佛黑人剧团里站在头排两端,正在大声巧辩的演员。到了晚九点,街上基本上就空荡荡了。

就算在领事馆,也不会经常有什么变化。基奥每天晚上都过来,因为科城最凉快的一个地方便是那座官邸朝海的小门廊。

白兰地总是流个不停;不到半夜,领事那自我放逐的心中便涌起一些愁绪。于是,他就会给基奥讲述他那段已经终结了的爱情故事。每天晚上,基奥总是耐心地聆听,随时准备好露出自己

ready with untiring sympathy.

"But don't you think for a minute" – thus Johnny would always conclude his woeful narrative – "that I'm grieving about that girl, Billy. I've forgotten her. She never enters my mind. If she were to enter that door right now, my pulse wouldn't gain a beat. That's all over long ago."

"Don't I know it?" Keogh would answer. "Of course you've forgotten her. Proper thing to do. Wasn't quite O. K. of her to listen to the knocks that – er – Dink Pawson kept giving you."

"Pink Dawson!" – a world of contempt would be in Johnny's tones – "Poor white trash! That's what he was. Had five hundred acres of farming land, though; and that counted. Maybe I'll have a chance to get back at him some day. The Dawsons weren't anybody. Everybody in Alabama knows the Atwoods. Say, Billy – did you know my mother was a De Graffenreid?"

"Why, no," Keogh would say; "is that so?" He had heard it some three hundred times.

"Fact. The De Graffenreids of Han-

那永不疲倦的同情心。

"难道你就从没想过"——约翰尼总是这样结束他那悲伤的叙述——"我真的是因为那姑娘而伤心吗，比利？我早就忘记她了。她再也没有进入我的脑海。就算她现在走进这扇门，我的脉搏也不会因此而跳得更快。事情已经过去很久了。"

"我还不知道这个？"基奥总是这样回答，"当然喽，你早把她忘的干干净净了。这才对嘛。她怎么能信那些没根没据的毁谤呢，就是那个——嗯——丁克·波森整的。"

"平克·道森！"——约翰尼的声调里包含了全世界的鄙夷和不屑——"白人里的垃圾！一个穷光蛋。是，他有 500 顷地；这个的确能算的出来。也许将来有一天我会找着机会回去收拾收拾他。道森家都是些无名鼠辈。住在亚拉巴马州哪个不认识阿特伍德家的人？！喂，比利——你以前知不知道我母亲是德·格拉芬里德家族的？"

"哎哟，不知道啊，"基奥总会这么说；"真的吗？"这句话他估计听了都有三百遍了。

"当然啦。汉考克县的德·格

cock County. But I never think of that girl any more, do I, Billy?"

"Not for a minute, my boy," would be the last sounds heard by the conqueror of Cupid.

At this point Johnny would fall into a gentle slumber, and Keogh would saunter out to his own shack under the calabash tree at the edge of the plaza.

In a day or two the letter from the Dalesburg postmaster and its answer had been forgotten by the Coralio exiles. But on the 26th day of July the fruit of the reply appeared upon the tree of events.

The *Andador*, a fruit steamer that visited Coralio regularly, drew into the offing and anchored. The beach was lined with spectators while the quarantine doctor and the custom-house crew rowed out to attend to their duties.

An hour later Billy Keogh lounged into the consulate, clean and cool in his linen clothes, and grinning like a pleased shark.

"Guess what?" he said to Johnny, lounging in his hammock.

"Too hot to guess," said Johnny, lazily.

"Your shoe-store man's come," said Keogh, rolling the sweet morsel on his

拉芬里德家族。不过现在我是绝不会再去想那姑娘啦，是不是，比利？"

"一点也不想，伙计。"丘比特的征服者最后总是听到这句话。

话说到这里，约翰尼就会渐渐进入梦乡，基奥便迈着悠闲的步子走回到他自己在广场边葫芦树下的小棚屋里。

才过了一两天，戴城的两个流放者就把戴尔斯堡的来信和他们的回信忘得一干二净了。可到了7月26日这天，那封回信有了结果，这真是个多事之秋。

运送水果的班轮安达多尔号定期回到科城，它驶入离岸不远的水域，抛锚靠岸。海滩上站了一排的看客，检疫医生和海关官员划船过去执行公务。

一小时后，比利·基奥穿着一件亚麻布衬衫，拖着慵懒的步子走进领事馆，看起来无比清爽，他咧嘴笑着，活像一头开心的鲨鱼。

"猜猜发生了什么？"他对正无精打采地躺在吊床上的约翰尼说。

"天太热了，不想猜。"约翰尼懒懒答话。

tongue, "with a stock of goods big enough to supply the continent as far down as Terra del Fuego. They're carting his cases over to the custom-house now. Six barges full they brought ashore and have paddled back for the rest. Oh, ye saints in glory! won't there be regalements in the air when he gets onto the joke and has an interview with Mr. Consul? It'll be worth nine years in the tropics just to witness that one joyful moment."

Keogh loved to take his mirth easily. He selected a clean place on the matting and lay upon the floor. The walls shook with his enjoyment. Johnny turned half over and blinked.

"Don't tell me," he said, "that anybody was fool enough to take that letter seriously."

"Four-thousand-dollar stock of goods!" gasped Keogh, in ecstasy. "Talk about coals to Newcastle! Why didn't he take a ship-load of palm-leaf fans to Spitzbergen while he was about it? Saw the old codger on the beach. You ought to have been there when he put on his specs and squinted at the five hundred or so

"你那位要开鞋店的人大驾光临了，"基奥说着，舌尖上还含着一块糖，"他还带来了一大批货，估计足够本大陆到火地岛的所有居民穿了。现在他们正用车把一箱箱的货往海关运呢。光是搬上岸的货就装满了六个驳船，而且他们还正划着小船去运剩下的货。哦，赞美圣人们吧！要是他们知道这是个玩笑，和领事先生面谈的时候，是不是会有什么好戏看呢？要是能亲眼看看那个好玩的场面，在这热死人的地方待九年也值了。"

基奥最爱轻松地享受快乐。他在铺着凉席的地方挑了个干净地方，躺在地板上。他的快乐让墙壁都颤抖了。约翰尼半转过脸，眨眨眼。

"不要告诉我，"他说，"有人傻到真的把那封信当回事了！"

"价值4 000元的货呢！"基奥气喘吁吁地说着，显得异常兴奋，"还说要把煤运到纽卡斯尔哩！趁着这个，他怎么不干脆运一整船棕榈树叶大扇子到斯匹次卑尔根群岛呢？我在海边看见那个有怪癖的老头儿了。你真应该去那儿看看，看看他是怎么戴上

barefooted citizens standing around."

"Are you telling the truth, Billy?" asked the consul, weakly.

"Am I? You ought to see the buncoed gentleman's daughter he brought along. Looks! She makes the brick-dust senoritas here look like tar-babies."

"Go on," said Johnny, "if you can stop that asinine giggling. I hate to see a grown man make a laughing hyena of himself."

"Name is Hemstetter," went on Keogh. "He's a – Hello! what's the matter now?"

Johnny's moccasined feet struck the floor with a thud as he wriggled out of his hammock.

"Get up, you idiot," he said, sternly, "or I'll brain you with this inkstand. That's Rosine and her father. Gad! what a drivelling idiot old Patterson is! Get up, here, Billy Keogh, and help me. What the devil are we going to do? Has all the world gone crazy?"

Keogh rose and dusted himself. He managed to regain a decorous demeanour.

"Situation has got to be met, Johnny," he said, with some success at seriousness.

眼镜斜眼瞅着他周围站的五百来个赤脚大仙的。"

"比利,你说的是真的吗?"领事虚弱的问道。

"真的吗!?你还应该看看那位被骗的先生带来的千金。那模样!她让本地那些肤色像砖粉的小姐们看起来像涂了焦油。"

"你接着说,"约翰尼说,"最好你能不要像驴子一样傻笑。我讨厌看见一个成年人这样傻笑个不停。"

"那人名叫赫姆斯特特尔。"基奥继续说道,"他是个——喂!怎么回事儿?"

约翰尼扭动着滚下吊床,他那双穿着软拖鞋的脚砰地砸在地板上。

"起来,你这个白痴,"他毫不留情地说,"要不然我就拿这个墨水瓶砸你的脑袋。那就是罗西娜和她爹!。老天!老帕特森真是个满嘴跑糊涂话的白痴!快起来,到这儿来,比利·基奥,帮帮我。咱们到底该咋办呢?是不是全世界都疯了?"

基奥站起来,拍拍身上的尘土。他尽量让自己看起来严肃些。

"事已至此,只能面对了,约翰尼。"他说着,看起来正经

"I didn't think about its being your girl until you spoke. First thing to do is to get them comfortable quarters. You go down and face the music, and I'll trot out to Goodwin's and see if Mrs. Goodwin won't take them in. They've got the decentest house in town."

"Bless you, Billy!" said the consul. "I knew you wouldn't desert me. The world's bound to come to an end, but maybe we can stave it off for a day or two."

Keogh hoisted his umbrella and set out for Goodwin's house. Johnny put on his coat and hat. He picked up the brandy bottle, but set it down again without drinking, and marched bravely down to the beach.

In the shade of the custom-house walls he found Mr. Hemstetter and Rosine surrounded by a mass of gaping citizens. The customs officers were ducking and scraping, while the captain of the *Andador* interpreted the business of the new arrivals. Rosine looked healthy and very much alive. She was gazing at the strange scenes around her with amused interest. There was a faint blush upon her round cheek as she greeted her old admirer. Mr. Hemstetter shook hands with Johnny in a

了一些，"你要是不说，我可是想不到她会是你那位姑娘哩。首先，应该替他们找个舒服的地方住。你下去听听海涛声吧，我现在跑到古德温家去，看看古太太会不会让他们住在她那儿。他们的房子可是这城里最像样的。"

"上帝保佑你，比利！"领事说。"我就知道你会帮我的忙。这个世界一定会玩完的，不过也许咱们能拖上它个一两天。"

基奥撑着伞朝古德温家走去。约翰尼穿上外套，戴上帽子。他捡起白兰地酒瓶，没有喝就丢下了，勇敢地迈向海滩。

在海关楼墙壁的阴暗处，他看到了赫姆斯特特尔先生和罗西娜，他们正被一群目瞪口呆的当地居民团团围住。海关官员躲开人群，悄悄地往后退，而安达多尔号船长正在向人们说明新来的人做的是什么买卖。罗西娜看上去很健康，神采奕奕的。她饱含兴致地注视着周围前所未有的景象。和自己旧日的爱慕者打招呼时，她那圆圆的脸蛋儿上浮起了淡淡的红晕。赫姆斯特特尔先生

very friendly way. He was an oldish, impractical man – one of that numerous class of erratic business men who are forever dissatisfied, and seeking a change.

"I am very glad to see you, John – may I call you John?" he said. "Let me thank you for your prompt answer to our postmaster's letter of inquiry. He volunteered to write to you on my behalf. I was looking about for something different in the way of a business in which the profits would be greater. I had noticed in the papers that this coast was receiving much attention from investors. I am extremely grateful for your advice to come. I sold out everything that I possess, and invested the proceeds in as fine a stock of shoes as could be bought in the North. You have a picturesque town here, John. I hope business will be as good as your letter justifies me in expecting."

Johnny's agony was abbreviated by the arrival of Keogh, who hurried up with the news that Mrs. Goodwin would be much pleased to place rooms at the disposal of Mr. Hemstetter and his daughter. So there Mr. Hemstetter and Rosine were at once conducted and left to recuperate from the fatigue of the voyage, while

十分友好地和约翰尼握了握手。他年纪有点大了，总是不切实际——他属于那群为数众多的想法奇怪的生意人，这类人永不知足，总是寻求改变。

"真高兴见到你，约翰——我能叫你约翰吗？"他说。"很谢谢你那么快就答复了邮政局长写的询问信。是他自告奋勇要替我给你写信的。那时候，我正另寻他路，看看有什么买卖能赚更多的钱。我在报纸上看到这个沿海地区成了投资者的焦点啦。听到你建议我到这儿来，我真是感激得不得了。我把我有的东西都卖了，然后买来了北美能买到的各式各样的鞋。你们这地方风景还真是不错呢，约翰。我希望买卖会像信中说的那么好。那封信可是让我大长信心呢。"

基奥的到来可是让饱受痛苦难熬的约翰尼缓了口气。基奥急急忙忙地带信儿过来，说古德温太太很高兴为赫姆斯特特尔先生和他女儿提供住处，请他们随意。于是，赫姆斯特特尔先生和罗西娜马上就被领到那里去休息，以消除旅途的疲劳，约翰尼则去确

Johnny went down to see that the cases of shoes were safely stored in the customs warehouse pending their examination by the officials. Keogh, grinning like a shark, skirmished about to find Goodwin, to instruct him not to expose to Mr. Hemstetter the true state of Coralio as a shoe market until Johnny had been given a chance to redeem the situation, if such a thing were possible.

That night the consul and Keogh held a desperate consultation on the breezy porch of the consulate.

"Send 'em back home," began Keogh, reading Johnny's thoughts.

"I would," said Johnny, after a little silence; "but I've been lying to you, Billy."

"All right about that," said Keogh, affably.

"I've told you hundreds of times," said Johnny, slowly, "that I had forgotten that girl, haven't I?"

"About three hundred and seventy-five," admitted the monument of patience.

"I lied," repeated the consul, "every time. I never forgot her for one minute. I was an obstinate ass for running away just because she said 'No' once. And I

认那些鞋箱子是不是安全地搁置在了海关的仓库里，因为它们还等着海关官员检验呢。基奥呢，他像鲨鱼一样龇牙咧嘴地笑着，四处寻找古德温，打算跟他说，先别让赫姆斯特特尔先生知道科城鞋市场的真相，好让约翰尼有机会挽救局势，如果还有可能的话。

当天晚上，在领事馆夜风徐徐的门廊上，领事和基奥孤注一掷，商讨对策。

"把他们送回家。"基奥揣摩着约翰尼的心思，开口说道。

"我会的，"一阵沉默之后，约翰尼回答；"可是我一直在骗你，比利。"

"没什么。"基奥友善地说。

"我给你说过无数遍了吧，"约翰尼慢慢说着，"说我已经把那姑娘给忘了，是不是？"

"也就 375 遍吧。"耐心纪念碑承认说。

"我说谎了，"领事说道，"我每次都在说谎，我一秒钟也没忘记过她。就因为她有一次拒绝了我，我就像一头倔驴一样从

was too proud a fool to go back. I talked with Rosine a few minutes this evening up at Goodwin's. I found out one thing. You remember that farmer fellow who was always after her?"

"Dink Pawson?" asked Keogh.

"Pink Dawson. Well, he wasn't a hill of beans to her. She says she didn't believe a word of the things he told her about me. But I'm sewed up now, Billy. That tomfool letter we sent ruined whatever chance I had left. She'll despise me when she finds out that her old father has been made the victim of a joke that a decent school boy wouldn't have been guilty of. Shoes! Why he couldn't sell twenty pairs of shoes in Coralio if he kept store here for twenty years. You put a pair of shoes on one of these Caribs or Spanish brown boys and what'd he do? Stand on his head and squeal until he'd kicked 'em off. None of 'em ever wore shoes and they never will. If I send 'em back home I'll have to tell the whole story, and what'll she think of me? I want that girl worse than ever, Billy, and now when she's in reach I've lost her forever because I tried to be funny when the thermometer was at 102."

家里逃掉了。我又是个傲气的傻瓜,所以不愿回去。今天晚上,我在古德文家同罗西娜聊了一会儿。我发现了一件事。你记不记得那个一直追她的乡巴佬?"

"丁克·波森?"基奥问。

"平克·道森。啊哈,他在她心里什么也算不上。她说他对她说的那些贬低我的坏话她压根儿就不信。可是,比利,我现在完了。就算我本来还有机会,也被咱俩发的那封愚蠢至极的信给毁了。等她发现她老爸成了这个玩笑的牺牲品,她肯定会轻视我的,因为一个正派的、有教养的男人是不会开这种玩笑的。这么多鞋!要是他在科拉里奥这里开20年的店,还卖不掉20双鞋可怎么办。你把那些加勒比人或黑皮肤的西班牙孩子找一个来给他穿上鞋,他会怎么样?铁定是头朝下,两脚朝天,尖叫着直到把鞋踹掉。他们以前没穿过鞋,将来也不会穿。要是我把他俩送回去,我就得说实话,那她会怎么看我?比利,我可是比过去任何时候都想得到她,现在她触手可得,可我却永远失去了她,都是因为我,温度都升到102度了我却还想逗乐儿。"

"Keep cheerful," said the optimistic Keogh. "And let 'em open the store. I've been busy myself this afternoon. We can stir up a temporary boom in foot-gear anyhow. I'll buy six pairs when the doors open. I've been around and seen all the fellows and explained the catastrophe. They'll all buy shoes like they was centipedes. Frank Goodwin will take cases of 'em. The Geddies want about eleven pairs between 'em. Clancy is going to invest the savings of weeks, and even old Doc Gregg wants three pairs of alligator-hide slippers if they've got any tens. Blanchard got a look at Miss Hemstetter; and as he's a Frenchman, no less than a dozen pairs will do for him."

"A dozen customers," said Johnny, "for a $4,000 stock of shoes! It won't work. There's a big problem here to figure out. You go home, Billy, and leave me alone. I've got to work at it all by myself. Take that bottle of Three-star along with you – no, sir; not another ounce of booze for the United States consul. I'll sit here to-night and pull out the think stop. If there's a soft place on this proposition anywhere I'll land on it. If there isn't there'll be another wreck to

"别难过。"基奥乐观地说道,"就让他们开店吧。我可是忙活了一个下午了。不管怎样,咱们暂时能掀起一阵鞋具热。等他一开张,我就一口气买它 6 双鞋。我还到处跑了跑,找了些熟人,和他们说了咱俩闯下的这场大祸。他们都打算买好多鞋呢,好像他们长了蜈蚣那么多的脚一样。弗兰克·古德温打算一口气买几箱。格迪夫家也想买 11 双。克兰西打算把几个星期的积蓄都用来买鞋,就连老多克·格雷格也说,要是他们有 10 美元一张的钞票的话,他也要买 3 双鳄鱼皮拖鞋哩。布朗沙尔看了赫姆斯特特尔小姐一眼;他可是个法国佬,不少于一打的鞋才够他穿呢。"

"十来个顾客,"约翰尼说,"就要买下价值 4 000 元的货!这顶不了什么事。现在还有个大问题要解决。你回去吧,比利,让我一个人待会儿。我得自己想办法把问题解决了;顺便把那瓶三星酒拿走——我决不再,先生,合众国领事决不再喝酒了。今晚我就坐在这儿,知道想出个办法来。要是有一个能解决任何问题的傻瓜之乡,无论它在哪儿,我都要去。要是没这种地方,美丽

the credit of the gorgeous tropics."

Keogh left, feeling that he could be of no use. Johnny laid a handful of cigars on a table and stretched himself in a steamer chair. When the sudden daylight broke, silvering the harbour ripples, he was still sitting there. Then he got up, whistling a little tune, and took his bath.

At nine o'clock he walked down to the dingy little cable office and hung for half an hour over a blank. The result of his application was the following message, which he signed and had transmitted at a cost of $33:

TO PINKNEY DAWSON,

Dalesburg, Ala.

Draft for $100 comes to you next mail. Ship me immediately 500 pounds stiff, dry cockleburrs. New use here in arts. Market price twenty cents pound. Further orders likely. Rush.

无双的热带就会再增加一艘沉船了。"

基奥走了,他觉得自己也帮不上什么忙。约翰尼将一把雪茄搁在桌上,靠在一张甲板躺椅上舒展四肢放松下来。当曙光出现,给港口水面镀上一层银色的波纹时,他还坐在那里。然后,他站起身,哼着小调,洗澡去了。

9点钟的时候,他走进脏乱窄小的电报室,拿着一张空白的电文纸,磨蹭了半个钟头。到最后,他签上了自己的名字,花了33块钱,发出了下面这份电报:

致平克尼·道森
亚拉巴马戴尔斯堡

我会在另一封信里给你寄100元汇票。请尽快给我发运500磅结实的干欧龙牙草。最近这里有工艺上的用途。市价每磅20分,可考虑续订单,马上。

30. THE PASSING OF BLACK EAGLE
30. 黑鹰的消逝

For some months of a certain year a grim bandit infested the Texas border along the Rio Grande. Peculiarly striking to the optic nerve was this notorious marauder. His personality secured him the title of "Black Eagle, the Terror of the Border." Many fearsome tales are on record concerning the doings of him and his followers. Suddenly, in the space of a single minute, Black Eagle vanished from earth. He was never heard of again. His own band never even guessed the mystery of his disappearance. The border ranches and settlements feared he would come again to ride and ravage the mesquite flats. He never will. It is to disclose the fate of Black Eagle that this narrative is written.

The initial movement of the story is furnished by the foot of a bartender in St. Louis. His discerning eye fell upon the form of Chicken Ruggles as he pecked with avidity at the free lunch. Chicken was a "hobo." He had a long nose like the bill of a fowl, an inordinate appetite for

有一年，一个凶残的强盗连续几个月骚扰着得克萨斯州边境到里奥格兰德一带的地区。这个臭名昭著的强盗长得很震慑人的视觉神经。他的个性为他赢得了这样一个称号："黑鹰，边境恐怖分子。"他和他手下的弟兄们有很多令人生畏的传闻被记录在案。突然，才一分钟的时间，黑鹰就从地球上消失了，从此再没有了他的消息。甚至他手下的匪徒们也解不开他消失的谜团。边境的农场和村落都害怕他会卷土重来，洗劫他们的牧豆灌木地。但他不会再来了。写下这篇故事就是要揭开黑鹰的命运。

故事从圣路易斯的一位酒吧侍者那里开始。当他正贪婪地啄食他那免费的午餐时，他精明的目光落在契肯·拉格尔斯的身体上。契肯是个"流浪汉"。他长着一只鸡嘴一样的长鼻子，对家禽的胃口超常的大，还习惯不花

poultry, and a habit of gratifying it without expense, which accounts for the name given him by his fellow vagrants.

Physicians agree that the partaking of liquids at meal times is not a healthy practice. The hygiene of the saloon promulgates the opposite. Chicken had neglected to purchase a drink to accompany his meal. The bartender rounded the counter, caught the injudicious diner by the ear with a lemon squeezer, led him to the door and kicked him into the street.

Thus the mind of Chicken was brought to realize the signs of coming winter. The night was cold; the stars shone with unkindly brilliancy; people were hurrying along the streets in two egotistic, jostling streams. Men had donned their overcoats, and Chicken knew to an exact percentage the increased difficulty of coaxing dimes from those buttoned-in vest pockets. The time had come for his annual exodus to the south.

A little boy, five or six years old, stood looking with covetous eyes in a confectioner's window. In one small hand he held an empty two-ounce vial; in the other he grasped tightly something flat and round, with a shining milled edge. The scene presented a field of operations com-

分文来满足这个胃口，正是基于这些原因他的流浪同伴们给他取了契肯（鸡）这个名字。

医生们都说吃饭的时候喝酒不是一个健康的做法。酒吧里却有人奉行着相反的一套保健方法。契肯没有理会医生的说法，他点了一杯酒来下饭。那位侍者绕出柜台，用一只柠檬榨汁器抓住这位不懂保健的客人的一只耳朵，把他揪他到门口，然后一脚把他踢到大街上。

这样一来，契肯的脑子才被迫感受到了冬天来临的种种迹象。夜晚寒冷；星星发出不近人情的光芒；人们在街上匆匆而过，无暇顾及他人，形成两道拥挤的人流。男人们已经裹上大衣，契肯百分之百地清楚，要从那些钮扣朝里的大口袋里哄出几个钱来，是越来越难了。他一年一度迁往南方的时间到了。

有一个小男孩，五六岁的样子，正站在糖果店的橱窗前，眼睛里充满着羡慕。他的一只小手握着一个两盎司容量的空瓶子，另一只手紧紧地攥着一个又扁又圆的什么东西，它的边缘已经被磨得发亮。这幅情景为冒险精神

mensurate to Chicken's talents and daring. After sweeping the horizon to make sure that no official tug was cruising near, he insidiously accosted his prey. The boy, having been early taught by his household to regard altruistic advances with extreme suspicion, received the overtures coldly.

Then Chicken knew that he must make one of those desperate, nerve-shattering plunges into speculation that fortune sometimes requires of those who would win her favour. Five cents was his capital, and this he must risk against the chance of winning what lay within the close grasp of the youngster's chubby hand. It was a fearful lottery, Chicken knew. But he must accomplish his end by strategy, since he had a wholesome terror of plundering infants by force. Once, in a park, driven by hunger, he had committed an onslaught upon a bottle of peptonized infant's food in the possession of an occupant of a baby carriage. The outraged infant had so promptly opened its mouth and pressed the button that communicated with the welkin that help arrived, and Chicken did his thirty days in a snug coop. Wherefore he was, as he said, "leary of kids."

提供了一片天地，让契肯的天才和大胆能得到相宜的施展。他扫视了一遍四周，确信没有政府的工作人员在周围巡视之后，便悄悄地上前和他的猎物搭讪。那男孩早就被教导要用怀疑的态度看待看起来对自己有好处的事，就没怎么搭理对方的提示。

于是契肯明白了，他必须作为一个绝望的、落魄的人挺身去投机，财富有时需要那些能赢得财富宠爱的人。五分钱就是他的本钱，他必须用它冒险去赢得那紧紧捏在小孩胖乎乎的手中的东西。契肯知道，这次试运气是可怕的。但他必须使用计策来完成这次行动，因为他有过一次可怕的用暴力抢劫儿童的经历。有一次，在公园里，由于饥饿的驱使，他向着一瓶放在一架婴儿车里的胨化乳婴儿食品发起了攻击。那个被激怒的婴儿如此迅速地张开嘴巴对着天空大喊大叫，结果援兵马上就来了，契肯在一个整洁舒适的监狱里待了30天。为此他是这么说的，"提防小孩。"

Beginning artfully to question the boy concerning his choice of sweets, he gradually drew out the information he wanted. Mamma said he was to ask the drug store man for ten cents' worth of paregoric in the bottle; he was to keep his hand shut tight over the dollar; he must not stop to talk to anyone in the street; he must ask the drug-store man to wrap up the change and put it in the pocket of his trousers. Indeed, they had pockets – two of them! And he liked chocolate creams best.

Chicken went into the store and turned plunger. He invested his entire capital in C.A.N.D.Y. stocks, simply to pave the way to the greater risk following.

He gave the sweets to the youngster, and had the satisfaction of perceiving that confidence was established. After that it was easy to obtain leadership of the expedition; to take the investment by the hand and lead it to a nice drug store he knew of in the same block. There Chicken, with a parental air, passed over the dollar and called for the medicine, while the boy crunched his candy, glad to be relieved of the responsibility of the purchase. And then the successful investor, searching his pockets, found an overcoat button – the extent of his winter

一开始他狡诈地问这个孩子喜欢什么糖果，然后慢慢地套出他想要的信息。妈妈告诉他到卖药的人那里去买一毛钱的镇痛药装到瓶子里；他要一直把那一块钱捏在手心里；在街上他不能同任何一个人讲话；他一定要让药店里的人把零钱包起来，装到他的裤子兜儿里。实际上，裤子有兜儿的——两只兜儿！还有他最喜欢奶油巧克力。

契肯走进商店，摇身一变成了一名投机者。他把全部的本钱投在这支糖果股上，完彻彻底底地为接下来去冒更大的风险而开路。

他把糖给了孩子，并满足地发现小孩对他已经建立起了信任。接下来，要掌握远征的领导权就容易多了；于是他手里牵着投资的财产，把它带到位于同一街区里一家他了解的还不错的药店。在药店里，契肯做出一副家长的样子，把那一块钱递过去，叫来了药，与此同时，那小孩正嘎扎嘎扎地嚼着糖，很高兴不用再担负买药的职责了。接着，这位成功的投资者翻遍了他的口袋，找到了一只外衣钮扣——他

trousseau – and, wrapping it carefully, placed the ostensible change in the pocket of confiding juvenility. Setting the youngster's face homeward, and patting him benevolently on the back – for Chicken's heart was as soft as those of his feathered namesakes – the speculator quit the market with a profit of 1,700 per cent. on his invested capital.

Two hours later an Iron Mountain freight engine pulled out of the railroad yards, Texas bound, with a string of empties. In one of the cattle cars, half buried in excelsior, Chicken lay at ease. Beside him in his nest was a quart bottle of very poor whisky and a paper bag of bread and cheese. Mr. Ruggles, in his private car, was on his trip south for the winter season.

For a week that car was trundled southward, shifted, laid over, and manipulated after the manner of rolling stock, but Chicken stuck to it, leaving it only at necessary times to satisfy his hunger and thirst. He knew it must go down to the cattle country, and San Antonio, in the heart of it, was his goal. There the air was salubrious and mild; the people indulgent and long-suffering. The bartenders there would not kick him. If

冬天包袱的一部分——并小心地把它包好，把这假零钱放进深信不疑的小孩的兜儿里。他让孩子面转向回家的路，慈爱地拍拍他的背——契肯的心肠软得就像和他同名的长毛的动物(chicken，鸡)的心肠一样——这个投机分子带着他用本钱赚到的百分之一千七百的利润离开了市场。

两小时后，一台铁山的货运列车从车场费力地开出来，驶向得克萨斯，机车后面拖着一串空的货车车厢。在一节运牛的车厢里，契肯有一半身子埋在细刨花里，躺得很舒服。在他身旁，放着一瓶一夸脱的廉价威士忌和一包面包和奶酪。在他的专用车厢里，拉格尔斯先生正在朝南方旅行，以避开冬季。

在一周的时间里，火车沉重地驶向南方，有移动、也有短暂的停留，一切都由车辆控制着，不过，契肯坚持呆在车上，只有在不得已要解决饥饿和口渴时才离开它。他知道，火车一定是南下至牛区的，圣安东尼奥就在这个区的中心，那儿是他的目的地。在那儿，空气有益于健康且气温适度；人们宽厚并且长期受苦。那儿酒吧里的侍者不会踢他。如

he should eat too long or too often at one place they would swear at him as if by rote and without heat. They swore so drawlingly, and they rarely paused short of their full vocabulary, which was copious, so that Chicken had often gulped a good meal during the process of the vituperative prohibition. The season there was always spring-like; the plazas were pleasant at night, with music and gaiety; except during the slight and infrequent cold snaps one could sleep comfortably out of doors in case the interiors should develop inhospitability.

At Texarkana his car was switched to the I. and G. N. Then still southward it trailed until, at length, it crawled across the Colorado bridge at Austin, and lined out, straight as an arrow, for the run to San Antonio.

When the freight halted at that town Chicken was fast asleep. In ten minutes the train was off again for Laredo, the end of the road. Those empty cattle cars were for distribution along the line at points from which the ranches shipped their stock.

When Chicken awoke his car was stationary. Looking out between the slats he saw it was a bright, moonlit night. Scrambling out, he saw his car with three

果他吃得太久或在一个地方出现得太频繁,他们会像念经一样毫无激情地咒骂他。他们骂得如此慢气吞声,在吐完丰富的词汇之前,他们几乎就不停顿,以至于契肯常常在辱骂的空当吞下一顿美餐。那里四季如春;购物广场的夜晚是愉快的,充斥着音乐和欢乐;除了轻度的不常有的寒流的天气,其他时间他都可以一个人舒舒服服地睡在户外,以防室内不欢迎他。

在特克萨卡纳,他的车厢换到了国际大北铁路公司的轨道上,然后继续向南驶去,直到终于爬过位于奥斯丁的科罗拉多大桥,像离弦的箭一样直奔向圣安东尼奥。

当火车停在这座城市时,契肯睡得正沉。10分钟之后,火车又离站开向铁路的终点拉雷多了。那些空的运牛的车厢就沿途分散在了多个装运点,大农场就从这些地方把牲畜装上车。

契肯醒来时,他的车厢已经停了。从板条间望出去,他看到的是一个晴朗的、月色照耀的夜晚。他爬出去,看见他的车厢和

others abandoned on a little siding in a wild and lonesome country. A cattle pen and chute stood on one side of the track. The railroad bisected a vast, dim ocean of prairie, in the midst of which Chicken, with his futile rolling stock, was as completely stranded as was Robinson with his land-locked boat.

A white post stood near the rails. Going up to it, Chicken read the letters at the top, S. A. 90. Laredo was nearly as far to the south. He was almost a hundred miles from any town. Coyotes began to yelp in the mysterious sea around him. Chicken felt lonesome. He had lived in Boston without an education, in Chicago without nerve, in Philadelphia without a sleeping place, in New York without a pull, and in Pittsburg sober, and yet he had never felt so lonely as now.

Suddenly through the intense silence, he heard the whicker of a horse. The sound came from the side of the track toward the east, and Chicken began to explore timorously in that direction. He stepped high along the mat of curly mesquit grass, for he was afraid of everything there might be in this wilderness – snakes, rats, brigands, centipedes, mirages, cowboys, fandangoes, tarantulas,

另外三节车厢一起被扔在一条小岔线上，四周是荒凉寂寞的乡野。在铁轨的一边，有个牛栏和一条牲畜通道。铁路把辽阔而朦胧的草原分成了两半，在它的中央，站着契肯和他微不足道的车厢。他束手无策，就像鲁宾逊当年和他的内陆船所处的境况一样。

铁路旁边有一根白色的标桩。契肯走上前去，看到最上边写着：圣安东尼奥，90。拉雷多差不多和南方一样远。他离任何一个城镇几乎都有100英里的距离。郊狼开始在他周围神秘的海洋中长嗥。契肯感到了寂寞。他住在波士顿时没上过学，在芝加哥时没有紧张过，在费城时没有过睡觉的地方，在纽约没喝过酒，在匹兹堡没醉过，可是，他可从来没有像现在这样经受过孤独。

突然，在万般寂静中，他听到了一匹马的嘶鸣声。那声音从铁路一侧向东传过来，契肯开始谨慎地向那个方向探望。他用脚尖踩着波浪般厚厚的牧豆草垫，因为他害怕这荒野中一切可能有的东西——蛇，老鼠，土匪，蜈蚣，海市蜃楼，牛仔，方丹戈舞，狼蛛，玉米粉蒸肉——他曾在故事书里读到过它们。很显然马受

tamales – he had read of them in the story papers. Rounding a clump of prickly pear that reared high its fantastic and menacing array of rounded heads, he was struck to shivering terror by a snort and a thunderous plunge, as the horse, himself startled, bounded away some fifty yards, and then resumed his grazing. But here was the one thing in the desert that Chicken did not fear. He had been reared on a farm; he had handled horses, understood them, and could ride.

Approaching slowly and speaking soothingly, he followed the animal, which, after its first flight, seemed gentle enough, and secured the end of the twenty-foot lariat that dragged after him in the grass. It required him but a few moments to contrive the rope into an ingenious nose-bridle, after the style of the Mexican *borsal*. In another he was upon the horse's back and off at a splendid lope, giving the animal free choice of direction. "He will take me somewhere," said Chicken to himself.

It would have been a thing of joy, that untrammelled gallop over the moonlit prairie, even to Chicken, who loathed exertion, but that his mood was not for it. His head ached; a growing thirst was

惊了，一声喷鼻声，一阵雷震般的猛冲，吓得他直发抖，只好围着一丛高高的仙人树打转，那仙人树把它奇异的长满吓人的刺的球竖得老高。马又跳开了有50码，然后重新开始吃草。不过，有一样荒漠里的东西契肯是不怕的。他是在一个农场里被养大的，他管过马，懂它们，并且还会骑马。

他跟在这个动物身后，慢慢地靠近它，抚慰地说着话。这匹马在刚才的一阵腾跳之后，显得温和极了，使拖在身后草地上的20英尺长的套马绳安然无恙。他需要的只不过是一点时间，照着墨西哥骑士的做法，设法抓住巧妙设计的马笼头的绳子。过了一会儿，他已骑上了马背，威风凛凛地小跑开了。他任凭马儿自由地选择方向。"它会把我带到某个地方，"契肯自言自语道。

即使对讨厌努力的契肯来说，在月光照耀下的大草原上骑着马自由自在地奔跑，也该算得上是件愉快的事了，但他没有心情来享受。他感到头痛；他越来

upon him; the "somewhere" whither his lucky mount might convey him was full of dismal peradventure.

And now he noted that the horse moved to a definite goal. Where the prairie lay smooth he kept his course straight as an arrow's toward the east. Deflected by hill or arroyo or impractical spinous brakes, he quickly flowed again into the current, charted by his unerring instinct. At last, upon the side of a gentle rise, he suddenly subsided to a complacent walk. A stone's cast away stood a little mott of coma trees; beneath it a *jacal* such as the Mexicans erect – a one-room house of upright poles daubed with clay and roofed with grass or tule reeds. An experienced eye would have estimated the spot as the headquarters of a small sheep ranch. In the moonlight the ground in the nearby corral showed pulverized to a level smoothness by the hoofs of the sheep. Everywhere was carelessly distributed the paraphernalia of the place – ropes, bridles, saddles, sheep pelts, wool sacks, feed troughs, and camp litter. The barrel of drinking water stood in the end of the two-horse wagon near the door. The harness was piled, promiscuous, upon the wagon tongue,

越口渴；这匹幸运的坐骑可能会让他将去的"某个地方"充满了凄厉的偶然。

现在，他注意到这匹马正朝着一个确定的目标奔跑。这一带草原平坦，他让马直线前进，就像一支箭一样朝东方射去。绕过小山或干枯的河道，或是走不通、长满棘的灌木丛，凭着它向来正确的本能的指引，马又畅快地奔跑起来。最后，在一个缓坡上，它突然减慢了速度，得意洋洋地踏着步子。投石之距以外，有一小丛序缨树；树下有一间小茅屋，有点像墨西哥人的建筑——垂直木桩撑起的只有一间屋的房子，用泥巴糊的墙，用草或芦苇盖的房顶。凡是有阅历的眼睛都会看出这里就是一个小牧羊场的指挥中心。在月光下，旁边围栏里的草地看起来很模糊，被羊蹄碾得平平展展的。到处都随随便便地扔着各种牧场必备的物品——绳子，马笼头，马鞍，羊皮，装羊毛的袋子，饲料糟啦，还有营地的杂物。在靠近门的双马马车后面，有一只饮水桶。挽具杂乱地堆在马车的辕杆上，吸收着露气。

soaking up the dew.

Chicken slipped to earth, and tied the horse to a tree. He hallooed again and again, but the house remained quiet. The door stood open, and he entered cautiously. The light was sufficient for him to see that no one was at home. The room was that of a bachelor ranchman who was content with the necessaries of life. Chicken rummaged intelligently until he found what he had hardly dared hope for – a small, brown jug that still contained something near a quart of his desire.

Half an hour later, Chicken – now a gamecock of hostile aspect – emerged from the house with unsteady steps. He had drawn upon the absent ranchman's equipment to replace his own ragged attire. He wore a suit of coarse brown ducking, the coat being a sort of rakish bolero, jaunty to a degree. Boots he had donned, and spurs that whirred with every lurching step. Buckled around him was a belt full of cartridges with a big six-shooter in each of its two holsters.

Prowling about, he found blankets, a saddle and bridle with which he caparisoned his steed. Again mounting, he rode swiftly away, singing a loud and tuneless song.

契肯滑下马,把马拴到了一棵树上。他一遍又一遍叫着"你好?有人吗?",可房屋仍保持着安静。房门开着,他小心翼翼地走进去。光线还好,足以使他看清没有人在家。这正是那种单身牧人的房间,主人满足于生活的必需品。契肯机灵地翻箱倒柜,找到了他几乎没有敢想过的东西——一只棕色小壶,壶里还有接近一夸脱他渴望的东西。

半小时之后,契肯——现在成了一个好斗的游戏对手——步子摇摇晃晃地从房子里走了出来。他穿上了不在家的农场主的全套行头,换下了自己褴褛的衣衫。他穿着一套粗糙的棕色衣服,上衣是西班牙男短样式,挺时髦的。还穿上了靴子和靴刺,每走一步就嗡嗡直响。他的腰上扣上了一根皮带,皮带里装满了子弹,还有两个手枪皮套,每个皮套里都有一只六发式左轮手枪。

四下寻觅,他又找到了几条毯子,一副马鞍和马笼头。他把这些东西披挂在他的战马上。他再次跨上马,飞驰而去,还大声唱着一支走调的歌。

Bud King's band of desperadoes, outlaws and horse and cattle thieves were in camp at a secluded spot on the bank of the Frio. Their depredations in the Rio Grande country, while no bolder than usual, had been advertised more extensively, and Captain Kinney's company of rangers had been ordered down to look after them. Consequently, Bud King, who was a wise general, instead of cutting out a hot trail for the upholders of the law, as his men wished to do, retired for the time to the prickly fastnesses of the Frio valley.

Though the move was a prudent one, and not incompatible with Bud's well-known courage, it raised dissension among the members of the band. In fact, while they thus lay ingloriously *perdu* in the brush, the question of Bud King's fitness for the leadership was argued, with closed doors, as it were, by his followers. Never before had Bud's skill or efficiency been brought to criticism; but his glory was waning (and such is glory's fate) in the light of a newer star. The sentiment of the band was crystallizing into the opinion that Black Eagle could lead them with more lustre, profit, and distinction.

由恶棍，逃犯，牛马盗贼组成的巴德·金团伙住在弗里奥河岸上一个隐蔽的地方。在里奥格兰德县城，他们掠夺的坏名声越来越响，他们的胆子没有人能比得过。金尼中尉的巡警队已经奉命前来搜剿这帮家伙。巴德·金，这个聪明的头领，并没有为执法者劈开一条紧追不放的道路，而是像他的弟兄们希望的那样，暂时迅速撤退到弗里奥多刺山谷这个要塞中去了。

虽然这是一次谨慎的撤退，不可与巴德出了名的勇气同日而语，但是在这一点上这一伙弟兄却有了争议。事实上，当他们如此不光彩地藏在灌木中时，紧接着巴德·金的弟兄们就关起门来，就他是否适合当领导人的问题进行了争论。在这以前，巴德的能力或本领从没遭到过批评；但他的荣耀在一颗新星的光芒下淡去了（这正是荣耀的命运）。大家的情绪具体化为一种意见，即黑鹰能带领他们获得更大的光荣，更多的利益，变得更加出色。

This Black Eagle – sub-titled the "Terror of the Border" – had been a member of the gang about three months.

One night while they were in camp on the San Miguel water-hole a solitary horseman on the regulation fiery steed dashed in among them. The newcomer was of a portentous and devastating aspect. A beak-like nose with a predatory curve projected above a mass of bristling, blue-black whiskers. His eye was cavernous and fierce. He was spurred, sombreroed, booted, garnished with revolvers, abundantly drunk, and very much unafraid. Few people in the country drained by the Rio Bravo would have cared thus to invade alone the camp of Bud King. But this fell bird swooped fearlessly upon them and demanded to be fed.

Hospitality in the prairie country is not limited. Even if your enemy pass your way you must feed him before you shoot him. You must empty your larder into him before you empty your lead. So the stranger of undeclared intentions was set down to a mighty feast.

A talkative bird he was, full of most marvellous loud tales and exploits, and speaking a language at times obscure but never colourless. He was a new sensation

这个黑鹰——又名"边境恐怖分子"——加入到这个团伙中才大约三个月。

一个晚上,这群家伙正在圣米格尔河水洼上的营地里,一位骑手骑着一匹标致的骏马冲到了他们中间。这个新来的人外貌凶险,令人震惊。一只鹰钩鼻,带着掠夺性的曲线,从一大堆又短又硬的、深蓝色的胡须中伸出来。他的眼睛凹陷下去,目光凶狠。他穿着马刺、阔边毡帽、靴子,配有左轮手枪,醉得不轻,无所畏惧。在里奥布拉沃河浇灌下的这个村子里,没人敢独自侵犯巴德·金的营地。但这只凶猛的鸟无畏地闯到他们这儿,还嚷着要吃的。

在草原上的村子里,好客是没有止境的。就算你的敌人经过你的地盘,在向他开枪之前你也得给他吃的。腾空你的子弹之前,你必须先腾空你的食物,来塞饱他的肚子。因此,他们给这位来路不明的陌生人安排了一桌盛宴。

这个人讲起话来滔滔不绝,嘴里装满了非常奇异的惊险故事和英勇传奇。他用的语言有时候

to Bud King's men, who rarely encountered new types. They hung, delighted, upon his vainglorious boasting, the spicy strangeness of his lingo, his contemptuous familiarity with life, the world, and remote places, and the extravagant frankness with which he conveyed his sentiments.

To their guest the band of outlaws seemed to be nothing more than a congregation of country bumpkins whom he was "stringing for grub" just as he would have told his stories at the back door of a farmhouse to wheedle a meal. And, indeed, his ignorance was not without excuse, for the "bad man" of the Southwest does not run to extremes. Those brigands might justly have been taken for a little party of peaceable rustics assembled for a fish-fry or pecan gathering. Gentle of manner, slouching of gait, soft-voiced, unpicturesquely clothed; not one of them presented to the eye any witness of the desperate records they had earned.

For two days the glittering stranger within the camp was feasted. Then, by common consent, he was invited to become a member of the band. He consented, presenting for enrollment the prodigious name of "Captain Montres-

真不好懂，但绝不会没有趣味。对巴德·金那些不怎么能接触到新的刺激的人来讲，他使大家耳目一新。他们很着迷，兴高采烈地听他自吹自擂，他那下流陌生的黑话，他那对生活、世界、遥远地方的带着轻蔑的熟悉，以及他那表达感情时极度坦荡的坦荡。

同他们的客人相比，这群歹徒简直就像是一群乡巴佬。他就是在"蹭东西吃"，就像他在农舍后门口讲些故事来哄顿饭吃一样。说真的，他们的无知也并不是没有理由，因为西南的"坏人"是不走极端的。那些强盗可能刚正正当当地去参加了气氛融洽的小型乡村炸鱼宴会，或小型山核桃集会。他们举止文雅有风度，步子收敛小心，声音轻细温和，穿戴普通低调；他们之中没一个人会让别人看出来，自己曾经干过无法无天的事情。

一连两天，这个光彩照人的陌生人都在营地里被宴请招待。之后，经过大家的认同，他被邀请加入这个帮派。他同意了，想以"蒙特雷索上尉"这个惊人的名字入帮。然而这个名字立刻被

sor." This name was immediately over-ruled by the band, and "Piggy" substituted as a compliment to the awful and insatiate appetite of its owner.

Thus did the Texas border receive the most spectacular brigand that ever rode its chaparral.

For the next three months Bud King conducted business as usual, escaping encounters with law officers and being content with reasonable profits. The band ran off some very good companies of horses from the ranges, and a few bunches of fine cattle which they got safely across the Rio Grande and disposed of to fair advantage. Often the band would ride into the little villages and Mexican settlements, terrorizing the inhabitants and plundering for the provisions and ammunition they needed. It was during these bloodless raids that Piggy's ferocious aspect and frightful voice gained him a renown more widespread and glorious than those other gentle-voiced and sad-faced desperadoes could have acquired in a lifetime.

The Mexicans, most apt in nomenclature, first called him The Black Eagle, and used to frighten the babes by threatening them with tales of the

匪徒们否决了，给换成了"小猪皮格"，以恭维主人那可怕而难以满足的胃口。

就这样得克萨斯边境就接受了它有史以来在它的丛林中穿行的最放光彩的强盗。

接下来的三个月，巴德·金像往常一样做着生意，避免撞上执法官员，满足于那些合理的利润。这一伙人在这片牧场偷走了好些马，又从里奥格兰德的对岸平安地偷了几群肥壮的牛，用它们换到了相当数量的钱。这帮强盗经常骑马冲进小村庄和墨西哥人的聚居地，胁迫居民，掠走他们需要的粮食和弹药。正是在这些没有见血的掠夺中，皮格凶悍的外表和骇人的声音为他挣得了名声，并且远比那些轻声细气，表情忧郁的匪徒们终身才能得到的名声更响亮。

最擅长命名的墨西哥人，一开始就把他叫做墨鹰。他们往往为了吓唬小孩，就讲起这个可怕的强盗的故事，说他会用他的长

dreadful robber who carried off little children in his great beak. Soon the name extended, and Black Eagle, the Terror of the Border, became a recognized factor in exaggerated newspaper reports and ranch gossip.

The country from the Nueces to the Rio Grande was a wild but fertile stretch, given over to the sheep and cattle ranches. Range was free; the inhabitants were few; the law was mainly a letter, and the pirates met with little opposition until the flaunting and garish Piggy gave the band undue advertisement. Then Kinney's ranger company headed for those precincts, and Bud King knew that it meant grim and sudden war or else temporary retirement. Regarding the risk to be unnecessary, he drew off his band to an almost inaccessible spot on the bank of the Frio. Wherefore, as has been said, dissatisfaction arose among the members, and impeachment proceedings against Bud were premeditated, with Black Eagle in high favour for the succession. Bud King was not unaware of the sentiment, and he called aside Cactus Taylor, his trusted lieutenant, to discuss it.

"If the boys," said Bud, "ain't satisfied

喙把孩子们叼走。很快，这个名字就传开了，黑鹰，边境恐怖分子，报纸上夸张的报道和牧场上的闲言碎语也都认可了它。

纽埃希斯河到里奥格兰德河一带，是原始而肥沃的大片原野，为牛羊们提供了牧场。牧场辽阔无边；而居民却寥寥无几；法律大致是一纸空文，这些强盗们很少遇到阻力，直到爱夸耀，穿得花哨的皮格给这伙匪徒做了太多广告宣传之前，劫掠几乎没遇到过抵抗。接着，金尼的巡警队开向了那些区域，巴德·金明白，这意味着有一场突如其来的讨厌的交战，或者一次暂时的撤退。他认为没有必要去冒险，于是就把匪帮撤到弗里奥河岸上的一个别人几乎找不到的地方，因而，如前面所说，暴徒中升起了不满情绪，弹劾巴德的行动也在策划，大多数人都支持黑鹰来继任。巴德·金不是没有意识到这种情绪，他把卡克图斯·泰勒，他信任的副官，叫来商量这件事。

"如果弟兄们，"巴德说，"不

with me, I'm willing to step out. They're buckin' against my way of handlin' 'em. And 'specially because I concludes to hit the brush while Sam Kinney is ridin' the line. I saves 'em from bein' shot or sent up on a state contract, and they up and says I'm no good."

"It ain't so much that," explained Cactus, "as it is they're plum locoed about Piggy. They want them whiskers and that nose of his to split the wind at the head of the column."

"There's somethin' mighty seldom about Piggy," declared Bud, musingly. "I never yet see anything on the hoof that he ex-actly grades up with. He can shore holler a plenty, and he straddles a hoss from where you laid the chunk. But he ain't never been smoked yet. You know, Cactus, we ain't had a row since he's been with us. Piggy's all right for skearin' the greaser kids and layin' waste a cross-roads store. I reckon he's the finest canned oyster buccaneer and cheese pirate that ever was, but how's his appetite for fightin'? I've knowed some citizens you'd think was starvin' for trouble get a bad case of dyspepsy the first dose of lead they had to take."

"He talks all spraddled out," said

满意我,我愿意让出位置。他们反对我对他们的指挥。特别是,当萨姆·金尼的人马逼近时,我决定放弃在丛林出击。我让他们免吃子弹或者逃脱了依法坐牢,他们却群起而攻之,说我不行。"

"没到那个地步,"卡克图斯解释说,"只不过是他们崇拜皮格简直要疯了。他们要用他们的胡须和他的鼻子去开路,抵挡巡警先锋队的挺进。"

"皮格根本没什么了不起的,"巴德边想边说。"我从没看见他拿出过什么真本事来说明他有那么大的能耐。他只会大喊大叫,他把马骑走,留下你在哪儿站着。不过,他倒是从不吸烟,你知道的,卡克图斯,自从他入了我们的伙,我们就没吵过架。皮格是可以去吓唬吓唬墨西哥的小孩,去十字路口的店铺搞搞破坏的。我想他是有史以来最出色的牡蛎罐头海盗和奶酪海盗。但是,他的仗打得怎么样呢?我知道,你会认为有的公民迫切想吃一场严重消化不良的麻烦,他们得先服一剂子弹。"

"他老说他那些事迹,"卡

Cactus, "'bout the rookuses he's been in. He claims to have saw the elephant and hearn the owl."

"I know," replied Bud, using the cowpuncher's expressive phrase of skepticism, "but it sounds to me!"

This conversation was held one night in camp while the other members of the band – eight in number – were sprawling around the fire, lingering over their supper. When Bud and Cactus ceased talking they heard Piggy's formidable voice holding forth to the others as usual while he was engaged in checking, though never satisfying, his ravening appetite.

"Wat's de use," he was saying, "of chasin' little red cowses and hosses 'round for t'ousands of miles? Dere ain't nuttin' in it. Gallopin' t'rough dese bushes and briers, and gettin' a t'irst dat a brewery couldn't put out, and missin' meals! Say! You know what I'd do if I was main finger of dis bunch? I'd stick up a train. I'd blow de express car and make hard dollars where you guys get wind. Youse makes me tired. Dis sook-cow kind of cheap sport gives me a pain."

Later on, a deputation waited on Bud.

克图斯说，"他跑出去敲诈蒙骗的事；还声称见过大象，听到过猫头鹰叫。"

"我知道，"巴德说，用的是牛仔那种意味深长的充满怀疑的措辞，"不过，那听起来是在和我对着干！"

谈话是在营地里的一个晚上进行的，这个时候，匪帮中的其他成员——有 8 个人——手脚伸开围躺在火旁，慢慢地吃着晚饭。当巴德和卡克图斯说完时，他们听到了皮格可怕的声音，他正如往常一样滔滔不绝地对其他人说话，他同时也忙着填充他那贪婪而饥饿的胃口，虽然从来没有填饱过。

"那有什么用，"他正说着，"转了成千上万英里，就为了去追那些小红牛和马？简直一点儿用也没有。骑马穿过灌木丛和刺丛，口渴得连一个啤酒厂也止不住，还吃不上饭！我说！如果我来当这帮人的头儿，你们知道我会干什么吗？我会去抢火车。我会让特快列车开花，搞到实实在在的美元，从中也少不了你们的好处。你们这样的干法把我搞烦了。像逮牛这样低级的消遣让我感到很痛苦。"

They stood on one leg, chewed mesquit twigs and circumlocuted, for they hated to hurt his feelings. Bud foresaw their business, and made it easy for them. Bigger risks and larger profits was what they wanted.

The suggestion of Piggy's about holding up a train had fired their imagination and increased their admiration for the dash and boldness of the instigator. They were such simple, artless, and custom-bound bush-rangers that they had never before thought of extending their habits beyond the running off of live-stock and the shooting of such of their acquaintances as ventured to interfere.

Bud acted "on the level," agreeing to take a subordinate place in the gang until Black Eagle should have been given a trial as leader.

After a great deal of consultation, studying of time-tables, and discussion of the country's topography, the time and place for carrying out their new enterprise was decided upon. At that time there was a feedstuff famine in Mexico and a cattle famine in certain parts of the United States, and there was a brisk international trade. Much money was being

稍后,一个代表团的人伺候着巴德。他们翘起一只脚站着,嚼着牧豆树的嫩枝,说话时绕来绕去,因为他们不愿伤害他的感情。巴德早就看出了他们的用意,于是没有为难他们。他们想要的,无非是更大的冒险和更丰厚的红利。

皮格关于抢火车的建议,燃起了他们的想像,增加了他们对他的冲劲和胆略的崇拜。他们是一群如此简单,没有心机,习惯了在丛林里混的匪徒,以至于以前他们从没想到过要把他们的惯例延伸,而不仅仅是偷盗牲畜和枪杀他们的熟人这类冒险。

巴德"公正"地表示,黑鹰应该接受一次担任领导的检验,之后他同意在匪帮中做一名下属。

经过大量的查阅咨询、研究火车时刻表,并讨论了地区的地形之后,实施新事业的时间和地点被定了下来。在那个时候,墨西哥正闹着饲料饥荒,美国的某些地区在害牛荒,但国际贸易却欣欣向荣。好多好多的钱在连接这两个共和国的铁路线上运送着。大家一致认为,最佳的预期

shipped along the railroads that connected the two republics. It was agreed that the most promising place for the contemplated robbery was at Espina, a little station on the I. and G. N., about forty miles north of Laredo. The train stopped there one minute; the country around was wild and unsettled; the station consisted of but one house in which the agent lived.

Black Eagle's band set out, riding by night. Arriving in the vicinity of Espina they rested their horses all day in a thicket a few miles distant.

The train was due at Espina at 10.30 P.M. They could rob the train and be well over the Mexican border with their booty by daylight the next morning.

To do Black Eagle justice, he exhibited no signs of flinching from the responsible honours that had been conferred upon him.

He assigned his men to their respective posts with discretion, and coached them carefully as to their duties. On each side of the track four of the band were to lie concealed in the chaparral. Gotch-Ear Rodgers was to stick up the station agent. Bronco Charlie was to remain with the horses, holding them in readiness. At a spot where it was calculated the engine would

抢劫地点是埃斯皮纳,那是国际大北铁路上的一个小站,大约位于拉雷多以北 40 英里以外的地方。火车要在那儿停一分钟;周围的乡野荒无人烟;在车站只有一座代理人住的房子。

黑鹰的团伙在夜色的掩映下,骑马出发了。到达埃斯皮纳附近以后,他们让马躲在一个离车站不过几英里的灌木丛中休息了一天。

火车按点应该是晚上 10:30 到达埃斯皮纳。他们可以抢劫火车,然后赶在第二天天亮以前,带着他们的战利品远远地越过墨西哥边境。

为黑鹰说句公道话,他对被授予的责任重大的荣誉,丝毫没有表现出退缩。

他谨慎地把他的人分派到各个岗位上,并仔细地把任务布置给他们。在铁路每一侧都有四名暴徒埋伏在灌木丛中。戈齐尔·罗杰斯将负责去抢车站代理人。布朗科·查理负责照看马,让它们做好撤离的准备。火车停下时,算出引擎会停在那儿的哪个位

be when the train stopped, Bud King was to lie hidden on one side, and Black Eagle himself on the other. The two would get the drop on the engineer and fireman, force them to descend and proceed to the rear. Then the express car would be looted, and the escape made. No one was to move until Black Eagle gave the signal by firing his revolver. The plan was perfect.

At ten minutes to train time every man was at his post, effectually concealed by the thick chaparral that grew almost to the rails. The night was dark and lowering, with a fine drizzle falling from the flying gulf clouds. Black Eagle crouched behind a bush within five yards of the track. Two six-shooters were belted around him. Occasionally he drew a large black bottle from his pocket and raised it to his mouth.

A star appeared far down the track which soon waxed into the headlight of the approaching train. It came on with an increasing roar; the engine bore down upon the ambushing desperadoes with a glare and a shriek like some avenging monster come to deliver them to justice. Black Eagle flattened himself upon the ground. The engine, contrary to their cal-

置,一侧由巴德埋伏,黑鹰自己则埋伏在另一侧。他俩将先发制服火车司机和司炉工,迫使他们下车,走到车尾去。然后,这列特快列车将被洗劫,接下来就是逃跑。在黑鹰鸣枪发出信号之前,任何人都不可以行动。这个计划完美无缺。

离火车到站还有10分钟时,每个人都各就各位,好好地藏到了长得几乎高到铁轨的浓密的荆棘丛里。夜色乌黑,阴云密布,从海湾飘来的流云洒下了蒙蒙细雨。黑鹰蜷伏在离铁路不到五码的一丛灌木后面,两支六发式左轮手枪拴在他的皮带上。他不时地从口袋里掏出一只黑色的大瓶子,举到嘴边。

一颗星星出现在铁路的那一头,很快就变大了,成了正在驶来的火车的前灯。火车越来越近,吼声越来越猛;火车前灯射出耀眼的光芒,呼啸着向埋伏的匪徒们逼近,就像来复仇的怪兽一样,要把他们送上的法庭。黑鹰紧紧地贴在地面上。同他们的估计不一样,火车的引擎没停在他和巴

culations, instead of stopping between him and Bud King's place of concealment, passed fully forty yards farther before it came to a stand.

The bandit leader rose to his feet and peered through the bush. His men all lay quiet, awaiting the signal. Immediately opposite Black Eagle was a thing that drew his attention. Instead of being a regular passenger train it was a mixed one. Before him stood a box car, the door of which, by some means, had been left slightly open. Black Eagle went up to it and pushed the door farther open. An odour came forth – a damp, rancid, familiar, musty, intoxicating, beloved odour stirring strongly at old memories of happy days and travels. Black Eagle sniffed at the witching smell as the returned wanderer smells of the rose that twines his boyhood's cottage home. Nostalgia seized him. He put his hand inside. Excelsior – dry, springy, curly, soft, enticing, covered the floor. Outside the drizzle had turned to a chilling rain.

The train bell clanged. The bandit chief unbuckled his belt and cast it, with its revolvers, upon the ground. His spurs followed quickly, and his broad sombrero. Black Eagle was moulting. The

德·金的埋伏点之间，而是向前冲了足有 40 码之后才停住。

这个强盗首领从地上爬起来，穿过灌木丛窥探着。他的人们全都静静埋伏着等待信号。黑鹰面前有一样东西立即引起了他的注意。这不是一趟定期的旅客列车，而是一趟旅客和货物混合的列车。在他前面是一节货车车厢，车厢的门不知怎么地开着一道缝。黑鹰走上前去，把门推开了一些。一种气味扑面而来——一种潮湿的、腐臭的、熟悉的、发霉的、醉人的、他所钟爱的气味，强烈地搅动着他关于从前那些快乐的日子和旅行的回忆。黑鹰闻着这股迷人的气味，就像归家的流浪者闻着童年时家里的小屋周围环生的玫瑰一样。怀旧的愁绪抓住了他。他把手伸进去，细细的刨木花盖在地板上——干爽，有弹性，又卷，又柔软，又让人心动。外面，细细的毛毛雨已经变成了冷飕飕的雨点。

火车的铃声叮叮地响起来了。这个强盗首领解开他的皮带扣，把它连同左轮手枪一块儿扔到了地上，他的马刺和阔边帽也

train started with a rattling jerk. The ex-Terror of the Border scrambled into the box car and closed the door. Stretched luxuriously upon the excelsior, with the black bottle clasped closely to his breast, his eyes closed, and a foolish, happy smile upon his terrible features Chicken Ruggles started upon his return trip.

Undisturbed, with the band of desperate bandits lying motionless, awaiting the signal to attack, the train pulled out from Espina. As its speed increased, and the black masses of chaparral went whizzing past on either side, the express messenger, lighting his pipe, looked through his window and remarked, feelingly:

"What a jim-dandy place for a hold-up!"

随之被扔掉。黑鹰在脱掉他的羽毛。火车嘎吱颤动了一下，便启动了。曾经的边境恐怖分子爬进货车车厢，把门关上了。舒服地伸直了手脚躺在细细的刨木花上，黑瓶子紧紧地贴在他的胸口。他闭上双眼，傻傻的，幸福的微笑在他那张可怕的脸上展开。契肯·拉格尔斯开始了回家的旅程。

火车毫发未伤，开出了埃斯皮纳站，而这帮无法无天的匪徒们还在一动不动地趴着，等待着进攻的信号。随着车速加快，一丛丛黑黝黝的荆棘从车厢两侧嗖嗖划过，这特快列车的信使点燃了他的烟斗，望这窗外，颇有感触地说：

"多好的一个抢劫地点啊！"

31. ONE THOUSAND DOLLARS
31. 1 000 美元

"One thousand dollars," repeated Lawyer Tolman, solemnly and severely, "and here is the money."

Young Gillian gave a decidedly amused laugh as he fingered the thin package of new fifty-dollar notes.

"It's such a confoundedly awkward amount," he explained, genially, to the lawyer. "If it had been ten thousand a fellow might wind up with a lot of fire-works and do himself credit. Even fifty dollars would have been less trouble."

"You heard the reading of your uncle's will," continued Lawyer Tolman, professionally dry in his tones. "I do not know if you paid much attention to its details. I must remind you of one. You are required to render to us an account of the manner of expenditure of this $1,000 as soon as you have disposed of it. The will stipulates that. I trust that you will so far comply with the late Mr. Gillian's wishes."

"You may depend upon it," said the young man politely, "in spite of the extra

"1 000 美元，"托尔曼律师又重复了一遍，口气郑重而又严肃，"给你。"

小吉利恩用手指头点着薄薄一叠50美元一张的崭新的钞票，爽朗地笑了笑，他被逗乐了。

"这真是一笔让人既搞不懂，用起来又不方便的钱，"他欢快地对律师说。"如果这是一万美元，接受它的人可能会放许多烟花奖赏一下自己。就算是50美元也不会惹来这么多的麻烦。"

"你叔叔的遗嘱宣读的时候你已经听到了，"托尔曼律师一本正经地说道，"我不知道是否你留意到了其中的一些细节，但是我必须提醒你其中一点。一旦你把这1 000美元花完，你就得向我们详细地解释一下这笔钱花到哪里去了，遗嘱就是这样规定的。我相信，你会遵从去世的吉利恩先生的遗愿。"

"您尽管放心，"年轻人客气地说，"尽管这会导致额外的花销。我可能需要请个秘书。因

expense it will entail. I may have to engage a secretary. I was never good at accounts."

Gillian went to his club. There he hunted out one whom he called Old Bryson.

Old Bryson was calm and forty and sequestered. He was in a corner reading a book, and when he saw Gillian approaching he sighed, laid down his book and took off his glasses.

"Old Bryson, wake up," said Gillian. "I've a funny story to tell you."

"I wish you would tell it to some one in the billiard room," said Old Bryson. "You know how I hate your stories."

"This is a better one than usual," said Gillian, rolling a cigarette; "and I'm glad to tell it to you. It's too sad and funny to go with the rattling of billiard balls. I've just come from my late uncle's firm of legal corsairs. He leaves me an even thousand dollars. Now, what can a man possibly do with a thousand dollars?"

"I thought," said Old Bryson, showing as much interest as a bee shows in a vinegar cruet, "that the late Septimus Gillian was worth something like half a million."

"He was," assented Gillian, joyously,

为我对管理账目并不擅长。"

吉利恩来到他的俱乐部，在那儿四处寻找，终于找到了一个被他叫做老布赖森的人。

老布赖森有40岁了，处变不惊，是一个退隐的人。他正在角落里看书，看见吉利恩走来，他叹了口气，把书放下，摘下眼镜。

"老布赖森，醒一醒，"吉利恩说，"我要给你讲一个有意思的事情。"

"我倒希望你到弹子房里去随便找个人讲，"老布赖森说，"你知道我有多讨厌你那些事。"

"这一次可不一样，比以前的好玩多了，"吉利恩一边说一边卷烟，"我很高兴跟你讲讲这件事。要是在噼里啪啦的弹子房里讲这种事就太不像话也太可笑了。我刚从我已故的叔叔开的那家合法的海盗公司回来，他留给我整整1 000美元。你说，一个人能用1 000美元做什么事呢？"

"我想，"老布赖森说着，并露出了一种掉进醋缸里的苍蝇所展示出来的兴趣，"去世的塞普蒂默斯·吉利恩的财产大约有50万美元吧。"

"是的，"吉利恩表示同意，口气很欢快，"这就是最有意思

"and that's where the joke comes in. He's left his whole cargo of doubloons to a microbe. That is, part of it goes to the man who invents a new bacillus and the rest to establish a hospital for doing away with it again. There are one or two trifling bequests on the side. The butler and the housekeeper get a seal ring and $10 each. His nephew gets $1,000."

"You've always had plenty of money to spend," observed Old Bryson.

"Tons," said Gillian. "Uncle was the fairy godmother as far as an allowance was concerned."

"Any other heirs?" asked Old Bryson.

"None." Gillian frowned at his cigarette and kicked the upholstered leather of a divan uneasily. "There is a Miss Hayden, a ward of my uncle, who lived in his house. She's a quiet thing – musical – the daughter of somebody who was unlucky enough to be his friend. I forgot to say that she was in on the seal ring and $10 joke, too. I wish I had been. Then I could have had two bottles of brut, tipped the waiter with the ring and had the whole business off my hands. Don't be superior and insulting, Old Bryson – tell me what a fellow can do with a thousand dollars."

的事了。他把全部的金币都留给了一种微生物。具体来说，一部分钱留给了那个发现那种微生物的人，剩下的钱用来建一所医院以消灭这种微生物。还有一两笔不值一提的遗产。男管家和女管家各得了一枚印章戒指和 10 美元。他的侄子得了 1 000 美元。"

"你以前总有花不完的钱，"老布赖森察言观色地说道。

"非常多的钱，"吉利恩说。"在零花钱这方面，我叔叔就像仙女教母一样大方。"

"他还有其他继承人吗？"老布赖森问。

"没有。"看着手中的香烟，吉利恩皱起了眉头，烦躁不安地朝长沙发椅的外层皮革踢了一脚。"还有那个住在我叔叔家的海登小姐，我叔叔是她的监护人。她性格文静，爱好音乐，是某个不幸成为我叔叔朋友的人的女儿。刚才我忘了说，她也得到了印章戒指和 10 美元，也是这笑话的一份子。我希望我也是其中一份子。那样我就可以喝完两瓶酒后把戒指给服务员当小费，而不会摊上这一堆烦心事。别摆出那副傲慢无礼高高在上的样子，老布赖森——告诉我，一个小伙子

Old Bryson rubbed his glasses and smiled. And when Old Bryson smiled, Gillian knew that he intended to be more offensive than ever.

"A thousand dollars," he said, "means much or little. One man may buy a happy home with it and laugh at Rockefeller. Another could send his wife South with it and save her life. A thousand dollars would buy pure milk for one hundred babies during June, July, and August and save fifty of their lives. You could count upon a half hour's diversion with it at faro in one of the fortified art galleries. It would furnish an education to an ambitious boy. I am told that a genuine Corot was secured for that amount in an auction room yesterday. You could move to a New Hampshire town and live respectably two years on it. You could rent Madison Square Garden for one evening with it, and lecture your audience, if you should have one, on the precariousness of the profession of heir presumptive."

"People might like you, Old Bryson," said Gillian, always unruffled, "if you wouldn't moralize. I asked you to tell me what I could do with a thousand dollars."

"You?" said Bryson, with a gentle laugh. "Why, Bobby Gillian, there's only

应该怎样花掉这 1 000 美元。"

老布赖森擦擦眼镜笑了。一旦老布赖森微笑,吉利恩就知道,他肯定比以往更让人讨厌。

"1 000 美元嘛,"他说,"既很多又很少。一个男人可用它买个幸福家庭,可以嘲笑洛克菲勒。另一个男人会用它把老婆送往南方拯救她的生命。1 000 美元可以给 100 个婴儿买纯牛奶,在 6 月、7 月、8 月三个月期间养活他们,还可以让其中的 50 个继续活下去。你可以用这些钱在戒备森严的美术馆,玩上半小时的法罗牌戏。也可以让一个有志气的孩子受到较好的教育。听别人说,在昨天的拍卖会上,一幅绝对是真品的柯罗画就卖了这个价。有了这笔钱,你可以搬到新罕布什尔城去住,在那儿体面地生活个两年。你也可以用这笔钱租麦迪逊广场花园一个晚上,如果有任何一个观众的话,你可以发表关于假定继承人的不稳固性的演讲。"

"人们也许会喜欢你,老布赖森,"吉利恩用几乎平静的语气说道,"要是你不总是说教的话。我想请你告诉我,我能用 1 000 美元做什么。"

"你?"布赖森说,脸上露

one logical thing you could do. You can go buy Miss Lotta Lauriere a diamond pendant with the money, and then take yourself off to Idaho and inflict your presence upon a ranch. I advise a sheep ranch, as I have a particular dislike for sheep."

"Thanks," said Gillian, rising, "I thought I could depend upon you, Old Bryson. You've hit on the very scheme. I wanted to chuck the money in a lump, for I've got to turn in an account for it, and I hate itemizing."

Gillian phoned for a cab and said to the driver:

"The stage entrance of the Columbine Theatre."

Miss Lotta Lauriere was assisting nature with a powder puff, almost ready for her call at a crowded matinee, when her dresser mentioned the name of Mr. Gillian.

"Let it in," said Miss Lauriere. "Now, what is it, Bobby? I'm going on in two minutes."

"Rabbit-foot your right ear a little," suggested Gillian, critically. "That's better. It won't take two minutes for me. What do you say to a little thing in the pendant line? I can stand three ciphers

出和蔼的微笑。"难道你不知道吗？博比·吉利恩，你能做的合乎情理的事情只有一件。你可以用这笔钱去给洛塔·劳里埃小姐买条钻石项链，然后直奔爱达荷的大农场。我建议你去个牧羊场，因为我对羊有一种特殊的憎恶。"

"谢谢你啊，"吉利恩说着站起身。"我就知道我可以依靠你，老布赖森。你提出了一个绝妙主意。我想把这笔钱一次全部花光，因为我不得不交一份账单，而我讨厌一条条的列出清单。"

吉利恩打电话叫了辆出租车，对司机说：

"科隆比纳剧院舞台入口。"

就在洛塔·劳里埃小姐用粉扑为自己的脸蛋增光添彩，马上准备登上座无虚席的午场戏的舞台的时候，服装员通报说吉利恩先生来了。

"让他进来，"劳里埃小姐说。"你有什么事吗，博比？再过两分钟我就要登台演出了。"

"给你的右耳添件小小的兔足，"吉利恩端详了她的脸庞，提议道，"那你就会更加漂亮了。这不会花两分钟的。喜不喜欢在项链上加个小挂件？我还能花得起这笔钱，三位数以内，第一个

with a figure one in front of 'em."

"Oh, just as you say," carolled Miss Lauriere. "My right glove, Adams. Say, Bobby, did you see that necklace Della Stacey had on the other night? Twenty-two hundred dollars it cost at Tiffany's. But, of course – pull my sash a little to the left, Adams."

"Miss Lauriere for the opening chorus!" cried the call boy without.

Gillian strolled out to where his cab was waiting.

"What would you do with a thousand dollars if you had it?" he asked the driver.

"Open a s'loon," said the cabby, promptly and huskily. "I know a place I could take money in with both hands. It's a four-story brick on a corner. I've got it figured out. Second story – Chinks and chop suey; third story – manicures and foreign missions; fourth floor – pool-room. If you was thinking of putting up the cap –"

"Oh, no," said Gillian, "I merely asked from curiosity. I take you by the hour. Drive 'til I tell you to stop."

Eight blocks down Broadway Gillian poked up the trap with his cane and got out. A blind man sat upon a stool on the

"好，就这样办吧，"劳里埃欢乐地说，"把右手套递给我，亚当斯。我说，博比，那天晚上你看到德拉·斯泰西戴的那条项链了吗？那个在蒂芬尼珠宝店里标价要2 200美元呢。不过，当然——把我的腰带稍稍朝左边拉一点点，亚当斯。"

"开幕曲开始，劳里埃小姐登台！"催场员在外面喊道。

吉利恩出去，走向正在等候他的出租车。

"要是你有1 000美元，你会做什么？"他问司机。

"开家沙龙，"司机声音粗哑地立即回答道，"我知道一个我可以双手奉上钱的好地方。那是一座位于街角的四层砖楼。一切都计划好了。二楼——中国菜和炒杂烩菜；三楼——美甲师和外交使团；四楼——弹子房。如果你在想打它的主意的话——"

"啊，不，"吉利恩说，"我只是因为好奇才问的。一直开，我喊停的时候再停，我会按小时付车费的。"

车沿着百老汇驶了八个街区后，吉利恩用手杖敲了敲扶手，然后下了车。人行道上，有一位

sidewalk selling pencils. Gillian went out and stood before him.

"Excuse me," he said, "but would you mind telling me what you would do if you had a thousand dollars?"

"You got out of that cab that just drove up, didn't you?" asked the blind man.

"I did," said Gillian.

"I guess you are all right," said the pencil dealer, "to ride in a cab by daylight. Take a look at that, if you like."

He drew a small book from his coat pocket and held it out. Gillian opened it and saw that it was a bank deposit book. It showed a balance of $1,785 to the blind man's credit.

Gillian returned the book and got into the cab.

"I forgot something," he said. "You may drive to the law offices of Tolman & Sharp, at — Broadway."

Lawyer Tolman looked at him hostilely and inquiringly through his gold-rimmed glasses.

"I beg your pardon," said Gillian, cheerfully, "but may I ask you a question? It is not an impertinent one, I hope. Was Miss Hayden left anything by my uncle's will besides the ring and the $10?"

盲人坐在凳子上卖铅笔。吉利恩朝他走去径直走到他的面前。

"打扰一下，"他说，"请问，要是你有 1 000 美元，你会用它来干什么？"

"刚从出租车上下来的是你吧？"盲人问。

"是的，"吉利恩说。

"我猜你身体健康，"铅笔商人说道，"大白天还要坐出租车。要是你愿意，看看这个。"

他从外衣口袋里掏出一个小本递过来。吉利恩翻开一看，是一个银行存折。上边显示的余额是 1 785 美元，是这个盲人的存款。

吉利恩把存折还给他，上了出租车。

"我忘了件事，"他说，"开车到托尔曼夏普律师事务所，在——百老汇。"

托尔曼律师的眼睛在金边眼镜后面滴溜溜地转，面带敌意。

"打扰一下，"吉利恩满面春风地说，"我可以问你个问题吗？这不是个莽撞的问题。我叔叔除了留给海登小姐印章戒指和 10 美元，还给她什么了嘛？"

"一分钱也没有，"托尔曼

"Nothing," said Mr. Tolman.

"I thank you very much, sir," said Gillian, and on he went to his cab. He gave the driver the address of his late uncle's home.

Miss Hayden was writing letters in the library. She was small and slender and clothed in black. But you would have noticed her eyes. Gillian drifted in with his air of regarding the world as inconsequent.

"I've just come from old Tolman's," he explained. "They've been going over the papers down there. They found a – Gillian searched his memory for a legal term – they found an amendment or a post-script or something to the will. It seemed that the old boy loosened up a little on second thoughts and willed you a thousand dollars. I was driving up this way and Tolman asked me to bring you the money. Here it is. You'd better count it to see if it's right." Gillian laid the money beside her hand on the desk.

Miss Hayden turned white. "Oh!" she said, and again "Oh!"

Gillian half turned and looked out the window.

"I suppose, of course," he said, in a low voice, "that you know I love you."

先生说。

"太谢谢您了,先生,"吉利恩说完立即走回出租车前,把他的已故叔叔的地址给了司机。

海登小姐正在书房里写信,她身材娇小,苗条修长,一身黑衣。但你仍然会注意到她的眼睛。吉利恩漫步进去,脸上带着一副愤世嫉俗的表情。

"我刚从老托尔曼的事务所过来,"他解释道,"他们一直在那儿整理文件。他们找到了一份"——吉利恩绞尽脑汁想找出一个法律术语——"关于遗嘱的修正文件,或者说是补充说明什么的。看起来是我的叔叔,这个老男孩转念一想,大方了一些,留给了你1000美元的遗产。我正好顺路过来,托尔曼就让我把钱捎给你。就是这些。你最好点点看是否有差错。"吉利恩把钱放到桌子上,靠着她手边。

海登小姐脸色变得苍白。"啊!"她惊叹道,又叫了一声"啊!"

吉利恩侧过身,向窗外望去。

"我想,当然,"他压低了声音说道,"你知道我爱你。"

"I am sorry," said Miss Hayden, taking up her money.

"There is no use?" asked Gillian, almost light-heartedly.

"I am sorry," she said again.

"May I write a note?" asked Gillian, with a smile, He seated himself at the big library table. She supplied him with paper and pen, and then went back to her secretaire.

Gillian made out his account of his expenditure of the thousand dollars in these words:

"Paid by the black sheep, Robert Gillian, $1,000 on account of the eternal happiness, owed by Heaven to the best and dearest woman on earth."

Gillian slipped his writing into an envelope, bowed and went his way.

His cab stopped again at the offices of Tolman & Sharp.

"I have expended the thousand dollars," he said cheerily, to Tolman of the gold glasses, "and I have come to render account of it, as I agreed. There is quite a feeling of summer in the air – do you not think so, Mr. Tolman?" He tossed a white envelope on the lawyer's table. "You will find there a memorandum, sir, of the *modus operandi* of the vanishing of the

"我很抱歉，"海登小姐说，并把钱收好。

"这不好吗？"吉利恩问道，而语气几乎是轻松愉快的。

"我很抱歉，"她重复道。

"我可以写个便条吗？"吉利恩微笑着问。他在书房里大大的写字桌旁边坐下来。她递给他纸和钢笔，然后又回到自己的写字台前。

吉利恩开出 1 000 美元的花费账目，内容如下所示：

"为了永恒的幸福，败家子罗伯特·吉利恩将上天恩赐的 1 000 美元送给世界上最好最亲爱的女人。"

吉利恩把便条塞进信封，匆匆对她鞠了个躬，就再次上路了。

出租车再一次停在托尔曼夏普的办公室旁。

"我已经花掉了那 1 000 美元，"他兴奋地对带金边眼镜的托尔曼说，"我来把我承诺过的账单交给你。有一种夏天的感觉洋溢在空气中——你发现了吗，托尔曼先生？"他把一个白色信封扔在律师的桌子上。"你会发现里面有一张便笺，先生，它会告诉你这些美元是如何消失的。"

dollars."

Without touching the envelope, Mr. Tolman went to a door and called his partner, Sharp. Together they explored the caverns of an immense safe. Forth they dragged, as trophy of their search a big envelope sealed with wax. This they forcibly invaded, and wagged their venerable heads together over its contents. Then Tolman became spokesman.

"Mr. Gillian," he said, formally, "there was a codicil to your uncle's will. It was intrusted to us privately, with instructions that it be not opened until you had furnished us with a full account of your handling of the $1,000 bequest in the will. As you have fulfilled the conditions, my partner and I have read the codicil. I do not wish to encumber your understanding with its legal phraseology, but I will acquaint you with the spirit of its contents.

"In the event that your disposition of the $1,000 demonstrates that you possess any of the qualifications that deserve reward, much benefit will accrue to you. Mr. Sharp and I are named as the judges, and I assure you that we will do our duty strictly according to justice – with liberality. We are not at all unfavorably dis-

托尔曼先生碰也没碰那个信封，而是走到另外一个门口去叫他的合作伙伴夏普。他们一起探索着大保险箱的洞穴，他们搬出一个蜡封的大信封，如同搬出一件挖掘到的胜利纪念品。他们用力地把信封打开来，把信放在鼻子底下，摇头晃脑地打开。托尔曼成了发言人。

"吉利恩先生，"他一板一眼地说，"除了你叔叔的遗嘱之外，还有一个遗嘱附件，他也把它托付给了我们。他规定，当你交给我们 1 000 美元遗产花费的清单后，这个文件才能公开。只有当你履行了上述条件时，我和我的合伙人才能宣读遗嘱附件。我不想用法律术语来妨碍你的理解，但是我会把大意说给你听。"

"如果你是以一种值得奖赏的方式来处理这笔钱的话，那么你将获得巨大的好处。夏普先生和我被指定为仲裁人，我向你保证，我们会严格、公正、慷慨地履行这一职责。绝对不会不利于你，吉利恩先生。不过让我们回到遗嘱附件上来吧。如果你对

posed toward you, Mr. Gillian. But let us return to the letter of the codicil. If your disposal of the money in question has been prudent, wise, or unselfish, it is in our power to hand you over bonds to the value of $50,000, which have been placed in our hands for that purpose. But if – as our client, the late Mr. Gillian, explicitly provides – you have used this money as you have money in the past, I quote the late Mr. Gillian – in reprehensible dissipation among disreputable associates – the $50,000 is to be paid to Miriam Hayden, ward of the late Mr. Gillian, without delay. Now, Mr. Gillian, Mr. Sharp and I will examine your account in regard to the $1,000. You submit it in writing, I believe. I hope you will repose confidence in our decision."

Mr. Tolman reached for the envelope. Gillian was a little the quicker in taking it up. He tore the account and its cover leisurely into strips and dropped them into his pocket.

"It's all right," he said, smilingly. "There isn't a bit of need to bother you with this. I don't suppose you'd understand these itemized bets, anyway. I lost the thousand dollars on the races. Good-day to you, gentlemen."

这笔遗产的处理是审慎的、英明的、无私的，那么，我们有权转交给你价值 50 000 美元的债券，这些债券暂时由我们保管。但是，倘若——正如我们的委托人，已故的吉利恩先生清晰明白地阐述的那样——你像过去那样花掉这笔钱——引用已故的吉利恩先生的原话来说——再和你那些不体面的朋友过着该受到谴责的放荡不羁的生活——这 50 000 美元就将立刻交给已故的吉利恩先生所监护的米里亚姆·海登。现在，吉利恩先生，夏普先生和我将要审查这 1 000 美元的账目。我认为你提交的账目是书面形式的。我希望你可以信任我们。"

托尔曼先生伸手去拿信封。吉利恩的动作比他们还快了一步。他拿起信封，从容不迫地把账目和信封撕成一条一条的，然后塞到口袋里。

"好了，"他微笑着说。"完全没有必要因为这点小事打扰你们。我想你们不会弄明白这些赌金的详细清单。我在赛马中输掉了这 1 000 美元。日安，先生。"

Tolman & Sharp shook their heads mournfully at each other when Gillian left, for they heard him whistling gayly in the hallway as he waited for the elevator.

吉利恩离开了，托尔曼和夏普痛惜地向对方摇了摇头，因为他们听到了他在门厅等候电梯时愉快地吹着口哨。